BAD BOY

INVERTARY BOOK 5

JANET ELIZABETH HENDERSON

Abby, aged twelve
"When I'm grown, I shall do what is expected of me as a
Montgomery-Clark."

Flynn, aged thirteen
"When I grow up I want to be a professional footballer. Or a stud.
Probably both."

CHAPTER 1

"I'm going to make a prediction—it could go either way." Ron Atkinson, former England soccer player and manager

"What are they doing, Muma?"

Five-year-old Katy's nose was pressed up against the kitchen window. Her attention firmly focused on the raucous crowd gathered on the plot of land Flynn Boyle had bought from Abby. The gorgeous flat land that ran between Abby's Victorian house and the stream. The same land that would soon hold his no doubt monstrous house and block her view of the water.

Abby took a deep breath. No one had put a gun to her head and told her to sell to the bad boy of European soccer. Nope. That particularly stupid decision was all on her. She'd been swayed by his movie-star good looks and the fact her bank account was deep in the red.

Clenching her teeth, Abby tried to think beyond the noise. The *incessant* noise. When Flynn turned up with his grotesque RV, her peaceful life had shattered. Squealing giggling girl-women, loud, thrumming music, men shouting at sports on TV and revving engines now filled her days. The noise was never-ending. Day in, day out. Night and day. For two long, long months. She was losing her mind from it.

Abby put down the paring knife she'd been using to slice a carrot and rubbed her temple. It made no difference. The tension headache was still there, taking over her personality, driving her insane.

"Muma." There was a tug at the sleeve of her cream-coloured silk blouse. Her daughter frowned up at her. "What's he doing? Is it another party? Why didn't he invite us? How come he never invites us?"

Katy folded her arms over her blue Elsa princess dress, which she'd teamed with luminous orange gumboots and a yellow woolly hat with a Minion face on it. She had purple eye shadow on her eyebrows and at least twenty strings of sparkling multicoloured beads around her neck. It other words, it was a normal day in the world of Katy fashion.

"It's rude not to invite us to his party." She pouted. "I would invite him to mine. Everybody knows you need to ask the people who live beside you. It's a rule."

Abby ran a hand over Katy's chestnut-coloured hair. There were moments when love for her daughter assaulted her. The depth of it stopped time itself leaving Abby breathless in wonder. This little, perfect person was hers. Time started again and she smiled at her grumpy little girl.

"It's an adult party, baby. Little girls don't go to adult parties."

Katy waved her arms dramatically. "That isn't fair. It isn't even my bedtime yet. Adult parties are supposed to happen when I'm asleep."

Abby couldn't argue with her logic, although she'd rather the party didn't happen at all. The thought of lying awake for yet another night listening to her inconsiderate neighbour was really too much to bear. "Why don't you play with your Lego? Dinner won't be long."

Katy gave her a look of disgust, one clearly implying her mother wasn't doing enough to get her into the party, and then she stomped off. Abby picked up the paring knife. The vibrations from the thumping bass of Flynn's music worked their way through her body, leaving tense muscles in their wake. She was exhausted. Wound tight enough to snap. And she was so incredibly fed up with cleaning up after the mess Flynn Boyle left in his wake. From dealing with hysterical women banging on her door at midnight, demanding Abby find them a taxi, to mending the fences mown down by his drunken friends after they'd joyridden through her paddocks —Abby was up to her ears in the fallout from selling land to Mr Boyle.

She glared out the window at her hateful neighbour, and froze. Katy was stomping across the field towards the RV, a look of grim determination on her face. Without a second thought, Abby ran to intercept her daughter.

Forgetting she still held the paring knife in her tightly clenched fist.

FLYNN KEPT a grin pasted to his face and thanked God his sunglasses hid the fact the smile never made it to his eyes. The Ball Babes were in the inflatable pool, whooping it up for the watching men. Their tiny bikinis barely covered their pricey assets, which he appreciated. Although he found himself wondering when plastic had become a valid substitute for the real thing. Sometimes he got to second base with a woman and felt like he had his hands on a waterbed. And what was with all the white-blonde hair? Was there a rule all soccer groupies had to bleach their hair? And why the hell did it bother him when they did?

Some genius had thought to empty a bottle of bubble bath into the pool. It was now filled with foam and frolicking women. He looked around at the leering faces of his former teammates and felt disconnected. This was boring. *He* was bored. And didn't that sum up his mental state. There were near-naked women playing around for his benefit and he'd rather they went home. He wanted to be alone. Alone with his broken leg and broken dreams. He scoffed at himself. Now even his pity party was too pathetic to tolerate.

"Whoa. Grumpy princess alert." Michael, Arsenal's best defender and a legend in the making, pointed his beer bottle in the direction of Abby's house.

Flynn swallowed a groan. Abby McKenzie was a wet dream walking—unfortunately, she had ice in her veins and a deep desire to kill all his joy. She was the fly in his ointment. He thought about it for a minute. Who the hell gave a crap about ointment? She was the fly in his beer. Yeah, much better. She was the rain on his parade. The hair in his soup. The bug up his…

A tiny figure appeared in front of him. Oh hell, it wasn't the ice queen, it was her mini-me. Flynn sat up straight. Where was her owner? Shouldn't she be in a pen, locked up tight with lots of plastic dolls? He flicked his gaze to the women in the pool at the thought of plastic dolls. It was official. He was losing his mind.

The girl folded her arms. Frowned with purple eyebrows and pursed her lips. "It's rude to have a party and not invite me."

"Oh, she is so cute," one of the Ball Babes squealed.

Aye, cute like a piranha.

Flynn blinked at the kid. How the hell was he supposed to deal with this? He had a minimum age limit for dealing with the female species—nineteen. His maximum was twenty-two. Anything younger was alien to him. Anything older wasn't worth his effort.

She tapped the toe of her orange gumboot and waited for his answer. "Well? Why didn't you invite me?"

Flynn rubbed his jaw, absently noting he hadn't shaved in…a while? Hell, he couldn't remember the last time he'd bothered. It didn't seem worth the effort. Very little did anymore.

"I didn't invite you because I didn't want you here, kid."

She narrowed her eyes at him. "That's rude. Are you always this mean? Muma says you're proof pretty isn't the same as nice or smart."

There was laughter. The guys were getting a kick out of his mini-tormentor.

"I don't need to be smart. Your mum is smart enough for all of us." Pretty too, but he wasn't sharing that thought with the kid. "Don't you have to go to bed or something?"

"It isn't even dinnertime. I don't go to bed for hours." She put her fists on her hips. "Don't think I'm going to invite you to my party." She said it like it was a threat.

"I'll live."

She opened her mouth to say something else, but stopped when a loud whoop came from the pool. One of the Ball Babes decided she wasn't getting enough attention and took off her bikini top. She swung it above her head as she jumped up and down in the water, ensuring everybody present got an eyeful of her foam-covered tits—including the kid.

Flynn groaned as the mini-terrorist's eyes went wide. Her jaw dropped. She pointed at the girl and shouted. "I can see her boobs!"

"You have got to be kidding me." Abby's clipped upper-class tones cut through the laughter.

He didn't need to look at her to know she was oozing

disapproval. Where he was concerned, Abby always oozed disapproval. Flynn's chin dropped to his chest. He could not get a break. He took a deep breath, let out a sigh and turned his head to the ice queen.

And stopped dead.

Flynn's easy charm faltered and his heart stuttered. The sight was not what he had expected. Abby had transformed. Gone was the calm, controlled demeanour he was used to dealing with. In its place was a wild woman. Her hair was flying, her cheeks were flushed and her eyes sparkled with fury. The ice queen had melted. Flynn felt his shorts tighten with raw hunger at the sight of her replacement. For the first time in months he got a glimpse of the passionate woman he'd spotted at his uncle's funeral. He'd known she was in there somewhere. The sight made him want to grab her and hold on tight.

At least it did until he spotted the knife in her hand.

Flynn struggled to his feet, holding his weight on his good leg. He held out his hands in a placating gesture. Behind him the voices were deadly silent.

"Now, Abby, don't do anything rash."

Her eyes flashed at him before scanning the scene in front of his motorhome. Picnic tables were covered in empty beer bottles and discarded food. The grass was littered with trash. The giant inflatable pool overflowed with bubbles as three Playboy Bunny wannabes stared wide-eyed at the wild woman. Aye, so it didn't look good. It wasn't his fault. He had too much on his mind to keep the place tidy. As for the women…he shook his head. Okay. There was no excuse for them.

The tiny terrorist's arm shot out. She pointed straight at Flynn. "He said he didn't want me at his party."

"Tattletale," Flynn grumbled at her, and she stuck out her tongue.

With an irate wail, Abby stormed into his RV. There was a loud crash and the music stopped dead. Well hell, that wasn't good. A moment later she appeared looking even crazier than seconds before.

Her lips thinned, her gaze focused on the pool and she strode purposely towards it. Flynn rushed to get into her path, but tripped over his weak leg. Michael's hand shot out to grab him before he hit the dirt. The defender thrust Flynn's walking stick into his hand. Flynn looked at it in disgust before turning his attention back to Abby. He was too late to stop her. He could only watch in shocked awe as she repeatedly stabbed the inflatable pool.

The Babes screamed, high-pitched and girly. The noise made him wince. They scrambled out of the side of the pool furthest away from the mad woman. As the pool deflated and water flooded the field, Abby whirled towards Flynn.

"Now, don't do anything you'll regret." Flynn's eyes were on the knife.

She let out a seriously scary screech as she caught sight of the topless woman sneaking towards the RV. "You!" She pointed at the half-naked Babe. "Get dressed. Get some self-respect. Stop flashing yourself at mindless men. Do something with your life."

The Babe gasped before running into the RV. She'd wisely decided to do what the woman with the knife ordered.

Abby spun to him. "You!" She closed her eyes for a second while she worked to control her breathing.

Flynn watched her closely as he willed her success. Control would be good. Really good.

"You," she said again, "will stop playing loud music." She took a step towards him. Her whole body vibrated with fury, making him notice the curves under her prim, yet seriously sexy, dress. "You won't shout in the middle of the night. And neither will your friends. You won't rev engines. Or scream.

Or bang around. You will remember that normal people sleep at night and remain respectfully silent." She took another step, making Flynn's eyes drop to her feet. She was wearing drop-dead sexy heels. They were nude coloured, with a peep-toe that flashed her pale pink nails. He shook his head. What the hell? There was a crazy woman with a knife and he was admiring her feet. He needed to cut back on his pain meds.

She pointed at him. With. The. Knife. "You will stop messing the place up. You will stop throwing orgies in plain view of the neighbours. You will be mindful of the child living next door to you."

Said child gave him a smug smile. He rolled his eyes at her.

Abby stepped closer until he could see the gold flecks in her blazing hazel eyes. "You will stop being an inconsiderate, immature, misogynist moron and grow up. You will do this right now. This minute." Her eyes narrowed. "And if I hear one more peep out of you, or your friends, you won't be pleased with my reaction. Do you understand me?"

For the first time since the tackle that'd destroyed his career, Flynn felt his interest in life spark. No. His interest in *Abby* sparked. A slow smile curved his lips as his hand snapped out to curl around her wrist. She jerked with shock. He held the hand clenching the knife as he leaned in to whisper in her ear.

"You are seriously sexy when you're mad."

Her back went ramrod straight. "This isn't a game, Mr Boyle. My patience with your childish antics, and inconsiderate behaviour, has reached its limit. I won't tolerate it anymore."

"I know." He squeezed her wrist, making her drop the knife.

He could almost feel his teammates' shoulders slump with

relief. Flynn ignored them as he held Abby's gaze with his. They stared at each other for a millennium, as Flynn wallowed in the passion and heat glittering in her eyes.

"Mr Boyle…" she started, but he noticed a waver in her voice, born of the awareness sparking between them.

"Call me Flynn." He slid his hold down her hand and over her fingers before releasing her.

Want flashed in her eyes before she took a wary step away from him.

"Let's go." She held out a hand to the kid.

With one last unreadable look at Flynn, Abby grasped her daughter's hand and stalked back to her house. The kid turned back to him and stuck out her tongue. Flynn couldn't stop a laugh from erupting.

As he watched Abby's curvy behind sway, Michael came up beside him.

"That's a helluva neighbour you've got there. You never mentioned she was so freaking wild. Hot too. Kate Middleton hot. Classy. I like that in a woman."

Flynn noted the lust-filled interest in his teammate's voice and scowled. "She's off limits."

Michael raised an eyebrow at him. "Are you sure?"

"I am now." Flynn watched Abby shut the door quietly behind her. As though the stately Victorian house was too refined for slamming doors.

"Did you get that?" An excited voice snapped his attention back to the people who invaded his space. "Please tell me you got it. That woman just propelled this documentary into the stratosphere. This is BAFTA material."

Flynn let out a disgruntled sigh. He'd forgotten about the damn camera crew. He turned to the producer.

"You can't use the footage."

The slimy weasel grinned. "You signed a waiver. Full access to your life for the duration of the shoot. The only stipulation you made was that we had to stay in this one-horse town. Everything else is fair game." He cast a lecherous glance towards Abby's house. "Looks like this shoot is going to be more interesting than I thought."

"My neighbour didn't sign a waiver. She isn't part of your show."

"She was on your property. Attacking your belongings. Shouting at you." The weasel laughed. "Seeing as this programme is about your life, she's just become part of the show." He turned to his mousy assistant. "Find out all you can about the neighbour. We need to come up with a way to give her more airtime." The terrified girl nodded, but her eyes darted nervously to Flynn.

"This documentary is about my life after injury. It isn't about my neighbour." Flynn kept his tone even. Cold. It was the voice he used to scare the crap out of opponents.

The weasel was too far gone with thoughts of BAFTA Awards to care. "You said it—your life. And she's in it." He turned his back on Flynn. "I want highlights on the web within the hour. Contact the news. Maybe we can get it picked up in time for the ten o'clock slot. People are going to see this teaser and wet themselves with excitement." He rubbed his hands together.

Flynn clenched his fists and took a step towards the man. A firm palm hit his chest to halt him.

"Not worth it," Michael said. "Call your lawyer. Agent. Whatever. Get the suits to sort it out."

"My agent got me in this mess in the first place." And wasn't Flynn the prize fool for letting it happen.

Michael shook his head. "I told you at the time you needed to spend some energy on vetting a new agent instead of screwing around. I told you about the rumours. Barney had some dodgy deals going on. The guy is only interested in money."

"Thanks for the I-told-you-so. It's always really helpful when I get them." Flynn rubbed a hand over his face. "You're right, though. I shouldn't have signed with the first agent who sucked up after Gerry retired."

"Barney saw a cash cow and went for it." Michael's nod was knowing. "The guy can be convincing."

"Aye, but I made it easy for him. I wasn't exactly paying attention." His memories of the months before his old agent retired were a little hazy. He remembered a buxom brunette, a vintage Corvette, too much Italian wine and a speeding ticket outside Milan. But he didn't remember much about screening new agents.

"He probably set this show up because he's pissed you cut off his cash supply."

"My heart bleeds for him, how he must have suffered when I got injured out of the game." He glared at Brian. The look of glee on the guy's face made Flynn's fingers twitch. "I want to hit him."

Michael's eyes were hard as he stared at the producer. This wasn't the first time the team had dealt with the man. "We all do. Call your people. Just don't hit the guy on air. No matter how tempting it is."

Flynn took a deep breath. His old teammate was right. Flynn losing his cool would just make better TV. He needed to end this. Not help it along. With a grunt of frustration, he grabbed his phone and made the call.

CHAPTER 2

*"I spent a lot of my money on booze, birds [women],and fast cars—
the rest I just squandered."* Georges Best, former Manchester United
player

Somehow Abby managed to swallow her fury long enough to
get through Katy's nighttime routine of dinner, bath and bed.
She smiled and nodded as her daughter ranted on about how
rude Flynn was and how ladies shouldn't be topless in a field.
It took all of Abby's stretched thin self-control to keep her
comments to herself. After what seemed like an eternity,
Katy was tucked under her Minnie Mouse comforter,
cuddling her tatty stuffed giraffe and sleeping. It was time for
Abby's breakdown.

She grabbed a bottle of cheap white wine from the fridge
and unscrewed the top. She didn't bother with a glass.
Taking the bottle into the sitting room, she picked up the
phone. With a groan at the ceiling, she lay in the dark on her
back on the rug in the middle of the floor. She wanted to

wail, but the thought of waking Katy stopped her. Propping herself up on her elbow, she gulped down some wine then speed-dialled her best friend. She lay back down while the phone rang in her ear.

"What's up?" Jena said by way of hello.

Abby was silent for a minute as she stared into the darkness. How did she answer? Maybe calling wasn't such a hot idea after all.

"Katy?" Jena's voice softened. "Is that you, baby? You need to remember to talk when you're on the phone."

Abby swallowed hard. "It's me, Jena."

"Are you okay?" Jena's voice was instantly alert.

"No." Abby heard the quaver in her voice. "I stabbed Flynn's pool to death and threw his stereo out the window."

There was a pause. "I'll be right there." The phone went dead.

Abby clicked it off, lifted her head and gulped down more wine. A field separated Abby's house from Jena's newly built home. She wouldn't take long. Sure enough, a few minutes later the front door crashed open. Jena barrelled into the living room. She was followed by her husband, Matt Donaldson. Abby tried to smile at the man. It was difficult. The last person Abby wanted to see was the town's only cop—especially as he was also Flynn Boyle's cousin.

"Oh, honey." Jena plopped on the floor beside Abby. She held Abby's hand tight in hers.

Abby cast a nervous glance at Matt, which Jena caught. She nodded towards her huge husband, who was leaning against the doorjamb, perfectly at ease.

"Don't worry about him," Jena said. "He's here in case we need a babysitter. Or in case he needs to arrest Flynn."

Abby jerked with surprise. "Flynn? Not me?"

Matt barked out a laugh. "Hell no, not you. I've known

Flynn a lot longer than you have. If there's trouble, it's his fault."

Jena giggled, which made Abby relax, slightly. A tear escaped unexpectedly and ran down the side of her face to settle in her hair.

"I'll be in the kitchen," Matt mumbled, before heading off.

Jena brushed the tear from Abby's cheek. "Now, tell me everything. What do you mean you stabbed a pool?"

Abby took a deep, shuddering breath and told her sordid tale. Jena gasped, laughed and whooped with encouragement. Slowly, Abby began to relax. She sat up and leaned back against the sofa with her legs stretched out on the rug.

"I snapped," she said. "I couldn't take any more." She gave Jena a beseeching look. "I don't scream. I don't brandish a knife. I don't destroy other people's property. I talk calmly. I show anger with cold words and a chilly attitude. The teachers at my finishing school would turn in their graves."

"Are they dead?"

Jena's question took a minute to register. Abby found herself smiling. "They should be."

Jena grinned as she lifted the wine bottle. It was empty. "Matt. We need more wine."

There was a grunt from the direction of the kitchen.

Jena settled beside Abby and patted her hand. "It's a miracle you didn't lose it before now."

Abby groaned and let her head fall back onto the cushion behind her. "I made a fool of myself."

"Nuh-uh, honey. The woman flashing her wares made a fool of herself. You, on the other hand, stood up for yourself."

"I should have called Matt. I should have politely complained."

"You've been polite for well over a month and it didn't get you anywhere. Maybe going psycho on his ass will. I would have done a whole lot worse in your place."

"Let's face it, princess," Matt said as he came into the room carrying a tray. "You would have tripped, fallen on the knife and bled on the grass while you waited to be rescued."

To her surprise, laughter burst out of Abby. Matt had a point. Jena was the most accident-prone person Abby had ever known. Matt placed the tray on the floor in front of the women. He flicked on a table lamp and left without another word. There was no wine on the tray. Instead there was a pot of coffee and a plate of peanut cookies Abby had made earlier.

"Guess we're getting cut off." Jena reached for a cookie.

"Probably for the best. I don't need any more alcohol." Abby glanced at the clock. It was past ten already. Soon she'd fall into bed only to start all over again in the morning. Another relentless day of reacting to other people's needs, of trying to get ahead and of dealing with Flynn. "I can't believe I was attracted to the man."

"Flynn?" Jena sat up straight. "When were you attracted to Flynn? You didn't tell me."

Abby groaned. "I saw him at Matt's dad's funeral. It was before his injury. He was wearing a suit and he was devastating. Of course, I didn't know then he was also Satan."

"Oh, I remember." Jena grinned. "That was around the same time you announced to the pub your hoo-ha was working again and you were desperate for a man."

"I did not!" Abby smacked her friend's arm. "I said my libido was awake after years lying dormant. I didn't mention anything about being desperate. And I certainly didn't say the word hoo-ha." Although, to be honest, Abby's memories of the night in the pub were filtered through too much wine. She wasn't sure what she'd confessed to her friends.

"So." Jena's eyes narrowed, scheming. "Your hoo-ha wants Flynn."

"No! And stop talking about my hoo-ha."

"He's the first man you've mentioned being attracted to since I met you. He must be pretty special."

Abby scowled. "Stop it. Stop whatever's in your tiny mind. I don't want Flynn."

"I think the lady doth protest too much."

"I think I should never have bought you a book on Shakespeare." Abby pushed the cup away from her. "It's too late for coffee. I have problems sleeping as it is."

"Want me to get you some tea?" Jena's face transformed from mischievous to concerned, and Abby wondered again how she would have managed if her American friend hadn't come to the Scottish Highlands.

"No. Thanks, though."

"Don't worry about Flynn, honey. This whole thing will blow over."

No. It wouldn't. "Maybe, but I still need to apologise to Flynn. I'll go over first thing in the morning."

Jena stopped dead, the cookie halfway to her mouth. "If you apologise, I'll find a new best friend. One with a backbone."

"I made a fool of myself. I set a bad example for Katy and I embarrassed my neighbour in front of his friends. I *have* to apologise." Being polite was practically wired into her DNA. She wasn't sure she could *not* apologise.

"He's the one who should be sorry. Not you."

"I know you don't understand, but I won't be able to live with the guilt of letting this lie." She held a hand up to stop Jena from saying anything else.

Jena's expressive eyes couldn't hide her emotions even if she tried. "I don't like it."

Neither did Abby, but it was the right thing to do, and no matter how hard she tried she couldn't break the brainwashing of her childhood—a Montgomery-Clark *always* did the right thing, even if the thought of it made her want to gag.

The doorbell rang, and before Abby could struggle to her feet, Matt passed the living room. "I'll get it."

"Did you call anyone else?" Jena asked.

"Who else would I confess my bad behaviour to?"

"Good point."

A moment later, Matt appeared in the living room doorway. He was grim. "The idiot is here to talk to you."

"I know a lot of idiots," Abby said. "You'll need to be more specific."

A man stepped into view behind Matt and the wind went out of Abby. Great. *That idiot.* Flynn wore a faded blue tartan shirt that hung open, revealing his toned chest. A pair of blue sports shorts showed off one muscled leg and one with a chunk missing from the calf and the rest of it covered in angry red scars. He leaned on crutches, his easy charm absent.

Flynn hobbled into the room without being asked— another mark against him. He was a couple of inches shorter than his cousin, which made him about six feet tall. He didn't have the same bulk as Matt, who stood behind Flynn with his arms folded over his wide chest. Nope, Flynn was all lean, corded muscle and toned power. Abby resisted the urge to count his abs. She'd been staring at his chest for weeks now. She didn't need to count to know there was a perfect six-pack waiting to be ogled.

Abby scrambled to her feet and sucked in a quivering breath. No way was she going to sit on the floor to deal with the man.

"I'm sorry." Her words came out as a sharp bark that sounded nothing like a genuine apology. She cleared her throat and tried again. "I'm sorry about earlier. There was no excuse for it. I will, of course, replace your stereo and pool."

She straightened her back and raised her chin, as she was taught to do. He gave her a rueful smile.

"Yeah, about that." He licked his lips and glanced at Matt.

Everything within Abby went on alert. She knew, with every fibre of her being, that she wasn't going to like what came out of his mouth next.

His mesmerising silver eyes captured hers. "I have something I need to tell you. It isn't good. Are you going to make a run for a knife? Do you need to be restrained?"

She narrowed her eyes at him before catching herself and replacing the expression with one of cool derision. "I think I can manage to control myself."

"Yeah. Right." He didn't look convinced.

"Well?" she prompted, folding her arms. Jena came up beside her and put a hand on her shoulder in silent support. It was welcome.

Flynn rubbed a hand over his unshaven jaw. "It's like this. There's a sports network doing a documentary on me right now. They're following me around for the next few weeks." His eyes flicked to Matt before returning to her. He let out a sigh, heavy with resignation. "Your visit was taped. They put some of it on the internet. You've gone viral."

Jena gasped. Matt cursed. Flynn's attention remained firmly on Abby. He studied her like a science experiment gone wrong, waiting for her to blow. His muscles were tense, poised ready for flight. Abby blinked. She felt as though her focus was zooming in and out. As though the room was moving.

"I'm sorry?" Her voice was eerily soft and calm. "Did you just tell me my behaviour was filmed and made public?"

He nodded.

The afternoon's events flashed through Abby's brain in vivid colour and detail.

"And"—Flynn's voice sounded as though it was coming

from far away—"there's more, but maybe you should sit down first."

She felt Jena's hand clench on her shoulder. Abby couldn't sit. She couldn't move. As in at all. Not an inch.

"Spit it out, Flynn," Matt said with a growl.

"Okay." Flynn actually took a step back from Abby. "The promotional clips were picked up by the news media. We made the ten o'clock news." He paused. "All channels."

That was when the world stopped. Abby blinked twice. Her breath faltered. Everything faded as stunned silence filled her brain. She felt herself falling.

And then she felt nothing at all.

"You broke Abby!" Jena wailed as she caught her friend before she hit the floor.

Flynn rushed forward to help, but his damaged leg gave way and he almost fell on his face in front of her. *Bloody useless leg.* Holding on to the back of an armchair, Flynn watched as Matt lifted Abby onto the couch.

Jena glared up at him. "When her husband died, she didn't faint. When her business collapsed, she didn't faint. When her family disowned her, she didn't faint. When Katy was sick and rushed to hospital, she didn't faint. You spend two months living next door to her, she's acting like a crazy woman and passing out in her living room. You broke my best friend, Flynn Boyle." She snapped her head towards Matt. "Hurt him, baby." She pointed at Flynn. "Break something. I'll be compassionate. You can break something he doesn't use." She glared back at Flynn. "Like his head."

Matt looked like he might follow his wife's orders. "If you weren't already injured, I'd kick your arse."

"Okay," Flynn said. "I probably deserve that."

"No probably about it, dirt-for-brains. You definitely

deserve to be beaten to a pulp." Matt wore his cop face, the one that made it clear he didn't tolerate idiots.

"Look." Flynn gestured to the unconscious Abby. "It's not my fault she came storming over to my place and went all Xena on my pool. If she'd given me a chance, I would have told her there was a camera crew."

"Not your fault?" Jena jumped to her feet. Her curves were poured into cut-off jeans and a bright pink baby tee. Long honey waves flew around her face. She strode to Flynn. "Not your fault?" She poked him in the chest. It hurt. Were her nails filed into talons? "This is *all* your fault." She swung back round to Matt. "He's the dummy in the family, right?"

That stung. It hit the same nerve people had been tweaking his whole life. The assumption being his brother Harry was a genius but all Flynn could do was kick a ball.

"Right now he is."

"Thanks, cuz," Flynn said.

Jena pointed at the sofa. "Abby has been through hell for years. While you were playing ball, she was taking care of her dying husband and baby girl. While you were screwing half the models in England, she was raising a daughter and running a struggling business. She got through all of that then you waltz in, party under her nose and drive her insane. You broke her. And now you need to fix her." She folded her arms.

"How the hell am I supposed to do that?" He knew coming back to Invertary was a dumb idea. The town attracted nutjobs.

"I don't know." Jena poked him in the chest again as Abby groaned. "All I know is you'd better do it. Or I'll kick your ass."

He almost laughed at the thought of the tiny ex-dancer trying to kick his ass. Then he caught Matt's steely gaze. Yeah. Jena might try to kick his arse. But Matt would make sure she was successful. Abby moaned as she struggled to sit up, drawing everyone's attention.

"Hey, honey." Jena went to help her. "Water, Matt."

He nodded and headed out of the room, growling low in his throat as he passed Flynn. Not a good sign.

Flynn watched as Jena helped Abby to sit on the sofa. She put her elbows on her knees and rested her face in her hands. Huh, maybe he had broken her after all. She'd only just started to show some spark, the thought it was over made him feel strangely responsible. A feeling he was not used to at all.

Matt handed Abby a glass of water, which she sipped. Her head hung in defeat.

"Are you okay, honey?" Jena brushed Abby's shoulder-length chestnut hair away from her face. Thick, shiny waves hung past her shoulders. It was the kind of hair a man wanted to wrap his fists in.

"I'm fine," Abby said. "This is what happens when you drink cheap wine on an empty stomach. Plus, I haven't had any decent sleep for months. I guess my system just overloaded."

"I can see why." Jena glared at Flynn. "Do you remember what happened?" she asked Abby.

There was a snort of derisive laughter. "Oh yes, I remember every detail."

She looked up at Flynn. Her eyes were filled with anger, resentment and pain. He shifted in place.

"Show me," she said.

He stared at her blankly.

"Show me the internet clips."

Oh. He hesitated. "I'll go get my iPad."

"Use mine." She pointed to the side table at the end of the sofa.

Matt helpfully handed the iPad to him. With an unusual

feeling of trepidation, he brought up the BBC news. They were running the clip on their sports and entertainment sections. Without a word—because seriously, what could he say?—he handed the tablet to Abby. She watched silently, without moving a muscle. Jena wasn't so still. She gasped and glared at him. Aye, the editing made it look worse.

"I don't know what to do about this." Abby's voice was barely a whisper, and it sounded so defeated that Flynn felt something he hadn't felt in a long, long time—guilt. It stirred in his chest and reminded him a lot of heartburn.

Jena and Matt frowned at him. Obviously expecting something. The problem was, Flynn wasn't sure what.

"I spoke to my lawyer," Flynn told them. "He told me the contract is airtight. There was nothing I could do to stop the segments from being aired."

Matt shook his head slowly. Disgusted. Disappointed. He turned to Abby, who still stared at the iPad. "Call Mitch," he said. "He'll know what to do. He's an entertainment lawyer as well as Josh's manager."

Big brown eyes, the colour of melted chocolate, peered up at Matt. "I can't afford Mitch."

Matt's lips thinned. "He'll probably do it for free, but if there are costs, Flynn will pay." His tone assured her there would be no argument on Flynn's part. Flynn wisely kept his mouth closed.

Jena handed Abby the phone.

"It's too late to call," Abby said.

"Now isn't the time to be polite, honey." Jena dialled then placed the phone in Abby's hand.

Slowly Abby raised the phone to her ear. As she spoke, her eyes focused on Flynn.

"Hi, Mitch, I'm sorry to bother you so late," she said. "I have a problem. A big problem, and I need your help."

Aye, Flynn didn't need a neon sign over his head to know

he was the problem. With a sigh, he flopped down into the armchair behind him. His leg hurt. His head ached and he knew the night was just going to get worse.

"Got any beer?" he asked Matt.

His answer was a set of three identical glares.

CHAPTER 3

"I'd been ill and hadn't trained for a week, and I'd been out of the team for three weeks before that, so I wasn't sharp. I got cramp before halftime as well. But I'm not one to make excuses."
Clinton Morrison, Exeter City player

"You didn't have to sit on the naughty step. I don't think that's fair."

Flynn opened the door of his RV to find Katy on his front step. After Mitch had turned up at Abby's house the night before and told everyone the best he could do was make sure the camera crew didn't film the kid, it had become clear Flynn was persona non grata in his hometown. Apparently nothing could be done to stop Abby being filmed. Nothing except keep her away from Flynn. Which suited him fine.

"Are you listening to me?" the tiny terrorist demanded. "I said it isn't fair you don't have to sit on the naughty step."

Flynn let out a heavy sigh as he walked out into his field.

Why wouldn't people just leave him alone? He looked down at her. People *and their spawn*, he amended.

"Go away. I'm busy here." The last thing he needed was for Abby to come storming over to retrieve the kid. "Shoo!" He waved her away with his hands.

She frowned. "When I'm naughty, I have to sit on the step."

Flynn let out a longsuffering sigh. "Don't you have something to do, kid? Play with dolls? Nap? Snack? Watch Mickey Mouse? Shouldn't you be with your mother? Doesn't she have a leash for you?"

She rolled her eyes with mega drama. "I'm too old for naps."

"Look, kid, your mum is going to be seriously cheesed off when she finds out you're over here. Do you want to upset her?"

"She's in a meeting. She won't know I'm gone."

Flynn tuned her out, because there was little else he could do. With the camera crew hovering at the edge of his property waiting for something to happen, he didn't want to attract attention. The weasel would love to lure his sexy neighbour from her house.

"This place is a pigsty." The kid folded her arms and shook her head.

She wasn't wrong. The Babes had gone shopping in Glasgow and his ex-teammates had headed back to London, leaving a field of debris in their wake. There was no way he could get down to the ground to pick up all the crap. It felt like a knife spiked through his knee every time he bent his leg. Crouching would probably knock him out entirely. There was nothing he could do but wait until the Babes got back to clean the place up. Unless...

He eyed the kid. "Want a job?"

"Cleaning?"

"Yeah."

"No."

"Kids are no bloody use," Flynn grumbled.

"That's a strange balloon." The kid pointed at something on the grass. "I have rainbow-coloured balloons at my parties. They're better than your ones."

Flynn frowned as he looked where she pointed. Hell, someone had dumped a condom on his grass.

"That's not a balloon, it's a…" He looked down at her wide-eyed attention and decided there were some things she didn't need to know. "Why are you still here? Go back to your cage."

"I came to get you to take you to the naughty step. Yesterday you were badly behaved. You made my Muma cry. It's not fair you don't have to sit on the naughty step."

A stab of pain shot through his chest at the thought of Abby crying. Worse still, the thought of him being responsible for her crying. He didn't know what to do with the strange emotion, so he buried it deep. "Life isn't fair, kid. Get over it."

She folded her arms. "I'm not leaving until you come with me and take your punishment."

Flynn stared at the sky for a minute. He was being punished, all right. He stared down at his tormentor. She was dressed in a purple dinosaur onesie, silver princess shoes and a tiara. Her cheeks were coloured with bright pink blush, her eyebrows were blue and her lips had red lipstick, applied with a heavy and shaky hand. She looked like a transvestite Barney.

"Has anybody ever told you that eye shadow doesn't go on your eyebrows?"

"Has anybody ever told you, you smell like baby poo?"

He lifted an arm and sniffed his pit. Okay, he could use a shower. He hadn't felt much like doing anything since he'd come back to town. Even showering seemed like an onerous chore. "If you don't like the smell, go back home."

"Not unless you come and sit on the step."

Talk about a dog with a bone. This kid had one thought in her head, and he was damned if he knew how to get another one in there to replace it. He let out a sigh. "Fine. What will it take to make you go away?"

She scrunched up her nose. She actually seemed to be thinking about it. She opened her mouth and he held up his hand. "And before you say it again. I'm not sitting on any damn step."

Her mouth snapped shut, but a calculating gleam appeared in her brown eyes. "You have to come to my tea party."

"Not happening. Try again. Do you want money? I have money. I'll give you fifty pounds to leave me alone."

She stuck her little nose in the air. "You have to come to my tea party. And you have to be nice. And you have to stay there for a long time. Like, seventeen or fourteen minutes."

"A hundred pounds. Last offer. A hundred pounds will buy a lot of Barbies."

She licked her lips. "How many Barbies?"

"A gazillion."

He watched her think it over. At last she nodded. She held out her hand palm up.

"I don't have my wallet on me."

"Then you'll need to come to my tea party."

It was worse than negotiating his contract with Arsenal. He pointed to the motorhome. "It's in there. On the bedside table. Go get it."

She ran off as fast as her sparkly-heel-clad feet would let her. Flynn flopped onto the lounger behind him. It was going to be a long, long day. He needed a beer. With the Ball Babes out for the day, there was no one to fetch him things when he needed them. He opened an eye and stared at the motorhome speculatively. No. He couldn't ask the kid to fetch him beer. Could he?

Before he could ponder his way through the latest moral dilemma to intrude on his happy place, the kid came running out of the camper wearing last season's Arsenal shirt over her dinosaur onesie. It came to her ankles and fell off her shoulders. She held it up in one hand, like a full-grown woman would hold up a ball gown. In her other hand she held his wallet.

"Can I have this T-shirt?" She handed him the wallet.

"No."

Her eyes narrowed. "You're not using it." She pointed to his bare chest. "You never wear shirts."

Flynn was past caring. He wanted her gone. His head was starting to ache from the mental gymnastics of dealing with her. "Fine. You win. Take it. Take whatever you want. Just leave me alone." She beamed at him. He opened his wallet and pulled out two fifty-pound notes. "Here. Go buy Barbies. And don't come back."

She grabbed the money, spun away from him and ran towards her house without another word, taking his favourite shirt with her.

Flynn plopped back in the lounger. He wanted a beer, but he sure as hell didn't want to drag his backside in to get one. He was having a bad leg day. Every time he moved pain sliced through him, making his stomach lurch.

"We should never have agreed to exclude the girl from the show." The weasel's voice sliced right into Flynn's already aching brain.

"Don't even think about it. She isn't part of the programme."

The weasel pointed at Abby's house. "The kid's visit is the most interesting thing to happen here all day. If you don't do something soon, this will be the most boring documentary ever made."

Flynn shrugged. "Fine with me." He shut his eyes and listened to the slimy guy stomp away.

Brian the weasel was short and skinny. A guy who was made up of lots of sharp angles, kind of like a Picasso painting Flynn had seen once at some hoity-toity party. Brian had perpetually narrowed eyes and a disdainful smirk on his face. He was the guy other men felt nervous turning their backs on. Nothing about Brian engendered loyalty or respect. If the weasel was having problems with the shoot then that was fine with Flynn. He didn't want to do the show anyway. His agent had sold it to him as a serious piece, an interview on his career with some life shots for filler. It was the exact opposite. He felt like Matthew McConaughey in that movie—*EDtv*. He glanced down at himself and wondered if his abs were better than Matthew's.

The answer wasn't forthcoming.

BRIAN FLANNIGAN WATCHED Flynn laze on the lounger in the middle of the perfectly nice field he'd turned into a dump. He sneered. Must be good to have so much money you could bum around all day, every day. It pissed him off. Guys like Flynn got all the luck. All they did was kick a ball around and look pretty, while men like Brian, men with brains and talent, had to work damn hard to make it through the month. It made him sick.

"What did you dig up on the neighbour?" he asked his whiny, terrified assistant. She was the walking, talking equivalent of beige wallpaper.

She cleared her throat and addressed her answer to her shoes. Her dull brown shoes.

"There isn't much. She comes from a wealthy, connected

family. Her mother is still alive; her father passed away a few years ago and his title went to her older brother. She doesn't have any contact with her family. The rumour is they disowned her when she married her late husband. He was an agriculture graduate who moved here to open a mushroom farm in the old mine. As far as I can tell, he was hardworking and well liked. People were really upset when he died. It was a brain tumour. Abby tried running the business herself, but it was going under even before the explosion a few months ago made the mine collapse."

Brian stilled. "Wait a minute. Go back a bit. You said 'his title'? Her father was a peer?"

The beige wonder nodded, still unable to meet his eyes. "A lord. Her brother is now Lord Montgomery-Clark. The family estate is in Kent."

"A lord?" He felt his heart race. He could see the documentary title now: *Class Warfare in the Highlands.* It was the edge he needed to take his documentary from mundane to spectacular. Instead of ninety minutes featuring a self-obsessed pretty boy, the programme would be a social commentary on the struggles of a failing British class system and the lower class' obsession with football. His mouth salivated at the thought of all the accolades that were bound to come his way.

"They're distant cousins of the Queen," the mouse said, breaking into his vivid daydream.

Holy hell. Brian bit back a laugh. This couldn't get any better even if he wrote it himself. After this, people would be queuing up to get him in on their projects. His name would be gold.

"Does the family know their daughter is slumming with the bad boy of UK soccer?"

The beige wonder's eyes snapped up to his, briefly. It

made him wonder if she had a backbone after all. "She isn't doing anything with Flynn. They're just neighbours."

He couldn't contain the grin that split his face. "The family doesn't know what Flynn is to Abby. If her family disowned her for marrying an educated and respectable working-class man, they'll go ballistic when they find out she's setting up home with *that* waste of space." He smiled over at Flynn. It was cold. He knew it. He didn't care.

"I, I don't think—" the mouse started.

"You're right. You don't think." He spun towards her, deliberately crowding her space. "I want you to make sure the unedited footage of Abby's meltdown gets to the family. I want this to happen anonymously. And I want you to include a note saying you're worried about the child growing up around all this debauchery. You can hint about Abby's parenting skills being substandard. Let's see what the Montgomery-Clarks do with that."

The mouse paled. Her pasty skin turned ashen. "I can't. You can't—"

"Get it done." He stared at her, letting his feelings for her leach into his gaze. She was nothing. Less than nothing. He held her career in his hands. "If you can't get it done, I can find someone who can."

She swallowed hard. Her eyes were back on her shoes, where they belonged. "I'll do it." Her words were barely a whisper.

"Now, mouse, do it now." He spun on his heels and headed for his car. This was turning out to be the best job of his career. He would make his name on this job. He'd be set for life. Fame. Fortune. It was all his for the taking—as it should be.

Watching Flynn Boyle crash and burn on national TV was just the icing on the cake.

CHAPTER 4

*"The ball is like a woman—she loves to be caressed."Eric Cantona,
former national soccer player for France*

Abby was meeting with the women of Knit or Die when Katy
burst into the room.

"Muma, you need to take me to the shop!"

"Don't interrupt, Katy." Abby was firm, but she smiled at
the same time. She wanted her daughter to learn manners,
not to have her personality subdued. "It isn't polite to interrupt. Wait until I finish talking with the ladies."

Abby turned her back on her impatient and grumpy
daughter. She was in the middle of presenting her knitwear
designs to the local knitting group. She hoped they would
work with her by making the designs a reality. This new
business had seemed like such a great idea during the planning stage. It would combine the skills she'd learned in
college with hours to fit around raising Katy. Now as she
looked at the uncharacteristically quiet demeanours of the

women in front of her, she worried she'd overreached. It'd been years since she'd studied textile design at art college. She was rusty. Out of date. She wasn't talented enough. Or smart enough. What had she been thinking? This was stupid idea.

The presentation fizzled out as Abby's cheeks heated. She'd made a fool of herself. She knew it. She forced her head high. She'd be polite, let the women off the hook and forget she'd ever come up with this foolish plan. Mind made up, she opened her mouth to speak. Kirsty's mum, Margaret Campbell, beat her to it.

"I am stunned," she said.

Abby's stomach lurched. She could hear the rest of the woman's comment before it came out of her mouth. *I am stunned you think such a childish plan will work. Your designs are pathetic. You've wasted our time.* She took a deep breath. It was okay. She'd be okay. She'd get a job at the supermarket. It wasn't like she hadn't heard this stuff before. Her father had been very vocal about her lack of ability and talent.

"Abby?" Margaret said. "Are you listening to me?"

Abby lifted her eyes to look at the woman. "I'm sorry, Margaret, my mind wandered. I didn't mean to waste your time. I'll just clear this mess up." She motioned to her designs. "Then I'll make everyone a nice cup of tea."

She rose from her seat, but a hand on her arm stopped her. Matt's mother, Heather, gave her a look of confusion. "Sit back down, Abby. You've completely missed what Margaret said." She turned to Margaret. "Say it again."

"I said"—Margaret looked at Abby—"these are the most amazing designs I've seen in a long time and I'd love to be a part of your new business."

Abby stilled, unsure she'd heard correctly this time. Heather patted her arm in reassurance.

"I'm sorry?" Abby said. "You *want* to work with me?"

"We all do," Shona said with a laugh. "You're going to make us rich with your patterns. They're gorgeous, absolutely gorgeous."

"I like the idea of local wool supplies and ancient dyeing methods," Jean added. "I like that it's going to be completely Scottish."

"I love the bags," Margaret said. "Who would have thought of designer bags in knit? They look so classy."

"The mix of textures is wonderful. Is that felting?" Heather pointed to one of the sketches.

Abby nodded, still too stunned to speak. They wanted to work with her? They didn't think she was reaching too high? They thought she had talent? It was a little too much to process.

"What are we calling this company?" Jean asked. "If we're going to be partners, I want us to have a good name."

Abby blinked a couple of times, still in shock. "I haven't thought of a name yet. I was more focused on the designs."

"Don't worry about it," Jean said. "We're great at coming up with names."

"I came up with the name for our knitting group—Knit or Die," Shona said proudly. "Best name in Scotland."

The women gave her a round of thumbs ups.

Abby eyed each of them in turn. The youngest woman in the group was in her fifties. These women had lived through a lot of life—losing husbands, losing children, losing jobs. They understood what it meant to start again.

"You really mean it? You want to do it? You want to start a business with me?"

"Of course we do, silly girl," Heather said with an understanding smile. "Now go make some tea and we'll hash out the details."

"Can I talk now?" Katy wailed.

Abby grinned at her, her head giddy with the women's generous approval. "Of course you can, sweetie."

"Great. I need to go shopping." She waved two fifty-pound notes in the air. "I need to buy a gazillion Barbies."

Abby's eyes shot between her daughter's beaming face and the huge amount of money clutched in her fists. She felt herself still. "Where did you get the money, Katy?" She tried to keep her voice steady.

There was silence in the room. All attention focused on Katy.

"Mr Boyle gave it to me to make me go away." She scrunched up her nose. "I wanted him to sit on the naughty step because he was badly behaved yesterday, but he wouldn't do it."

Abby felt her blood turn to ice. "Mr Boyle gave you a hundred pounds?"

"Uh-oh," one of the women mumbled.

Katy nodded. "Uh-huh, and a T-shirt. But I kept tripping over the T-shirt so I put it in my bedroom. I think I'll give it back to him. He probably needs it because he never has enough clothes to wear."

Abby's vision blurred. She was going to kill the man. She wasn't sure how she would do it, but it would happen. As soon as she calmed down, she was going to Google how to murder someone.

"Honey," she said to Katy, making sure her voice was soft. It wasn't her five-year-old's fault their neighbour was an idiot. "You can't keep the money. Mr Boyle shouldn't have given it to you. It's rude to pay people to go away. And that is an awful lot of money for a little girl. You need to return it."

"No!" Katy clenched the money to her chest. "It's my money. He gave it to me. I'm not giving it back. You told me it's rude to return presents. You're making me be rude."

"Katy, listen to me. The money wasn't a gift—it was a bribe. It needs to be returned."

"I won't do it!"

With a wail, her daughter ran from the room. There was stomping and a door slammed. Katy was locked in her room. Thankfully, Abby had a key. Once Katy calmed down they'd have another chat. In the meantime, there was someone else she needed to talk to.

"Excuse me, ladies." Abby stood calmly. "I need to speak to my neighbour."

"Don't mind us, dear." Margaret Campbell had a wicked gleam in her eye. "You go sort him out."

"We'll look after Katy," Heather said. "Give my nephew a good piece of your mind. He shouldn't be handing out cash without talking to her mother first."

"No. He shouldn't." Abby felt her lips thin as she stalked out of the room.

THIS IS THE LIFE, Flynn thought as he kicked back on the lounger. The sun warmed his skin and bleached his eyelids. It was so quiet he could actually hear the birds. And if he kept his eyes shut he wouldn't see the mess all around him. It was a win-win situation.

The production crew were sitting over at their van having lunch. Their quiet voices didn't bother him. Their weaselly producer was glued to his phone as he paced back and forth beside the stream. From the angry glances the weasel cast in his direction, Flynn could only assume the conversation was about him and it wasn't going well. In two weeks the jerk, along with his cameras, would be gone. In the meantime, Flynn planned to do a whole lot of nothing for them to film. He was going to kick back, enjoy his quiet time and relax.

"Mr Boyle, I need a minute of your time."

And there went his relaxed state.

Abby McKenzie's voice was a pin to his happy balloon. Flynn kept his eyes shut and hoped she'd go away. A shadow blocked out the sun. She wasn't taking the hint. He peeked out one eye.

"Abby," he drawled. "You're blocking the sun, sugar. Could you move a couple of steps to the right?"

Her cheeks flushed and her eyes narrowed. But she didn't move.

"Mr Boyle." Her tone was ice. "You can't give my daughter money. You certainly can't give her a hundred pounds. I want you to go over there and explain you made a mistake. In the meantime, here's your money." She placed five twenty-pound notes on his bare chest.

"That isn't my money, sugar. I gave the terrorist two fifties."

Her jaw clenched. "Take the money and get up. You have a mess to sort out. I need you to explain things to Katy."

He shrugged. It was hard to keep his focus on her words. The woman was seriously hot when she was riled. "Explain what? We had a deal. Why is this different from paying another kid to mow my lawn? She did a job. I paid her."

"You paid her to go away."

"Going away was the job."

"You paid her one hundred pounds to go away."

"Was worth twice the amount." He eyed her speculatively. "How much will it take to make you go away?"

She made a little growling sound that went straight to his groin. Damn, but he wanted to hear her make that sound under *very* different circumstances.

"Get up and fix this." Her words were clipped. Polite. Strained. She was cute.

"Nope. I'm busy. Got to keep up my tan." He shut his eyes

and blocked her out, almost sad he didn't get to see the steam coming out of her ears. "The Ball Babes will be back from their shopping spree soon and there won't be any peace to lie in the sun. Got to take advantage when I can."

There was a strangled sound and ice-cold water hit his face. "What the hell?" He sputtered as he shot to sitting. He was now wearing the jug of water he'd left on the grass beside him.

"You are the most infuriating man on the planet." She put her hands on the hips of her formfitting dress. It was perfectly respectable, knee length, capped sleeves and high neck, yet it hugged her curves as though it was silk lingerie. It was damn distracting. "You can't bribe a five-year-old. What kind of example do you think this sets for her? You need to get your lazy bum off that chair and sort this out."

"I don't think so. It took a lot of effort to get my bum back in this chair." He was exhausted after the energy it took to take a shower. Fear his foot would slip on the wet floor made his muscles lock. Muscles already screaming with pain. It had taken all the strength he had left to make it back to his seat. There was no way he was moving now.

"Will you please take this seriously?" Her exasperation worked like an aphrodisiac on his sluggish libido—probably not the effect she was aiming for.

Before he even knew what he was going to do, he reached out, grasped her wrist and yanked her into his lap—biting back a flinch when a stab of fresh pain hit as she landed on his knee. He shifted her into a more comfortable position. Well, more comfortable for him, anyway. She fit like she was custom made for him. And she smelled like summer. Delicious.

For a few seconds Abby was too stunned to move, but Flynn knew what was coming. He waited her out, and sure enough, she blew.

"What do you think you're doing?" She struggled to free herself, and he clamped his arms around her to hold her tight.

"Got a crick in my neck from looking up at you."

"Let me go this instant." She wriggled in his hold.

"Sit still, sugar, you're hurting my leg." And damn if she didn't do as she was told.

She glared at him. "Let me up."

He ignored her because even though she was angry, she couldn't hide the spark of curiosity in her eyes.

"Okay," he said. "I can see this is important to you, so how about I talk to the kid about the money"—he paused as he curved his hand over her hip and tugged her closer to him —"in return for a kiss."

Abby's eyes flew to his lips. A split second's hesitation that betrayed her interest. It was gone in a flash. She glared up at him. All fury and defiance. "No. This isn't something you can bargain your way out of. You need to do the decent thing here."

Flynn chuckled. "Sugar, hasn't anyone told you I'm far from decent?"

He nuzzled against the smooth column of her neck. Her scent was subtle and incredibly feminine. If he could bottle the fragrance, he'd make a mint. He heard her breath hitch and noticed she didn't make any effort to get out of his lap.

"You aren't taking this seriously," she said. "I don't know why I bothered coming over here."

"Because you can't keep away from me?" He had the same problem. Like a kid, he did things he knew would bring her over to complain, just so he could see her.

She gave an unladylike snort. "This conversation is over. Let me up."

"Come on, Abby, one little kiss and I'll do whatever you say. It's the bargain of the century." He nuzzled the sweet spot behind her ear as he poured promises of decadence into his words to tempt her. "Aren't you even a little bit curious to see what it would be like? I sure as hell would love to know how you taste. I bet you're delicious. Addictive." He trailed his lips over her jaw and felt her pulse beat a staccato rhythm under his touch. "I know you've thought about it."

"I have not." He heard the lie for what it was, a defence against her own desire.

"One kiss," he whispered against her lips. "One tiny kiss. What harm can it do?"

He saw the hesitation in her eyes. Saw the war between want and reason. Her tongue flicked out to wet her lips.

"You promise you'll sort the money thing out?"

He wanted to pump the air in victory. "If you kiss me, sugar, I'll do whatever you want me to."

Her breath left her in one long whoosh of air. "Okay," she whispered.

It was all he needed. He threaded his hand through her hair at the back of her head, angled her mouth and sipped at her lips. If this was the only taste he'd get of Abby McKenzie, he was damn well going to make it count. The sensation of her petal-soft lips against his jolted through him. With gentle licks at her bottom lip, he teased his way into her mouth. Abby was stiff in his arms, but her shallow breaths and dark, needy eyes said something else was happening in her oh-so-intelligent mind.

"You're delicious." His words were a breath against her lips. "If I was a condemned man, I'd want you as my last meal. I've been thinking about having my mouth on you since I saw you at the funeral. It's better than I imagined it would be."

Her eyes went wide, the lashes so thick and long they made him weak. He groaned and pressed his lips to hers again. And then magic happened. She softened in his arms.

Not by degrees, either. One minute she was tense and defensive, the next she was limp and needy. Flynn couldn't help the tiny possessive growl that escaped when she made a little mew of surrender.

He heard the blood rush through his veins. One sensuous lick and he was addicted, flying high on pure, unadulterated Abby. She angled her head as her arms slid around his neck. Her body pressed into him, soft curves and giving flesh.

He'd known it would be like this. From the minute their eyes had met in his uncle's dining room and the air turned static. And every time since when the heat in Abby's eyes betrayed an attraction she thought was hidden behind cold words and proper behaviour. It was never hidden. He knew she wanted him. Because he'd felt the same undeniable need to touch her too.

"That's telling him, Abby," a voice shouted, breaking through his daze.

Abby froze in his arms. Her body rigid. Her lips stiff against his.

"Aye, he'll never give Katy money again," someone else called. "You've taught that boy a lesson."

"Ah, hell," Flynn murmured against her mouth before he heaved a sigh of resignation.

His hold loosened and Abby was out of it in a split second. She stared at him, her breath ragged, her chest flushed, her eyes glistening with desire and shock. Flynn leaned back onto his elbows and forced a laidback smile when he felt wound tight enough to snap. He clenched his fists to stop from reaching for her. To stop himself pulling her back into his lap.

"Now aren't you glad you said yes?" he drawled.

She made a sound, part scream, part groan, then spun on her sexy heels and stormed back towards her house. Flynn grinned after her as he watched her hips sway.

"Don't get too smug over there," someone called from Abby's house.

He followed the voice and shook his head. His aunty Heather was standing on Abby's front steps, along with half the Knit or Die women.

"I'm telling your mum on you," Heather shouted.

Flynn groaned and flopped back onto the lounge chair. He was six months away from turning thirty and people were telling tales to his mother. He was in the middle of asking himself why he'd returned to Invertary when he heard the weasel ask his camera guy if they got the whole thing on tape.

Damn. Not again.

CHAPTER 5

"Our team was on the edge of a cliff, but we managed to get our act together and take a step forward."
Joao Pinto, former player for Portugal's national soccer team

"Are you angry with me for taking money from Mr Boyle?" Katy asked over lunch the following day. "I didn't mean to take his money. He made me do it."

Abby smiled at her daughter. She was surprised Katy had taken so long to ask about the money incident. But then they'd been busy all morning as Abby got things ready for her new business and Katy painted her toenails in various glitter colours.

"No, I'm not angry with you. I'm angry with Mr Boyle. He shouldn't give children money without making sure it's okay with their parents. He should have talked to me first."

Abby dished up vegetable soup and homemade bread, placing the bowl in front of Katy. She went back to the kitchen counter to get her own meal.

"If you're angry with him, why did you kiss him?"

Abby stilled as she poured tea into her cup from the china pot. "You were watching from your bedroom window?"

"Uh-huh." Katy nodded, her mouth full of food.

Fabulous. It seemed like half of Invertary was watching Abby make out with Flynn. She still wasn't sure how it happened. One second she'd been so mad she could have wrung his neck, the next she was panting for more of him. Hormones. It had to be hormones. They were making her terminally horny to the point where even Flynn Boyle was too much temptation to resist. It took her a minute to realise Katy was still waiting for an answer as to why she'd kissed Flynn.

"It was an accident," she said as she sat at the kitchen table beside her daughter. "I didn't mean to kiss him."

Katy looked puzzled. "How can you kiss someone by accident?"

"You'll understand when you get older." *When your hormones start overruling your brain.* Oh yes, Abby could *not* wait for that phase of her parenting life. She eyed her daughter speculatively and wondered how old you had to be to enter a convent.

Katy let out a huge sigh. "You always say that. I'm fed up waiting to get older. I want to know now."

"And what would you do with all this knowledge?" Abby pointed a piece of bread at Katy.

Her daughter narrowed her eyes. "Rule the world."

Abby was still laughing when she heard a car approach. She was in no mood to tolerate another one of Flynn's get-togethers. The last lot had only just left, and she'd been hoping for a few days' reprieve before the next round of partying started. A moment later she heard the car veer up her gravel driveway instead of heading up Flynn's dirt road.

"Someone's coming," she told Katy. "You stay here. Finish your lunch."

That earned her another frown. Abby walked down the long hallway, past the staircase with its carved wooden banister, to the front door. When she opened it, she stopped dead.

Her elder sister was climbing out of a black Bentley. Abby froze, her hand on the door, her eyes glued to her sister. It'd been seven years since she'd seen her last. Seven years since Victoria had come to tell her their parents had disinherited her and she shouldn't come home unless she came back as a single woman. They'd wanted to annul her marriage. Divorce was *so* common. Too common for the Montgomery-Clarks. But if it took a divorce to divest Abby of her lower-class husband, they would live with it. Better divorce than an unsuitable match that brought shame on the family name.

The driver's door opened and a man she didn't recognise stepped out. He was pristine in a tailor-made charcoal suit, Italian leather shoes and crisp white shirt. There was grey at his temples and laugh lines around his eyes. He gave her a smile tinged with sympathy. It made her heart sink.

Her sister brushed her palm over the front of her navy shift dress. An understated Gucci bag hung at her elbow, matching shoes in mulberry on her feet. Her hair was perfectly styled in a chignon. Her makeup subtle. Her jewellery expensive and tasteful, as befitting a lady. She looked much younger than her forty-four years, yet her attitude made her seem older. Victoria's eyes slowly turned to Abby, and Abby's mouth went dry.

"Hello, Abigail," Victoria said. "I apologise for the inconvenience of visiting unannounced. May we come in?"

Abby found it hard to speak. The words seemed to stick in her throat. Her eyes prickled with tears she wouldn't dare shed. Family. She never thought she'd see them again. She never imagined they'd want to see her.

Abby cleared her throat. "Of course." She gestured for them to come inside.

She eyed the man. He wasn't quite six foot tall, although he was solidly built and carried an air of someone who was used to giving orders—and being obeyed. Victoria gestured towards the man.

"May I present Lawrence Maynard, or Maynard-Fraser-Grayson."

Abby felt panic solidify in her stomach as she recognised his name. It felt like a rock, indigestible and heavy, weighing her down. She was shaking hands with the family lawyer. There could be no good reason he would come to Scotland. None. She swallowed her fear and smiled politely.

"Pleased to meet you," Abby said automatically as her training kicked into place.

"It's entirely my pleasure, Abigail." Lawrence held out his hand.

"Please, call me Abby. No one calls me Abigail anymore. Come in and join me for tea."

Her sister's lips pursed before thinning into obvious disapproval at the nickname. "Tea would be lovely." Victoria's voice was frosty.

"This way." Abby's led them past the living room and study to the kitchen at the back of the house. The bright pastel colours she'd used to decorate her home seemed inappropriate for such a heavy event as a visit from family.

She opened the kitchen door for them. Victoria took two steps into the room and stopped dead. Abby ignored the unspoken censure at having taken them to the kitchen. She looked past her sister to find Katy standing on a stool, rooting around in the pantry. She had a pack of chocolate buttons in her hand, chocolate smeared around her mouth and a guilty look on her face. Lawrence coughed. When Abby's eyes shot to him it looked like he was hiding a laugh. Victoria stared at Katy, her expression unreadable, but the tension in her shoulders radiated disapproval.

"Katy." Abby jerked herself into action. "What do you think you're doing?"

"It wasn't my fault." Katy blinked huge doe eyes intended to melt Abby's heart. The little master manipulator. "My tummy made me do it. It needed chocolate. I tried to tell it you said no chocolate till after lunch, but it wouldn't listen." She held her hand to her mouth and whispered loudly, "My tummy doesn't like the soup."

There was another cough from Lawrence. Abby took the chocolate from her daughter's hand, put it back on the top shelf and picked her up. She walked back around the marble-topped counter to the dining table and put Katy in her chair.

"I don't care if your tummy doesn't like the soup. Your mouth is going to eat it all up. Are we clear?"

"Yes, Muma." Katy sounded like she'd been given a life sentence. With heavy, slow movements, she picked up her spoon. "Jonathan doesn't have to wait to eat chocolate. He gets chocolate for breakfast, lunch and dinner. *His mum* says chocolate is healthy and he'll get sick if he doesn't eat it all up." She blinked with exaggerated innocence.

"I wonder if Jonathan has to sit on the naughty step for telling all those lies?" Abby said. "I think children who tell lies should definitely sit on the naughty step. What do you think, Katy?"

Katy lifted the spoon to her mouth and slurped up some soup. "My tummy says it's changed its mind. This soup is yummy."

Abby stroked her daughter's hair. "Well, isn't that convenient."

Katy gave her a huge, heart-melting grin before she

spotted the visitors. She looked up at her mum then stared back at them, practically buzzing with her need to know who they were.

"Katy, this is your aunt Victoria and her friend Mr Maynard." She turned to her sister. "This is Katy, my daughter."

Lawrence smiled widely at Katy. Victoria showed no emotion whatsoever. Katy let her jaw drop dramatically before bouncing with excitement.

"Really? You're really my aunty? I never had one before. I always wanted one. Even when I was really little. Jonathan's got about a million aunties and uncles. They always bring him presents when they visit." She batted those eyelashes again.

Victoria seemed stunned by Katy's blatant wheedling.

Lawrence barked a laugh. "Sorry, little one, we didn't realise we were supposed to bring a gift."

Katy's whole body sagged with disappointment.

"Perhaps we could remedy the oversight later?" Lawrence said. "Maybe you could tell me what sort of gift an aunt usually brings and I'll help Victoria arrange for one."

Katy perked right up. "I can do that. But you have to remember I'm a girl. I don't like the same presents as Jonathan. He got a pirate costume last time his aunty and uncle visited and it had no sparkles on it. It was a really yucky brown. If you get me a pirate costume it has to have sparkles."

"I'll make sure to remember." Lawrence smiled widely.

Katy nodded, obviously pleased Lawrence could be trained. Abby looked at him cautiously. Surely if he were the bearer of bad news he wouldn't be so nice to Katy. Surely this was a good sign. She wasn't reassured.

"Please, sit." Abby gestured to the table.

Lawrence didn't hesitate. He pulled out a seat beside Katy

and commented on how delicious her soup looked. Victoria sat as far away from Katy as was possible, yet still remain polite. Abby felt her chest squeeze. What happened to the woman who used to hug her when she was a child? Who laughed and played? Who twirled her around the nursery as they danced? With an aching sadness, she filled the kettle and prepared a tray with teacups.

The last time she'd heard from her family was when her father had suffered a heart attack. Charles, her older brother, had called and demanded she visit her father's deathbed. Unfortunately, Abby was nursing her terminally ill husband and caring for her infant daughter at the time. It wasn't possible to rush to the bed of a man who'd made it clear she was nothing more than an inconvenience and disappointment to him. A man who had disinherited her and hadn't been interested enough to tell her himself. A man she'd still loved—more fool her.

She cleared her throat. "Is Mother well?" Her insides spasmed at the thought of losing another family member. Even one who didn't want her.

"Quite well, thank you." Victoria's voice was emotionless.

Abby's stomach unknotted. Slightly.

"What brings you to the Highlands?" She tried to sound casual, but there was a wobble in her voice. She cringed at the sound. Aware of the vulnerability it revealed.

"It's best if we don't speak of the reason for our visit in front of the child," Victoria said.

Abby turned slowly. "Her name is Katy."

Victoria's eyes jerked away from Katy. "Yes," was all she said.

Lawrence gave Abby a sympathetic smile. "Perhaps when Katy is finished her meal, she wouldn't mind playing in another room for a while?"

"I want to stay here," Katy complained straight away. If there was gossip, she didn't want to miss it.

Abby pulled out the big guns. "How about you watch *Peppa Pig* in the living room?"

"Really?" Katy's whole face lit up then she frowned. "Jonathan says only babies watch *Peppa Pig*."

"I watch *Peppa Pig*, am I a baby?" Abby said.

"No." Katy giggled.

"See? Your best friend doesn't know everything, does he? Eat up and I'll put the TV on."

The hated soup was finished in record time. Abby settled Katy in front of the TV with a drink, closed the living room door and went back to the kitchen. For a second she felt like she'd interrupted something. Victoria was glaring at the far wall, her mouth pinched, her back straight. Lawrence's cheeks were flushed as he stared at Victoria with undisguised frustration.

"Tea, then." Abby faked a lightness she didn't feel.

"Tea can wait, Abigail." Victoria frowned. "*Abby.* Please, join us."

Abby changed direction away from the kitchen counter to sit facing her sister. Her hands clenched tightly in her lap. Lawrence's eyes softened. He looked at Victoria, who gave him an irritated glance before turning back to Abby.

"Mother was upset to discover you'd made an appearance in the tabloids."

Abby's hands began to tremble and she hoped Victoria didn't notice. What else could they do to show their disapproval? They'd already disowned her. She fought to hold her chin high. Victoria's emotionless eyes held hers.

"Mother is anxious to ensure your daughter is receiving the care befitting a Montgomery-Clark."

Abby flicked the tip of her tongue over suddenly dry lips. "Katy isn't a Montgomery-Clark, she's a McKenzie."

Victoria stared at her for a minute. Her expression gave nothing away. "There are concerns over the influences in your daughter's life. It's clear your association with Mr Boyle, and his friends, exposes your daughter to dangerous and undesirable examples of behaviour."

Abby couldn't breathe. Couldn't move. The world had stopped. "What do you mean? Get to the point, Victoria."

Victoria's lip curled slightly. "Our mother wishes to start proceedings to remove your daughter from those undesirable influences. She feels a more appropriate environment can be provided at Montgomery Hall."

Abby's hands hit the edge of the table. Her nails bit into the wood as she held on tight. It wasn't anchor enough. She needed something stronger to hold her in place.

"You want to take my daughter?" The words were a whisper. The thought too horrific to be spoken any louder.

Victoria gave a curt nod. "If that's what's needed." Her eyes were unwaveringly cold. "You didn't think Mother would allow another generation of Montgomery-Clarks to stray, did you?"

No, one generation was enough. *Abby* was enough. Abby fought the urge to vomit as her lunch curdled in her stomach.

"Is that why you're here?" She turned on Lawrence. "To serve notice?"

He shook his head. Grim. The man was grim. "As I explained to your family, no court would willingly remove a child from her mother unless the situation was extreme." He gave Victoria a sharp look. "In my opinion, this situation is nowhere near extreme. I was able to persuade your mother to wait before proceeding with legal action. Her concession came with one condition—a family member must assess the situation in lieu of a visit from your mother. That is why Victoria is here. I'm here as your mother's legal representative." His jaw clenched. "I'm also here to give an unbiased opinion on the matter. It was a condition I insisted upon."

Lawrence Maynard, a partner in her mother's firm, was here to monitor Victoria? To make sure Abby wasn't railroaded? She swallowed hard. He was an ally. She had an ally. Her shoulders relaxed slightly.

"Lawrence's opinion will not factor into the report I give to mother," Victoria snapped.

"I can give my own report, Vicki," Lawrence snapped back.

Vicki? No one called Victoria Vicki. Abby felt like she'd walked onstage in the middle of a play and she didn't know her lines. No, that wasn't true. She knew one line. The only one that mattered.

"You won't take my daughter."

"It's all about what's best for the child."

Abby slapped the table. "I'm what's best for Katy. Me. Her mother."

"I agree," Lawrence said.

Victoria scowled at Lawrence. She hooked her handbag over her arm as she stood. For a second, Abby thought she saw her sister's hand tremble. "You have one week to prove this is an environment fit for a Montgomery-Clark."

"Are you insane?" Abby felt the blood drain from her face. "I won't be bullied into complying with your demands. You have no right to assess me on anything, let alone how I care for my child."

Abby stood to face her sister. Every muscle in her body vibrated with outrage.

"Do you really want to take on Mother, *Abigail*? You know how ruthless she can be when she wants something. Nothing matters more to her than the good name of the family. Lawrence might not agree with her, but he isn't the only lawyer in his firm, and his firm isn't the only one in London.

Do you really want to go up against the team of lawyers Mother would assemble? Do you want your life raked through the courts? Do you want your daughter to suffer the stress and insecurity of your actions? A stressful litigation could drag on for years. If things are as idyllic as you say they are you have nothing to fear in allowing Lawrence and I access over the next seven days. Wouldn't that be the most sensible course of action?"

The kitchen door burst open and Katy barrelled in. Her cheeks were rosy from running fast—her only speed. She smiled widely as she ran straight into Abby's arms.

"I'm done with *Peppa Pig*. Now I want to make art."

Abby wrapped her arms around her whole world and held on tight. Her eyes caught her sister's and she thought there was a flash of envy in Victoria's gaze. It was gone much too quickly to be sure. Abby turned back to her daughter. "Why don't you go set up your paints on the table in the living room?"

"I want you to watch me." Katy pouted. "I'm making a *Peppa Pig* world."

"I'll come watch you as soon as Victoria and Lawrence leave." She scowled at her sister. "Which will be in just a minute."

Katy ran off to do as she was told. Abby faced her sister. "Is this what you want, Victoria? You want to help Mother take away my child?"

Victoria's face was expressionless. "As you well know, Abigail, when it comes to dealing with Mother, personal desires are irrelevant. What I want is irrelevant. My purpose is to protect the legacy of the Montgomery-Clarks. It's what we were born to do. It's what you should have done. You know as well as I do just how harsh the consequences are when you disagree with Mother. Take my advice and comply with her wishes. It is pointless fighting."

"What happened to you?" Abby wanted to shake some sense into her sister. "What happened to the woman who laughed and played with me when I was a child?"

Victoria's head snapped back as though she'd been struck. "She learned the hard way that there is only one possible course of behaviour for a Montgomery-Clark—the one Mother deems acceptable."

Abby shook her head in disgust. "I can't deal with you right now. You need to leave."

Victoria's back was stiff, her face unyielding. "I'll be in touch in the morning for your decision." Without another word, she turned on her heels and strode to the front door.

A strong hand patted Abby's shoulder. "I'm sorry, Abby. I did what I could and I won't stop trying. Your mother is incensed over this, but that doesn't make her right."

"What about Charles—what does my brother have to say about mother's latest plan?"

Lawrence let out a sharp laugh. "Charles would very much like for this matter to be resolved. He informed me he has better things to do with his time than listen to your mother whine about it." Lawrence's eyes gentled. "Your brother cares only about himself. You won't find an ally there, I'm afraid."

Abby wasn't surprised. Charles had always been nothing more than the mouthpiece of their parents. "I can't let them take my baby," she whispered.

"No, *we* can't. Let's deal with this one step at a time. We have a week to work on Victoria, and I have a few tricks up my sleeve."

"Why are you doing this, Lawrence? Surely helping me is a conflict of interest. Won't this get you into trouble?"

He smiled sadly. "I've found more and more lately this job of mine leaves a bad taste in my mouth. This situation is the last straw, so to speak. I think it may be time to make some changes in my life." He squeezed her shoulder. "Try not to worry. This isn't a done deal. Nowhere near it."

With one last reassuring smile, he followed Victoria out of the house.

"Look." Katy barrelled into the room, holding a drawing she'd already made of a pig. "It's Peppa!"

"It's gorgeous, baby. You're a clever little artist."

Katy gave her mum a speculative look out of the corner of her eye. "You know, it's super-hard work making art."

"Is it?" Abby pulled her daughter into her embrace.

Katy nodded. "I used *loads* of energy." She leaned back to look in Abby's eyes, placing a tiny hand on each of her mum's cheeks. "I've completely run out of energy."

"How awful." Abby smiled in spite of the fear gripping her. "How do you think we could fix it? Is there a way we could replenish your energy before you fall over in a heap?"

Katy nodded solemnly. "I think chocolate would do it." She batted those long, dark lashes.

Abby smiled, hugged her tight and kissed her cheek. "Well, you better go get the chocolate before it's too late and you collapse."

She was off her mum's knee and running for the pantry before the sentence was out of Abby's mouth, proving once and for all that her energy was *entirely* depleted. Abby chewed her bottom lip as she stared at the door her sister had stalked through.

She wouldn't let them take Katy. It was unthinkable. As much as she wanted to tell Victoria to go to hell, one week was a small price to pay if it meant her daughter wouldn't get upset. Katy had been through so much already in her short life. She deserved the security of knowing she wouldn't lose her only remaining parent. And Abby would do whatever it took to give her child security.

Even if it meant making a deal with the devil.

Abby reached for the phone, hands shaking, and dialled Jena. "I need help," she said by way of hello. "My family want to take Katy away from me. They're using Flynn's bad behaviour against me. They didn't like my appearance on the news. I need help talking to Flynn. I need him to be on his best behaviour this week while my sister is here, assessing me."

There was a silence for a moment. "I think you've already seen Flynn's best behaviour, honey," Jena said. "I'm not sure what else we can do."

Abby felt tears prick her eyes. She blinked them back. Now wasn't the time to fall apart. She listened as Matt asked what Abby wanted and Jena explained.

"Give me the phone," she heard Matt bark. "Abby?" he said in her ear. "Don't worry about it. We've got this. Be at Flynn's parents' house tomorrow morning. I'll sort Flynn out for you."

Before she could say a word, he hung up. Abby spent a few minutes staring at the phone. She quietly placed it in the dock and sat on the chair behind her. She really hoped Matt's confidence wasn't misplaced. If she lost her baby to her cold-hearted family all because Flynn Boyle couldn't behave like a grownup for one single week, she would… She would do nothing. If they took her baby, they would take everything. And Abby wasn't sure she'd survive long enough to exact vengeance on Flynn.

CHAPTER 6

*"I've had fourteen bookings this season—eight of which were my
fault, but seven of which were disputable."*
Paul Gascoigne, former England national soccer player

Flynn waited until the camera crew had gone home for the
night before he went round to the back of his van and bent
over to open the hatch underneath it. He smiled into the
darkness when he heard the tiny squeaks.

"Look who's hungry." He picked up the three miniature
hedgehogs and placed them on the grass.

The babies were about five weeks old, as far as he could
tell. He'd found them beside their dead mother one night
when he'd been out walking in the woods. Well, hobbling in
the woods. He wasn't sure what killed the mother, but the
babies had been mewing softly beside her, hungry and
scared. Flynn had scooped them up, as he'd done with many
an injured animal over the years, taken them back to his van
and set up a home for them in the cabin under it. In a couple

of weeks they would start foraging for their own food, but for now they still needed him.

Flynn fetched their food from his kitchen, sat on the grass beside them and hand-fed the hoglets. They would have been fine eating straight from the dish, but he needed the comfort of caring for them more than they needed the comfort he could provide. For a precious few minutes they helped him forget his life was screwed up six ways to Sunday.

"Wouldn't it be great if everything was as simple as dealing with you guys?"

Pulling his phone from his pocket, Flynn called his agent's number again. Professional athletes didn't tend to keep office hours so Flynn knew there would be someone to take his call.

"I'm sorry, Mr Boyle," the secretary said. "As I told you earlier, he's unavailable."

Flynn ground his teeth together as he stared out into the darkness. "He's been unavailable for days. I keep leaving messages, but he doesn't get back to me."

"I'm afraid all I can do is take another message." The woman sounded as though she'd rather boil her eyeballs.

"Great, take another message. Tell him, *again*, that I want him to get me out of this documentary shoot. I've had enough. I want it done. He needs to talk to the sports studio and break the contract."

"No problem, Mr Boyle." The line went dead as the damn woman hung up on him. Again.

Flynn let out a stream of curses, most of which he'd learned on the soccer pitch, and let his head thud back onto the van behind him. His agent was dodging him. Michael was right: now there were no huge contracts in his future, or megabuck endorsements, his representation had lost interest in him. If this kept up he'd have to go to London in person and camp on his doorstep until he dealt with him. He pinched the bridge of his nose as the pain in his leg spiked. Powerless. He was so bloody powerless. The injury had robbed him of his career and the respect it garnered. He'd been so used to having a voice. People fell over themselves to listen to him. Now, he couldn't even get his agent on the phone.

One of the hoglets demanded his attention by trying to climb over his leg. Flynn smiled and helped the little guy. Life was so much simpler with animals than it was with people. Maybe he'd take the money he'd made from investing in his brother's big brain and buy an island somewhere. He'd fill the place with all sorts of animals and become a hermit. Aye, it was a great idea. No more people. No more criticism, or whining, or bullying. No more living up to someone's expectations or disappointing them when he didn't. The more he thought about it, the better the idea became.

Flynn closed his eyes, listened to the noises of the night and planned a future away from it all.

THE WALLS WERE CLOSING in on Abby. As soon as Katy was asleep, she locked the house up tight, snatched the baby monitor and made the short walk across the corner of Flynn's property to the stream. She knew from experience she would hear Katy perfectly from her spot by the water and could be back at her side in a moment if needed.

The darkness folded around her like a blanket. The weight of the night soothing to her nerves. Behind a copse of trees, hidden by the overgrowth, was a fallen log. Abby brushed her fingers over the worn wood. Years she'd come here to sit. First with her husband and then alone. She remembered the times she'd sat wrapped in David's arms as they whispered their hopes for the future. He'd had such wonderful dreams. All of which revolved around having a family, something he hadn't known as a child. He'd wanted a house full of laughing children, a thriving business, a place in the community and to love her for the rest of his life. They were simple desires, but each one infinitely precious. Remembering David's whispered hopes brought back the gnawing pain deep in Abby's chest. The pain that never quite left her. The one throbbing with memory.

Abby sat on the log and stared out over the water. The soothing sounds of it trickling over the pebbled bed eased her clenched muscles somewhat.

"I'm screwing up, David," she whispered to the water. "If you were still here, everything would be okay. You would know what to do about Victoria." She scoffed at herself. "If you were here, this situation wouldn't have happened in the first place. You would have dealt with Flynn before everything got out of hand. He would have listened to you. Everyone did. You had a way with people. Charming, you were so charming, David."

She pulled her feet up onto the log in front of her and wrapped her arms around her knees.

"If you'd been here, we probably wouldn't have had to sell the land to Flynn to start again. You would have thought of a way to keep the mushroom farm going, even after the cave-in." She closed her eyes. "I'm so sorry, honey. I wish I could have saved your farm for you. I know how much it meant to you."

She worked to steady her breathing for a minute or two. Listening to the water and the night noises as small creatures rustled through the edge of the wood.

"I kissed him," she whispered.

The breeze on her cheeks was all the answer she received.

"I liked it." She let out a long groan. "I feel as though I shouldn't have liked it. As though I've been unfaithful to you. But you aren't here, David. You left me, my sweet man. I miss you so much. I miss your arms around me. I miss your sweet kisses. I hate having another man's kiss to compare to yours. I hate that I liked it so much. I hate that it made me feel. At the same time, I desperately want to feel like that again. Like I'm actually living my life, rather than treading water, trying to keep afloat, trying not to drown. I'm sorry about this too. I'm sorry I have to move on from you." She let out a sharp laugh. "Although probably not with Flynn." Her fingertips traced over her lips, as though it was possible to still feel Flynn's touch there. "I did like his kiss, though."

An owl cried out, breaking into the memory of Flynn's warm, firm lips on hers. Of his taking control of the kiss, of her body, of her. It was delicious. More so, because she felt it was almost forbidden. Her heart had thudded with the teenage excitement of kissing a bad boy. What a cliché! She was a mother, with responsibilities, not a hormonally driven teenager with time to lust after an inappropriate boy. She had no time to think about kissing anyone. She had to focus on her daughter.

"Victoria wants Katy." The words burned like acid in her throat. "Well, Mother wants Katy. Not to spend time with her, no, that wouldn't be proper enough. She wants to send her to boarding school, teach her how to be a proper lady, raise her to be reserved and constrained—exactly as she did with me. It kills me to think it's even a possibility."

Abby put her feet down and stared at the black water. The only light came from the moon above and the glow from the house behind her. The world was painted in shades of grey, and for some reason the lack of colour made it feel intimate. This place, this log, was the only spot where Abby felt like she was comforted. Here she could feel David with her. Here she could let go of her responsibilities and fears, if only for a moment. She gave voice to her worries. Only here, where there was no one to judge, or condemn, or to scare.

"I wish you could see Katy," she said. "You would be totally in love with her. More than you were before you went away. She is priceless. Smart, funny, full of life and love. She makes me laugh, David, even when my heart is breaking or my stomach is roiling with fear. I never know what she's going to say next, which could be a huge problem right now. I dread to think what she might tell Victoria. It will be a miracle if Victoria doesn't condemn my parenting on Katy's tales alone. I need to figure out a way to censor Katy. She's so young. Too young to understand her words can be used against us. I don't know what to do. I wish you were here to help me. I wish it wasn't just me. Alone. Fighting everything alone."

Abby stood, dusted off her dress and blinked back tears she didn't have time to shed.

"I'm being pathetic. There's no time to wallow in self-pity. There are things to deal with." She smiled out over the water. "I wish she knew you, darling." Her voice broke on the words. "I wish that the most. I wish she had you."

She wiped a stray tear with the back of her hand as she turned to leave. She couldn't stay away from the house too long. That would be irresponsible. And as much as Abby's responsibilities pressed down on her, making her buckle under the weight, she couldn't ignore them. No, she could never escape for longer than a few stolen minutes. With one last glance at the log that held so many of her private memories, good and bad, she crept silently back to her house. And back to the problems mounting as they waited for her to deal with them.

FLYNN WATCHED Abby walk back to her house. He hadn't meant to listen. He'd intended to tease. To make her eyes blaze with passion and coax her into another kiss.

And then she'd started to talk.

At her first word, Flynn took a step back and let the darkness swallow him. Loneliness and fear oozed from her, like blood from a seeping wound. He was used to an Abby who was controlled, responsible and sensible. Not one who was scared of the future and insecure about herself.

And he was to blame.

There was no denying it. He'd been blamed for other people's problems in the past. It didn't have much effect on him. But this was something else. Something new.

He rubbed his chest where it started to ache. It took him a minute to realise why he was in pain. It wasn't heartburn.

It was guilt.

CHAPTER 7

*"The rules of soccer are very simple, basically it is this: if it moves,
kick it. If it doesn't move, kick it until it does."*
Phil Woosnam, former Welsh football player and manager

It was early. Too early for Flynn. Especially seeing as he'd been awake most of the night trying to come up with a way to help Abby—and hopefully get rid of the pain in his chest at the same time. His brother didn't care about Flynn being knackered. Nope, Harry ignored his pleas and dragged him over to their parents' house. Apparently there was a family meeting and his attendance was mandatory. Flynn didn't understand why it couldn't have waited an hour or two. At least until he'd had a pot of coffee and his brain was working properly. He never got up before nine unless he was training. Which meant he was never getting up before nine again. Now there was a cheery thought to start the day.

His brother, Harry, pushed him into his parents' dining room and Flynn stopped dead. The room was packed. This couldn't be good. There was Matt and his wife Jena, Harry and his fiancée Magenta, Claire and her fiancé Grunt. Seriously? Grunt? On what planet was Grunt an acceptable name? Flynn shook his head. His parents were there. His aunt Heather was there. The only one missing was Megan, the other half of the nightmare twins. Everyone in the room was frowning at him. Well, except for Magenta, she was grinning. It wasn't pleasant. It was the same look he imagined on the face of Jaws just before he ate the boat captain.

"Got any coffee, Mum?" Flynn plopped into one of the two free chairs.

"Coffee later. Talk first," his father said.

He'd used the same tone each time Flynn had screwed up as a kid. It set off all sorts of alarm bells in Flynn's head. He suddenly worried he wasn't just an attendee at the meeting, but the subject of it.

Jena looked up from her phone and spoke to Matt. "That was Abby. She's running late and isn't sure when she'll get here."

"Should we wait for her?" Matt frowned and Jena shook her head.

"Why does Abby need to be at a family meeting?" Flynn asked.

"Because, dirt-for-brains," Matt said, "this involves her too."

Yeah, Flynn was right. This wasn't a run-of-the-mill family get-together. He was about to get roasted. His dad confirmed his suspicion when he looked right at Flynn and said, "Let's get this over with."

As if everyone knew something Flynn didn't, all eyes turned to Matt, who sat beside Flynn. Matt glared at Flynn as he spoke.

"Abby's sister is here to assess whether or not she's a fit

mother. She's got one week to prove Katy lives in a good environment. A stable, quiet and civilised environment."

Right, now Flynn knew why he was there. He was obviously the unstable, noisy and uncivilised element that needed to be fixed. Excellent. And all of this without a cup of coffee. He opened his mouth to tell them he already knew about Abby's problem and was working on it, when Matt's glare dared him to speak. Guess he wasn't allowed to talk. Fine. He folded his arms and waited for the rest of it.

"If," Matt continued, "at the end of the week, her sister decides Abby isn't a fit mother, or the living environment isn't healthy, the family is going to bring legal action and try to take Katy away from Abby."

Everyone in the room stared at Flynn. The air of disapproval was palpable. He stared back. They wanted him silent. They were bloody well going to get silent. There were groans of frustration.

"You're the reason her family is here, dirt-for-brains," Matt said. "They saw Abby losing her mind on the ten o'clock news. They think living next to you is going to warp the kid. You need to clean up your act and behave like a civilised person."

Aye, Flynn was done being quiet. "Look who's talking. You wouldn't recognise civilised if it bit you on the backside. Don't forget, I was by your side for most of your delinquent behaviour. I know exactly how uncivilised you can be. You might want to shove the superior attitude before you say anything else." Flynn sure as hell wasn't going to share about his intent to help Abby now.

"This isn't about Matt," his dad said. "It's about you."

"We've had enough, son," his mum said. "We're worried about you. And now we're worried about Abby and Katy."

"It's time to grow up," Matt said, making Flynn's fists clench with the need to pummel him. "We're sick of cleaning up after you and dealing with the fallout from your life. People are really beginning to suffer, and it's pissing us all off that you don't seem to give a flying fart about the damage you cause. This situation with Abby and her daughter is serious, and you influence the outcome of it. We're all worried about it. We're not sure you won't blow it for her. You're a mess. You're out of control and it's time that changed. It's time *you* changed. We're here today to make sure you get the message."

Flynn stared at his cousin's angry face. "Seriously?" To hell with coffee. There wasn't enough caffeine in the world to deal with this. "You've staged an intervention? For me?"

"Call it what you like." Matt crossed his arms. "We've all had enough of you. You've been back home two months and you're driving everyone insane. Especially Abby. It's time you quit behaving like a teenager."

"My behaviour isn't any of your business. I don't go around telling you how to live."

Matt let out a cold bark of laughter. "You don't have the right to tell *anyone* how to live."

Flynn clenched a fist. It'd been a good few years since he'd gone head to head with his older cousin. Maybe it was time to rectify that.

"Your behaviour affects everyone around you," his mum said. Her pixie-shaped face, which had very few lines considering her age, radiated distress. "You might think it's only about you, but it isn't. I thought I taught you better than this. I thought I raised you to understand that your actions have consequences, for you and for those around you. I don't know where I went wrong."

Great. Mother guilt. Just what he needed. The woman had been taking lessons from Aunty Heather. Again. He cast a glance at Heather and watched as she nodded her approval at his mum. Yeah, they'd definitely teamed up.

"We had the tabloids camped on our doorstep for days when the paternity story broke," his dad said. "Your mum couldn't even go to the local shop without getting harassed about your love child."

"I didn't father that woman's kid. The claim was bogus." Great. Now he was being blamed for things outside his control.

"That's not the point," Harry chimed in. "The point is there wouldn't have been any paternity case if you weren't living like Hugh freaking Hefner."

Flynn rolled his eyes. Hef *wished* he could live like Flynn. There was no comparison.

"People keep calling me." Matt scowled. "Every time you get into trouble, they want my reaction. As though your cop cousin would step in and sort it out. Even if I could, I wouldn't. You know, life isn't all about you. You aren't the only one in town the paparazzi find fascinating. Josh, Kirsty and Harry here are trying to live quietly. You're screwing it up for them."

This little attack on his character was getting out of hand pretty damn fast. "You want me to leave town?"

Aunty Heather shook her head. "We want you to grow up."

Well, that sucked.

Flynn worked at controlling his anger. This situation needed to be defused, and fast. It was time to charm his way out of trouble. He gave them the smile that showed his dimples and used the same self-deprecating head tilt that worked with aggravating reporters during interviews.

"You're making a big deal out of nothing," he said. "I'm just having some fun. A little downtime while the leg heals. So I've had a few friends over. And yeah, things might have gotten a little out of hand, but seriously, you lot need to lighten up." He congratulated himself on his tact.

His mother straightened her shoulders and pursed her lips before she spoke. "You have three half-naked women living with you in your motorhome. Rumours are rife. Your women do their best to keep those rumours going. We've had a magazine reporter asking if the town as a whole was alternative when it came to relationships. The woman hinted we were free and easy with our..." She trailed off, suddenly finding the tablecloth really interesting.

"With our sex lives," his dad finished for her, practically barking the words.

"It's embarrassing seeing you live with three women," his mother said.

Flynn thought it probably wasn't the time to explain there was nothing going on with the Babes. They'd needed somewhere to have fun; he'd needed the distraction and asked them to stay. There were no multiple girlfriends. No group sex. In fact, no sex at all. Being in pain all the time didn't exactly put him in the mood. Not to mention he'd been in and out of hospital for months. He knew he had a reputation with the ladies, but seriously asking him to perform after orthopaedic surgery was pushing it a bit far. He opened his mouth to confess about the women, saw the glares coming at him and decided no one was really in a listening mood. They were leaning more towards a ranting mood. So he kept the information to himself.

Jena glared at him. "Then there are your visits to the pub. Dougal is losing business because no one wants to eat around your entourage. You're noisy, rude and disruptive."

"Not to mention the town is overrun by bimbos," Magenta said. "Every week brings a new wave of bleach-blonde stick insects with inflatable boobs. We're tripping over them. They're all here to vie for the honour of getting into your pants, probably for the money in your pocket, because it sure as hell couldn't be for anything else."

Flynn scowled at her as his brother high-fived his fiancée. It was painful to think he was stuck with her in his family for the rest of his life. She'd been a pain in his backside when she was a kid. She'd only gotten worse with age.

"It isn't just the women," Aunty Heather said. "You leave a trail of destruction wherever you go. There's rubbish from parties. Women's clothing hanging on bushes by the stream. One of your friends got drunk and drove through three fields taking out the fences. Fences people had to fix. It's costly, time consuming and downright annoying to clean up after you."

"I want to talk about the noise," Jena told him. "We live on the other side of the field and we can still hear the racket you make. People shouting at all hours. Loud music. Car horns. It isn't only Abby you affect with your wild behaviour, it's all of us. And you don't listen when people complain. Abby has spoken to you time and again. Matt has been over to your place several times and yet you haven't changed one thing."

Matt's lips thinned. "I've been cutting you some slack seeing as you're family. But from now on I'm going to arrest your hairy backside for disturbing the peace, littering, being naked in public—whatever I can come up with. You can have your film crew sit with you in your jail cell. I'm sure it will make great TV."

"Okay." Flynn barely managed to keep a lid on his temper. "I think I've had enough of this intervention. Thanks for making my morning memorable, but I'm done here."

"We're not done." Matt put a hand on Flynn's shoulder.

"Nowhere near done," Jena added.

"We need to talk about the state you're in," Harry said. "You look like crap."

That was pretty offensive coming from a guy who thought an Einstein T-shirt was high fashion. He sneered at his brother. Harry ignored him.

"You drink too much."

"I haven't been drunk in ages."

"Not since your last DUI." His father frowned. "At least you don't have your licence back yet. One less thing to worry about."

Flynn just stared at him. Talk about an overreaction. One DUI and everybody freaks out.

"You don't shower," Harry carried on. "And you've stopped buttoning your shirts. What's with that? We don't live in the Mediterranean. We're in Scotland. Sure, it's summer, but it's still bloody freezing. It's like you think you're Matthew McConaughey. Or maybe the Hef thing is spot on. Are you going to start wearing pyjamas next?"

"And cover this?" Flynn looked down at his bare chest. "Abs like these shouldn't be hidden."

He'd thought it was funny. He'd even hoped the mood would lighten. It didn't. There were groans of frustration.

Jena threw up her hands in disgust. "You aren't listening to a word we're saying. You really don't care how you're affecting your family and friends, do you?"

It was plain no one was willing to listen to anything he said. Flynn pushed to his feet.

"Thanks for the chat," he told them as he headed for the door. "It was a blast. Let's *not* do it again sometime."

"That's it? That's your reaction? You're just going to run away?" his dad barked.

"Run? I'd be ecstatic if I could run. No, Da, I'm just going to hobble away. Feel free to continue the character assassination once I'm gone."

His dad started to bluster as he rose from his seat.

"Let him go," Matt said. "I knew this was a waste of time. Flynn only cares about Flynn. And right now he's too busy feeling sorry for himself to notice anyone else. I just hope he can live with himself when they take Abby's kid from her."

Flynn clenched his jaw at Matt's words. To hell with him. To hell with all of them.

He stalked down the hall, threw open the front door and barrelled straight into Abby.

"Sorry," she said as he caught her around the waist to stop her from stumbling.

Her cheeks were flushed as though she'd been running. Flynn's fingers curled into soft flesh as he fought the urge to bury his nose in the crook of her neck and breathe deeply. He knew Abby's scent would wash away the hour he'd spent being attacked. He knew it would bring him peace.

Big chocolate eyes looked up into his. "Did I miss the meeting?"

He snorted. "You mean the character bashing? Aye, you missed it."

The look of uncertainty she gave him made him want to hug her close. She licked her rose-coloured lips. "Did they tell you I need help?"

"Mainly they told me to grow up. Then they detailed my humiliating and annoying behaviour, just in case I missed any of it while it was happening." He clenched his jaw as the words from earlier swam through his mind. "But aye, they told me about your sister's visit."

Abby let out the breath she'd been holding. He noticed she hadn't moved from his hold. He wondered if she even realised she was still wrapped in his arms. It felt natural for her to be there. It felt right.

"Why didn't you just talk to me yourself? Why the three-ring circus?" He nodded behind him to his parents' house.

She let out a frustrated sigh. "Would you have listened? I've been traipsing over to your place for weeks asking you to turn down your music and you never paid any attention."

"I didn't think you were serious."

The look she gave him was half incredulity and half anger. "Really? That's what you thought?"

He relaxed slightly at the sight of her passion. "Okay, maybe I didn't want to take you seriously. Plus, I liked watching you tell me off in that prissy tone of yours."

"Now that sounds more like it." She stuck her nose in the air. Pleased she was right. It was cute.

"But this is different, Abby. You think I'd just ignore you asking for help with your sister? You think I wouldn't care about someone wanting to take the terrorist from you?"

"Flynn." She patted his chest above his heart, and he was suddenly sad that this was one of the few days he'd buttoned his shirt. He would have killed to feel her touch on his skin. "I know you don't understand this, but I don't really know you at all. Of course I thought you'd ignore me. You ignored everything else."

He frowned down at her.

She cocked an eyebrow and it made him grin.

"This situation is different. Of course I'll help you keep your kid." He'd already decided he would. Which he would have told his damn, interfering family if they'd shut up long enough to listen.

Abby's lips trembled, and he realised just how much she was holding inside. For someone who normally didn't notice other people's feelings, the sudden insight into Abby's fragile emotional state almost knocked him off his feet.

"Really?" she said quietly. "No more parties, loud music, cars and rubbish? No more half-naked women?"

He noticed the dark circles under her eyes. She'd tried to cover them with makeup, but they were still sorely out of place on her creamy skin. The circles bothered Flynn more than they probably should have. He traced one with his fingertip.

"No more noise. No more parties. No more Ball Babes.

It's done. I'll be good. I won't screw things up further for you and the kid." *I hope.*

His body trembled slightly as panic hit him. This was insane. How the hell was he supposed to keep his word? What was he thinking? He felt Abby's fingers clench on his chest as she leaned into him. Her relief was so obvious it made Flynn heady with the knowledge he'd done something right—for once.

"Good," she said. "That's good."

He took a deep breath and gave her the rest of it. She deserved honesty. Even he knew that much. "You need to know, I'm not sure I can pull this off. But I'll try."

Wide eyes stared up at him. She blinked solemnly. "Just remember I own a set of very sharp chef's knives and I'm not afraid to use them. Think about those if you're tempted to backslide into debauchery."

Flynn burst out laughing. Although he had a slight suspicion she wasn't joking.

He was about to pull Abby closer when his younger cousin Megan raced up.

"Damn it, I'm too late. Have they told you off yet?" She stared between Abby and Flynn. "They have, haven't they?" She faced Flynn. "It's not too late. You need to hear my point of view too before you make up your mind about turning over a new leaf. I just wanted to say, whatever you're doing, keep it up. In fact, feel free to get worse. You're making me look good. I haven't had any hassle at all from the family since you came back."

"Megan!" Aunty Heather shouted with outrage, and the three of them snapped around to see they had an audience peering at them from the living room window. Great. Just what Flynn needed—more family interference.

"What?" Megan shouted back. "He needs to hear all sides of the argument so he can make an informed decision."

Aunty Heather pursed her lips at Megan. Flynn figured his cousin had an intervention of her own to get through in the near future.

The door opened behind them.

"I take it from the fact you're wrapped around Abby that you plan to help her out," Matt said.

Abby jerked in his arms as though suddenly realising where she was. She took a step back, dropping her hands from him and leaving him cold.

"Thanks a lot," he said to Matt.

"Flynn's turning over a new leaf," Abby said.

"Thank the Lord," his mother said. "This calls for cake. I've got a chocolate one in the fridge. Who's making tea?"

At the mention of chocolate cake, everyone rushed for the kitchen.

"Don't screw this up," Matt warned him.

Flynn's fingers tingled with the urge to make fists as he looked at his cousin. "Soon as my leg is better, you and me are going to spend some time in the ring."

"Bring it on, ball-boy. I'll wipe the floor with you. Again." With a laugh, Matt headed into the house, leaving Flynn alone with Abby.

Flynn glared after him.

"Thank you," Abby whispered, bringing his attention back to her pale face.

Flynn jerked at the words. They made him feel something he'd never felt before. It took a minute to recognise what it was and when he did, he wasn't pleased.

It was responsibility.

He felt responsible for Abby.

And the thought terrified him.

CHAPTER 8

"Playing against a defensive opponent is just as bad as making love to a tree." Jorge Valdano, former general manager of Real Madrid

Abby was sitting politely sipping morning tea, while Victoria quizzed Katy about her life. What she really wanted to do was rip out her sister's hair and send her running back to mummy.

"So you don't attend school?" Victoria said.

"No, silly," Katy said. "It's summer holiday. I start school after the holiday. I'm going to be in Jonathan's class. He's my best friend. He doesn't like slugs, but worms are okay."

"Your best friend is a boy?" One of Victoria's eyebrows twitched upwards, and Abby wondered if Katy's choice of friend was going to be a black mark against her too.

"Uh-huh. We met in kindy. He wants to marry me, but I don't know if I want to marry him. He's funny and entertaining, so I probably will. If I wait too long to decide I might end up with a naughty boy, and I don't want that."

Victoria seemed a bit too stunned to ask anything more. Fortunately for her, Katy didn't actually need any encouragement to talk.

"Muma says I don't need to get married if I don't want to. She says I can do what I like, that I shouldn't let Jonathan force me to do something I don't want to do. I told her not to worry. I beat Jonathan in fights all the time. If he won't listen to me, I'll just punch him."

"Katy!" Abby wanted to sink through the floor. This was exactly what she was worried about. She had no way to control what came out of Katy's mouth. "What did I say about punching?"

Katy stopped just short of rolling her eyes. "I shouldn't hit anyone. Ever. Unless I'm in danger." She thought about it. "Isn't it dangerous if someone wants to make you marry them?"

"I told you this before. No boy can make you marry him."

"Uncle Matt made Aunty Jena marry him."

"He did not."

"Did too." Abby put her fists on her hips. "It's the only way he could keep her in Scotland. If he didn't marry her he had to arrest her and put her in jail for being an eagle in-the-grunt."

Abby's shoulders slumped. This was not going well at all. "Illegal immigrant," she corrected automatically. "It means someone who doesn't have permission to live in this country."

"See!" Katy folded her arms in triumph. "That's why he made her marry him. If he didn't, she'd have to go to jail."

Victoria's complexion paled as the conversation progressed. Abby caught her sister's eyes and smiled in a way she hoped conveyed that children were cute but not to be trusted.

"I thought your husband didn't have any family," Victoria said. "I thought he was orphaned and grew up in foster care."

"Jena's my best friend. Matt is a police officer. The only one stationed in town."

"She was here illegally?" Victoria's nose rose at the thought.

"Accidentally. She hadn't realised her visa had expired." *Mostly. Kind of.* Mainly Jena hadn't bothered to look into what kind of visa she needed when she moved to Scotland from America. And Matt *had* kind of bullied her into marriage. "Matt and Jena are very much in love," she felt the need to add.

"They kiss all the time," Katy said in disgust. "Muma kissed Mr Boyle the other day. She said it was an accident, but Jonathan said it means they have to get married now. Do I have to kiss Jonathan if I marry him?"

Kill me now! Abby looked towards heaven.

She gave Victoria a weak smile. "She's five." She really hoped the explanation was enough to cover everything pouring from Katy's mouth.

"You're romantically involved with your neighbour? The soccer player? The one who lives in a bus? The one whose influence caught mother's attention?" The icy nature of Victoria's tone made Abby want to burst into the song from *Frozen. Let it go...*

"No. Of course we aren't involved. Children don't always understand what they see." She stood up. "Right. Time for your bath, Katy."

"But I always have a bath after dinner," she whined.

"You're having yours before lunch today. Now upstairs right this second."

Katy grumbled and dragged her feet, but she did as she was told. Abby turned to Victoria.

"Lawrence mentioned you wanted to spend the afternoon

in town. I hope you enjoy your visit." *In other words, please get out of my house.*

"Yes." Victoria stood. Today's designer shift was grey silk. "I'd like to talk to some of the locals. Get a feel for the place."

Dig up information on me, you mean. Abby smiled politely. "I'm sure you'll find they are absolutely charming."

Without a backwards glance at Abby, Victoria headed for her car completely unaffected by the devastation she'd wrought in her wake.

Abby rested her forehead against the cool wood of her front door. This was so much worse than she'd thought it would be. There was no way she could keep Victoria away from Katy, and there was no way she could censor Katy's conversation. It was hopeless. They were doomed.

BEING GOOD SUCKED. Flynn had only been doing it for a couple of hours and he could already tell it wasn't nearly as much fun as being bad.

"I don't understand," one of the Ball Babes whined. "Why do we have to leave?"

He'd been having this same argument with the three women for half an hour and his head was beginning to hurt. It wasn't that they were stupid—one of them was on summer break from uni, where she studied physics, of all things. He considered the three wide-eyed bleached-blondes and hoped to hell the one studying physics never got near anything nuclear.

"I explained this, honey." Flynn was seriously losing his patience. "I'm through partying. It's time to concentrate on my recovery, and to do that, I need quiet."

"We can be quiet," Mindy said. At least he thought she was Mindy. The three of them had names that rhymed. Something like Mindy, Sindy, Bindy. Who the hell knew? Whatever it was, they probably spelled it with an i and dotted the letter with a little heart.

Old. He felt old.

"I know you can, honey, but it's time to move on. I've arranged for you to go hang out with Michael. He's renting a house down in Edinburgh. There's more life in the city anyway, and you girls definitely need more to occupy you than a beat-up footballer."

"But we *like* our beat-up footballer." Mindy/Sindy/Bindy Number Two knelt up on her chair, pouted collagen-enhanced lips and ran her palm over his chest.

His abs twitched beneath her touch, and he wondered again if he should just keep them. They could be quiet. If they tried. No. He was going to be good if it killed him. He shook his head and gently removed the hand heading steadily south to his shorts.

"I'm sorry, honey, but all good things must come to an end. That's the way the cookie crumbles. But every cloud has a silver lining." Somebody needed to slap him upside the head. Could he squeeze any more clichés into this conversation?

"But I want to stay with you." Mindy/Sindy/Bindy Number Three pouted.

"I know you do. But you can't always get what you want, sometimes you get what you need." He mentally rolled his eyes at himself as she nodded sagely. The vacant look in her eyes led him to suspect she was the one who *didn't* attend uni.

"Can we come back and visit?" Number One said.

He was distracted momentarily by the fact her baby tee barely covered her ample rack. But instead of wondering about getting her out of the shirt, as he usually did when around women who were scantily clad, he was wondering if she shopped in the kid's section. What was wrong with him?

"Course you can," he crooned at Number One. "You know

the Ball Babes are always welcome here." Damn, wrong thing to say. "Except right now, when you have to go." Smooth. Real smooth.

Number One's eyes twinkled with mischief. "You look really tense, Flynn. Maybe you shouldn't make this sort of decision until you're relaxed. The girls and I could give you a massage." She licked her lips. "It would help clear your mind."

Every cell in his body screamed, *Yes please!* They gave damn good massages. He'd been indulging in them for weeks, hoping their touch would help him heal. Mentally and physically. Yeah, he liked those massages a lot. He wondered if his family would appreciate everything he was sacrificing to please them. He doubted it. He closed his eyes and waited until his breathing slowed.

"That's a really kind offer," he said at last, "but I booked a car for you and it will be here in a little while. Anyway, wouldn't you rather stay in an Edinburgh penthouse than in a dusty old van in the middle of a field?" He glanced around at his luxury, top-of-the-line, two-bedroom motorhome. Okay, maybe dusty old van was pushing it. "Now, go pack up your things. Michael's really looking forward to your visit. He's planning a team party around it."

"He is?" Number Two perked right up.

"Absolutely," Flynn lied. Well, it was kind of a lie. He was sure Michael would plan a party as soon as he knew the women were heading his way, which would be about ten minutes before they rang his doorbell. Flynn had this relocation timed down to the second, like a military manoeuvre.

"Well, if you're sure." Number Three hung her head in resignation.

"I'm sure. Now, I'll just hang outside until you're ready to leave." Before they could say another word, he turned and hauled himself out of the van, pushing the camera guy out in front of him.

He was about to heave a sigh of relief when he spotted the weasel waiting. His arms were folded tight across his bony chest. The perpetual frown was in place. "You're sending them away? Right now, they're all this documentary's got going for it. What are we supposed to shoot now? Your hairy arse lounging around all day?"

Flynn shrugged rather than punching the weasel's face. The camera was still rolling, and he knew anything he did would be edited for effect. "I didn't know you were that interested in my arse, Brian."

The weasel grabbed his phone from his pocket and stabbed at it with bony fingers as he stomped to his car. Seemed like the whole town heaved a sigh of relief when the car sped away, leaving behind a cloud of dust and a peaceful gap where the man once stood.

The camera guy snickered as Flynn hobbled past him to his lounger. As he stumbled over discarded beer bottles and empty chip packets, he realised his mistake. He should have sent the women away *after* he got them to clean up. Now he'd have to hire someone to do it for him.

Half an hour later, the car arrived to take the women to Edinburgh. They came out of the van laden with luggage. Each of them primped and sparkled, ready for travel. He stood to accept hugs, kisses and fake tears of farewell.

As Number Two and Number Three climbed into the car, Number One gave him an extra squeeze. "Take care of yourself, Flynn. Don't let it get to you." She nodded towards his leg.

He smiled politely, because that was what you were supposed to do when people said stuff like that. "I won't, promise."

She put a hand on each of his shoulders, went up on tiptoe and kissed his cheek. "Remember, you aren't only a guy who kicks a ball. You've got a brain, Flynn, and you're a decent guy when you try. It'll be okay."

He nodded, suddenly eager to hold her tight, rather than let her leave. As she walked away, she looked over her shoulder at him and smiled with luminous white teeth. "And for the record, my name is Joyce." She gave him a wink before she climbed into the car.

Now she mentioned it, he distinctly remembered the day he'd met her and she introduced herself as Joyce. It made him feel even more foolish over calling her Mindy/Sindy/Bindy for the past two months. As the girls waved and the car disappeared, he felt a sudden surge of panic. He was alone and the future was a huge mountain in front of him. One he didn't know how to climb. He rubbed his chest at the thought before he remembered his every move was being recorded.

Plastering a lazy smile to his face, he headed towards the stream.

"You can take a break," he told the camera guy. "I'm gonna snooze beside the water for half an hour. I'll get you when I wake up."

The guy lowered the camera. "Thanks, dude." He lumbered towards his van.

Flynn worked hard to push away the feelings of despair nipping at his mind. He didn't have time to wallow. He needed to be proactive. He had to come up with a plan for his future. Pity his mind went blank the instant he thought the word "future"—as though his brain was terrified to go there.

As Flynn neared the water, he heard a distressed noise. There was rustling from one of the bushes. With a wince, he crouched down to investigate. Gently pushing back the leaves on a nearby bush, Flynn came face to beak with a terrified duck. There was fishing line wrapped around its wing and the hook was embedded in its side. Flynn cursed under his breath as he reached for the cowering wreck.

"Let's get you cleaned up, buddy. You're in a worse state than I am."

The duck quacked its agreement as Flynn carried it, like it was precious cargo, back to the van.

As he shushed the duck to quiet her, an idea hit Flynn like a bolt of lightning. He knew how to help Abby. He could take away one of her problems. He had the resources. He grinned widely. He was a fricking genius. Now all he needed was a minute alone with Katy—and a wallet full of cash.

CHAPTER 9

*"We must have had ninety-nine percent of the game. It was the
other three percent that cost us the match."*
Ruud Gullit, former Dutch national soccer player

Abby was entrenched in hell. After another sleepless night
where she tossed and turned with worry, she had the pleasure of her sister's company again for morning tea. She was
holding on to her sanity by a hair, waiting for Katy to say
something that would seal their fate. There was no way she'd
make it through another five days of this. She wasn't even
sure she'd make it to lunch.

When the doorbell rang, Abby was busy serving tea for
her unwanted guests. At least Lawrence was pleasant—when
he wasn't giving Victoria looks of disapproval. Although
Abby appreciated his effort on her part, it didn't do anything
to lighten the tension in the air.

"I'll get it." Katy ran to open the door, and a moment later,
she came back trailing Flynn behind her.

Abby froze, teapot angled as she poured for Lawrence. It was a miracle she didn't pass out on the spot. The chances of someone saying the wrong thing had just doubled. She couldn't monitor Katy *and* Flynn. She had to get rid of him. Now.

Katy cocked a thumb over her shoulder at Flynn, in a move stolen from Matt. "I told him he wasn't allowed in here, but he says he is. Is that right, Muma? Are we letting him in now, or is he telling big hairy fibs?" She glared back at Flynn, who bugged his eyes out at her.

A hand on her arm brought Abby's attention back to the tea. Lawrence smiled up at her. His cup had overflowed, leaving him with a saucer of tea.

"I'm terribly sorry," Abby said, "let me get you another one."

"How about I deal with the tea and you deal with your guest?" Lawrence stood, taking the overflowing cup and saucer with him.

Abby smiled with fake gratitude. She didn't want to deal with her guest. She didn't want to deal with *any* of her guests. What she did want to do was tell them all to go to hell then slam the door shut behind them.

"Flynn," she said through a clenched-teeth smile. "What brings you here, *of all places* you could be right now that *aren't* here?" Okay, not very subtle. It was still better than screaming the place down. So, it was a win.

"I came to introduce myself to your lovely sister and her friend. I'm just being a good neighbour." Flynn's grin was pure charm. It dazzled. She squinted at his mouth. Were those teeth artificially whitened? She shook her head.

"How lovely. I know how busy you are. It's kind of you to fit us in—especially when you have *that thing* you need to get to this morning. Remember the urgent business you told me about. The business you have to do right now. Away from here." Abby silently communicated, using telepathy, bug eyes and thinned lips that he'd damn well better invent a pressing engagement toot sweet. He seemed not to get the message. Instead he turned to her sister.

"Doesn't look like Abby wants to introduce us." He flashed a charming smile. "I'm Flynn Boyle." He held out a hand to Victoria.

"I'm sorry," Abby said in a tone clearly revealing she wasn't. "This is my neighbour." She glared at Flynn, who ignored it. "This is my sister, Victoria Montgomery-Clark. And this is Lawrence Maynard, my mother's lawyer."

Abby watched as Flynn's mouth twitched when Victoria gave him a limp handshake using barely more than her fingertips.

Flynn's eyes sparkled a little too much when he looked back at Abby, making her stomach clench in fear. "You don't need to worry about *that thing* I had on this morning. It was cancelled. Seems it wasn't urgent after all." His lips twitched with clear mischief. He was up to something. This was *not* the time for him to be up to something! He eyed the table, taking in the tea and cake. "Mind if I join you?"

Yes! I mind! Every fibre of Abby's being screamed at him. Unfortunately, it was silent and he missed it.

"We're feeding him now?" Katy protested loudly.

"You're such a joker, kid." Flynn ruffled Katy's hair, making her growl.

He just grinned and shook hands with Lawrence. Abby stood frozen. She couldn't speak. She couldn't think of a way to get Flynn out of her house. Her eyes darted between Katy and Flynn. The two of them together had the potential for Armageddon.

Katy stomped over to Flynn's side, folded her arms and scowled at him. "Why are you here? You can't be here to be friendly. Muma said you'd only be nice to us when all the rivers in Scotland dried up, and I saw the stream this morning. It still has water."

Abby gave an obviously fake, and clearly hysterical, laugh.

Flynn reached out and tugged Katy's ponytail. "Isn't she a cute kid?" he asked Victoria. "Almost too cute to be allowed out in public." He turned to Abby. "Maybe you should keep her in her room?" Although he was grinning, Abby wasn't sure it was a joke. She watched as he gave Katy a narrow-eyed glance.

"There's rules for coming into my house," Katy said. "You need to wear clothes. And you need to stop kissing my Muma."

Lawrence made a choking noise as he sat back down at the table.

Abby stopped breathing. Stared at the ceiling and pleaded once again for a meteor to strike the house.

"Clothes?" Victoria asked in a strangled voice.

"She means T-shirts," Abby said. "Flynn likes to sunbathe, so he rarely wears them. Got to keep up the tan, eh?"

Flynn cocked an eyebrow at her, making it clear he thought she was the one who was nuts.

"You're a funny kid," he said to Katy. "Cute and funny. Great sense of humour. Bet you get to sit on the naughty step a lot with all those tales you tell."

Katy leaned in to him. "You need to sit on the naughty step, not me. You need to sit there for about a year. You let a woman show her boobs at a party. And you're noisy. And messy. And Muma said you're a pig."

"Katy!" Abby felt the floor disappear beneath her feet. She held on to the table to stop the room from spinning. This conversation alone was enough for Victoria to file for custody. What made her think she'd get away with a week of good behaviour from Flynn? What made her think Katy would keep her knowledge to herself? It was a disaster.

"You know what?" Flynn stood. "Katy promised to show me her new Barbies. How about we do that now, kid? While your mum makes some coffee. There's only tea here, and I'm not much of a tea drinker."

Katy and Abby opened their mouths to protest at the same time, but Flynn beat them to it. "You know, I think I've got another football shirt you'd like, Katy. Why don't I tell you about it while we look at the new Barbies?"

Katy's back snapped straight as her eyes narrowed. Her tongue licked across her bottom lip in a gesture that could only be described as calculated.

"My Barbies are in the living room." Katy turned on her heels, head held high, expecting him to follow.

"Kids." Flynn shook his head and grinned at her family before following Katy.

Abby was stuck to the spot, torn between running after them to rescue Katy from Flynn, or Flynn from Katy, depending on what was happening. And staying with her sister in an attempt to make the whole visit seem normal. When Victoria eyed her with disapproval, staying won out. It was time to do damage control.

"Flynn has a strange sense of humour." Abby forced a smile. "I'm told it's worse since the injury. His cousin thinks he may have suffered brain damage from lack of oxygen on the operating table. It's a terrible waste. But we have to show compassion to those less fortunate than ourselves, don't we?"

Lawrence started choking again while Victoria's eyes went wide.

"Now, who would like a slice of Bakewell tart?"

FLYNN HOBBLED into the living room closely behind the five-year-old terrorist. They stalked into the centre of the room. Katy spun towards him, arms folded and the usual glare on her face. Flynn stayed standing too, even though it hurt his knee, because he didn't want to give ground to the monster.

"Okay, kid, what will it take for you to be nice to me while your aunt and her friend are here?"

"I don't want to be nice to you. You're mean. Smelly. And stupid."

"Did your mum teach you to talk to adults like that?" Flynn knew damn well Abby wouldn't tolerate Katy's behaviour. Katy was nothing but respectful around adults—when she wasn't running off at the mouth.

"You're not an adult."

And there was the answer. "You might be right, kid, but we need to get along this week. So what will it take to see some good behaviour from you? You need to be friendly too." He thought about it. "And you can't go telling everybody's secrets to your mum's sister. She's not from around here; she won't understand how things work."

Katy stuck her nose in the air. "That's a lot of work." Her cheeks flushed as her eyes calculated. "It's going to cost you lots."

He folded his arms to mimic her. "Name your price. I came prepared. I have money in my pocket."

She thought about it while tapping one finger to her chin. It would have been cute if she wasn't a master manipulator. Hell, she could give his aunty Heather a run for her money—and she was the town's current queen of manipulation.

Katy straightened her back and smiled sweetly. "I don't want money. I want my own swimming pool. I want you to come to forty-seven tea parties with my dolls. You need to read me ten bedtime stories." She thought about it. "No, eleven-teen stories. I want chocolate every day—and you can't tell Muma about it. I want a puppy and a new Barbie house for all my new Barbies. And I want you to teach me how to play football so I can beat Jonathan." She grinned in triumph. "I want to score my own goal. Jonathan scores own goals all the time. I want one too."

Flynn groaned. What were they teaching kids these days? "Own goal means you scored against your own team, kid. It isn't a good thing. It's a bad thing. You don't want one of those."

She narrowed her eyes. "I want it all."

Time was ticking, and they had to get back into the kitchen before someone came to find them and ruined negotiations.

"I can do the pool, the Barbie house and the chocolate. There's no way I'm sitting through tea parties with your dolls, I can't play football because of my leg and if I give you a puppy your mum will kill me."

Katy stared at his leg. "When will it be fixed?"

Flynn bit back the urge to shout never. "Soon. Maybe. Who knows? But I can't run after a ball right now."

She nodded. "I want a pool and a Barbie house and chocolate and bedtime stories and ten tea parties."

He shook his head. "No tea parties. No bedtime stories."

She stamped her tiny foot. "Then I'm going to tell on you to Aunty Victoria. I watch you all the time when my Muma puts me to bed at night. She thinks I'm sleeping. I can tell Aunty Victoria all about your parties."

"How old are you, kid? Because you act like a forty-year-old lawyer."

She just smiled. It was scary.

"Katy? Flynn?" Abby shouted. She sounded brittle enough to snap.

"Coming," Flynn shouted back. "Fine. Everything except the football and the puppy." He figured seeing as she couldn't count, she wouldn't know if he kept his end of the bargain regarding how many times he endured a story or tea with the dolls.

"Deal." She bounced on the spot. "And no more kissing my Muma."

"That's a deal breaker, kid. I'm going to kiss your mum. If it was so important to you, you should have mentioned it first on your list of demands."

"Are you two coming?" Abby was near hysterics.

"Let's go," Flynn said. "And remember, you need to act like we're friends. And keep other people's business to yourself. Stop telling tales."

"I'm going to tell Muma all about this," she threatened, ignoring his order not to tell tales.

"That's the one exception to keeping things to yourself. You should tell your mum. You shouldn't keep secrets from your mum. It's the other people I'm worried about. We need to keep secrets from them. And anyway, don't you think your mum will figure out our deal when a pool turns up?"

She rolled her eyes as she ran from the room. "I want a really big pool. Not one of those baby ones."

With a shake of his head, he followed her. He'd intended to help Abby, but he suspected his interference might be causing more harm than good.

CHAPTER 10

"My parents have been there for me, ever since I was about seven."
David Beckham, former English national player

It was the Mad Hatter's tea party and Abby was playing Alice. Victoria was the Red Queen. At any minute, Abby half expected her to point to Flynn and demand Lawrence remove his head. Katy was grinning like the Cheshire Cat. And Flynn, Flynn was the Hatter.

"Damn shame about your leg," Lawrence said. Lawrence didn't belong at the Hatter's tea party. Abby was beginning to think her mother's lawyer was the only sensible person in the room. "I saw you play at Wembley last year. Great game. I follow Chelsea myself."

Victoria looked disgusted at this confession, and Abby had to admit she was surprised too. She'd figured Lawrence for a cricket man.

"Ah, Chelsea." Flynn grinned mischievously. "The pet football team of a Russian billionaire. Boys and their toys."

Lawrence laughed, as though that was hilarious. "They *did* win the league last year."

Flynn shook his head. "It's amazing what money can buy you these days."

Lawrence raised an eyebrow. "Are you saying they bought the win?"

"I'm saying if you throw enough money at a club you can buy guys with skill. There's no denying there are amazing players on the Chelsea side, but are they a team? Nope, just a bunch of egos chasing limelight and money."

"They still won."

Flynn shrugged but his jaw tightened. "It's not the way I like to see football run. Look at Man City. The Emirati come in and buy them up, throw money at them like it's going out of fashion and the team are edging out Manchester United." Flynn leaned forward. "But where's all this taking the game? Isn't it better to be part of a club that nurtures its players, that fosters real team spirit, that enhances the national side and creates football that's a joy to watch?"

"Like Arsenal?"

Flynn grinned widely. "Like Arsenal." He sat back in his chair as though he'd won a debate.

Abby shook her head to clear it. She had definitely fallen down the rabbit hole. She didn't understand the conversation at all.

"Arsenal?" Abby said, mainly because she felt she should say something rather than sitting there quietly and politely. As though she were a character from a Jane Austen novel who didn't concern herself with "manly" topics. Great, now she was jumping genres—*Alice in Wonderland* to *Pride and Prejudice.* What was next? *War and Peace?*

Lawrence gave her an indulgent smile as he pointed at Flynn. "Flynn is a Gunner."

Yeah, now she was totally lost. She looked at Flynn, aware her ignorance and confusion were written large on her face.

His eyes flashed with pain and anger, but it didn't seem to be directed at anyone in the room. The look was quickly covered with his trademark lazy smile.

"Used to be a Gunner," he corrected.

Lawrence shrugged. "With your record, you'll always be a Gunner. You scored more goals for that team than any other player this decade." He turned to Abby. "The Arsenal players are called Gunners. Flynn here has been with the team since he was a teen. You were in their academy, weren't you?"

"Yeah, moved down there when I was thirteen."

"Thirteen?" Abby stared at him. "You went to live in London at thirteen? To play football?"

Flynn's eyes sparkled at Abby's astonishment. "I started out with Rangers when I was ten. Was picked up by one of their scouts and played off and on in their academy. A guy from Arsenal spotted me during one of those games and offered a better opportunity. I have relatives in London, Dad's brother. So I went to board at the academy and my aunt and uncle took care of me. It wasn't like I was sold into slavery, sugar—I wanted to do it. Hell, I was begging to do it. Do you have any idea how many great players went through the Arsenal academy? I owe them everything. They're my team. The only one I ever wanted."

He looked down at the table, suddenly overcome by his thoughts. It took Abby a minute to realise he was grieving. He'd lost his team, his life, when he'd lost the use of his leg.

"I'm sorry, Flynn," she said.

He gave her a soft smile that melted something within her.

"What's she sorry for?" Katy asked with a mouthful of cake.

Flynn cocked his head towards Katy. "Remember I told

you I couldn't play football because I hurt my leg? Well, your mum is telling me she feels sorry for me. She knows how much I enjoyed playing. She knows I miss it."

Understanding flashed in Katy's face. She placed a tiny hand on his arm. "Don't worry, Flynn, you can always play other games with me. Like swimming and tea parties."

She batted her lashes at him and Flynn narrowed his eyes in her direction, although he looked strangely impressed.

"Well played, kid," he said, making her giggle.

"Is it that bad?" Lawrence said to Flynn, taking his attention from Katy. "The leg. Are you going to make a recovery?"

Victoria's disapproving gaze shot to Lawrence. Polite people did not ask personal questions. The lawyer ignored her. Abby wished she could do the same when she was on the receiving end of her sister's glare.

"I won't recover enough to play." Flynn's answer was flat. "My team already let me go."

Abby was beginning to understand that the more something meant to Flynn, the flatter his voice became. This had to mean a whole lot to him. Everything, she suspected.

Lawrence nodded as though the news was a blow to him as well. He gave a sad little smile. "Broke my heart that you couldn't play for England. We could have used your skill."

"I love playing for Scotland, representing my country, but it would have been nice to make it to the World Cup."

"And we might have won had you been there."

They smiled at each other, sad but warm.

"Well," Victoria said in that clipped voice of hers. "I think it's time to take another walk around town." She stood. "Are you coming, Lawrence?"

"Going to check up on Abby?" Flynn said.

Abby's mouth dropped. She suspected he thought his charming smile would defuse the question.

Victoria stuck her nose in the air and looked down at him. "I don't see why that is any of your concern, Mr Boyle."

"Seems to me it's definitely my concern. Far as I can gather, you came rushing up to Scotland because Abby got caught up in the documentary being filmed about my life."

Victoria sneered at him. "We came here because Abby's behaviour was unacceptable for a Montgomery-Clark. It had nothing to do with your little television programme."

Flynn leaned forward to clasp his hands on the table. His steely gaze was focused on Victoria. "You know damn well Abby is perfectly behaved. She's an amazing mother. A valued member of this community. She is nothing but respectable. So she had one little freak-out. I don't think that gives you the right to judge her—especially seeing as it was my fault. I pushed her to it. Ask anyone. My behaviour would make a saint lose his cool."

"Flynn, I can handle this. Please…" She wanted to tell him not to interfere. She wanted to tell him this was none of his business. But she couldn't do it in front of her sister. It would make everything an even bigger deal.

"It's okay, Abby," Flynn said. "Your sister needs to know you're above reproach. And yeah, I know words like that. Lots of them." He grinned at Abby before turning back to Victoria. "Here's another one for you—libel. Coming here, accusing Abby of being anything but the perfect mother, neighbour and friend is tantamount to libel and slander."

Lawrence grinned. "I knew I liked you," he told Flynn. "He's not wrong," he said to Victoria. "If I was representing Abby, it's an avenue I would definitely investigate."

Flynn nodded at Lawrence, but spoke to Victoria. "Everyone makes mistakes. Abby's happened to be caught on film, which is unfortunate, but still, it was just a mistake. No court in the land would use it as a measure of her character. You know it. I know it. Hell, everyone knows it."

Victoria chilled even further. Her words were ice. "My sister attacked a party with a knife. In front of her child."

"Your sister punctured a pool filled with foam and topless women. She was saving her child from being subjected to bad influence. I should know. I was the bad influence. She was doing what any good parent would do. Making sure her kid was safe and protected."

"And yet you're still here. In her home. Spreading your bad influence." The words came out like bullets. Short. Sharp. Hitting the mark.

Flynn stood slowly. He leaned over the table towards Victoria, his palms flat on the surface. "We all make mistakes. All of us. Even you."

Victoria's back snapped straight enough to break in two. A slight flush appeared on her cheeks. It was so subtle most people would have missed it. Flynn's eyes narrowed slightly.

"I wonder what mistakes you have hidden in your deep, dark past?" he murmured to Victoria. "Should we judge you on them? Should we set a pack of lawyers on you over them? Mmm, Victoria. What are you hiding?"

Victoria's eyes flashed wide with fear before she was once again under perfect control. "It was an experience meeting you, Mr Boyle," she snapped. "I'm sure I won't be seeing much more of you during our stay, so I'll say my goodbyes now." She nodded at him before turning her back and gliding out of the room. The message was clear. It was an order. She didn't want to see Flynn again and he was to obey.

"Beer and football some night?" Flynn called after Lawrence as he followed Victoria.

Lawrence flicked a glance at Abby before grinning at Flynn. "It would be my pleasure."

And then they were gone.

CHAPTER 11

"Rugby is a game for barbarians played by gentlemen. Football is a game for gentlemen played by barbarians."
Oscar Wilde, amateur football player

"What do you think you're doing?" Abby's hysterical question hit Flynn as soon as the door shut on her sister. It distracted Flynn from his speculation about the sister. There were skeletons in her closet. Possibly ones that would help Abby's cause.

"I'm helping. Like I told you I would."

"This is helping?" Her voice became a high-pitched screech. Not attractive.

"Flynn's in trouble, Flynn's in trouble," Katy sang. "Make him sit on the naughty step. He never sits on the step."

"What did we talk about, kid? You're supposed to be nice to me."

"Only when Aunty Victoria is here, and she's gone." She turned back to her mother. "Make him sit on the stair!"

"That's it," Flynn told her. "No story tonight. If you can go back on the deal and freak the hell out, I don't need to read stories."

"Children!" Abby shouted then flushed red when she realised what she'd said.

The look on her face would have been funny—if he hadn't been the one she was calling a kid.

Katy smirked, and Flynn resisted the overwhelming urge to stick his tongue out at her. Huh, maybe Abby had a point?

"I mean," Abby said with forced calm, "you two stop it." She pointed at Katy. "She has an excuse. She's a preschooler. What's your excuse?"

Flynn couldn't resist. He pointed at Katy too. "She made me do it!" He burst out laughing.

Abby ran her fingers through her hair, obviously forgetting it was tied in a bun at the base of her neck. Her fingers caught and the hair came loose, hanging lopsided at her shoulder.

"Damn it." She pulled out the rest of the pins.

Katy's hands flew to cover her mouth, her eyes wide. "She said the D-word," she whispered to Flynn.

"Aye." Flynn pretended disappointment. "Her behaviour is deteriorating. Maybe *she* should sit on the naughty step?"

Katy's giggle told him she thought it was a brilliant idea. Meanwhile, Abby was muttering something about cats and hatters. Flynn actually began to worry; yet another emotion he was unfamiliar with. He wasn't sure how many more times Abby could lose the plot before she lost it for good. She was English. The English dealt with trauma by drinking tea. He could make tea.

"Sit down," he told the pacing woman. "It's all going to be fine. I'll make you a nice cup of tea and you'll feel a lot better."

"I'll help," Katy shouted.

Whatever. Flynn headed for the kitchen counter with the terrorist at his heels. Abby ignored his soothing advice and continued with her muttering and pacing. Although, he had to say, he enjoyed the pacing. She wore a pale pink dress that skimmed her curves and ended below her knee. It had a high neck, long sleeves and was in no way revealing. Yet on her, it was sexy as hell. Especially seeing as it cupped her curvy backside with every angry step she took. And damn. Those heels. The pink peep-toes were sex in shoe form. He almost groaned at the sight.

"You fill the kettle," Katy said. "I'll get the tea bags."

Flynn dragged his eyes away from her mother, to see Katy climb on a stool and retrieve some tea bags from the cupboard. There was an open box of tea on the counter. Flynn pointed at it.

"Why aren't we using this tea?"

Katy looked at him like he was the idiot. "That's loose tea. I don't know how to work it. Teabags are easier."

She had a point. Flynn didn't know what to do with loose tea either. Katy arranged a cup and saucer, then put a bag in it while they waited for the kettle to boil. Flynn leaned against the counter and watched Abby mutter.

"Is this normal?" he asked Katy.

"No." Katy shook her head. "She once threw a pot at the wall. And a long time ago she cried. I think that was when my daddy died. Muma usually smiles. Except when she's mad at you. You made her cry too. But only a little bit. Not like the last time. And usually she talks to real-life people. I don't know who she's talking to right now."

"Neither do I," Flynn said.

Suddenly Abby stopped pacing and spun to them. Her eye twitched. Not a good sign. "Katy." He voice was saccharine sweet. "Could you go play in your room for a little while? Muma needs to talk to Mr Boyle."

"It's okay to call him Flynn. He's not really a grownup."

The eye twitch grew more noticeable. "Honey, go play in your room."

"Okay." Katy huffed as she stomped to the door. "But no kissing while I'm gone."

"We're not going to kiss," Abby snapped at the same time Flynn said, "I'm not promising anything, kid—that wasn't part of our deal."

"Deal?" Abby's attention zoomed in on him.

Flynn winced. Yeah, maybe now wasn't the best time for this discussion. Unfortunately, the terrorist wasn't on the same page as he was.

"Flynn's going to buy me a swimming pool if I pretend I like him and I stop telling Aunty Victoria all about everybody's business."

Abby didn't move for a long minute as she stared off into space. She was frozen. System overload. Where was her reboot button? He needed to call a doctor.

"Go. Play." Her words were even. A quiet command brooking no argument.

With a dramatic slump of her shoulders, Katy did as she was told. Abby stared after her for a long time before turning to Flynn.

"I can explain." He held up his hands in a reassuring gesture while eyeing the area around her for weapons.

"Yes. You can and you will. Start now."

Man, she was hot with a capital H when she got all bossy. Flynn dragged his mind out of his shorts and focused on defusing the bomb that was Abby.

"I was trying to help."

She let out a strangled scream. He carried on regardless.

"I'll be the first to admit I'm not used to helping people. And maybe I don't know what I'm doing. But I should at least get credit for effort."

He looked at her hopefully. She glared back. Flynn charged on, hoping to get the explanation out before Abby went hunting for a knife.

"I thought your sister should know you're a really respectable person and the blame for any uncharacteristic behaviour rests with me."

She lips formed words, but no sound came out. She was counting to ten silently. "And you thought coming over here, confronting my sister, being rude and corrupting my child was the way to go about helping me?"

"Okay, when you put it like that, it doesn't sound so good."

"And you bribed my daughter?" The scary high-pitched tone was back again.

Flynn lowered his voice to compensate for it, hoping it would soothe her. "Look, we both know you were having problems with the things Katy was saying. I thought I'd help. Now she'll keep her mouth shut around your sister."

Wrong thing to say. Abby's eyes snapped to his. "How do you know that?"

Flynn looked around the room, hoping an answer would present itself. It didn't. He had no choice but to go with honesty. "I heard you at the stream."

Abby gasped. Her hand flew to her chest. Her face went pale. Flynn's muscles tensed, ready to run for her if she looked like she was going to drop. He'd pay for it later—his leg didn't want to run; it barely wanted to walk—but he couldn't let her topple to the floor. Again.

"Take nice, easy breaths, sugar. It's going to be okay. Why don't you sit down? There's a chair right behind you. That's right," he encouraged as she plopped onto the chair.

"You heard me?" Her voice was a trembling whisper. Her eyes were glassy. Oh hell. It wasn't fainting. It was crying. Flynn wanted to run now for sure. Except this time he didn't want to run to her rescue—he wanted to head out the door and keep going until he was back in London.

"It's okay. It's fine. Nothing to worry about." He aimed for the same gentle tones he'd once used years earlier when he'd talked an injured dog out of a corner.

"You heard me?" she whispered again, and a tear ran down her cheek.

Oh hell. The dam had cracked. With a grimace, Flynn limped over to her. He bit back a grunt of pain as he knelt on his good knee in front of her. Awkwardly, he patted her shoulder.

"There, there." He was pretty sure that was what people said in situations like this. He was equally sure that the words he'd used with the dog—*"Come on, boy, be brave and I'll get you a juicy bone"*— wouldn't help here. "It's okay," he said instead.

"It's not okay." Her big chocolate eyes were melting. "I wasn't talking to you. I was talking to David. You weren't supposed to listen. No one was supposed to hear."

At the sight of more tears, Flynn broke out in a cold sweat. Would she be okay for a minute alone? He just needed enough time to call Matt or Harry. They had women. Either of them would know what to do. Right? Abby's big brown eyes looked up at him, and he knew he couldn't leave her side. There was no choice but to grit his teeth, comfort the woman and hope like crazy he didn't screw things up further. *What to say? What to say?* Inspiration struck.

"It's a good job I heard you. Your husband isn't in any fit state to help out, but I can. I want to." Okay. So that didn't come out the way he'd intended. He pushed on. "Aye, it shocks the hell out of me too. But I do want to help. I got you into this mess. I want to help get you out of it. Sure, your kid is the spawn of Satan, but you like her so you should get to keep her. I'd feel bad if she went away. It's not like you have a backup. She's the only one you have."

Abby blinked several times as though stunned. Did hearing he wanted to help send her into shock? Was that even possible?

Flynn ran his hand down her back in what he hoped was a comforting gesture. "There, there," he said again, then gave himself a mental eye roll. "I'm going to do what I can to fix this. I promised you I'd clean up my act. That's why I'm here. To help you out."

"By buying my daughter a pool?" She seemed confused. Was that a symptom of shock?

"It's just a pool. It's no big deal." He didn't think it was a good time to mention the other items on the little terrorist's list. "And if it gets her to stop dropping information bombs this week, it's worth the money. I only want to help. Let me help."

"But…" She closed her eyes for a moment before looking back at him. "I don't think I can trust you. This situation with Victoria is delicate. You could really screw it up."

Okay, that was a slap in the face. He decided her reaction was just another symptom of her obviously shocked state, and carried on regardless.

"I'm turning over a new leaf. I'm growing up. You should know it's a painful process, but I'm embracing it." He caressed her cheek with his palm, while his other hand continued to rub her back. "Let me help, Abby. I feel bad and I can't stand it. I'm not used to guilt and I don't know what to do with myself. Let me help."

"You drive me crazy. I'm not even sure I like you." Still, she relaxed under his touch.

He quirked a smile. "Aye, I know, but you do like my kisses. And you like me to touch you. Don't you, Abby?" There was a rumble of desire undercutting his words. It was impossible to be around this woman and not feel desire. She was beautiful, and good, and clean and kind and…well, everything Flynn wasn't. And she owned a closet full of sexy shoes. He was defenceless against her.

Her cheeks burned red as her gaze fell to her knees. "You weren't supposed to hear that either."

"I'm glad I did," he whispered, leaning in closer to her. His thumb stroked over her full bottom lip. "I like kissing you too, Abby." She shuddered under his touch, making him instantly ravenous to taste her. "Don't worry about things so much. Go with the flow. Let me help you. Let me touch you. It's all going to be fine."

"You're a dangerous man, Flynn Boyle." But it was said with resignation. Acceptance. Desire.

He felt heat flare throughout his body. "So I'm told." His words were a breath against her lips.

And then he was kissing her. Gentle. Soft. Slow. Everything their last kiss hadn't managed to be. Her taste and scent stole his mind. His arm clamped tight around her. He felt her nails dig into his shoulders and almost wished the flannel shirt was gone so he could feel the bite in his skin. She tilted her head slightly as she sipped at his mouth. Her tongue darted out to taste, a nervous little move. He slanted his mouth over hers, met her tongue with his and kissed her slowly and thoroughly.

Never before had kissing a woman felt so perfect. He could stay like this for hours. Tasting her, listening to her panting breaths and tiny whimpers of need. It was bliss.

"I told you no kissing!" The shout from the door had Abby jerking away from him.

Katy stood with her arms folded and her face like thunder. The look was somewhat ruined by the pink tutu and yellow gumboots.

"No more kissing," she ordered. "If you kiss him you have to marry him, and I don't want him as a daddy."

Even though Flynn didn't want to be her father either, the words stung. What was wrong with him? He'd make a great dad. Probably. Maybe.

"It was an accident..." Abby began, which was pretty insulting.

"Another accident?" Katy screeched. "Stop having accidents." She glared at Flynn. "This wasn't in our deal." Suddenly her thunderous face turned into a calculating smile and Flynn felt genuine fear. "I'll let you kiss my Muma if you buy me a pony."

"Katy!" Abby was on her feet and heading towards her daughter before he fully registered the words.

Flynn laughed as Abby lectured Katy on how she couldn't sell her mother for a pony. He caught the terrorist's eyes and gave her a thumbs-up gesture. If a pony was what it took to get his lips on Abby again, he'd gladly buy the kid one.

CHAPTER 12

"I'm going to ask you again to reconsider," Lawrence said as he drove back into the centre of town. "You have the power here. You can spend the rest of the week getting to know your sister and your niece before you go home and tell your mother there's no reason to bring in the lawyers. Wouldn't that be preferable to carrying out your mother's orders? You know as well as I do, she's in the wrong. She has no right to interfere in Katy's life."

Victoria stared out of the window at the passing scenery. If it wasn't for the tight set of her lips, he would assume she wasn't listening. He let her be for a moment. He'd known Victoria most of her adult life. She needed time to think through things. A trait he normally admired.

Abby's house was nestled at the base of the lush green hills that cradled Invertary. It wasn't so far away from town to be isolated, but far enough to be quiet and private. It made him reconsider his Waterloo apartment, which he'd bought after his divorce purely because it was close to the office and had a view of the Thames. He had every luxury in his apartment, yet still felt like he was living in a box. One of many boxes piled on top of each other. All filled with busy little worker bees who put in long hours in order to pay for their box. He smirked at himself. Middle age was getting to him. Next thing he knew he'd purchase a motorbike and get his ears pierced.

"Mother won't listen," Victoria said at last. "She never listens. You know this better than most. She wants to make Abby pay for embarrassing the family, and the best way to do that is to take her daughter away."

Her voice was dead, as though she was stating an irrevocable fact of life. Something over which she had no influence. Her lack of emotion made Lawrence burn. There was always the option to fight.

"You can try to make her see reason. I will too. Together, we'll make her listen. This action against Abby is baseless and will be costly. Surely your mother will understand that?"

Victoria let out a dry laugh. Admittedly, Lawrence's time spent with Victoria had been limited to business meetings in the office, but he couldn't remember ever seeing her smile. He thought hard, but no images of Victoria with a genuine smile on her face came to mind. The realisation was shocking.

"Mother only listens to Mother. Even when Father was alive, his opinion only mattered when it matched hers. She's ruthless, conniving and completely without compassion. All she cares about is getting what she wants." Victoria turned back to him, and he saw pain in her eyes. It stole the air from the car. He was so used to the emotionless veneer she presented to the world that the sight staggered him. "You deal with her more than most, Lawrence. You know it's the truth. The best thing Abby can do is to give in quietly, hand over Katy, negotiate to spend time with her daughter and then get on with her life."

"You don't believe that." He *hoped* she didn't believe that. It was too horrific to contemplate if she did.

Lawrence turned into the top of the high street, a cobblestone road flanked by mismatched whitewashed houses. At the bottom of the road, the loch sat glistening in the sun, enticing everyone who looked at it to give up on their tasks and laze beside it.

"I know exactly what she's capable of." Victoria's small voice sliced through him like a knife to his soul. "I know from experience, the faster you surrender, the more painless it is. She will win anyway. She always wins."

Before he could stop himself, Lawrence reached out and patted her knee. She jerked back at his overly familiar touch.

"Not this time, Vicki. This time she's up against the both of us. I have a good reputation and an excellent track record. The firm doesn't need your mother's support. We will manage fine without her business. We're all wealthy men. If it comes to it, our partnership will cut ties and we'll fight her on this."

Victoria's eyes went wide. They were an exact match to Abby's. Except where Abby's eyes gleamed with laughter and life, Victoria's only held dead acceptance and fear.

"Why?" she whispered.

He noticed she didn't remove his hand from her knee. It sent warmth flaring throughout him.

"Because it's the right thing to do, Vicki. Because it's the right thing to do."

Her cheeks flushed pink and something like hope flared in her eyes before she turned back to look out the window. Lawrence returned his hand to the steering wheel and concentrated on the drive. Wondering all the while what Victoria would look like if she smiled. He bet she would be beautiful.

CHAPTER 13

"Julian Dicks is everywhere. It's like they've got eleven Dicks on the field." Sports commentator for Metro Radio

The call from Flynn's agent came through at last. And the timing was perfect. It gave him a reason to run from the McKenzie house. Well, hobble from the house. He left Abby and Katy arguing about whether there would be a pool or not, while he answered the call.

"What the hell are you doing?" Barney shouted. "Are you trying to kill me here? We made a deal with these TV guys. You're not keeping your end of it. You're supposed to be figuring out your future *on camera*. That's why they're following you around. They're trying to get an insight into the mind of an athlete when he's dealing with injury. You're screwing this up, boy."

Flynn leaned against the rail leading up to Abby's front door. "What do you want me to do, Barney? Make a Power-

Point listing all my options as a washed-up footballer? Ask them for ideas on what to do with my life next? Cry into my beer about my career ending with a foul tackle and let them film the tears? What should I be doing here? Tell me, because I thought I was supposed to live as I normally do and they'd edit for what they needed."

"Do all of those bloody things," Barney yelled. "Do anything. The producer is nagging my ear off. Hours of footage showing you working on your tan isn't good TV."

"I don't give a crap about good TV. When I signed you said it was a couple of interviews, some filler footage of me in my hometown and the rest would be archive material showing my career. Instead I'm stuck in *EDtv*. I want out of this contract."

"Not going to happen. The contract is ironclad." Barney let out a loud sigh. "Look, son, this isn't about you. It's about your fans. Don't they deserve to know how you're doing? They're worried about you."

"The hell it's about the fans. It's about the money. The huge amount of money they're paying me to do this, of which you get a hefty cut."

"So sue me for wanting to get paid for doing my job. Suck it up, Boyle. Get the job done. You're only committed for two more weeks. Give the guy what he wants and get this over with. Stop acting like a baby. I don't have time for this crap." The phone went dead.

Without thinking, Flynn threw the phone towards his van. It bounced off the boundary fence with a loud snap. Damn it. Now he needed a new phone. They didn't make phones the way they used to. One wee tap and the screen snapped.

He stomped, as best he could, to the RV. Once inside, he plopped onto the armchair in front of the driver's seat. His leg ached. He looked down at the pale, scarred mess and traced his finger over the spot where his broken bone had torn through skin. He'd known before they told him that his career was over. The pins holding his bone together had been his first clue. The fact his knee would likely never have a complete range of motion was another. The orthopaedic surgeon had clasped Flynn's shoulder, looked him in the eye and said, "Think about the future, son. You don't come back from this sort of injury."

Flynn covered his face with his palms and laughed. It sounded hollow. Think about his future? He'd done nothing but think about it since the dirty tackle took him down. What the hell was he good for except chasing a ball? He was too unpredictable for commentating. No TV station would risk him on air when they didn't know what would come out his mouth next. Coaching was out. He didn't think he could bear helping guys do what he wanted to do so badly. Management was a joke—even if someone was daft enough to hire him, he had no patience for the politics of the sport. That left what? Charity work? Charities would worry about the publicity he attracted. Start a business? Go back to school? Move to Rio and live on a beach? He'd thought he had years before he'd need to think about life after football. He was only twenty-nine. He was in his prime. And his life was over.

He rolled his eyes at himself. As one of the Babes would say, "drama much?" Thinking about this was driving him nuts. He needed to stop going around in circles and be proactive. He swivelled towards the built-in table and pulled the laptop towards him. A minute later he had a new document open. He made two columns. One headed *skills,* the other headed *interests.* He'd break down what he could do and see where he would go from here. He felt good. It was a practical plan.

In the skills column he wrote, *ball skills, game strategy, game analysis.* He turned his attention to the interests column and wrote, *football.* He thought about it for a minute then added *women* to the list. That was when his mind went blank. He couldn't think of even one more skill or interest.

There was no avoiding it. He was screwed.

"That's all you've got for skills? Man, that's sad. Why isn't your degree on the list?"

At the sound of Harry's voice, Flynn clutched his chest. "Damn it, are you trying to give me a heart attack? It isn't on the list because it isn't a proper degree. I got it online."

Harry blinked at him. "Through Open Uni, nutjob. It's the same as any other uni."

Flynn ignored him. "Why are you here anyway? Shouldn't you be at home putting Elvira into her coffin for the night?"

His brother grinned. "Vampires sleep in daylight. And I'm telling Magenta you're calling her Elvira again."

Harry sprawled on the couch that ran along the wall of the living room area. He took up pretty much all of the space.

"Seriously? Why are you here?" Flynn closed the laptop with a snap. "I've had my intervention. I'm being good. You can back off now."

"As much fun as that was, I'm here to take you out." He looked around the motorhome. "You live in a shoebox. If you don't get out now and then, you'll start making homemade bombs or collecting cats."

"Those are the only options for my future? Cats and bombs? Fan-bloody-tastic. And for your information, moron, this shoebox is top of the line. I have everything I need at my fingertips. And when I get fed up with the scenery, or the people"—he pointed at his brother—"I can drive off and park somewhere more interesting."

Harry didn't acknowledge the dig. He rarely did. "Aren't

you supposed to be building a house? Shouldn't you talk to an architect or something?"

"I will as soon as I get rid of the film crew." Although he had to admit the idea didn't have the same appeal it'd had when he'd first bought the land from Abby. "Right now, I have other things to do. I need to hire someone to put in a pool."

Harry's eyebrows shot up into his unkempt hair. "You're putting in a pool before the house? Not sure that's going to help your new image, bro."

"Bro? Where are we? The hood?" Flynn shook his head at Harry's grin. "It's not for me. It's for Katy. I was thinking I'd get her one of the blow-up ones, like the one Abby destroyed, then I thought about the fact you can't really swim in them. If you're going to have a pool, you should be able to swim in it, right? If I get a decent-sized proper pool we can do laps."

Harry sat forward, ran his fingers through his hair and stared at Flynn as though he'd lost his mind. "I don't even know where to start with this."

Flynn had no idea what he was talking about, so he ignored Harry and took the few steps between his chair and the fridge. He pulled out two bottles of Belgian beer and handed one to his brother. By the time he'd dragged himself back to his chair, Harry's brain had formulated a reply. For a guy with a genius IQ, it often took a long time for Harry to have a conversation with mere mortals.

"Okay, first, you're building a pool for Katy? I didn't even think you noticed the kid, let alone liked her enough to buy her a pool. Second, does Abby know about this? Is she okay with it? Third, what do you mean when you say 'we can do laps'? You don't plan to share the pool, do you?"

Flynn wiped his mouth on the back of his hand. "You offend me. Of course I notice the kid. She's always here, poking her tiny nose into my business. She negotiates like a shark. You can't get anything past her." He grinned with pride when he remembered her skills. He liked to think he'd played a part in helping her develop them. "She negotiated for the pool. It's a bribe to make her behave while Abby's family is around." He took another swig from the icy bottle. "Plus, she needs to pretend we get on. Trust me, the pool is the least of it. She wants a pony as well. At least Abby knows about the pool. I'm not sure how to break the news that I've ordered a pony. Maybe after her sister leaves."

Without a word, Harry got up, opened the cupboard above the sink that held Flynn's medication and proceeded to put the bottles of pills onto the counter.

"Hey, what are you doing?"

Harry cocked an eyebrow at him, a move he'd obviously stolen from Lake. "I'm checking your meds. Either you're overmedicating or something here is reacting badly with something else, because everything you just said was insane." He started counting pills.

Flynn let out a sigh. "Knock yourself out." He'd only find there were more pills than there should be. Flynn was trying to cut back on the pain meds. He didn't like the fuzzy way they made him feel. They impaired his thought process, and he couldn't help thinking they were at least in part to blame for all the things he'd let slide recently. Only partly to blame, though. The rest of the blame for his poor decision making was all on him.

"Okay." Harry finished counting. "It isn't the pills. What's going on, for real?"

"For real." Flynn made no attempt to hide the fact he was fast losing patience. "I'm bribing the kid next door to help her mother, because I feel bad about causing problems for Abby. And I thought while I'm forking out for this bribe, I may as well go the whole hog, make it a decent-sized pool, put it along the fence we share so we can share the pool too. It isn't rocket science, although you might have grasped it a whole lot faster if it was. It's no big deal. You wanted me to grow up." He spread his arms wide. "Well, welcome to the grownup version of your big brother."

Harry did a great impersonation of a fish. "This is you being a grownup?" He stared at Flynn for a minute or two before he burst out laughing.

Flynn flipped him off before opening his laptop to Google pool builders. Pool diggers? Pool providers? He'd figure it out.

He was deep into his search by the time Harry stopped laughing. Flynn looked over to see his red-faced brother wiping his eyes. And that was when the duck quacked. Flynn stared at the screen, hoping Harry didn't notice.

"Was that a duck?"

Come on, Flynn demanded skyward, *give me a break here. I'm trying!*

"It's nothing. Probably some ducks under the van again. It happens. I live beside a stream." Flynn kept on typing, two-fingered, at his keyboard. There was another quack.

"Sounds like it's coming from inside." Harry headed towards the back of the van, where Flynn's bedroom and bathroom were situated.

"Just leave it," Flynn called after him. "I'm sure it's nothing."

Too late. Harry opened the bathroom door. Flynn could do nothing but watch as Harry stared into his bathroom. It took his brother a minute to process. Then, eyes gleaming, grin wide, he turned back to Flynn. He pointed into the bathroom.

"There's a duck in your shower. She's floating in a baby bath with the cutest little bandage on her wing." Harry started to laugh again. "Friend of yours, bro? You holding out on me? I thought you said you weren't seeing anyone?" He doubled over in hysterics.

Flynn did his best to ignore him, while he picked out the perfect pool to share with Abby and the kid.

CHAPTER 14

*"Football is a simple game; twenty-two men chase a ball for ninety
minutes, and at the end, the Germans win."*
Gary Lineker, former player for England's national team

Abby was making animal-shaped pancakes for breakfast
when a huge rumble shook the house. For a second she
panicked, thinking there was another problem with the
mine. The last time the earth shook, the mine had collapsed
—taking her business with it. She rushed to the front door,
threw it open and tripped over her feet at the sight.

There were trucks, diggers and an assortment of equipment heading to the spot in her garden that lay beside
Flynn's land. And standing beside their shared fence was
Flynn. Arms waving directions to the trucks. A guy in work
gear stood beside him holding a large sheet of paper and a
clipboard. Another guy was pinning little sticks into the
ground and stringing a line between them.

Abby felt steam come out of her ears as she stalked towards them, with Katy on her heels.

"What's going on?" she demanded as soon as she was within speaking distance. "Who are these people? Why are they on my property? What are you up to?"

"Surprise!" Flynn threw his arms wide.

He was wearing a long-sleeved shirt in army green, over a pair of grey cargo shorts that came to his knees. The shirt was tight across his chest, which was more than a little distracting. It was criminal he could look so good while being so unreasonable. Everything—his intense eyes, sexy grin and broad shoulders—made her mouth water. And distracted her from her anger towards him. She narrowed her eyes at him. Did he know he had such power over her? Oh my goodness, she hoped not. The man would be a devil with it.

"Surprise?" She stopped in front of him, put her hands on her hips and glared.

"Yes. Surprise?" Katy copied her action while standing at her side. In her tiger onesie and bunny slippers, she managed to undermine Abby's dramatic gesture. As confirmed by the chuckles of the watching men.

"I'm giving you a pool, remember?" Flynn pointed to the guy measuring out the area. "Ta-da."

Abby started to count to ten. One, two... Oh, to hell with it. "You're doing what?" Yes, it was a shriek. She wasn't proud of it, but there was no way she could have stopped it. "I thought the pool comment was a joke." Was he out of his mind? "Are you out of your mind? You can't give a kid a pool. Especially not without talking to her mother about it first. And this is Scotland." She pointed at the ground. "That's an outdoor pool, which means the weather will be warm enough for it to be used maybe four days a year." Okay, she was shouting now. She needed to calm down.

"It's top of the line," the idiot said. "It's heated. There's a Jacuzzi section. An automatic cover. The whole shebang. We'll be able to use it year round."

"In the rain? The snow? Have you thought about this at all?"

He glanced at the guy beside him. "Bob here says it'll be fine. He's the expert."

"Bob probably just wants the business." She gave the man a tight smile and pretended she hadn't just called him a liar. "No offence, Bob."

He didn't seem offended. From his smile, he seemed to be entertained.

"Maybe we should build an indoor pool?" Flynn said to Bob.

Abby wanted to scream. "Not on my property, you aren't. Who's going to pay the huge monthly bills for heating and maintaining a top of the line pool?"

He actually had to think about it. Honestly!

"I guess I'll take care of the running costs, since it's my gift to the kid."

Enough of this. She folded her arms. "Send them away. Stop this now. You can't give a child a pool. I'm putting my foot down. Enough is enough."

"Abby, Abby, Abby," Flynn said with a shake of his head. "Any parent worth their salt knows you don't make promises to kids unless you intend to keep them. Otherwise it breaks their wee hearts and sets them up for a lifetime of dealing with trust issues. Do you want that for your child? Now, tell me honestly, do you?" He actually batted his eyelashes at her, while a smile quirked at his lips. "I need to give the kid her pool. I promised."

Was it wrong that she wanted to superglue those damn eyes shut? And maybe his mouth too? Definitely his mouth. His mouth was the part of him that caused the most trouble.

"Yay, I'm getting a pool! I can't believe I'm getting a pool," the traitor at her side yelled—as though she hadn't arranged the whole thing. She squealed loudly and did an excited dance.

"I don't know why you sound surprised, kid." Flynn seemed genuinely perplexed. "You were the one who demanded a pool."

"I didn't think you'd give me one." Katy rolled her eyes but couldn't contain her glee. "I thought if you did I'd get one of those kids' pools. Not this. This is gonna be a real pool. Isn't it?" She looked up at him, suddenly uncertain. "Is it going to be a real pool, Flynn?"

Abby watched as Flynn's eyes warmed before he rolled them dramatically, in an imitation of Katy. He awkwardly patted her head, the way someone else would pat a strange dog.

"Yeah, it's going to be a real pool, you numpty. We can't swim in a kids' pool. And by we, I mean us separately. You swim at your time. I'll swim at mine. You can swim, right?" Flynn looked up at Abby. "Can she swim? Is she old enough? How old are kids when they learn to swim?"

Abby shook her head. "Yes, she can swim. No, she shouldn't be around a pool unsupervised. That's not the point. The point is, I don't want a pool." She turned to Bob. "We can't accept this. I'm sorry, but you have to leave. I don't give you permission to put in a pool."

The guy looked unsure. His eyes shifted to Flynn.

"Give me a minute, Bob," Flynn said.

He walked the few steps to Abby, threw his arm around her shoulders and led her away from the work crew. As though this was his property and he had a say in what happened on it.

"Abby, sugar, give the kid her pool." He spoke softly against her ear.

"Not going to happen, Flynn. Make them pack up. This is worse than the money you gave her. You can't give a five-year-old a pool just because she asked for one."

Flynn's thumb caressed her shoulder, momentarily distracting her. "I'm not giving her a pool. This isn't a gift. It's a deal. With a miniature terrorist organisation." He leaned into her, the heat of his body having a strange effect on her ability to breathe. "This is the cost of her help. The kid has been through a lot. All she wants is a pool. Give the kid a pool, Abby."

For a moment she swayed towards him, her focus on those luscious lips of his before she caught herself. What was she doing? His insanity was contagious. She pushed away from him and folded her arms over her navy twinset. Yes. Twinset. She didn't care what it said about her, she liked wearing them.

"I'm not bribing my daughter with a pool, Flynn."

"It will be great. We can all use it."

"You want a pool, put one on your property. And make sure it's properly fenced. And has a roof to keep out the snow. But there is no way you're giving my five-year-old a pool. I don't care what deal you made with her. She's five. She can't even tie her own shoelaces, let alone understand what she's asking for. This is not happening."

Flynn studied her face for a moment before nodding. She must have looked as immovable on the topic as she felt, because he caved. She didn't know whether to sigh with relief of pump the air with joy. He nodded once before walking back to the men.

"Change of plans. We're moving the pool over the fence. Same size, just a few feet that-a-way." He pointed at his land. "And we're going to make it an indoor pool. Make sure there's a door on this side for Abby and her daughter. They'll need their own private entrance, as I have no problem sharing *my* pool with them." He grinned at her.

She narrowed her eyes.

The men set about moving their equipment to the other side of the fence as Katy ran up to Flynn. "If you put it over there it won't be my pool. And you promised me a pool."

"You didn't specify where the pool would be. It could be anywhere. This is still your pool. It will just sit on the other side of the fence. We'll make a sign. We'll call it Katy's Pool. Good enough for you, kid?"

Katy tapped her finger to her chin as she considered his offer. "Can the pool building be pink?"

"No."

"Can the pool be pink?"

"No."

"What about some pink blow-up stuff to put in the pool?"

"That we can do."

"Then it's okay for the pool to move," Katy said solemnly.

Abby felt a headache start. She stepped towards her neighbour. "This isn't what I meant. I told you I didn't want a pool. I told you that you can't give Katy a pool."

"And I'm doing exactly what you said. It's my pool, on my property and I'm calling it Katy's Pool." He reached out and high-fived Katy, who was still jumping up and down with excitement.

The noise of a car roaring up the drive stopped the argument. Her heart sank when she saw it was her sister, back for another round of Prove Abby is a Terrible Mother. She didn't have enough brain space to deal with all of this.

"You're undermining me, Flynn Boyle, and I'm not happy about it. We're going to have a long talk about this later." She made the words a threat.

He seemed unaffected. "Looking forward to it, sugar."

"Abby." Victoria's icy voice preceded her as she strode towards them. "What's this?"

Abby sighed—quietly, she hoped.

"I'm putting in a pool," Flynn said. "For physio. Nothing better than swimming to recover from an injury. The water takes the strain off the joints."

Victoria's cold gaze made Abby squirm, even when it was directed at Flynn. "And this pool of yours is going to be in Abby's garden?"

"Bit of a mix-up with the work crew." Flynn smiled. "It's all sorted now." He dismissed Victoria with a nod before winking at Abby. "Catch you later, sugar."

"Flynn," Katy shouted as she ran up to them. "Don't forget my bedtime story. You promised."

Abby gaped at her daughter. Katy's lips were set in a determined pout. And from the pained look on Flynn's face, there was no way he wanted to read to her at bedtime. She almost grinned. Let him suffer. He deserved it.

"You promised you'd do it every night this week and you haven't even read to me once," Katy pointed out.

"Yes, Flynn." Abby couldn't resist. "We both know how important it is to keep our promises to children. We wouldn't want her to grow up with trust issues, now would we?"

Flynn growled at Abby. "Fine. But I'm picking the book. We're having none of that pink princess rubbish."

With one last frown, he strode away, barely limping, which told her his leg wasn't so bad today. He really should use his crutches more. Abby shook away the thought. He was a grown man. He could take care of himself. She bit her lip. Maybe. She sighed. He most definitely couldn't look after himself. She made a mental note to talk to him about the crutches when she next saw him. If the man wanted to recover, he'd better use the things.

"Abby?" Victoria's voice made her realise she was staring at Flynn's rear.

She blushed as she turned to her sister. "Tea?" she said lightly.

Without waiting for Victoria's answer, she called for Katy and headed to her house.

FLYNN WISHED there was an AA-type group for guys who were trying to behave. He could see it now, him at the front of a room: "Hi, my name is Flynn. It's been forty-eight hours since I last behaved like an asshole." And then they'd all shout, "Hello, Flynn." Yeah, he definitely needed a support group. He was trying hard here. Being good was exhausting —and boring. Plus, he felt he wasn't getting enough credit. Actually, *any* credit.

He'd hired a cleaning crew to sort the place out. He'd started buttoning his shirts. He was showering every day. He'd sent everyone away, except the camera crew that he couldn't get rid of no matter what he did. He'd sat down for a very serious interview with a magazine, where he answered dumb questions like: "What do you find most attractive in a woman?" He'd made sure his answer was mature and politically correct, even though what he wanted to do was sneer and say a talent with her tongue. Because, seriously, would it hurt someone to ask him a decent bloody question?

On top of all this, he'd been lying low. Resting his leg. Watching TV. Being bored out of his mind in an effort to please everyone around him. And no one noticed. Would it kill his family to tell him he was doing well? To give him some encouragement? A pat on the back, maybe?

"Hey, you in there?" There was a thump at his door.

Flynn turned to see his cousin Claire stick her head in. She smiled when she saw him. Claire had always had a soft heart, and for a minute Flynn thought she'd come to give him some praise. He was wrong.

"Got a minute?" she said.

"For you? Never."

She ignored him and chewed her bottom lip. "I've got something for you. It's outside."

Now Flynn was curious. He followed her out of the RV and stopped in his tracks at the sight of Grunt holding a small fluffy goat against his chest. His overly muscled arms made the goat seem tiny. The guy had to be taking steroids, because that kind of bulk was not normal.

"You got me a goat?" He stared between the goat and his cousin.

She shuffled in place. "Someone gave it to the kindy as a pet, but it's getting too wild with the children and we can't keep it. I thought you could keep it here." She batted her eyelashes at him, and Flynn wondered if that crap worked on her fiancé.

"You're giving me a goat?" Aye, it wasn't sinking in.

The goat bleated.

"Well." Claire toed the grass. "Harry said you were collecting pets now. He said you had a duck. We thought with all your space, you wouldn't mind having a goat too."

Bloody Harry. Flynn was going to kill his brother. "I don't have a pet duck."

Claire gave him a look that said she knew otherwise. "If I go in there, will I find a duck in the bathroom?"

"It's sick. I'm looking after it. The nearest vet is in Fort William. It isn't a pet. As soon as it's better, I'll put her back in the stream."

"Have you named her?" Claire looked like she wanted to laugh.

"Hell no, I haven't named her."

"Harry said you called her Daisy and bought her a pink bow."

"There's a good chance you had your last conversation with Harry. I hope you said goodbye. His life is about to end."

Claire grinned widely. "Okay, I believe you. Harry was wrong. You don't have a pet duck. But can you take the goat? At least until we find another home for her. You're the only one with enough space. She's no trouble at all. Honest."

Flynn eyed the goat sceptically. He knew nothing about goats. He could see another evening Googling animal care in his future. He let out a sigh. "Fine. I'll keep the goat. But you better look for another home. This is temporary."

"You're the best." Claire bounced in front of him before giving him a kiss on the cheek.

He wasn't sure about being the best, but he was definitely the most gullible. Claire nodded to a spot behind Flynn and he felt the hair on his neck jump to attention.

"Will the goat be on TV?" she said.

Yeah, his neck had nailed it. The camera crew were back. They'd wandered off to interview people at Rangers Football Club in Glasgow, to fill in some backstory for the documentary. He'd been hoping they'd forget to wander back.

"Let the goat free, baby," Claire said to Grunt.

The big buy opened his arms and dropped the goat.

"Not like that," Claire shouted. She wrapped her arms around the animal and cooed in its ear. "Poor baby. It's okay."

Flynn shared a look of bewilderment with Grunt. It was their first male bonding moment. Flynn felt like they should mark the occasion with beer or something.

"Done here," Grunt said.

Guess beer was out, then. Claire blathered instructions about goat care as Grunt grabbed her hand and dragged her back to his SUV. A minute later Flynn was left standing in a field with a camera crew and a strange goat.

The goat bleated at him. She then headed for the lounger and proceeded to eat the padding off the seat. Flynn pretended he didn't see anything and went back into his van.

As soon as he stepped inside, the duck let out a loud protest quack.

Flynn put his hands on his hips and hung his head.

This was his life. And people wondered why he acted out.

There was another knock at his door, this one a lot more timid than the last. With a heavy sigh, Flynn went to open it. The shy assistant to the producer stood staring at her shoes. Flynn felt for the woman. She was always taking crap from the weasel, probably because she was the only member of the crew with a conscience.

"What's up, honey?" He remembered the Ball Babe dig about him not bothering to learn their names and felt bad. "What's your name again?"

She was startled by the question, as though she didn't rate him knowing her name. It made him feel even more like a self-obsessed asshole than he'd felt before.

"Julia," she whispered.

"Well, Julia, what can I do for you?" Flynn plastered a charming smile on his face, even though the woman was still staring at her feet.

"It's time for your interview."

"Interview?" He was trying his best to avoid the documentary crew—why would he want to take part in an interview?

"Your agent spoke to my producer. They arranged for a formal session where you would answer questions about your career." Wide eyes looked up at him. They were pretty eyes, but they weren't stunning. Not like Abby's were. "Originally the questions were going to be seeded into a more relaxed situation. As though you were conversing with friends as part of your everyday life. But Mr Flannigan is getting a little impatient. So your agent thought a formal interview might be better. We're setting up for it now."

Flynn clenched his jaw. It was round about now the old Flynn would lose his temper, shout at the girl, shout at the producer, then call up his agent and shout at him too. But he was the new Flynn. He was being mature. Rage bubbled inside him, but he swallowed it down.

"I'll get changed and meet you outside." The words almost stuck in his throat.

Julia blinked hard. "You're going to do it? Without a fight?"

It was a direct hit. Flynn smiled at her. "Contrary to popular belief, honey, I'm not always a dick."

She giggled, then flushed red when she realised she'd let a laugh slip.

"Go on. I'll be out soon. Can't do a formal interview in a T-shirt. Got to get into a suit."

"I don't think you need to—"

He held up a hand to stop her. "I know press calls, honey. I'm wearing a suit." A suit was armour in these situations. There was no way he was letting the weasel pry into his head without armour.

She nodded, mumbled something, then left. Keeping a tight rein on his fury, Flynn went to retrieve his phone so he could chew out his agent. He got two steps before he remembered he'd killed the phone after the last talk with his agent. He stared at the ceiling and tried to slow his breathing.

Being good was so bloody hard.

CHAPTER 15

"What's he doing, Muma?" Katy said with her nose pressed
up to the kitchen window.

Those words struck fear into Abby's heart. Had Flynn
backslidden already? Were the women back? Was there going
to be more noise? She caught Victoria staring at her from the
corner of her eye and gave Katy a serene smile, when she felt
far from serene.

"I don't know, darling. Let me see." It took effort not to
rush to the window in an attempt to head off whatever Flynn
was up to.

The sight took her breath away. Flynn in a pair of tatty
shorts and an old flannel shirt was gorgeous. Flynn in a
tailored suit was devastating. Abby experienced weakness in
her knees and a mouth-watering need to pet the man.

"What's happening?" Katy tugged at Abby's arm, snapping her from the Flynn daze.

Abby cleared her throat. "It looks like he's being asked questions for a TV show, sweetie."

Lawrence came up to stand beside them. His eyes sparkled with amusement as he spotted Abby's flushed cheeks.

"He cleans up well," Lawrence said.

"Yes. I'm sure he does. I hadn't really noticed." Abby's lie made her cheeks burn more ferociously.

Lawrence grinned knowingly.

"Can we go watch?" Katy bounced in place. Today's ensemble included pink jeans worn under a pink tutu, sparkling yellow play shoes, a red scarf tied around her waist and a faux-fur shrug—in luminous purple. Her face was makeup free. Her hair had three rainbow-coloured bows stuck in it randomly. "Can we? I want to. Can we?"

"I don't think so. This looks like a very serious interview. I'm sure he doesn't want anyone watching, or distracting him." Abby looked down at her hyperactive daughter. "They don't let people make any noise, baby. I'm not sure you can be quiet."

"I can. I really can. Can we go? Can we?"

Lawrence rubbed his perfectly smooth chin. "I wouldn't mind hearing what he's saying either. I don't see where the harm would be. We can stand well back. I'm sure we wouldn't be a distraction. Katy will promise to be quiet, won't you, little one?"

Katy made a zipping action at her lips. Yeah, like Abby believed that.

She chewed her bottom lip as she looked over at Flynn. He seemed to be acting as a magnet, pulling her in his direction. "I don't know."

"This is a fabulous idea." Victoria's words dripped

sarcasm. "Why don't we all go stand in a field to hear what pearls of wisdom Mr Boyle is sharing with the world? I'm sure he has much to teach all of us."

The condescending smile on Victoria's face made up Abby's mind for her.

"You're right, Victoria." She smiled brightly. "This is too good an opportunity to miss. Who knows what we might learn. Let's go hear what Flynn is saying."

Victoria started to protest, but Katy was already squealing and running for the door, followed closely by a beaming Lawrence.

"Abby, surely you realise these sort of decisions can't help your cause."

She sighed as she looked at her sister. "I don't know what happened to you, Victoria. I'm really sorry you changed. I miss the Victoria I remember from my childhood. The one who told the best bedtime stories and laughed easily. I want my sister back."

Victoria's face paled. "I'm not your sister," she said before walking away.

Pain sliced through Abby, cutting her in a way she didn't think was still possible when it came to her family. She blinked back tears and went to stand with her daughter. Victoria was right. Abby had lost her sister a long time ago. And there was no sign she was ever coming back.

Abby walked over to the fence she shared with Flynn. The summer sun was hidden behind a blanket of wispy white cloud. It was warm and peaceful, a perfect summer's day. As she neared the fence, Katy waved at her from her perch on top of it, held in place by Lawrence. She was so happy, so oblivious to the problems swirling around her, and if Abby had to sell her soul to achieve it, Katy would stay that way.

Burying the stress of dealing with Victoria, Abby turned her attention to Flynn. He was sitting on a tall chair, surrounded by lights and reflecting discs, yet he seemed laidback, at ease and totally in control. His slightly overgrown golden hair was back from his face. It sat in place, but still managed to look a little tousled—not much, just enough to make a woman's mouth water. He'd shaven, but left a sprinkling of designer stubble. He wore a three-piece navy suit with a fine grey pinstripe. His shirt was a crisp white, open at the neck, hinting at the chest Abby had seen many times. She wanted to flick those buttons open and follow the gap they made with her tongue.

"Holy guacamole." Jena's whisper broke into Abby's thoughts. She turned to find her friend standing beside her, flanked by Matt, who was in full police uniform. "What happened to the hobo?"

Abby shrugged her answer. She was thinking the same thing.

"This is his professional mode," Matt murmured to them. "Don't be fooled—he might act like an idiot, but my cousin is far from stupid. He knows how to do his job. And part of the job is dealing with the media."

"I thought his job was running up and down a soccer pitch?" Abby said.

Matt gawked at her. "Do you know nothing about the sport?"

She assumed it was a rhetorical question, and turned her eyes back to Flynn. He gave an easy smile in the direction of the camera as he answered the questions the pinched-looking producer threw at him. His voice was deep and self-assured in a way that sent shivers running along Abby's spine.

"Every footballer—every professional athlete—knows their career comes with a best-before stamp on it. I was lucky I had the run I did. There are players who injury out in their first season. I had a great career and have stored up a lot of good memories along the way."

Abby's jaw dropped. She shared an astonished look with Jena. Matt smothered a chuckle. "Told you," he whispered. "Not dumb."

"But he usually talks like he didn't even finish high school and doesn't care about it," Abby whispered.

Matt's eyes sparkled. "Flynn has an honours degree in Natural Sciences. It's not something he broadcasts, but he doesn't hide it either. He studied with Open University, distance learning while he played."

"You're pulling my leg. He's famous for his playboy ways. He's always in the press. When would he have time to study?"

"He's twenty-nine, Abby. He's had plenty of time to study. He only acts out when he's bored. He doesn't do it all the time." Matt gave a wry smile. "Although when he does act out, he tends to really make it count."

Abby turned her stunned face to her best friend. "Did you know any of this?"

Jena shook her head as she frowned. "No, but Matt and I are gonna have us a little chat about keeping secrets."

The producer's sharp voice cut through their whispered conversation.

"Are you trying to tell us you aren't bothered at all that your career is over? You were cut down in your prime by an illegal tackle. Exactly the kind of play that would make your head blow off if it'd happened to one of your teammates. Yet you're sitting there calmly telling me you're fine with how things turned out."

Abby swallowed at the steel in Flynn's eyes. "Now, there wouldn't be much point in losing my temper, would there? It won't undo the damage to my leg. The player who tackled me was dealt with by FIFA. As I said, players know their time in the game comes with an expiry date. Mine just arrived a few years sooner than I expected."

"So there are no hard feelings towards the player or his club?" The producer's tone said he wouldn't believe any answer Flynn gave.

Flynn looked straight into the camera. "None." He exuded sincerity. "These things happen. It's the risk you take when you play the game. It's why I was paid the big bucks. That and the fact I was damn good at the game."

The little man shifted in his seat. Each movement sharp and angry.

"What will you do with your time now? Any plans for the future?"

"There's always TV work," Flynn said with a wide smile. "I hear documentaries are easy to make. You don't need much skill to pull it off."

Jena slapped a hand over her mouth to smother her laugh.

"I beg to differ," the producer said. "Still, there's little chance any TV station would risk employing you. You don't have any experience and you're known for your unfiltered comments. Not exactly presenter material, wouldn't you say?"

Abby pursed her lips. Was he intentionally rude?

"But my sexy good looks more than make up for my runaway mouth. I'm sure the ratings would go up just having me on screen—even if all I did was sit silently and looked pretty."

Abby smiled widely at him, and for a second she could have sworn his eyes flickered in her direction.

The producer started to say something, but Flynn held up his hand to stop the man. Ignoring the producer, he stared into the camera. He'd clearly run out of patience with the interview.

"Let's not beat about the bush. Everyone knows I'm a

public relations nightmare." Flynn ran his fingers through his hair, making it seem even more sexily rumpled. "I'm too bad-tempered and impatient to go into coaching or management. I'm too much of a risk for TV. As you kindly pointed out, I don't have any outside interests, other than the sort of hobbies that make headlines." He gave a self-deprecating grin. "Last time I checked you couldn't make a career out of getting drunk, sleeping around and acting like an ass. So I'm left with a dilemma. What will I do with my life? And the answer is I don't know. I've been out of the game for six months now. My leg is still healing and I need to concentrate on recovery, rather than worrying about what I'll be doing in five years' time."

He stared at the producer. "We both know I have enough money to let me sit on my hands for the rest of my life. I don't need to do anything. Which puts me in the privileged position of having time to think. Time to recover. Time to reform."

"Reform?" the moronic little man interrupted. "You're reforming?" His laugh was sharp and bitter.

Flynn nodded, smiling at the man as though he were in on the joke. "It's been brought to my attention recently that it's time I grew up."

Abby sucked in a breath. She felt Jena and Matt still beside her.

"You're telling me there will be no more partying?" The producer was disdainful. "No more paternity suits. No more sex tapes. No more drunk driving or speeding. No more trashing hotel rooms. You're a new man? The injury was a sort of epiphany for you and now you're a born-again nice guy?"

Flynn's face went blank. "No. This is what I'm saying: I'm twenty-nine, and it's time to grow up. Time to take responsibility for my actions. I can't change the past, but from here on in I'm going to try to live a considerate life. I'm reforming. I'm going straight. No more bad boy of British football. Now there's just going to be Flynn Boyle. Nothing more."

He stood from the stool, buttoned his jacket and tugged at his cuffs. "We done?" he asked, but was walking away from the camera crew before anyone could answer. As he reached the camera guy, he smiled into the lens. "For the record, there was only one sex tape, and it was a piece of art."

Abby rolled her eyes. "This is him turning over a new leaf?" she asked Matt.

Matt chuckled. "Aye, this might be as good as it gets. So don't go expecting great things."

"I wonder if that tape is on the net?" Jena said.

Matt cocked an eyebrow at her.

"What?" Jena demanded.

Matt just shook his head at his wife.

They waited as Flynn limped over the uneven ground towards them. He was breathtakingly handsome in his suit. Abby had seen a meme on Facebook once where a photo of a guy in a suit was accompanied by the words "suits are to women what lingerie is to men." The sentiment was spot on. She licked her lips as Flynn came to a stop in front of their little group.

"How'd I do?" His grin was cheeky.

"I thought you did an excellent job," Lawrence said. "You might have been a bit hasty in your dismissal of a career in television."

Flynn looked appalled. "That's as long as I could control myself. I'd only be of use if the show that hired me lasted fifteen minutes tops."

"What's sex tape?" Katy piped up. "Is it like Sellotape? Is it good for art? Do we need some? I like making art."

Abby felt her cheeks flush as everyone else smothered their smiles.

"It's not for art, it's—" Flynn started.

Abby jumped right in, shouting over him. "It's a different kind of tape. Nothing little kids can use."

Flynn gave her a wry look. "I was going to say it was a sport thing. Not an art thing."

Matt turned his laughter into a cough.

"Okay." Katy had already moved on to the next topic in her little head. "Don't forget my bedtime story, Flynn. You can't hide anymore. You promised you'd do it today."

"I know." Flynn let out a sigh. "I told you I'd be there, kid. Take a chill pill. I'll bring the reading material. You do the sleep part."

Abby heard an alarm go off inside her head. "What reading material?"

"Don't worry," Flynn said, making her worry. "I loaned my latest copy of *Playboy* to Matt here. I'll have to bring something else to read."

"Your reading material had better be age appropriate."

"Yes, milady." He affected a bow.

"My sister-in-law is Lady Montgomery-Clark. I'm just plain Abby."

Flynn's smile was wicked. "There's nothing plain about you, Abby."

Abby rolled her eyes at him, gathered her daughter into her arms and headed back to her house. All the while a part of her hoped Flynn would wear the suit when he came over for Katy's bedtime story. Her cheeks were flushed by the time she made it into the house, and it wasn't because Katy weighed a tonne. It was from the memory of the gorgeously sexy Mr Boyle.

As her eyes caught Victoria watching them from the front porch, an uneasy acknowledgement coursed through Abby. She was dancing with fire spending time with Flynn, flaunting her familiarity with her neighbour in front of her sister. She squeezed Katy tight. Now wasn't the time to rebel. It wasn't the time to attract any attention to areas of her life she'd rather her sister didn't see.

She looked over her shoulder at Flynn. It definitely wasn't the time to get involved with a bad boy. No matter how irresistible that bad boy might be.

CHAPTER 16

"Without being too harsh on David Beckham, he cost us the match."
Ian Wright, former England national player

It was a surprise when Flynn actually turned up to read to Katy. Abby expected him to run and hide. Instead, he'd shown up wearing butter-soft faded jeans, a long-sleeved crew-neck tee in royal blue and beaten grey Converse on his feet. He sauntered into her house like he owned the place, rooted around in his gym bag for a minute, came out with a magazine then dumped the bag by the table.

"Where's the terrorist?"

"Not so fast."

She was trusting this guy with her child. So what if he came with stellar references from people she trusted? And okay, it *was* only a bedtime story—it wasn't like she was letting him take Katy to Disneyland Paris for the weekend. Still, Flynn was an unknown element—an irresponsible unknown element. At the very least Abby wanted to make

142

sure he wasn't going to warp Katy's little mind with his choice of reading material. She pointed at the magazine.

"What are you reading?"

Flynn's smile was devilish and did things to her heart rate she was sure would cause a coronary. He held up the magazine.

Abby's eyebrows rose. "*Sports Illustrated?*"

"Note, it isn't the swimwear edition. I put a lot of thought into this. There's a great article in here on the future of the Premier League."

"Premier League?"

"Her education has been sorely lacking, Abby. There's no way she'll learn about football from you. Someone needs to step up."

She shooed him away. "First door on the right at the top of the stairs. Here I was worried you'd wind her up and she'd be awake all night." She pointed at the magazine. "If you read that to her she'll be out like a light in under ten minutes."

"Heathen," he muttered as he climbed the stairs, holding tightly to the banister.

As Abby watched, she had a sudden flash of him racing up the steps three at a time. She couldn't imagine what it would be like to go from being confident in your physical ability to not trusting your own two feet.

"Leave the door open," she ordered as Flynn hit the top step. "I want to hear if you freak her out."

"No trust." He shook his head before stepping into the room. "Hey, kid. It's your lucky night." His voice echoed through the house, and Abby realised she needn't have left the baby monitor on in Katy's room. She'd hear everything anyway.

She walked into the kitchen, hoping to keep herself occupied by tidying up. Katy's voice came through the monitor on the bench.

"This better be a good story, Flynn. You owe me."

Abby smiled. Her child *was* a terrorist. Not that she'd ever admit it to Flynn.

"This is the best story ever," Flynn said with genuine enthusiasm. "It's about the best sports league in the world."

"Is there a princess?"

"Not unless you count Jesus Navas. He's a bit of a pretty boy."

"Boys can't be princesses." Katy was clearly disgusted.

"Whatever. Are you ready to learn something?"

"Yes." Katy sounded so solemn it made Abby laugh.

She listened in astonishment as Flynn read about the struggles in the Premier League, stopping every couple of sentences to shout about something he didn't agree with. He wasn't rude. He didn't swear. He also made no attempt to dumb it down for Katy. When there'd been silence for some time, Abby assumed her daughter had been bored to sleep. She was wrong.

"Jonathan's mum said David Beckham is better looking than you. She said David Beckham is the greatest player in Scotland."

There was silence for a minute. "Who is this woman?" Flynn sounded outraged. "I need to talk to her. Give me a name."

"Her name is Jonathan's mum."

"Not helping, kid." Abby heard him take a deep breath. "First, Beckham is not better looking than me. Did Jonathan's mum tell you Beckham is obsessed with hair gel? No. I bet she never mentioned that. Second, he couldn't be the greatest player in Scotland because he's English. And third, the guy is old. He retired years ago. Now all he does is model underpants."

"Oh, okay then, who is Scotland's greatest footballer?"

Abby rolled her eyes as she waited for Flynn's obvious answer.

"Hands down, it's Kenny Dalglish." Abby heard the awe in Flynn's voice, once she got over the shock of him not answering with his own name. "He's the best goal maker in Scottish history. He should have been a midfielder. He would have been legendary in midfield, but he played as a striker and was still world class. No one could place a ball like Kenny Dalglish. Not even your precious Beckham. Seriously, what is your mother teaching you? You should know this stuff. It's almost as important as knowing who Robert the Bruce is. Tomorrow, I'm going to bring over some of Kenny's games. After you watch him play you'll be able to tell Jonathan's mother all about Scotland's greatest player. Beckham?" He snorted in disgust. "Right, I'm done here. I'll deal with your ignorance tomorrow."

She heard chair legs scrape as Flynn moved.

"What about my kiss goodnight? You're supposed to kiss my forehead and tell me to sleep well. Don't you know anything about little kids?"

"Nope. Nothing. I'll send your mum up to do the kissing thing."

"Scaredy cat," Katy taunted. "I'm telling Jonathan's mum you were too scared to put me to bed properly."

"Why me?" Flynn groaned. "You are driving me nuts, kid."

Abby heard him thump around, and there was a short, sharp kissing noise. "Right. Go to sleep."

"Sleep well," Katy reminded him.

"Fine. Sleep well. Just sleep, will you?"

There was more thumping. "Am I supposed to shut the door?" Flynn asked.

"I'm sleeping," Katy said.

"I don't know why I bother asking you anything," Flynn grumbled. "I'll let your mum sort it out."

"Flynn?" Katy called. "Have you met Kenny Dog Leash?"

"It's pronounced *Dal-gleesh*," he corrected. "And yeah, I have." Abby could hear the grin in the words.

"Maybe you could take me to visit him, then I can tell Jonathan I met Scotland's greatest footballer. Do you think Kenny Dog Leash likes little kids?"

"I don't know about visiting him, but I'm fairly sure he likes kids. He's known for being patient with them and showing them how to play better."

There was a pause. "Do you think he'd make a good daddy?"

Abby's heart stopped dead. Her hand fluttered to her mouth.

"You looking for a dad?" Flynn's voice was calm as Abby's heart broke. "I think Dalglish is too old for your mum. You might want to look elsewhere."

"I thought about Uncle Matt, but he married Aunt Jena." There was a pause. "Can I tell you a secret, Flynn?"

"Nope. Time to sleep. Shut your eyes. And shut your mouth. Sleeping goes a lot better when you don't talk. "

"But I want to tell you my secret," Katy whined.

"I keep telling you, kid. Tell your secrets to your mum. That's what mums are for. You don't tell secrets to the guy who lives next door. Don't you know anything?"

Abby blinked back tears as she grinned at Flynn's admonishment.

"I'm telling you my secret and you can't stop me." She rushed the words before Flynn stopped her again, or walked away. "I moved Muma's stuff, and hid things so she would have to call the police. I wanted her to see Uncle Mattie. I thought if he saw she needed a policeman he'd move in here and marry her."

Tears slid down Abby's cheeks. For months she'd thought she was losing her mind. Things had moved from where she'd left them. She'd even thought someone was stealing from her, and her business. And it turned out it was her matchmaking baby. No wonder it'd stopped when Matt married Jena.

"Marriage doesn't work that way, kid. Grownups need to fall in love with each other. You can't make it happen. Your mum will find someone she likes one day. And if he's a nice guy she'll fall in love with him and they'll get married."

"If you know any nice guys can you tell me? I want to find one for my Muma. She wouldn't be so sad all the time if there was a daddy around here to help her." There was silence for a minute. "Jonathan has a daddy. He takes Jonathan to the park. He makes Jonathan's mum laugh."

"If he's so great, why does Jonathan's mum have a thing for David Beckham?"

Abby laughed through her tears.

"Will you look for a man for my mum?" Katy persisted. "A good one."

"Whatever it takes to make you go to sleep."

"I have a list of things a daddy needs to be able to do."

"I'm sure you do."

"You can't do any of them," Katy said. "I checked."

"I can't even begin to express my relief. Now, I'm going downstairs. This conversation is hurting my head."

"Don't tell my Muma my secret."

"I will if she asks. Little kids shouldn't have secrets from their mums. If they do their heads explode and it makes a mess of the walls."

Abby heard a door shut and Flynn stomp down the stairs. She wiped her eyes on the back of her hands, but they still felt wet. So she splashed her face with cold water and patted it with the purple hand towel she kept on a hook by the fridge. She fought to put Katy's words out of her mind until she was alone. Until it was safe to think about her daughter's need for a father who was long gone. A father who would have adored her and taken her to the park. And a husband who was a good man and never failed to make her laugh.

Flynn's chest ached from the conversation that would not end. He wasn't entirely sure why he felt like he was in pain. Maybe it was the fact Katy thought Matt would make a good father and he wouldn't. There was no way his cousin would beat him in the fatherhood stakes. When the time came, Flynn would be a great dad. He'd be the freaking cup winner of fathers. He'd beat Matt's ass at fatherhood any day of the week.

When Katy had gotten all doe-eyed and terminally cute, Flynn had shut it right down. Football he could discuss—and he would be discussing it at length, seeing as Katy didn't have a freaking clue about the sport—but emotional need? He wasn't equipped for that. What the hell did you say to a five-year-old so desperate for a dad she tried to set her mum up with Matt? *Matt?* Surely there were better options.

Abby was covering leftovers with cling film when Flynn entered the kitchen. Her eyes were puffy and red. He glanced at the baby monitor on the counter. He didn't need his brother's genius IQ to figure out Abby had heard everything her kid said. Yet again, he was chest deep in the emotional world of the McKenzie females. He wondered for a second if he was supposed to be polite and pretend he didn't notice she'd been crying. Then he remembered he was Flynn Boyle. He might be trying to be good, but it didn't mean he needed a complete personality overhaul.

"I'd cry too if I heard she was trying to set me up with Matt."

Abby burst out laughing, but a tear ran down her cheek. As her laughter turned to sobs, he gave into his need to comfort her. He cursed under his breath and crossed the room to pull her into his arms.

"I like this shirt," he said against her hair. "Try not to get snot on it."

She let out another strangled chuckle that turned into a sob. Flynn held her tight as he stroked her back. Strangely, holding Abby, comforting her, made the pain emanating from the exposed space within him ease. At last her sobbing tapered off. She hiccupped and looked up at him, still in his arms.

"I'm sorry?" she said.

He grinned. "You don't sound very sure."

Her smile was rueful. "I'm not sure if I really am. I appreciate you comforting me while I had a complete meltdown."

"You call this a complete meltdown? Sugar, you haven't seen a Premier League player lose his cool in the final when the referee makes a bad call. *That's* a meltdown. This is just a little emotional seepage."

"Emotional seepage?" She grinned widely, looking strangely beautiful, even with her puffy eyes and red nose.

"It's a technical term used for when women can't hold it together. You're English, shouldn't you stiff-upper-lip the life out of any feelings you have?"

"You can see why my family disowned me. I never did live up to the English ideal." Her eyes turned sad again and Flynn kicked himself for opening his mouth. It was just more proof he wasn't meant to deal with emotional crap. He was in over his head. A place he seemed to permanently live since meeting Abby.

"You look pretty ideal to me, Abby McKenzie." He waggled his brows and loaded the sentence with as much innuendo as he could muster.

With a playful slap to his chest, she pushed out of his arms. Flynn was confounded by just how much he didn't want to release her. Pushing away the need to grab her and return her to his embrace, he jammed his hands into his pockets and leaned against the counter. He should run before she decided to talk about her feelings. Or go over the conversation she'd overheard, picking at it like a dog with a chicken carcass. But for some reason he didn't want to leave her. Although he still didn't want to talk about any emotional stuff. He spotted the leftovers she'd been covering.

"Food looks good. Got any going spare? I'm starved. Your daughter takes a lot of energy."

For a second he thought Abby might reprimand him for bad manners. Which, to be honest, kind of made him hot, but she didn't. Instead she smiled.

"Sure, I have shepherd's pie."

"I love shepherd's pie."

"Flynn." She sighed. "You're a guy. You just love food."

"Not all of it. I don't like wheatgrass. Wheatgrass is just wrong. Should we really be eating something cows enjoy? Shouldn't we just leave it for the cows, and once they've eaten it, we eat them. It's life's perfect cycle. Taking the cow out of the equation messes with nature."

Abby blinked hard at him several times before she laughed. He liked the sound of it. It wasn't one of those high-pitched, girly giggles women thought men loved—it was deep and raspy. It was sexy as hell. It made him want to draw her to him and taste the lips that produced such a sound. It made him want to see what other sounds he could cajole out of her.

"How much do you want?" Abby pointed to the covered dish.

He paused. "That's a trick question, right?"

"All of it. Got it. Grab a drink from the fridge and take a seat while I heat this up."

Flynn intended to do as he was told. He could have

sworn his feet moved towards the fridge for two whole steps before they detoured towards Abby instead. She froze, container of food in hand when he appeared in front of her.

"I want dessert first," he said.

Her lips parted and her eyes darkened. "I don't think that's a good idea."

"I think it's the best idea I've had all day." He took the container from her hands and placed it on the counter behind her.

"Flynn..." The protest died on her lips as he stepped into her space.

There was something amazing about the way their scents mingled to produce something new and heady just for them. Flynn backed her against the counter, placing a hand on each side of her face.

For a minute, they stood there, staring at each other, sharing the same air. Anticipation curled around Flynn, intoxicating in its strength.

Slowly, he touched his lips to hers. A long breath left her lungs. Her fingers curled on his waist. Flynn intended to tease her, taste her, make the kiss last. Instead, it was like a match to kindling. One touch and reason was gone. He groaned at the taste of her, licking his path into her mouth, eager to devour. He felt Abby relax into him. Felt her cheeks heat under his palms. Heard her soft little moans as he deepened the kiss.

The moment broke when his stomach growled loudly. With a chuckle, he kissed her lips one last time. "Not my most romantic moment."

Abby tucked her hair behind her ear, lowering her head slightly in a move he hadn't seen her make before. "I'll get your food."

As she stepped away from him, he felt the distance

increase exponentially. Facing the microwave, she cleared her throat.

"I've been thinking."

His heart stilled. "Aye?"

"Now isn't a good time for this." Her dark eyes looked back at him, pleading for him to understand.

He did. But he sure as hell didn't want to.

"My sister is here this week," Abby rushed out. "I need to concentrate on her. And…" Her face flushed crimson.

"And if she sees you with me your chances of heading off a custody battle will be blown." He clenched his teeth tight enough to make his jaw ache.

Abby turned towards him. "Maybe, after…"

"Aye, no problem." Flynn recognised a brush-off when he heard one. He straightened his shoulders. "The food smells good."

Abby bit her bottom lip. "I need to focus on this situation with Katy."

"I understand." He forced a smile, worked hard to make it charming. "Don't worry about it."

"It's only for the week." She shuffled in place. "I mean, if you want to, later, if you still want, you know…"

His eyes snapped to hers only to find her studying her feet. The tight feeling in his stomach released. He stepped into her space, put his hand on her cheek and made her look up at him.

"Damn straight I want."

"So, maybe after Victoria leaves…" Her uncertainty brought a rush of anger.

"Definitely after Victoria leaves." He gently kissed her lips, never closing his eyes. "We haven't had our fill of each other. Nowhere near."

"But we need to wait until after this week."

"We can keep our hands off one another for a week." As the words left his mouth, he felt they were a lie.

"Yes. Yes we can." It was clear she wasn't convinced.

Flynn wasn't sure if her uncertainty comforted him or made him anxious. If she was half as desperate to touch him as he was her, they didn't have a hope in hell.

CHAPTER 17

"We didn't underestimate them. They were a lot better than we thought." Bobby Robson, former England manager

"I have a secret," Katy said. Victoria's face paled, making Lawrence chuckle. "You can't tell Muma." Katy looked towards the bank at the bottom of the high street where they'd left her mother to do her business. "You need to promise not to tell."

"I promise?" Vicki didn't sound so sure.

Katy cupped her mouth with her hands and whispered louder than she'd been talking. "Flynn bought me a swimming pool so I'd be well behaved in front of you. Am I being well behaved? It's important to keep your end of a deal. Flynn says so."

Lawrence laughed as he watched Katy undermine every effort Victoria made to keep the girl at arm's length. They were wandering the high street under the pretext that Abby had to shop for Katy's new school year—which was six weeks away. Lawrence suspected she just wanted to get them out of her house for an hour or two. She probably felt like she was under siege.

"I'm not supposed to tell you any more stories about other people's business either," Katy said. "Flynn said it isn't nice to talk about other people. He said they might want to keep their business secret. He said you wouldn't understand it anyway, because you don't live in Invertary. He said the people who live in Invertary are weird and other people don't always understand them."

Victoria looked utterly helpless as Katy spilled all of her secrets. It was the most vulnerable he'd ever seen the woman, and the look suited her.

"Do you talk to Flynn a lot?" Victoria said.

Katy shook her head. "Only since Muma stabbed his swimming pool. Before that I wasn't allowed to talk to him. Muma said he was a bad influence. But I watched him a lot. I can see his bus from my bedroom window and sometimes when Muma puts me to bed I get up and watch Flynn." She scrunched up her nose. "You aren't going to tell on me, are you, Aunty Victoria?" She batted her long lashes as she looked up at Victoria.

"No." Victoria caved embarrassingly fast.

Katy gave her a smile so dazzling it required sunglasses. She put her tiny hand in her aunt's and dragged her towards the shop selling toys. Victoria was so startled by the contact that she stared at the hand for a minute before clasping it tight. The sight made Lawrence's heart ache.

"I asked Flynn to help me look for a daddy." Katy was completely unaware her every move was breaking through walls her aunt had spent years erecting. "To get a new daddy, Muma has to marry a boy. I thought about Flynn, but I think he wouldn't make such a good daddy. He isn't really a grownup, he only looks like one."

Lawrence burst out laughing. Out of the mouths of babes. Victoria frowned her censure at him and he held up his hands in surrender. If this was a battle, Katy was winning. He saw it in the way Victoria's terrified eyes softened every time the child touched her.

"Flynn said he can't help me find a boy for Muma. He said she needs to do it herself. He says she can't marry someone unless she loves him. Do you think she loved my daddy?"

Victoria hesitated slightly. "Yes. I'm certain she did love your father." Lawrence heard truth in her words, and wondered how she knew about Abby's relationship. As far as he could tell, the Montgomery-Clarks cut off contact with the pair soon after they got together.

Katy nodded. "That's what I thought. Flynn has lots of parties." Following Katy's conversation made Lawrence's head ache, and from the look of it, Victoria was struggling to keep up too. "Every night there were lots of people in his garden. They made a lot of noise. Muma doesn't like noise. She said it made her want to kill the man. I think she meant kill Flynn." She thought about it for a minute. "Would Muma really kill Flynn?"

"No," Victoria answered instantly, looking slightly horrified. "It's just something people say when they are very annoyed."

"That's good." Katy visibly relaxed. "He might not be a proper grownup, but I think I like him. I'd like him more if he sat on the naughty step, but he's going to buy me a pony so he can kiss Muma, so I guess that makes up for it."

Lawrence was laughing so hard, he had to wipe his eyes. They stopped outside the little novelty shop that sold everything from real Highland souvenirs made in China to school supplies. Like all of the shops on the high street, it was an old converted house, whitewashed to make its crooked proportions blend in with the rest of the mismatched houses on the street.

"Maybe we should wait for your mother before we go inside." Victoria looked back down the street towards the bank. There was no sign of Abby.

"She'll catch up soon enough," Lawrence said. The woman deserved her short reprieve from relentless scrutiny.

Katy tugged at her aunt's hand, obviously annoyed about Victoria's attention straying.

"Hurry up, Aunty Vicki. They have Barbie houses in here."

As soon as they stepped into the tiny, overfilled shop, Katy dropped Victoria's hand and ran in the direction of the toys.

Victoria slumped slightly beside him. Her stunned expression made Lawrence want to put his arms around her to comfort her. Maybe later. He suspected if he were to caress Victoria in public, she'd faint from the trauma.

"I don't know what to make of any of this," Victoria confessed.

"Just enjoy it. She's five. She won't always be like this."

Such brutal, raw longing flickered in Victoria's eyes it made Lawrence forget to breathe.

"You know, there's no reason why you couldn't visit regularly after this week is over. Get to know Katy properly. Spend time with Abby. Would you like that, Vicki?"

Yes. He saw it. A brief flash of desperate need. Then it was gone.

"Mother wouldn't approve."

"Your mother doesn't need to know. You're a grown woman. You can do what you want."

She scoffed as though he were naive. "Not when she holds the purse strings. I am dependent on her for everything. Exactly how she likes it."

"Then get a job. Become more independent. You have skills, I assume."

"I know how to be a wife. It's what I spent my entire life training to become. The perfect socialite wife." Her smile was cold. "Ironic, considering I'm practically a professional spinster. Such a great disappointment to the family. A terrible waste of all that time in finishing school in Switzerland. I was supposed to marry well, keep home for my husband, sit on committees and lunch with the girls. Instead I spend my time catering to Mother's every whim. What kind of job could I get with those skills?"

"Surely you have some money of your own." Lawrence knew exactly how wealthy the Montgomery-Clarks were.

Victoria's laugh was brittle. "Very little, I'm afraid. Our family doesn't work on the principle of independent money. There are no trusts for the children. Charles has a job in the city, which affords him a tad more independence, but his house, his society parties and his wife's indulgences are all paid for at Mother's discretion. It's been like that for generations. The parents hold the purse strings."

"Abby broke away. You can too."

"Abby had David. She had an education. She fought hard to be allowed to go to art college. Even then, Father only paid her tuition fees. He refused to give her any money to live on. It was his way of making his disapproval known, making Abby work while she studied. He thought she'd give in and run home after just a few weeks. Of course, she didn't. In fact, it made her more independent. Abby worked several jobs while she was a student in order to pay her way. It wasn't easy for her. I wanted to help, but Mother and Father checked all of our transactions. If I'd been married, there would have been more leeway. But as you can see, I'm terminally single."

"I don't get it." Lawrence ran a hand over his face. "Why

not just leave? I'm sure you could get work somewhere. You aren't stupid. You'd manage fine. If it's what you want, Vicki, you should go for it."

"I learned a long time ago—I don't get what I want. And wanting only brings pain. I'd rather not want anything at all. It's much safer." She gave Lawrence a tight little smile. "I'm not like Abby. I'm not courageous. I don't have her confidence. I've tried to stand up to Mother in the past and it went terribly wrong. I learned my lesson. I shall just endeavour to do as I'm told until Charles is head of the family. I'm sure he won't care to boss me around. He has his own concerns to occupy him."

"That's your plan? Wait until Millicent dies until you have a life you want? It's not much of a plan, Vicki."

"It's not much of a life," she whispered.

Before Lawrence could say anything else, Katy ran over to them, waving a bright pink Barbie car. "Look what I found. Do you think Muma will let me get it for school?"

Lawrence watched as Victoria's face melted with longing. "I don't think you need a Barbie car for school."

Katy's whole body slumped. It took Victoria all of three seconds to crumble.

"But it is the sort of thing an aunt can buy her niece," she said.

Her reward was two small arms wrapped tight around her hips. "You're the best aunty ever." She squeezed hard before running back to the toys.

Victoria never took her eyes of her niece.

"Come work for me." The words were out of Lawrence's mouth before he knew they were coming.

Victoria's head snapped up. Her shock was priceless and he knew exactly how she felt. He didn't know who was more surprised by his offer.

"What?"

"Work for me." He nodded. The words felt right. In fact, the more he thought about it, the better the idea became. "I'll hire you. The firm will train you. You'll earn a decent wage. I'll help you to find somewhere to live. It's the perfect solution. Work for me. Change your life. Do it, Vicki, before it's too late." He let out a sigh. "There are things in my life I regret. Things I should have dealt with, but waited too long. It's how I lost my wife. I ignored my marriage and concentrated on building the firm. She wanted children, but I was too busy for them. Before I knew it she was gone, married to another man, starting a family with him. I don't have children. I'm fifty-seven. The time for children is past. Don't be like me. Don't wait until it's too late. You can change your life. You have no excuses now. If you want to work, if you want to move out from under your mother, then take my offer. Think about it."

Lawrence left her to it and stepped out of the shop. Heavy clouds were gathering over the hills surrounding the town and the air felt balmy. Summer storm, he thought. Although June in the Highlands barely counted as summer. His hands trembled as he thrust them into his pockets. The past was too fresh in his mind. The mistakes he'd made were still there, raw and unforgiving. It wasn't just the family he'd passed up on when he'd relentlessly chased his narrow-minded dream. It was a life he'd missed out on. His only friends were at work, and even then, they were more associates than friends. His family were long gone. His days were spent working. His nights spent lonely, locked up tight in his expensive box, looking out on a vista he never actually had the time to get out in and enjoy. He couldn't even remember the last time he'd had a holiday. It was all about work. And he was tired of it.

He looked around the small town that had welcomed them. Life in Invertary was different. Slower. People took time for each other. They knew each other. They enjoyed their town. As he said hello to a passing stranger, he thought about his words to Vicki. If it wasn't too late for her to make changes, maybe it wasn't too late for him as well. A small seed of an idea took root in his mind. His eyes fell on a sign in the empty shop facing him on the high street. And with a smile, he felt the seed begin to grow.

CHAPTER 18

"A football team is like a beautiful woman. When you do not tell her, she forgets she is beautiful." Arsène Wenger, Arsenal manager

It was a sign of how desperate Abby's life had become that a trip to the bank was almost a holiday. When her business with the bank manager concluded, too quickly for her liking, she found herself dallying outside the bank in the hopes of stealing a few more minutes to herself. That was when she spotted him.

Flynn stood at the water's edge facing out over the loch. He had on nothing but a pair of navy swim shorts, and his back rippled as he stretched his arms above his head. The sun caught the sheen on his skin, making Abby's mouth water to taste him. She tried to pull her eyes away. She had to focus on her mother's threat. Now wasn't the time to get distracted by her libido.

Flynn dove into the cool water, making barely a splash.

He sliced through the vast blue expanse, his strokes rhythmic, steady, powerful. *Oh my...*

"Here." A tissue appeared under her nose, making her jump. "For the drool."

Abby batted her best friend's hand away. "Idiot." It took serious effort to pry her eyes from Flynn to focus on Jena.

Her friend was decked out in work clothes—cut-off beige dungarees with a sparkly purple tee under them. She'd painted her nails to match the tee, and her hair was tied into a ponytail high on her head. She worked at the hardware store and had talked the owner into training her to become a handyman. She called it her apprenticeship, and she loved every minute of it. For a woman who looked like she belonged in a nail salon, Jena wielded a sledgehammer with glee.

"So you're still kissing him?" There was no censure in Jena's voice. No matter how annoying Flynn proved to be, if Abby wanted the man, Jena wouldn't judge. Her friendship was a gift.

"No, we've stopped." With a heavy sigh she pried her eyes from the loch. "We had a chat, decided now wasn't the best time to get involved." She thought about it for a minute. "Although I'm not sure we were getting involved exactly. Is three kisses enough to be involved?"

"For you, yeah." Jena hooked her arm with Abby's as she turned to walk back up the high street. "You don't do casual, honey. And right now you're under a lot of pressure. I'm worried you aren't thinking with your brain. I'm worried you're thinking with your—"

Abby smacked a hand over her best friend's mouth. "Don't say it. I beg you."

Jena grinned against her palm. Abby dropped her hand. "Say what? Hoo-ha?"

"You went there." Abby hung her head. "You just had to do it."

"So tell me." Jena nudged her with her hip. "How does he kiss? I bet it's good. I imagine dirty and forceful. Am I right? You can tell me."

"Jena Donaldson, are you perving over your cousin-in-law?"

"Yeah, that does sound a little twisted." She smiled wickedly. "It was good, though, huh?"

"He makes me lose my mind," Abby confessed, her cheeks heating at the memory. "I melt. I can't think. I get desperate. It's like I'm being set on fire from inside."

"Wow." Jena heaved an exaggerated sigh.

Abby snapped herself back to the present. "But this isn't the time to lose my mind. I need all of my faculties to deal with mother's latest plan."

"I get it, but you still deserve a little time for you. Some time to get your mind blown—even if it is with Flynn." Her smile let Abby know she understood the appeal. "How are things with Victoria? Are you coping? If you bring her by the hardware store, we'll put in a good word for you."

"Please, don't! Everywhere we go, someone feels the need to tell Victoria how virtuous I am. In the bakery this morning, Morag McKay said she was so impressed with me that she wouldn't mind having me as a member of her morality society."

Jena barked out a laugh. "Do all the members have to get poodle perms and wear polyester coats? Because if they do, say no."

"You're wicked."

"I know." Jena grinned widely. "But how are you really?"

"Don't worry. I'm coping. I came up with a new way to deal with the stress."

Sympathy wafted off Jena. "Denial? I hate to tell you, honey, but that method is tried and true."

"Not denial, organisation. I scheduled my worries into my planner. Today I'm scheduled to worry about getting the business off the ground. Tomorrow I'm going to worry about Victoria and Mother. The following day I'm going to worry about Katy starting school. And so on. See, it's perfect. Each day is booked, the worry is spread out and there's no danger of my head exploding."

Jena slapped her palm against Abby's forehead. "No fever. So it's not that." She frowned in concentration. "Are you hallucinating? Have you eaten something suspect recently? Dodgy mushrooms, maybe?"

"I'm not hallucinating. There's nothing wrong with my brain. In fact, I'd say it was working brilliantly, seeing as I came up with an amazing plan to reduce stress."

"Yeah, you scheduled it. That's not normal, honey."

"Like you can judge normal!" Abby grinned as she pointed at Jena's purple sparkly platform sandals—or as Jena liked to call them, her work shoes. "You do DIY dressed like a stripper. Normal people don't wear stripper shoes to plaster a wall." Which Jena had been doing all morning.

Jena's eyes sparkled. "As I keep telling Gordon, I'm bringing sexy back to DIY."

As Abby listened to Jena talk about her latest renovation project, Abby's eyes strayed back towards the loch. One week. She could push Flynn from her mind for one long week. How hard would it be to fight hormones? Women did it all the time. Right?

"Is it possible to die from sexual frustration?" she asked her best friend.

"No," Jena said. "But I hear it makes women stupid."

"Good to know." Abby decided she'd worry about that particular problem the following Wednesday.

CHAPTER 19

"I like the comfort of jeans, and the elegance of a suit. But above all, I love the sensuality and sexuality that emanates from leather. It multiplies one's sensations tenfold."
Emmanuel Petit, former French national player

How was it possible to crave a woman so badly after just a few kisses? Flynn suspected it was a case of reverse psychology. Ever since Abby had declared they couldn't touch, all Flynn could think about was touching. Touching, tasting, teasing…aye, he was going crazy with the images inside his head.

He'd thought a swim in the freezing waters of the loch would help take his mind off Abby. Instead, all it achieved was to make his unused muscles ache. He'd pushed himself too hard, forgetting his body didn't work the way it used to. And now he was paying for it. His leg felt like it was on fire, and it took all his effort not to strike out at anyone who crossed his path. After a lifetime having absolute confidence in his own body, the weakness he felt was humiliating. He hated the fact his body had let him down. Hated it wasn't perfect. Hated it all.

He opened the cabinet above his kitchen sink and pulled out the medication he'd been given. It was a combination painkiller and muscle relaxant. He'd been loath to take it, but now he had no choice. It was take the pills or spend the rest of the day in bed suffering.

"You in there?" A voice broke into his thoughts.

"No." What did a man have to do to get some peace?

"Flynn?" It was Megan.

"I don't have time for another lecture on how I'm screwing up everyone's lives. Come back another day." He was busy. He'd planned on spending the afternoon staring out at the garden, where the goat was currently eating his shirt, all the while brooding about having to keep his hands off Abby.

"That wasn't me," Megan said. "It was the rest of the family, remember? I'm on your side. I'm happy to support your screwed-up life."

"Thanks." Flynn swallowed the pills.

"Can you come out here? I need to talk to you."

"No."

"Flynn, stop being a grumpy old man. You really need to be out here for this."

Damn, he didn't like the sound of that. He limped towards the door, wondering why he'd fired his physio. He'd done it in anger straight after he'd gotten the word the club was letting him go. He hadn't seen the point of physiotherapy when he'd never play again. Now he kind of thought it might be nice to have help to just bloody walk without being in agony.

"What is it?" He threw the door open and gawked.

Megan was grinning up at him and she was flanked by

two ugly-as-sin donkeys. They looked to be about a hundred years old. Their ribs were showing and they were obviously depressed. Suddenly Eeyore made perfect sense. Megan held the reins out towards him.

"Claire said you're taking in animals. So here you are. This is Derek and this is Boris. They've been mistreated and need a good home. They're all yours."

Flynn stared at her then at the donkeys. He looked back at his younger cousin. She was grinning, but it was nervous.

"Do I look like a bloody animal shelter?" Flynn barked.

Megan scowled. "You look like an inconsiderate deadbeat who should be nice to his relatives. I brought you a gift. A nice guy would say thanks."

"You want me to thank you for two donkeys who are so old and knackered they should be turned into glue?"

She gasped before petting the animals. "Don't listen to the mean man. I'm pretty sure they don't turn donkeys into glue. He's just being nasty."

"Take them away." Flynn was done with this conversation.

He turned to go, but Megan stopped him with a pout. After a lifetime dealing with the twins, he should have been immune to the pout. But he wasn't. It was their superpower. One pout and men crumbled.

"Flynn, they need someone to look after them, and you have lots of space. You're already taking care of a duck and a goat. I hear you're doing a great job. You're the best person to take care of the donkeys. They won't be any trouble."

"That's what Claire said about the goat." He pointed at the animal, who had part of an Arsenal shirt hanging out of its mouth.

"Yeah, well, donkeys only eat grass." Megan worked at looking innocent. "Can you at least take them until I find another home? Please?"

"What are you doing with donkeys anyway?"

"A parent at Claire's kindy asked her to find a home for them. She was too scared to bring them herself after offloading the goat on you."

"Why is Claire suddenly the go-to person for homeless animals?"

Megan shrugged. "Word gets around. And Claire's a soft touch."

Flynn looked at the depressed animals and his shoulders slumped. Apparently Claire wasn't the only soft touch in the family. "Okay, I'll take them. But just until you and Claire find another home. And you better look for one."

"I will. Promise." She thrust the ropes at him and made a run for it, heading straight for the lime-green Mini Cooper she shared with her sister. The tiny car had a large horse trailer attached to it, which made Flynn shake his head. The trailer was three times bigger than the car. Matt would have a fit if he saw it.

Thinking of Matt made Flynn realise he wasn't the only one with land. Jena and Matt's new house sat on three acres. He'd been conned. Megan had chosen the easier relative, her wimp of a cousin over her scary big brother.

He looked at the animals. "As soon as it gets dark," he told them, "we're going to take a little walk over to Matt's place. You'll like it there. His grass is tasty."

The one on the left nuzzled him, and he couldn't resist patting it. He felt the bones under his hand and wondered who exactly had mistreated the animals. Once his leg was better, he'd pay them a visit. There was nothing wrong with his fists, and as soon as he could stand without toppling he'd put them to good use.

"Come on, guys. The grass by the stream is the best." He led the animals to the spot he had in mind, followed closely by the goat, who wanted to see what was happening. That goat was a nosey bugger.

"Here." He pointed to the grass as he looked around for somewhere to tie the donkeys. He stopped. Why couldn't they wander? With a shrug, he clipped off the leads, earning another nuzzle.

As Flynn walked back to his RV, he wondered if there was a supplement or something he could get for the animals. Something to build them back up. As soon as he was in his van, he put a call through to the vet in Fort William. He was now on first-name terms with the guy. While he was on the phone, he asked him how long he should keep the duck's wing in a splint. And what to do to stop the goat eating everything in sight.

As he listened to the vet's advice, he spotted the bloody goat chowing down on his limited edition Nikes. Flynn wondered if goat curry would be a better solution for that particular problem.

CHAPTER 20

"You can't score a goal if you don't take a shot." Johan Cruyff,
Dutch national player

Flynn dragged his aching backside over to Abby's house at seven o'clock sharp to read Katy a story. It would probably have been wiser to stay away, but he'd made a deal with the kid.

Plus, the more he thought about keeping his distance from Abby until her sister was gone, the more annoyed he became. Hadn't Abby put her life on hold enough already? Was it right that Victoria was making them jump through hoops? He was annoyed Abby wasn't strong enough to tell her sister to go to hell. No, he was annoyed he wasn't getting his way. And his way meant having Abby naked and screaming beneath him.

"She's upstairs, ready for her story," Abby said when she opened the door to him.

The fake cheer made Flynn almost as annoyed as the distance she put between them.

"Great." He knew it was a growl, and was unreasonably pleased when it resulted in a frown.

He felt like his skin was too tight. Like nothing sat right with him. He felt like the air was too heavy against him.

"Are you in a mood?" Abby cut through his bullshit, as usual.

"Aren't you?" He cocked an eyebrow at her.

"You know keeping our distance is the responsible thing to do." Her lips thinned.

"I hate being responsible."

"How would you know? Have you ever tried?"

"Have you ever tried saying to hell with it and doing what you want instead of what you should?"

"I don't need to. I can wait for what I want."

"Good for you. I don't have that much patience."

"For goodness' sake, grow up. It's only a week."

Flynn felt the hairs on his arms stand up straight. "Do you know what I hate more than having to be responsible? Being told to grow up."

Abby's eyes blazed as she pointed at the stairs. "Sooner you're done, the sooner you're out of here."

"I shouldn't have come." He was being childish. He knew it, but he couldn't seem to stop it.

"Nobody put a gun to your head to make you, Flynn." With a snap of her jaw, she turned and stalked away from him, making him focus on the lush curve of her behind. Damn, but she was breathtaking when she was mad.

Not exactly the right circumstances to help keep his hands off the woman. Which reminded him, how long was it since he'd touched Abby? Twenty-four freaking hours. He was pathetic. He was behaving like a teenager who was told to wait to get into his girlfriend's pants. He had more self-control than that. Surely?

Annoyed, Flynn dragged himself up the stairs and into the kid's pink room, and once again felt like he was swimming in a vat of Pepto-Bismol.

"I brought you a book." He tried not to sound like a grumpy old man.

"Yay!" Katy sat up in bed and started bouncing. "A book, a book, I love books."

"Great. This one is called *Famous Footballers*." He pointed at the cover. "Tonight we're going to learn all about someone called Pelé."

"That's a weird name."

"Some people think Katy's a weird name."

"Not smart people."

He shook his head, pulled up a chair and started to read the section on Brazil's greatest footballer. Possibly the greatest footballer ever.

"Are you still kissing my mum?" Katy said in the middle of his reading, proving she had no respect for the topic.

"Not right now." It came out like a blast from a cannon. Luckily, his tone had no effect on Katy.

"Jonathan says kissing somebody is how you get Germans."

"Why me?" Flynn appealed to the ceiling. "Not Germans. Germs. They're tiny bugs you can't see. They can make you sick."

"Invisible?"

"Yeah."

"How do you know they're there if you can't see them?"

"Okay, maybe not invisible, just really tiny. People with big magnifying glasses can see them."

"How do they make you sick?"

"They crawl up your nose, then fly through your body

kicking stuff until you feel sore. Then they have a party, overindulge and puke up a lot. That's what snot is. It's germ puke."

Her eyes went wide. Her hands flew to her nose. "How do you stop them getting up your nose?"

"You stop breathing."

She gasped. "If I don't breathe I'll die."

"And if you do breathe you'll get germs. Then you might get sick and die anyway. It's a chance we all take. It's life, kid."

"Flynn!" Abby's voice echoed through the house. "Get down here."

"I need to go."

She pointed at her forehead. "What do you do at bedtime?"

He rolled his eyes, kissed her forehead and told her to sleep well. Bloody terrorist. He left the football book beside her bed and went to see what'd wound Abby up this time.

He found her in the kitchen. She was chopping potatoes as though she had a personal grudge against them.

"You can't tell a five-year-old not to breathe. Are you insane? Do you want her to hold her breath until she turns blue? Or suffocate herself because she doesn't want to breathe in germs? Fix this."

Flynn barely resisted the urge to salute her. He bit his tongue as she pointed at the door, aware she had a knife in her hand. Beyond irritated, he thumped back up the stairs and opened Katy's door.

"Kid," he said. "Don't stop breathing. You need air. Don't worry about the germs. Your mum's got some special medicine that will kill the little buggers before they party in your nose."

"Flynn!" Abby shouted. He ignored her.

"Do I need to get the medicine now?"

"No. You're covered. Germs are scared of pink, and this room is full of it."

"Flynn! Get down here." Where she had a knife? He didn't think so.

"Thanks, Flynn," Katy said, and for some reason he wanted to pat her head and tell her it was all going to be fine.

He squelched the urge and dragged himself back to deal with her mother.

"I've changed my mind," Abby said as soon as he entered the kitchen. "Don't try to fix things. From now on, limit your conversations with Katy to football. That would be safest."

He was pleased to see she'd put down the knife. Her eyes blazed, her mouth pursed and her cheeks flushed with irritation. He found himself taking another step towards her.

"You're overreacting. She's not dumb. She wouldn't do anything stupid."

"She's five. She lives for stupid. It's the mission statement of all five-year-olds—find stupid, do stupid. She doesn't need any encouragement."

His brain told him to get out of the house before *he* did something stupid. Unfortunately, his mouth wanted to pick a fight. "Did you have to paint her room pink?" And apparently any topic would do.

He studied the counters for leftovers, even while he waited for her curt reply. Guess the rumours were true: men could really eat under any circumstances.

"Oh, for goodness' sake. There's a container in the fridge. Pop it in the microwave. And yes. It had to be pink. She's a girl. She likes pink."

Flynn pulled the plastic container out of the fridge. He popped the lid and inhaled. "Fettuccini?"

"Do you care?" She banged around in a cupboard. Smacking pots together as though they'd offended her.

"Nope." He popped it in the microwave and leaned back

against the counter. The position left him staring at Abby's back. It was a fine back, topped by luscious shoulders and a silky-smooth neck. But it all paled in comparison with her well-rounded backside. A well-rounded backside he wasn't allowed to touch.

"You know, I'm pretty sure she'd like other colours if you encouraged them. Maybe some blue to break up the pink."

"Will you stop talking about the décor in Katy's room? I don't care about it. You don't care about it. You're just trying to drive me mad."

"Is it working?"

Although she didn't turn around, he could have sworn she clenched her teeth. The microwave dinged. Flynn took the tub of pasta to the other side of the counter from Abby, pulled out a stool, grabbed a fork and dug in.

"Don't you want a plate?" she snapped.

"Does my lack of table manners offend you, your majesty?" He made a production of forking some pasta into his mouth.

Her strangled scream of annoyance made him smile. It wasn't a pleasant smile. It was the smile of a man pleased that someone was suffering alongside him.

He ate as he watched Abby bang around the kitchen. Barely contained rage radiated from the woman. Every move he made, every sound he uttered, had her head snapping in his direction, a frown on her face. It was a matter of minutes before they gave in to the tension and ended up shouting at each other about nothing at all.

This was stupid.

Flynn couldn't take anymore.

As Abby thrust her hands into a sink full of soapy water, Flynn left his seat and came up behind her.

"This is insane," he said.

"I don't know what you're talking about." Her tone was snippy.

Flynn wrapped an arm around her, splaying his palm flat across her stomach. She froze.

"What are you doing? We agreed. No more touching. Now isn't the time."

"Our agreement isn't working for me." He covered her back with his body, feeling his temper ease slightly as her warmth seeped into him.

"Flynn." Her tone was a warning.

"It isn't working for you, either." He used his free hand to pull her hair off her neck. Baring it to him.

"We agreed." It was an accusation. Her body still tense in his arms.

"It was a stupid agreement. We're going nuts here, snapping at each other when what we really want is to touch." He kissed the curve where her neck met her shoulder and felt her shudder. "We need a new agreement, a new plan."

She didn't speak, but he felt her heartbeat speed up under his lips.

"How about we touch, but we keep it a secret until your sister is gone?"

She stilled. Thinking. "Explain?" Her demand made him smile against the sensitive skin behind her ear.

"We'll have a secret affair. One that won't interfere with everything else you need to concentrate on. We'll get together in times like this. Times when no one knows and you don't have to deal with your sister."

He felt her relax slightly under his touch. "I don't know."

"We can't stay away from each other. It isn't working."

"We've only been trying for a day. For goodness' sake. We only kissed—"

"It shouldn't be this hard," he said, finishing the thought for her. "I know."

She sank into him and he knew he'd won. "Secret?"

"Promise."

Abby reached for the towel near her and dried her hands. Flynn took the opportunity to kiss his way down her neck and across her shoulder.

Slowly, she turned in his arms. Her hands fisted in the front of his shirt. "I'm worried I can't think rationally because I'm being swamped by hormones."

Flynn blinked at her. "Hormones?"

She nodded, totally serious. "Jena says I'm sexually frustrated, and women in my condition do stupid things."

Ah, the penny dropped. Flynn fought a grin. "And you think I'm one of those stupid things?"

She let out a heavy sigh. "I can't think straight around you."

He was pleased to know he wasn't the only one. "You shouldn't say that sort of thing to a man. It gives him too much power over you."

The look she gave him was pure innocence, tempered by hunger. "What will you do with all that power?"

"Whatever you want," he said. "I'll do whatever you want."

Gently he ran his nose down the soft skin of her neck to her shoulder and nipped at the muscle. The tension seeped from her body. Her hands snapped up to hold his shoulders. Her head swayed, falling backwards. He honestly couldn't remember the last time a woman had responded to his touch like Abby did. If any woman ever had.

He pulled her tighter to him, feeling her softness against his body. Wanting her closer still. He placed slow, lazy kisses along her collarbone. Her eyes were dazed with need. Her gaze dipped to his lips. The tip of her tongue popped out to run along her bottom lip. He waited a beat, wondering what she would do. Her teeth nibbled her full bottom lip, making him groan. Slowly, her fingers curled into his shirt.

"Kiss me?" she whispered.

"Always," he whispered back.

THE LAST THOUGHT Abby had before Flynn's lips met hers was that hormones had a lot to answer for.

Oh, but the man could kiss. His lips were soft and warm, yet firm and demanding. He had a way of taking control that, along with the strength of this body, made her crumble. She'd never felt like this before. The desire to surrender was strong. She ached to give herself over to Flynn and let him take her to heights she could only imagine.

Whether it was hormones, newly awakened needs she thought had died with her husband or just the reaction to everything Flynn, she couldn't say. And honestly, at that moment, she didn't care what made her want him so desperately. And it was desperation she felt. With his arms around her, his strength keeping her in place, his musky scent invading her senses and his touch stealing her reason, there was no space for thought. There was only need.

His tongue swept past her lips, dancing with her tongue. Mastering her. Claiming her with a kiss brutal in its relentlessness. When he pulled away, she felt weak, dizzy and alive. So alive.

"We'll hear her if she wakes, right?" He nodded to the monitor on the counter.

Abby wasn't sure what he was talking about. Her fingertips kneaded his biceps. Her gaze ran over the breadth of his shoulders and she sighed. She wanted to go up on tiptoe and nip at his strong jaw, but she couldn't move. Her legs were jelly. As her gaze met his mouth she licked her lips. He chuckled softly and her eyes flew to his. They were dark, full of desire. And amusement.

"Abby, sugar, will Katy wake up?"

She blinked a couple of times before his words sank in. "She doesn't usually."

"Will we hear her on the baby monitor if she does?"

She frowned her confusion. He chuckled again. Abby didn't care. She moved her palms to his chest and ran them over his muscles. Oh yeah. This was what she needed.

"What I mean is," Flynn said, his voice husky and low, "if I sit you on the counter and put my face between your thighs, is there any chance the kid will walk in on us?"

Heat raced through her. Her cheeks became unbearably hot. David never said things like that to her. Ever. She wasn't sure if she liked it or not.

"You can't say things like that," she whispered.

Flynn grinned, leaned forward and put his lips to her ear. "Yes, I can. And I will. I want my mouth on you. Tell me we won't be interrupted. Let me make you come, Abby. Let me make you feel good."

Oh my. Abby slumped against him. Talking was hard. Thinking was hard. She was swimming in a sea of sensation. Floating on desire. Flynn's hand caressed her back, his fingertips tracing the line of her spine until he trailed over her rear. He cupped her behind and pulled her up to him. His mouth on her neck, kissing, sucking, nipping.

"I'll make it simple," he murmured against her skin. "Answer yes or no. Will we hear Katy before she comes downstairs?"

He nipped her neck again. Her mind went fuzzy. What was he asking? Katy? Hearing Katy.

"Will we hear her, Abby?"

"Yes." It was a breathless whisper, but he heard it. His muscles stiffened.

"Do you want to take this further?"

Did she? Oh my goodness, yes. Yes. Yes. He laughed, a low, deep rumble.

"I need to hear the word, sugar."

"Yes," she breathed.

He practically vibrated against her. Good. Oh so good. His mouth moved back to her ear.

"Do you want me to lick you and taste you and make you purr?"

Her knees gave out. "Yes!" It was a gasp.

His hands clasped her face. She wrapped her fingers around his arms. The heat of his skin seared her. She stared into Flynn's eyes. The colour was gone, replaced by the blackness of heat and desire.

His smile was soft and secret, just for her. "It will be my pleasure, Abby."

And he kissed her. A deep, forceful, mouth-watering kiss. A kiss that stole the rest of her reason and left her alone with the dizzying sensations of his touch. One of his hands caressed her neck, across her collarbone and down to the curve of her breast. Without thinking about it, Abby arched her back in a silent plea for him to touch her there. Her breasts felt heavy, achy and desperate for his touch. He didn't make her wait. His palm skimmed over her nipple and she shuddered. He swallowed the tiny moan that escaped.

His touch was perfect. Firm, confident. It sent spikes of need straight through her body.

"Please," she whispered.

"I'll please you. You can count on it." His mouth trailed over her throat.

He rose to his feet. His hands grasped her waist. She found herself being lifted up to perch on the edge of the counter behind her. One of his hands covered her breast while the other cupped the back of her head. Abby felt herself being lowered backwards. Her back hit the cold marble of the countertop. Flynn's hands were everywhere. Nipping, caressing, kneading. She felt limp. Dizzy.

His mouth found her nipples and he took turns biting each of them through her shirt, making her press up into his touch. Her fingers twisted in his hair, pulling him closer. Needing more.

He kissed his way down her stomach as his strong hands slid over the curve of her hips and along her thighs. She felt his hands on the waistband of her skirt. Skilled fingers found the concealed zipper. He tugged it, then slowly pushed her skirt over her hips to let it crumple on the floor. He hooked his hands behind her knees, pulled her to the edge of the counter and widened her legs. All at once she felt exposed. Insecurity made the desire recede.

Flynn cupped her cheek and ran his thumb over her lower lip, sincerity in his eyes. "You're beautiful. Don't worry."

"I…" She wasn't even sure what she meant to say. It didn't matter anyway, because Flynn stole the words from her mouth with his talented lips.

"Please," she whispered against his lips.

"Shh, it's going to be okay."

She felt the cool air on the warm skin of her thighs and stomach as Flynn kissed down her body. He went to one knee in front of her. She felt a gentle kiss on her most private place, the heat of his mouth searing her through the satin of her underwear. Abby gasped. Her hands needed something to grasp. She wound her fingers through his unruly hair. She felt thumbs hook into the sides of her underwear and then it was sliding down her legs.

"So beautiful," he murmured.

She felt his breath against her sensitive flesh. Followed by the warm pressure of his tongue. A gasp. A moan. Her world disappeared. Her head flew back. Her neck arched. Desperate pants filled the air as Flynn's kisses intensified. Each stroke of his tongue was agony and ecstasy.

"Please, please, please…" Her words were a whispered chant. She could have been saying anything. She didn't care. All she cared about was Flynn and his touch. Her world had shrunk. There was only him.

He sucked her hard, as his finger slipped inside her. Every muscle in her body clenched with tension. Desperate gasps were punctuated with throat-deep moans. And then it was too much. The sensations of his lips, tongue and touch melded together to push her over the edge. Her shoulders pressed into the hard counter as her hips flew up towards Flynn. Her fingers clenched in his hair. She saw stars burst. The coiling sensation building in her body snapped as her muscles spasmed and flexed. As her moans turned to gasps. As ecstasy took over.

Flynn kissed her throbbing flesh gently as Abby's muscles collapsed and the world started to return. She felt him nuzzle her stomach before he placed a soft kiss on her belly button. She couldn't open her eyes. She couldn't speak. She lay there, replete. Relaxed. Satisfied.

She heard Flynn chuckle above her and opened her eyes a crack to find him looking down at her. A smile on his face. His weight rested on his hands, either side of her hips.

"Hi," Abby said on a sigh.

His eyes sparkled. "Hi yourself."

Abby blinked up at him. "Would you like a slice of lemon cake and some coffee?"

And Flynn burst out laughing.

CHAPTER 21

"I was saying the other day, how often the most vulnerable area for goalies is between their legs." Andy Gray, former Scottish national player

Abby served lemon cake for an amused Flynn, excused herself and headed for her bathroom. Where she was currently hiding. It wasn't mature and she wasn't proud of her behaviour. She also didn't plan to leave the room until Flynn ate his cake and went home. Yes, she was that pathetic.

She sat on the toilet seat with her head in her hands. She didn't even know where to begin sorting out her evening. She'd let Flynn... She couldn't even think the words. And worse than letting him was the fact she'd wanted him to do it. No. She'd been *desperate* for him to do it. And. It. Had. Been. Mind-blowing.

She groaned at her own stupidity. What about focusing on Victoria's visit? What about waiting? Where was her common sense? Heck, she'd settle for any kind of sense at all.

Common or otherwise. But no, there had been no sense. No protest. No nothing. He'd touched her, she'd melted and minutes later she was screaming his name. In. Her. Kitchen. With her baby asleep upstairs. With her sister in town to assess her. What kind of mother did that make her?

No. She couldn't think like that. Just because she was a mother didn't mean she didn't have needs or desires. It didn't mean she stopped being a woman. Right? Yes. That sounded good. But on her kitchen counter? She let out another groan.

"Are you going to stay in there all night, sugar?" Flynn's lazy drawl made Abby jerk up straight. "As flattering as it is to listen to you wail and groan after I rocked your world, it'd probably be more productive if we talked about whatever crazy thing is going on in your overactive head."

Her elbow hit the porcelain sink and she gasped. Could this get any more mortifying? Maybe if she was really quiet, he would think she was somewhere else? Maybe.

"Abby, I know you're in there. Pretending you're invisible isn't going to work."

It was as though he could read her mind. She stared at the door. Panic made her mouth dry.

"Abby? This is putting a serious dent in my ego. Usually woman run to me, not away from me. Especially when there's screaming in ecstasy involved."

She gaped at the door. Could his ego get any bigger? It was then she heard the chuckle. He was teasing her by making fun of himself. That was…kind of sweet. She cleared her throat.

"I think you should go home." Her voice was strong, confident, unwavering. It would have been really impressive if it hadn't come from within a locked bathroom.

"And I think you should come out of the bathroom." He sounded amused. "Do you think that's going to happen anytime soon?"

Abby thought about it for a good long minute. "No, I think I'll stay in here, thank you very much."

"Afraid you can't keep your hands off me? I get it. It's the same reaction a lot of women have. Trust me, I can fend you off if I have to. It's safe to come out."

She heard the grin in his voice. "Stop being nice to me. I can't handle it right now. I'm trying to figure out how we managed to break our agreement in under twenty-four hours. I'm trying to figure out how you talked me into letting you kiss me. There's no space in my head for anything else."

"You let me do a whole lot more than kiss you, sugar. Do you need me to remind you what we did?"

"No!" Her cheeks began to heat at the thought. The last thing she needed was him saying naughty things in that deep, husky voice of his. His voice was partly to blame for her current mess in the first place.

He chuckled. "Come out of the bathroom, Abby. This is crazy."

Great, his reasonable attitude made her feel even more foolish. But she still couldn't face him. She hung her head and closed her eyes.

"I need time, Flynn. You're the first man I've been physical with since my husband died. I thought he would be the last man I kissed. The last man who made me scream. The last man who held me in his arms while I came back to earth. This is a lot for me to process—even without adding the whole let's-have-a-secret-affair thing." She took a deep breath and let it out slowly. "I know I'm being an idiot, but I need time to think. Can you give me some time?"

"Aye, Abby, I can give you time." His voice was soft, low and unbelievably understanding. "I'll talk to you tomorrow."

ABBY SAT on the toilet for a long time after she heard his

footsteps fade into the distance. She wondered who the real Flynn was. The egomaniac who oozed confidence, or the sweet man who reassured her? The guy who teased her or the man who seduced her? Maybe he was all of them? Maybe she'd underestimated Flynn Boyle? Maybe everyone did. She rubbed her temples before heaving herself to her feet and exiting the bathroom.

The house was quiet. Flynn was gone. One small lamp lit her bedroom. Abby padded on bare feet to her dresser. She picked up the photo that had pride of place on top of it. It was framed in silver. A wedding gift. Abby traced a finger down the smiling face of her husband. While she'd been with Flynn she'd forgotten David. For the first time in years he'd been gone from her mind. She knew it was normal, part of the process of moving on with her life, but it still felt wrong.

She ached as she thought of two very different men. They were night and day. David was all sunshine and gentleness. Flynn was darkness and power. And maybe that was part of the attraction—the fact Flynn was nothing like her husband. She didn't want a replacement for David. There would never be another man like him. Her heart clenched at the thought.

Part of her was angry at him. Angry that his dying had put her in this situation where she was physical with another man, where she was moving on from him. Part of her hurt because her actions still felt a little like betrayal. David wasn't there, but the promises she'd made to him were still alive within her. She wasn't sure if she'd ever get past them. At the same time she knew she had to. Living without David hurt. Moving on without him would hurt even more.

"I'm so confused," she whispered to his image. "How can I touch someone else and still love you? How can I move on? How can I let someone else make me feel good? It feels right *and* wrong. It feels good *and* bad. I wish you were here to tell me what to do." She snorted as tears escaped to run down her cheeks. "How twisted is that? Wishing you were here to give me advice on Flynn."

Still holding the photo, Abby climbed fully clothed onto her bed. She hugged the frame to her stomach, letting it lie over the ache that never seemed to ease. The ache residing in the place David used to fill. The place Flynn had stirred with his kisses and touch. The place that made her want, at the same time as making her resent herself for wanting. As silent tears fell, Abby let exhaustion claim her. She fell asleep thinking of kisses filled with passion. Kisses, not from her husband but from the bad boy next door.

BRIAN FLANNIGAN STUBBED out his cigarette in Abby McKenzie's roses. He'd watched, helpless, as Flynn had walked into the house hours ago just to avoid the cameras. He'd listened in the darkness of her garden while Flynn got the widow off. The guy was screwing with him, by doing what he normally did—exactly what Flynn wanted. It didn't matter to Flynn that Brian was on a deadline. Or that he needed some decent material for his programme. No, all the asshole cared about was getting the pussy he wanted, when he wanted it. Rich bastard never had to work a day in his life. And yeah, he didn't count chasing a ball as work.

Time was running out and the project was sinking. Brian thought bringing Abby's family into the mix would stir up some drama, but so far there was nothing. He knew the mother wanted to take her grandkid back to the homestead, and he'd heard murmurs in town that the sister was giving Abby a week to prove her case. Which explained Flynn's sudden good behaviour.

It made him sick. How was he supposed to get any decent material when Flynn was mooning around and acting like a

Boy Scout? Brian stilled. He narrowed his eyes at the house. Unless…

The sister wanted evidence Abby was hanging out with a reprobate. And Brian could definitely help her see the real Flynn Boyle. The guy might have fooled everyone into believing he'd turned his back on his bad behaviour, but his bad behaviour was about to come calling on him instead.

He pulled out his phone, scrolled through his contacts and found the number he wanted.

"Peaches," he said when the woman answered. "You still looking for a father for that baby of yours?"

The woman was a football slut. She must have slept with Flynn at some point. Why not make it work for her? She might even manage to squeeze some cash out of the bastard if she was lucky. If not, the publicity would help her burgeoning career as a reality star.

He finalised his plans with the woman, then dialled the next name on his contacts.

"Ray? Hey, man, got a job for you. Flynn Boyle wants to throw the party of the century in his hometown. Nothing formal, just a few hundred friends, lots of women and plenty of booze. You know the hip-hop band you booked for the rave in Sheffield last year?"

"The one that got arrested?" You could practically taste Ray's excitement at the prospect of letting them loose again.

"Yeah, Flynn likes their sound. Thought they got a bad deal. Wants to give them a second chance. Can you arrange it?"

Ray hesitated. "When we talking about?"

"Saturday." Two days wasn't a long time to get everyone to Invertary. But it had to be Saturday—it was Victoria Montgomery-Clark's last day in town. If he wanted to show her Flynn's true colours, it had to be then.

"It's gonna cost him," Ray said.

"Name your price. Just be here." Brian would figure out the money later. He was pretty sure his boss would authorise it as an expense once he saw the footage Brian got from the band's appearance. Last he checked, the boys were banned from most radio stations and those feminist groups were camped outside their every gig. One song about rape was all it took to rile them. Couldn't those women take a joke?

"I'll sort it. Send me the details." Ray hung up.

Brian grinned widely as he walked back to his car. It was going to be a busy night. He had a lot more calls to make.

Saturday was going to bring a party the likes of which Invertary had never seen, one even Victoria Montgomery-Clark couldn't excuse.

Saturday was the day Flynn Boyle's charmed lifestyle would come to a crashing end.

Saturday was going to put Brian Flannigan on the map.

And he couldn't wait.

CHAPTER 22

"I think I am a man, but I don't believe I need to say it. But I could also be Peter Pan because I do things my own way and I am free."
Mario Balotelli, Italian national player

Abby didn't know what surprised her most on Thursday morning. The fact she woke wearing yesterday's clothes and mumbling Flynn's name, or the fact Victoria arrived bearing gifts for Katy. Her sister handed Katy the package in much the same way someone handed over a summons—as though they expected violence when it was opened.

"Goody!" Katy bounced. "Look, Muma, a present."

Abby barely had time to smile before the wrapping paper went flying.

"Rapunzel!" Katy squealed. She waved the doll in the air. "Look how long her hair is," she demanded of no one in particular. "Will you help me brush her hair, Aunty Victoria?"

Victoria nodded stiffly. "Of course."

"I'll get the hair stuff. I have glitter." Katy ran from the room.

Abby watched her sister. In her elegant clothes, she looked like a pinched and strained version of Audrey Hepburn. Her cheeks were slightly flushed and Abby could have sworn there was a glassy sheen to her eyes.

"Thank you for Katy's gift."

"It was Lawrence's idea."

Of course it was. "Please thank Lawrence as well. Is he coming over this morning?"

Victoria frowned. "He's busy." Abby thought the topic was closed, but her sister surprised her. "He has some fool notion he's chasing."

"Oh?" Was it possible Victoria was trying to have a conversation with her? Had the sky fallen?

Victoria shifted nervously. "He's talking to his partners today. He wants them to buy him out of their practice. He's got the idea into his head of moving to Invertary and starting a smaller practice here." She looked bewildered. "He wants to learn how to fish."

Abby didn't know what to say. She wasn't sure what this news meant. "The town does need a lawyer. We don't have one."

"That's what Lawrence said." Victoria stared at the wall. Abby thought the conversation was over. "He wants me to move here with him to run the office." The statement was so soft Abby wasn't sure she'd heard it. "Of course, I told him his idea was preposterous. Mother would never allow it."

"Does she have to allow it?" *What am I doing? Do I want a permanent spy living in town?* She looked at her sister and knew the truth. If she could have family nearby, if she could have a chance to get to know Victoria properly without their mother getting in the way, she wouldn't hesitate. "It's your life. It's up to you."

Victoria gave a most unladylike snort. "This hasn't been my life for years." She seemed startled when the words came out of her mouth.

Before Abby could say anything else, Katy ran into the room and straight to her aunt. "I have glitter, and colour, and hair clips, and ribbon, and face paint, and glue."

"Glue?" Victoria said.

Katy rolled her eyes. "In case we want to keep the hair in a nice shape."

"I'll get hairspray." Abby smiled at her daughter. "You confiscate the glue," she told Victoria.

Victoria nodded as Katy continued to talk a mile a minute. Abby left them to it as she headed upstairs to fetch the hairspray. As she passed the front door, someone knocked. Thinking it was Lawrence, she opened it. And found Flynn standing on her step. Her heart raced. Her cheeks warmed. And part of her, a secret part, softened just at the sight of him.

His jeans were worn and scuffed with age. They fit him like a second skin. The material of his shirt looked so soft she wanted to rub her face on it—right over his pecs where the fabric strained. He thrust his hands into his back pockets and rocked on his heels. He seemed nervous and unsure, which was kind of endearing.

"I was worried," he snapped, as though the statement was an accusation. He frowned at her. "About you."

Abby was bewildered. From his attitude it seemed he wasn't pleased to be worrying about her. Or maybe he just wasn't used to someone other than himself taking up space in his head.

"Thanks?" she said.

Flynn gave her a look of chastisement, took his hands from his pockets and walked into the house. As though he belonged there. Without thinking, Abby shut the door behind him. Seemed he wasn't the only one who thought his presence in her home, and life, was normal.

He turned towards her, crowding her space, making her back up against the front door.

"Are you okay?"

"Yes?" Why was everything coming out as a question?

He trailed a finger from her cheekbone to her jaw. "You said you needed time to process. Have you had enough? Because I really want to kiss you again."

Something inside her melted at his confession. She blinked up at him as her body swayed towards him. Her body didn't need time to process. Her body had no problem letting Flynn loose with it.

"I know how hard it is to move on from something you thought you'd have forever. I know you're confused about letting another man near you. But I'd really like the processing time to be over. Is it over, Abby? Can I taste you again?"

The way he whispered the words, not a hairsbreadth away from her mouth, made her wonder what kind of tasting he meant. Heat rushed through her body, followed very closely by desire. He was staring at her. He seemed to expect an answer.

"My sister is in the living room."

"We'll be quiet."

"Then I'm okay," she whispered. She couldn't tear her eyes from his.

"Thank you, Lord." He cupped her jaw in his huge hands, tilted her head and captured her mouth with his.

Every time Flynn was near, every time his scent engulfed her and his strength bracketed her, she turned to mush. Delighted, happy mush. One of his hands flattened against the small of her back to pull her into him. Abby softly moaned her approval into his mouth. Her arms felt weightless as she wrapped them around his shoulders. Her fingers entangled in the golden hair at the base of his skull. All the while, his lips and tongue teased, entwined, duelled with hers. Bliss. Mind-stealing bliss.

His kisses became less intense, until he gently nibbled at her lower lip.

"Damn, Abby, you're addictive." His breathing was ragged. "I feel like I'll never get enough of you."

She blinked up at him. Her eyelids felt unreasonably heavy. Her body was boneless. She didn't want to stop, but through the fog in her head she heard Katy chatting to Victoria. She let her forehead fall onto Flynn's strong chest. He clasped the back of her head and nuzzled the hair at her temple. She wanted to roll in his warm, masculine scent.

"I don't want to stop," he said.

His fingers curved around her chin and he lifted her head to look into her eyes. His emotions seemed raw, much as she expected her own were. "This isn't the time, but we're finishing this, Abby. You're going to be in my bed." He leaned into her, pressing his strength against her length. His lips caressed her ear, sending shivers through her. "And I'm going to be in you," he whispered. The words took what little strength was still in her legs, and she sagged against him. Flynn's silver eyes studied her. "If you don't want that, tell me now, Abby."

She stared up at him. She couldn't say the words. She couldn't deny him. Deny them. Against common sense. Against reason. She wanted the man until it burned.

"Yes?" he murmured.

"Yes," she whispered.

His arms clenched around her. "Damn, I don't know how I'm going to wait. I want you now."

"Yes," she said on a sigh. Or maybe it was a moan.

"You are killing me." He let out a rueful chuckle. "I can

hear your monster and your sister not ten feet from here. And I still want to pick you up and take you upstairs."

She blinked. "You'd just hurt your leg."

Flynn barked a laugh before calming to stare into her eyes with such intensity it humbled her.

"It'd be worth it."

Before she could reply, he released her and stepped away. She felt cold and her body swayed to follow him.

"Got anything to eat?"

"You are always hungry," she reprimanded with a smile.

"In more ways than one, Abby love." His eyes flicked to her lips.

She licked them, a deliberate tease, but took a step back from him. "There are croissants in the kitchen."

"Great." He cupped her cheek once again before turning and stalking to the back of the house.

Abby watched him go, a study in lean muscle and raw power. Did she really want him in her bed? Even though it wasn't the responsible thing to do? There was no doubt. No hesitation. The answer was instantaneous. Yes. She did. She wanted him badly. And the guilt that normally accompanied the thought was strangely absent. Mustering her energy, Abby climbed the stairs to her bathroom, splashed water on her face and grabbed the hairspray.

On her way through her bedroom, she spotted the photo of David. He seemed to be smiling right at her. And there wasn't any judgment in his eyes. With a fragile lightness she didn't want to examine too carefully in case it broke, Abby headed back downstairs.

Victoria was sitting in the play corner of the living room. The look on her face was a mixture of awe and fear as she listened to Katy's instructions on how to style Rapunzel's hair. There was no sign of Flynn, but she could hear banging around in the kitchen. Strange—the fact the man was making himself at home made her feel warm inside rather than threatened. A couple of minutes later, Flynn appeared in the doorway. A mug of coffee in one hand, two croissants in the other.

"Flynn!" Katy ran at him as though she hadn't seen him for a year. She wrapped her arms around his legs and hugged tight.

Flynn seemed bewildered. "We're hugging now?"

Katy looked up at him. "This is what normal people do, Flynn. You need to get used to it. Aunty Victoria isn't used to hugs either, but she's toilet training them for me."

"Tolerating," Abby corrected without much thought.

Katy scrunched her nose. "Toilet rating." She grinned up at Flynn.

He balanced the pastries on top of the mug and used his now empty hand to pat her head. His action was stiff and awkward. "Close enough, kid. We done here? I'm hungry."

"You're always hungry," Katy complained, but let him go.

"So your mum tells me." Flynn ignored Victoria's glare and plopped into an armchair. He thumped his feet onto the coffee table in front of him.

"Get your feet off my table, Flynn Boyle," Abby snapped.

He gave her puppy-dog eyes. "But my leg hurts. It's more comfortable if it's raised."

She rolled her eyes at him, grabbed a cushion from the sofa and put it under the ankle of his injured leg. She knocked his other foot off the table.

"I'll take what I can get." He grinned before biting off half a croissant.

"Does Mr Boyle live here now?" Victoria's voice was icy with disdain.

"Flynn lives in a bus," Katy said helpfully. "He's building a house."

"I don't see any building," Victoria said.

"It's in the planning stage." Flynn seemed unconcerned.

"You have an architect?" Victoria asked.

"I have a field. I'm still getting a feel for it. Wouldn't want to build something before I know what kind of house I want there. It needs to be comfortable." He looked around. "I like this house. I like the high ceilings and the spacious rooms. The big windows are good too. And those things." He pointed at the top of the wall.

"Cornices and moulding," Abby told him.

"Aye, I like those too. I might build something like this. But I'm in no hurry."

"You don't need a house," Katy said. "You can stay in your bus and use my pool."

"Exactly." Flynn polished off the rest of his croissant, then batted his eyelashes at Abby. "There are some croissants left. Do you need them?"

She shook her head, wondering where all the food went. If she could bottle his metabolism and sell it to women, she'd make her fortune.

"I'll get them." If she didn't, who knew what else he would eat while he was in there.

"Mm," Victoria said. "It certainly seems like Mr Boyle lives here now."

"I'm just being neighbourly, hanging out, being friendly. Getting fed," Flynn said. "Showing you how well behaved I am now, so you can see I'm nowhere near being a bad influence on the kid. Isn't that right, monster?"

Katy giggled. Abby bugged her eyes at him. *So not helping.*

"We'll see," was all Victoria said.

CHAPTER 23

"He's one of those footballers whose brains are in his head."Derek Johnstone, former Scottish manager and player

After lunch, Lawrence appeared to take Victoria into town. He wanted her to look at office properties. She was snippy about his quick decision making and very vocal about knowing nothing about offices. She still went with the man. Which made Abby wonder if there was something more going on between them.

Flynn refused to leave, even when the women from Knit or Die turned up for a meeting. He waved her away, sending her to the kitchen to talk to the women while he plugged his iPad into the TV and pulled up an old football game. Last she checked, Flynn was sitting on the sofa with Katy beside him. He alternated between shouting at the TV and explaining everything to Katy in excruciating detail. Katy seemed fascinated. Abby wasn't sure if it was with Flynn or football.

"Don't worry." Margaret patted her hand where it rested

on the kitchen table. "Katy's safe with Flynn. He wouldn't hurt a fly."

Heather, Flynn's aunt, snorted. "Not unless he got drunk, stole a car and ran her over while joyriding."

The other women nodded, which did nothing to alleviate Abby's worries.

"He was a wild child," Shona said. "Remember the time he stole the Paterson cow and tried to ride her like a rodeo bull? Poor cow sat there mooing, wondering what the hell was happening."

Jean laughed. "And the time he was going out with the McLean sisters—all of them. Three sisters at one time and they didn't know about each other. It's a town record."

Heather shook her head. "I thought Robert McLean was going to shoot him when the girls found out."

Abby stared at the women. "How could he do all this stuff when he was in London? Wasn't he sent away when he was thirteen? He told me he was with Arsenal by then."

"Aye," Heather said. "But he wasn't sent away. He was desperate to go. He went down there just before his thirteenth birthday. My sister-in-law cried for a month. She was worried sick about him, but it was his dream. What was she supposed to do? Stand in his way? Harry was only nine at the time, and such a shy wee boy. The only person he ever really talked to was Magenta. We were terrified if Harry was taken away from the security of his routine, he'd become one of those antisocial computer guys who sits in a shed and builds bombs."

Margaret nodded. "It was touch and go there for a while. Magenta was the only one who kept the boy in the real world. Flynn always seemed so much more capable. Nobody worried about him the same way as they did Harry."

"I think that's why he started acting out," Shona said. "Seeking attention. Feeling neglected."

Heather shook her head. "He got plenty of attention. His dad's brother kept a close eye on him and the family went down every chance they got. Not to mention he came home every break. He wasn't neglected. The problem is his brain."

Abby swallowed awkwardly and coughed. "His brain?" Fear rushed through her, sounding like wind in her ears. Was there something wrong with him? Memories of her husband struggling with tumours assaulted her.

"Oh, no." Margaret patted her hand again. "It's not like you're thinking. All Heather means is he was a smart boy and when he wasn't occupied he became easily bored. And when he's bored, he gets into mischief."

"That's putting it mildly." Heather reached for another slice of cake. "The boy is too clever for his own good. He's fine when he's playing and thinking about playing, but honestly, it wasn't enough of a challenge for him mentally. He calmed down a little when he was studying, but what he really needs now is a challenge. Something he finds hard. Those two boys are blessed with intelligence and good looks. Things come easily to them and they hate it. Luckily Harry always loved programming, which kept him out of trouble. But Flynn hasn't found his thing yet. He will, though, I'm sure of it."

"He's always thought he was stupid because Harry's IQ is off the charts. But Flynn's no dummy; he came top of his class in everything he studied. It just doesn't mean anything to him because he keeps comparing his efforts to Harry's," Margaret added.

Comparing himself to Harry didn't sound like the action of a smart man to Abby. Arguing from the direction of the living room drew her attention.

"Excuse me," she said wearily.

She pushed back from the table and went to investigate.

"You can't like the pink uniforms best," Flynn was saying.

"They're the referees. They aren't even players. They wear pink so the players can see them. There are no football teams with a pink uniform. Stop being such a girl and pick one of the proper teams."

Katy folded her arms and glared at him. "I want to support the pink men."

"You can't support them, you numpty, they aren't a team."

"Don't care. They're pretty."

Flynn threw his hands in the air. "How about you support Holland? You like orange, right? Orange is a pretty colour too."

Katy thought about it, then nodded. "Okay, I can support orange. But there should be a team with pink T-shirts. What about all the girls who watch football? I bet they'd like to watch some pink shirts."

Flynn grunted as he tapped on his iPad. "Trust me. The girls who are watching football aren't looking at the players' shirts. Right, enough rubbish." He pointed at the screen. "This is the international between Holland and England in…"

Abby backed out, a strange tightness in her chest as she left them to it.

"Everything okay?" Heather said as she returned to the kitchen.

"They're fighting about pink football shirts."

The women looked at each other then burst out laughing. Abby asked everyone if they needed more tea, and when they didn't they got down to business. The women were working their way through her patterns and had some suggestions and feedback. Meanwhile, Abby updated them on the suppliers she'd found and the progress of the website. They would be doing a lot of their selling online initially, but one day she'd love to open a store in town.

"About names for the business." Jean pulled out a legal pad. "We've been thinking and we have a few suggestions."

"Okay," Abby said slowly.

Jean cleared her throat and started to read. "This is what we have so far: Woolly Wonders, Kute Knits—with a K for cute. Highland Originals—but I think that's a bit bland—Fibre Fancies, Get Your Knit Off—I came up with that one. You know, as in Knit instead of kit? I thought it was sexy." She looked really proud. The other women were less impressed. "Then there's Purls of Wisdom, Knit Picking, Knit Tonight Josephine, To Knit or Not to Knit…"

Jean showed no sign of stopping. Abby held up her hand. "Wow, that's a lot to think about. I'll mull over those suggestions and get back to you."

Just as Jean opened her mouth to protest, Flynn sauntered into the kitchen, with Katy at his side. "We're hungry. What're you doing?"

Abby tried not to notice how sexy he looked when he folded his arms, making his shoulders bulge. "We're trying to come up with a name for my designer knitwear business."

Flynn shrugged. "McKenzie Made—luxurious knits, Highland style."

The women gaped at him as Flynn and Katy wandered into the kitchen area and started opening cupboards.

"Why didn't we think of that?" Shona said.

"I still think Get Your Knit Off is better," Jean grumped.

A minute later Flynn and Katy walked past, arms full of snacks. "Do any teams have purple shirts?" Katy said.

"Kid. The colour of the shirt is the last thing you focus on."

"Is there a purple team or not?"

They disappeared from sight.

"See." Heather pointed after them. "That's exactly what I mean. Flynn's got a quick mind. My nephew isn't an idiot."

"Are we going with McKenzie Made?" Margaret said. "I like it."

There were nods of agreement.

"I don't mind being called McKenzie Made, just so long as we can do an advertising campaign with Get Your Knit Off as a slogan," Jean said. "We can rope in some half-naked men in kilts for the artwork. Men in kilts can sell anything."

"So can a good set of abs," Shona said.

"And a tight bum," Margaret added.

The women nodded sagely.

CHAPTER 24

"We lost because we didn't win." Cristiano Ronaldo, Portuguese national player

As the afternoon progressed, Abby's tension grew.

Flynn hadn't returned to his motorhome. In fact, he seemed pretty settled inside her house. He padded around on bare feet, shouted at the TV and lectured Katy on soccer rules. He also ate everything in sight. Every time he was near her, her need ratcheted up a notch. When he smiled a secret little smile just for her, she felt it sing straight through her body, waking every cell and derailing her thought process at the same time. And when he reached into her space with one of those oh-so-casual touches, everything within her paused.

By the time dinner came around, she was wound up tight and barely able to breathe. They ate together, Flynn and Abby staring at each other over the wooden table as Katy chatted away, oblivious to the undercurrent of tension in the room. As Katy ran off to get changed for bed, Flynn helped

Abby clear the table. When he brushed against her, she blushed.

"Stop jumping every time I'm near you."

"I can't help it. I… My… I'm…" Nope, she had nothing.

"You're thinking about later." Flynn boxed her into the corner beside the fridge. "You're wondering how it will be with us. You're wondering when we'll get to touch. You're thinking it will be explosive." He nuzzled her neck, just below her ear. "I feel it too. It's anticipation."

Her fingers curled into his shirt at his waist. He brushed a stray lock of hair off her forehead. "Try not to worry. No pressure."

"Yeah, right," she scoffed.

Flynn's big hands cupped her jaw. There was no trace of the usual mocking amusement in his eyes. "I'm serious here, Abby. I want you. I can't hide it. But we go at your pace. I'm not the dickhead most people make me out to be."

"Well, not totally." Abby smiled up at him.

"No," he conceded. "Not totally."

He leaned into her and nipped her bottom lip, stealing her breath just as fast. As Abby clung to him, she wondered if it would always be like this with Flynn. If he would always steal her mind and strength with just one touch. She looked into his dark eyes, lost for a minute before she remembered there was no always, there was only now.

"You got it sorted?" he asked softly, as though he'd been party to her thought process.

"Yes," she whispered.

"Good." His mouth covered hers in a gentle kiss.

"I better get a pony, Flynn Boyle." Katy's voice cut through Abby's desire like a knife. She jumped back from him only to find her retreat blocked by the fridge. Flynn stepped away from her, but stayed close.

Katy had her arms folded over her Minion pyjamas. "You

promised me a pony if I let you kiss my Muma. You better not forget."

"Katy!" Abby stepped towards her daughter. "Flynn is not buying you a pony." She glared at Flynn. "Tell her."

Abby could tell Flynn was struggling with his answer. His eyes said he really wanted to tell Katy she could get a pony. He shuffled nervously.

"This is one of those things your mum has to decide," he said at last. "I'll talk to her about it, okay?"

Abby narrowed her eyes at him. Did he think it wasn't obvious he was plotting behind her back? She wouldn't be surprised if a pony mysteriously turned up on her doorstep one morning.

"Then you can't kiss her." Katy pointed at Abby. "She belongs to me and I get to say who can kiss her."

"No you don't, young lady." Abby scooped up her daughter. "Your mother chooses who she kisses."

"But," Katy said, "Jonathan said you have to marry the people you kiss, and I don't want you to marry Flynn. Jonathan said he wouldn't make a good daddy. Jonathan said a good daddy has a proper job and a house. Flynn doesn't work and he lives in a bus. Plus, he doesn't know how to play tea party." She glared at Flynn over Abby's shoulder. "And he ate all my snacks."

"If you're not fast you're last, kid." Flynn showed no remorse.

"I think he's got worms," Katy said. "Jonathan's dog had worms and he ate all the time, just like Flynn. His bum was itchy, too. Is your bum itchy, Flynn?"

As Abby stared at her daughter, Flynn reached around her and plucked Katy out of her grip. "I don't have worms. It's time for a bedtime story. Tonight we're going to learn all about a guy called Maradona. He was a great footballer, who not only ran rings around England during the World Cup in

'86, but cheated in the same match. That's not on. Cheating is bad. Remember that."

"What colour did he wear?"

"Pale blue."

"No pink?"

"No pink." Flynn looked utterly disgusted. He turned to Abby. "Give your mum a kiss and we'll go read the story."

While Flynn held Katy, she wrapped her arms around her mum's neck, squeezed tight and pressed a kiss to her cheek. "I know what to get Flynn for Christmas. A pink football shirt," Katy whispered loudly in Abby's ear before giggling.

"Enough of this," Flynn ordered. "Time to learn something useful. Like the fact you never ever use your hands in a football game. Especially when it's the quarterfinal in the World Cup and you're playing against a country you were at war with. Goals should be shot with your feet. Not your hands. Got it?"

"Got it, Flynn." Katy rested her head on his shoulder and he carried her up the stairs.

Abby felt her eyes tear up as she watched them go.

Flynn Boyle was stealing her baby's heart. And Abby worried hers was being stolen right along with it.

As she turned to go back into the kitchen, the doorbell rang. Abby detoured to open it and was hit by blinding light. She stepped back as she shielded her eyes against the light. It took her a second to blink enough to see again. That was when she spotted the camera aimed at her face. She was about to slam the door shut when a hand reached out to stop her.

Abby saw the long red fingernails first. Then she saw the woman. She was poured into a red minidress, her feet clad in sky-high matching stilettos. Her hair was long and teased out to give it lots of volume. Her makeup was perfect. Her eyes were calculating. And they were focused on Abby.

"I need to speak to Flynn." Her voice was sharp.

"Flynn?" Abby stepped back.

"Yes. I have something that belongs to him." She pointed at the porch beside her.

Having been blinded by the lights, Abby had missed the dark shape. It was a baby carrier. A car capsule. And in it, smiling up at her, was a beautiful little baby.

"Junior wants to meet his daddy," the woman said.

Abby blinked at the woman. At the camera. Then years of training snapped into place. Her back straightened. Her chin went up.

"Of course. Give me a moment and I'll fetch him. Excuse me."

She closed the door with a polite nod, leaned her head against it and closed her eyes.

Baby.

Flynn.

Cameras.

The air thickened, making it difficult to breathe.

Reality smacked her in the face. Even if Flynn was trying to change, he would still have to deal with the consequences of his past behaviour. Consequences Abby wasn't ready to let into her life. One look at the woman and her baby was like ice water over her brain. What was she doing? An affair with Flynn could never remain secret, and there was too much at stake to gamble that it would.

It was time to stop listening to hormones.

It was time to stop playing around with Flynn.

CHAPTER 25

"I have a number of alternatives, and each one gives me something different." Glenn Hoddle, former England manager

"Are you sure the baby isn't yours?" Matt asked again.

They were in Matt's newly built house, which was still being decorated. Boxes filled corners of the rooms, waiting to be unpacked. Flynn couldn't have the conversation on his own land, as he now had two film crews camped there. Crews Matt had been called in to move after Abby politely, and coldly, asked Flynn to deal with his problem.

"I'm sure it isn't mine." Flynn ran a hand through his hair. "I've never seen her before."

"You've slept with a lot of women," Matt said. "Do you remember all of them?"

Flynn clenched his jaw. No, he didn't remember all of them. "I would recognise her. I don't. Nothing about her is familiar. Plus, I'm not an idiot. I don't have unprotected sex. I made that clear during the last paternity claim."

"Accidents happen." Matt glared at him. "Especially when you court trouble."

"Thanks for your support." Flynn glared back. "It means a lot. I'm touched."

"You're touched, all right," Matt growled. "Touched in the bloody head."

Matt stalked off to stand beside his wife. Flynn's mother and Aunty Heather were making tea and sandwiches in the kitchen, even though everyone had told them they weren't hungry. His father was furious as he stared out of the window in the direction of the lights at Flynn's place. Harry was tapping on his laptop, Magenta beside him—unsmirking for once. The twins were sitting on the couch while Grunt stood guard behind them. And everyone was mad at Flynn.

Flynn stopped pacing and stared them down. "I did not have sexual relations with that woman." He pointed towards his land.

Harry was the only one who laughed.

"This isn't funny, son," his dad snapped.

"You think I find this funny?" Flynn laughed. It wasn't pretty. "This is my life. There's nothing funny about it. I've got people crawling out of the woodwork to use me as a stepping stone to get what they want. I'm tied into shooting a tabloid documentary loosely disguised as sports TV. My agent isn't taking my calls. He did record a special message just for me. It was two words. One began with F. There's a woman in professional makeup on my lawn and she's using a baby to get airtime. Abby closed the door on me and probably won't let me back in. She's upset and she won't even talk to me. My leg hurts like a mother. My career is over. My reputation is mud. I have no idea what to do with my life. And I'm trying damn hard to be good!"

Aye. So. He'd lost his cool. Fine. They could cope with it. Right? He scanned the astonished faces staring at him and wondered if he should move. Far away. Somewhere where family couldn't find him. Somewhere away from film crews. From gold diggers. Somewhere out of reach from his past. Like Neverland.

"Got it." Harry punched the air then grinned at everyone. "What'd I miss?" he said when he saw the stunned silence.

"Nothing." Flynn hobbled over to his brother. "What you got?"

Harry pointed at the screen. "Everything you ever wanted to know about Susan Muir."

"Who?" Flynn couldn't sit. He was too wired to sit. But standing made his leg ache. He resisted the urge to bend over and rub his knee. Instead he folded his arms, gritted his teeth and focused on Harry.

"The woman in your yard. Susan Muir. She's twenty-five, she loves the spotlight and she's better known as Peaches—from her stint as a Page Three girl." Harry looked up at his family. "Do they still have Page Three girls?"

"Unfortunately, some papers still think topless women are news," Magenta said dryly. "We protested against them a few years ago, didn't we?" She grinned at her two best friends, Flynn's twin cousins.

"Yep. We made placards and picketed the head office in London. We demanded the paper print men with their junk hanging out on page two." Megan shrugged. "Seemed only fair."

"Megan wanted to do the protest topless, but we wouldn't let her," Claire added.

Flynn stared at the women before addressing his father. "And you think I'm out of control?"

"Back to the issue," Harry said. "*Peaches* is currently filming her own reality show about life after Page Three. She's also written a book." He read some more as he grinned. "It's a novel called *Tits Up*."

Matt frowned at Harry. "What else?"

"Birth dates." His fingers flew over the keyboard before he sat back with a smirk on his face. "Flynn isn't the father."

"I told you this already." Flynn threw up his hands. "Doesn't anybody listen to me?"

His family proved his point by ignoring him.

"According to the dates"—Harry pointed at the screen—"Flynn here was in training camp during the time of conception and the lovely *Peaches* was filming another reality show in Ibiza. For months, they weren't even in the same country. There's no way he could be the baby's father."

"Is anyone listening to me?" Flynn was too sore to stand anymore. He pulled out a chair beside Harry and sat down hard. "The woman turned up with a camera crew. The producer from my show was smirking in the background. It doesn't take a genius to figure this out. The guy is pissed I'm not doing anything to make his programme more interesting, so he's stirring things up." He rubbed a hand over his face. "Look," he said on a sigh. "I'm not proud of it, but I'm used to this sort of thing. I know how to handle it. I'm not worried about me. I'm worried about Abby."

Claire faked fainting. The back of her hand hit her forehead as she swayed before flopping onto the couch behind her. "I'm fine, I'm fine," she said to her grinning fiancé. "For a minute there I thought Flynn said he was worried about someone other than himself. I must have been hallucinating, because that can't be right."

Magenta and Megan thought that was hilarious. Flynn didn't. "Abby's sister is still in town. This new crew filmed Abby's reaction to my alleged child. This could harm her and the kid. We can't let it get out. Like I said, I tried calling my agent. I'm getting nothing."

"You need to fire him," Harry said. "He isn't good for you or your career."

"That's a moot point now, considering I don't have a football career for him to manage."

"I'll talk to Mitch," Matt said. "He'll sort this." He pulled out his phone and pointed at Flynn with it. "You're paying his fee."

"Whatever." Flynn rolled his eyes. "Just make sure Abby is protected."

"There it is again," Claire said dramatically. "I'm definitely hearing things. I think I'm ill. I could have sworn I heard Flynn say he was looking out for someone else."

Flynn ignored the laughter. This wasn't a joke. He needed to protect Abby and clean house before his screwed up life caused any more problems for her.

Before Matt hung up on Mitch, Flynn motioned for the phone.

"I need help," he told the lawyer.

"From what I hear, you're asking the wrong person. But I can recommend a good shrink."

Flynn was in no mood for humour. "I need to get rid of my agent and lawyer. And I need it to happen fast." He let out a sigh. "You're the only one I trust to sort this out at short notice. So I'm asking for a favour."

There was silence. No jokes, no ribbing.

"Email the details." Mitch was all business. "I'll take care of it."

Flynn felt relief flood him. "Thanks, man."

"We're friends," was all Mitch said before hanging up.

Flynn looked around the room and suddenly it seemed different. Friends. Family. People in his corner. People who cared about him. Who worried about him.

An unfamiliar determination not to disappoint them swept through him. They deserved better than to deal with the fallout from his life. They deserved a better Flynn.

Suddenly the effort to be good didn't seem so onerous after all.

CHAPTER 26

"If history repeats itself, I should think we can expect the same thing again." Terry Venables, former England manager"

Come on," Lawrence told Victoria when she opened her hotel door on Friday morning. "We're going for a walk. It's a beautiful day."

She blinked at him as though he'd suggested they dance naked down the high street.

"It's just a walk. You'll enjoy it. Trust me."

"I'm reading." She motioned to her perfectly made bed with the paperback novel resting on the end of it. "I don't have time for a walk. I'm expected at Abby's house in an hour."

"Get your bag. Put on your shoes. We're going for a walk. You'll make it to Abby's house in time and the book can wait."

She wavered. Indecision clear in her eyes.

"Chop, chop," Lawrence said.

"Oh, all right." She turned back into her room, picked up her grey leather handbag, slipped on a pair of sensible low-heeled shoes, checked her reflection in the mirror over the dresser, patted her hair—which was in a tight bun at the nape of her neck—then turned back to him.

It was only when she closed her door behind her that she really looked at Lawrence. "You're wearing jeans." Her shock was endearing. She said it in the same way someone else would say, "I can't believe you invaded Russia."

"Got them this morning." Lawrence looked down at his new jeans. They were a bit pristine for his liking, but he planned to wear them in and mess them up. He also had on a long-sleeved shirt in the softest grey. The woman in the shop said the shirt was designed to be worn with the tails untucked. He'd done as she'd said, but he wasn't sure about it. He'd spent most of his adult life in pristine suits. It felt strange to let his shirt hang out. Even stranger not to wear a tie.

Victoria considered him for a moment, her expression giving nothing away. Her eyes hit his polished leather shoes. "You may need new shoes."

For a second he thought she was going to smile. "The woman in the shop suggested running shoes. She told me I needed to go to Fort William to buy them. I'm not sure running shoes are quite me, but Dougal told me to get deck shoes. He said they're casual, comfortable and stylish. He also offered to go clothes shopping with me, if I needed further advice."

The horror in Victoria's face was priceless. "Dougal? The hotel owner? The man who wears pink shirts with green tartan bow ties and matching vests?"

Lawrence laughed. It felt good, and reminded him he hadn't spent enough time laughing over the past few years.

"I hope you refused his offer." Victoria was earnest.

"Don't worry, Vicki. I have more sense than to shop with Dougal."

"Good." She nodded, but her cheeks flushed. "One thing..." Her hesitation was endearing. He softened further towards her. Reaching out, he took a chance and gently caressed her cheek. Her shocked eyes shot to his, but she didn't stop him.

"What is it, Vicki?"

"Your shirt." She pointed at his sleeves. "May I?"

"Of course." He dropped his arms to his sides and watched as Victoria rolled up each of his sleeves in turn until they sat beneath his elbows.

Her cheeks were pink when she looked back up at him. "This looks better."

"Thank you." And then he did something that stunned them both. He bent over and brushed his lips over hers.

For a second they stared at each other. The air frozen between them.

"Let's go for a walk," Lawrence said.

"Yes." Chin up, back straight, Victoria turned for the stairs.

And Lawrence smiled. He hadn't imagined the hitch in her breath. Or the tremble in her body. He hadn't imagined the desire in her eyes.

Nor the anxiety.

Victoria Montgomery-Clark was a puzzle. And Lawrence loved a good puzzle. Grinning, he followed the woman who captivated him.

ABBY SPENT Friday morning berating herself. She should have known better than to get physical with Flynn Boyle—especially while her sister was still in town. She wished she could blame hormones, or a rampant horniness, but really there was no excuse. The man just drew her to him. Like a bear to honey. Even now, knowing what was at stake, she still wished he was with her.

She peeked out from behind the curtains in her living room. The woman with the baby was back. This time in a lime-green minidress. She stood in the driveway just shy of Flynn's property boundary. The baby was currently being held and, from the looks of it, sang to by the shy woman who worked alongside Flynn's producer. Abby had only spoken to the woman once, but she'd seemed nice. Far too nice to be working for her boss.

"Can I go see the baby?" Katy asked from beside her. She was peeking out the window too, as though it was a game.

"No, sweetie."

"That's not fair." Katy frowned up at her. "I like babies." Her face transformed into the falsely innocent look she got when she wanted something. Abby waited for the other shoe to fall. "I'd really like a baby sister. Can I get one, Muma? Can I?"

"You need a Muma and a daddy to get a baby sister."

Katy's little nose scrunched up. "I need a daddy fast, don't I?" She let out a heavy sigh. "Can you still marry Uncle Matt?"

"No, he's married to Jena."

"What about Uncle Harry?"

"He's getting married to Magenta."

"Huh." Katy fell silent while she thought about it. "Can you marry Uncle Dougal?"

Abby blinked down at her. "Dougal?"

Katy nodded. "He's in charge of the whole town. If he was my daddy, I'd be in charge of the whole town too. And I bet he'd give me free chips every time we had dinner in the pub."

"I'm not marrying Dougal." Abby tried to imbue the word with firmness instead of horror.

"Because you don't want to kiss him, right?" Katy said solemnly.

"No, I don't want to kiss Dougal."

Katy let out a heavy sigh. "I'm just going to have to let Flynn be my daddy."

"What? No!" Abby stared down at her determined daughter. "You can't just pick a daddy. It doesn't work like that."

"I know, Flynn said you need to pick him. But you're already kissing Flynn, so you might as well marry him." She gave an exaggerated shrug. "He isn't so bad. I can probably train him. Jonathan said you can train daddies just like puppies. Can I get a puppy?"

"No." Abby felt like her head was spinning.

"Then I'll just have to make do with Flynn. A puppy would fetch a ball, but Flynn can teach me to play football. That's better than a puppy fetching a ball, isn't it?" She grinned up at her mum, who was trying hard not to hyperventilate. "I've decided you can marry Flynn. He can be my daddy and teach me to play football. But I want to play in a pink shirt."

Before Abby could say anything else, Katy was off running, pleased she'd worked everything out.

"Take off your shoes." Lawrence laughed at the shock on Victoria's face. "I didn't tell you to strip. Just take off your shoes. Feel the sand under your toes."

"Why?"

"For fun, Vicki. Don't you have fun?" Lawrence wanted to reach out and tug the woman into his arms. The look of utter confusion on her face broke his heart. He might have been stuck in an endless loop of work and sleep for the past several years, but there had been pockets of time where he'd lived. He suspected Victoria didn't even have those.

"I read," she said. "Reading is enjoyable."

"Take off your shoes." Lawrence stepped into her space, making her cheeks flush and her eyes dart around in confusion. "Reading is great, Vicki, but you can't live completely until you experience things for yourself. Look around you." He entwined his fingers with hers, making her jerk and her eyes go wide. "The loch is a rich blue, the warm scent of summer flowers is in the air and the sky is clear of clouds. Be present. Be here. Take off your shoes, curl your toes into the sand and breathe deep. No one will judge. No one is even watching. It's just the two of us, stealing a moment to live fully in a beautiful part of the world."

A flurry of emotion passed across her face. She nodded once, tersely, dropped his hand and bent to tug off her shoes. Lawrence felt like he'd won a great victory. He watched as she curled her toes into the warm sand and her obvious trepidation turned to joy. Her shoulders relaxed and she gave him a small smile. It was better than a medal.

"Move here with me," Lawrence said before he could stop the words from escaping. "Start a new life, here. In Invertary. With me."

She blinked in shock. "I can't."

He suspected those words were her standard answer to anything asked of her.

"Why can't you?" He stepped closer to her, standing behind her as she looked out at the loch. Water lapped gently in front of him, the sounds of the town fading behind them. Lawrence couldn't resist the pull of the woman any longer. He closed the distance between them and wrapped his arms around her shoulders. At once she stiffened, then slowly relaxed into him. "Why can't you stay, Vicki?"

"I don't understand why you *can* stay." There was genuine confusion in her tone. "How can you walk away from everything you've built? What makes you think you'll have a better life here?"

He nuzzled her temple as he considered her question. "When I called my partners and asked them to buy me out, do you know what they said? They said, 'About time.'" He chuckled. "They're happy for me. This move wasn't a surprise. I'd been making noises about changing my life for a couple of years now. One of the guys thought I might buy a house in Provence, but I like it better here than France. I like the people here. I want to get to know them. I want to slow down. I want to learn to fish. I want to feel the sand beneath my toes and listen to the locals rib each other over breakfast in the pub." He turned her in his arms. "I want to wake up each morning with a beautiful woman beside me." He ran a finger down her cheek. "With you beside me," he whispered.

She jerked against him. He tightened his hold. He wouldn't make it easy for her to escape.

"Why? Why me?" She twisted to look up at him. The absolute rawness he saw in her eyes made him want to crush her to him and never let her go.

"I see you." He touched the corner of her mouth with his thumb. "I see you trapped in there. I see all that emotion and need bursting to get out. I see a woman who's lost herself under the pressure of a tyrant. I see someone who needs to live, just as much as I do. We can do it together. Start again. Go slow. Here. In a place where they don't mind people who aren't quite normal."

"I don't know if I can." The words were barely a whisper. He had to strain to hear. "I don't know how to be any other way."

"We'll learn together. You want to spend time with Abby and you want to be a part of Katy's life. Don't deny it. I see it. You are full of wonder and joy when you're with them. But you're also afraid they won't want you. They will. Give them a chance. Give us a chance. Don't let your mother win. Have courage. Have a life. You can do it, Vicki, I know you can."

To his surprise, she wrapped her arms around his waist and pressed her cheek to his chest.

"I'm so scared," she told him.

"I know." He held her tight as he watched the beauty of the Highlands just gently be in front of him.

"I have secrets," she said as they relaxed into the breeze.

"We all have secrets."

"I've done things. Terrible things." She looked up at him, the absolute agony in her eyes utterly heartbreaking. "Things that will make Abby hate me if she finds out about them. It's too risky to stay here. She might discover my secrets."

"Every chance to be happy, to be free, comes with risk. And Abby is a very forgiving woman."

"I don't see how she could forgive me when I can't forgive myself." A lone silent tear rolled down her cheek and crushed his heart.

Lawrence pulled her tight against him. There were no words for her pain, but he offered what comfort and reassurance he could with the strength of his arms and his silent belief she was able to face the future by his side. No matter what the future held.

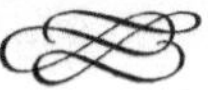

CHAPTER 27

"I can see the carrot at the end of the tunnel." Stuart Pearce, former England national player

"I didn't sleep with her." Flynn's voice sliced through the darkness surrounding Abby as she sat on the porch outside her kitchen door. The sun had long ago disappeared and the cool dark of the night had wrapped her in its intimate cocoon. Flynn sat down on the step near her, not looking at her, instead staring out into the black night. "I didn't father her kid."

Abby didn't speak. Really, what was there to say? Flynn looked up at her as she sat huddled in the corner of the old swing seat, a thin, but soft blanket covering her knees—more as reassurance than for warmth.

"It doesn't mean there aren't other women out there," Flynn said tightly. "It doesn't mean there haven't been mistakes. There might be children. I don't know."

Abby cleared her throat. "And if there are children?"

"Then I claim ownership. If I have kids, I want to be part of their lives. I don't want to run from them, Abby."

"They aren't dogs, Flynn. You don't own children."

"You know what I mean. I wouldn't turn my back on my kids, no matter how they came into being. This woman, though, she's lying. Her kid doesn't belong to me."

"I know." Abby let out a sigh. "Jena called and filled me in on the family meeting."

Flynn looked more serious than she'd ever seen him. "I have a past. It's not one I'm particularly proud of, it isn't one I regret either. It just is. I know my past is never going to go away. There will always be fallout from the choices I've made. If not this woman, then another. I thought I was careful, but you just don't know." He ran a hand through his hair, making it stand on end. "It isn't just the women. I was a he-slut. I get it. Those choices are bound to bite me in the arse. It's the rest of it, too. My career options are limited because of how I behaved. The weasel over there is out to get me because he thinks I deserve it." He laughed without mirth. "I probably *do* deserve it."

Abby didn't rush to reassure him. They were about the same age, and while she'd been worrying over the consequences of every decision she made, he'd been doing things without thought for the future. It was almost humorous. She'd grown up before her time, whereas he'd taken too long to grow up.

"I didn't care," Flynn said, breaking the silence. "I didn't care about the future, or if anything I did affected anyone else."

"And now you do?"

"I care what you think."

She felt like she'd been hit by lightning. The swing swayed as she leaned towards him, wishing he was closer so she could pet him. The man called to her on a visceral level, making it difficult to shut him out.

"We all make mistakes," she said. "We all have pasts that made us who we are now. It's up to you whether you let your past dictate your future, or whether you learn from it and change."

"You mean, stop screwing up and deal with the consequences like an adult. Be responsible. Be boring." He ran a hand over his face. "I know. You're right. I get it. But it sounds so bloody dull."

"I can't help you there. I only know how to be boring and responsible. I don't know how to have fun while I'm being a grownup."

His eyes sparkled in the low light coming from the kitchen. "Maybe we can help each other. You teach me to be responsible. I'll teach you how to have fun."

Everything inside of her jumped up and down with glee at the thought. She tried to squish the feeling, but it wouldn't stay down.

"Sometimes I feel so very old for twenty-eight," she confessed.

"Most days I barely feel like an adult. See, we're a perfect fit."

Abby couldn't help laughing at him. "Only in your head, Flynn, only in your head."

"My head is the only place that matters."

"And that right there is why you keep getting into trouble."

He got up on his knees and shuffled until he was kneeling between her thighs. She saw the wince when he manoeuvred on his injured leg and noted his weight was leaning heavily on his good leg. Silly man. He shouldn't be kneeling at all. Flynn placed his hands on her thighs and stared into her eyes. The intrusion into her personal space was wonderfully intimate.

"I promised myself I'd keep away from you," she said.

"You know what they say, promises are made to be broken."

"You tempt me, Flynn Boyle, but there's more at risk here than my neglected heart."

"I know, but I still want to lead you astray. You're walking temptation for me, Abby."

"I thought you wanted advice on behaving responsibly." His eyes were captivating. It was impossible to look away.

"How about I lead you astray and then you lead us back to adulthood?" He was playing with her. She knew he was teasing her, and yet a part of her wished it was real. He leaned forward, brushing his lips over hers before resting his forehead against hers. "I'm sorry about yesterday, Abby. I know you need to distance yourself from me and my mess this week. I'm sorry it landed on your doorstep. Again."

She couldn't help the smile. How did he manage to be dangerously sexy one moment and innocently cute the next?

"I'd better get back. Things are quiet right now, but who knows what's going to happen next. I'll stay away until your sister is gone. Like I should have done in the first place." He stood and backed away from her, making her shiver from the loss of his heat. "Tell the terrorist we'll carry on with her football education once this is all over."

Leaning over, he cupped the back of her head with his huge hand and pressed a kiss to her hair. Without another word, he turned and walked back down the steps towards his property.

Abby felt a surge of panic as she watched him go. Before she knew what she was going to do, she shot to her feet and chased after him. She grabbed his hand in hers and held it tight. Her body trembled as she stared up at him. Confusion clear in his eyes. The war between what she wanted to do and what she needed to do raged within her. She should let him go. It was the right thing to do. The adult thing. The risks of getting involved were just too high.

But the risks for letting him walk away were high too.

"Stay," she whispered.

"Abby?"

"Stay." She infused the word with confidence, but was betrayed by her trembling hand.

She wanted this. A moment stolen with Flynn. A moment when she didn't have to be an adult. Where worry didn't chase her every thought. She wanted him.

She swallowed hard and waited for his answer.

"What are you doing, Abby love?" Flynn gentled his voice, scared to spook her and make her run.

Wide eyes looked up at him through dark lashes. A flush coloured her cheeks.

"You said"—she licked her lips and almost undid him —"you'd do whatever I want you to."

He stopped breathing. Abby took a step towards him. Her touch was tentative when she placed her hand on his chest.

"I want you to come to bed with me, Flynn." It was barely a whisper.

Every muscle in his body went taut. He wanted to drag her up the stairs. He wanted her naked. He wanted her now. And yet…

"Your sister?"

She squeezed her eyes shut. "I need this. For me. Just tonight. No one will know."

His mouth went dry. Everything within him screamed to take what she offered before she changed her mind.

"What about the terrorist?" Sure, the kid was a pain, but she was growing on him. He didn't want to traumatise her.

"She sleeps like the dead." Abby gave him a shy smile that stopped his heart. "We'll lock the bedroom door and take the monitor into the room. I'll hear her if she needs me."

He should have been running for her bedroom, with her slung over his shoulder, ready for a no-strings-attached good time. In the past he would have been. But this was Abby. This was different. He couldn't screw this up.

"Are you sure?"

Her eyes narrowed slightly in irritation. "Do you want me to beg? Because I have to tell you, Flynn, I don't want you *that* much."

Flynn cupped the back of her head and angled her face up towards him. "Liar," he said before he claimed those plump lips as his own.

Her hands slid across his chest to entwine around his neck. The press of her lush curves against the firmness of his muscle was almost too much. His fingers grabbed the clasp keeping her hair in a knot at the back of her head and unclipped it. Soft, thick waves tumbled down around her shoulders. Flynn couldn't stop a guttural growl from escaping as he wound his fingers into the curls. He slanted his mouth over hers. His hands grasped her waist, clasping the curve of her hip, pulling her closer.

"Never going to get enough of you, Abby," he said against her mouth.

His tongue found hers and the sound of desire she made ignited his passion. He was quickly degenerating into one-word thoughts. Want. Need. Take. Mine. As he deepened the kiss, she did what she did every time he'd touched her: she melted. Complete, utter submission. It was the best aphrodisiac he'd ever known. It took all of his very limited self-control to break the kiss.

"I'd carry you up the stairs, sugar, but I'm in no fit state."

"Mmm," she said against his chest.

The sound made him squeeze her tighter. "If you want to do this in private, we need to go upstairs." He was about thirty seconds away from revoking the offer and taking her up against the wall. Or on the swing. Or sitting on the steps. Hell, anywhere. Everywhere. He just wanted Abby.

"Abby love." Eyes drowsy with lust looked up at him. "I promise I'll do the whole caveman thing when my leg gets better. Right now, if you want to do this in a bed, you've got to walk under your own steam."

She blinked at him a couple of times before his words sank in. "Oh." Her embarrassment was delightful. "Okay, yes." She looked around them, bit her bottom lip and stepped away from him. Her hand went to her hair and she seemed surprised to find it hanging loose.

Damn, she was beautiful.

"Come on, Abby love." He held out his hand for her and she took it without hesitation.

With a shy smile, she took the lead, walking him up the back stairs to her house. She locked the kitchen door, flipped the light switch and, without a word, led him through the house and up the stairs to her bedroom. It was across the hall from the kid's room, and Flynn wasn't so far gone with need that he didn't check the door was closed. Abby gave him a knowing smile when she saw him do it.

Without a word, she walked into her room, closing the door behind them. He stood in the middle of the room as he heard the snick of the lock. It was loud in the silence. Flynn watched as she moved to the bed, taking the decorative cushions and tossing them onto the floor.

He stepped up behind her, his hands circling her waist as he traced a line from her shoulder to her ear with his lips.

"Oh." Her head fell to the side to give him more space to work.

"Aye," he said against her skin. It came out as a growl.

He kissed and nipped and licked. She clutched the forgotten cushion tight against her chest as she swayed in his arms. He loved the way she lost herself in the moment.

Flynn's nimble fingers found the zipper at the back of her dress. He slid it down, caressing the skin it revealed, trailing fingertips over peach-coloured lingerie and silently blessing Kirsty for opening a shop in Invertary.

"Flynn?" Abby's voice was husky. "Can we both get naked this time?"

He chuckled as his hands swept the dress off her shoulders. It skimmed her body and fell into a crumpled heap at her feet.

"Aye, we're going to be naked." He kissed her shoulder before slipping the strap of her sexy lace bra down her arm. He repeated the move with the other strap, effectively trapping her arms at her side. Hands on her waist, he manoeuvred them so that he was sitting on the edge of the bed and Abby stood between his thighs.

"I don't think you need this." He grinned at her as he took away the cushion she had clutched to her chest. She seemed surprised to find it was still in her hands.

When it was gone, he sucked in a breath at the sight of her, all curves and softness. The blush on her cheeks spread down her throat and across her chest. He looked up to find her chewing at her bottom lip. Was she nervous? Daft woman.

"You are so beautiful," he told her.

The red on her cheeks deepened. "I have stretch marks and cellulite, and I think my boobs are beginning to droop."

He burst out laughing. "Thanks for the rundown, love.

You have got to be the first woman I've had in this position who pointed out her faults."

Her eyes gleamed as irritation cut through desire. "Really? You're going to compare me to your many, many other women. Really?"

With another laugh, he bent forward and nipped the upper curve of her breast.

"Hey!" She smacked him on the head, making him laugh harder.

"Behave," he told her. "You're distracting me."

"From biting me?"

"From admiring your beauty."

She rolled her eyes. "Yeah, right."

He sobered. "Aye. Right. Look at you. You are so freaking gorgeous."

He ran a hand over the curve of her hip and round to her backside. It was lush in his grip.

"Oh." Abby's face softened, her eyelids drooping.

"Stunning."

He reached up and tugged the cup of her bra down to expose her breast. It pushed it upwards and out towards him.

"Doesn't look droopy to me."

"Idiot." But it lacked any rancour.

"Mmm." He licked around the pink areola and tightened his hold on Abby as she swayed in place.

Nipping at the taut bud, he listened to her little mewls of delight. Her fingers curled into his shoulders, biting skin, reminding him he still had his shirt on.

He let go of her hip long enough to pull his shirt over his head.

"Oh yes," she whispered as Flynn's head dipped back to her breast.

. . .

ABBY GRASPED the firm muscles of Flynn's shoulders, using his strength to hold herself upright. Her head fell forward and her breath stuttered at the erotic sight of Flynn's lips on her breast. His eyes looked up and caught hers before he sucked hard and deep. She gasped and her knees gave way.

With a chuckle, Flynn twisted and lowered her to the bed. She felt the clasp of her bra pop.

"As much as I love this lingerie, I want it gone."

His voice was a growl. It made her burn. She loved hearing how affected he was by what they were doing. She felt deep satisfaction knowing she wasn't alone in being swept up into this whirlwind of need.

"We're in this together," he whispered, as though reading her mind.

"Yes," she whispered back.

And then he was devouring her. His lips and tongue mastering her. His touch possessive as his hands slid over her body. She felt the rasp of his jeans against her thighs. The bite of the buttons against her stomach.

"Naked," she demanded, but it was barely a murmur into their kiss.

His reply was to pop the buttons of his jeans. A second later he was kissing her again and the jeans were gone. Deep, desperate kisses that gave her no space to think. Her hands grasped warm muscle. His scent engulfed her senses, blocking out everything else. There was only Flynn. His weight pressing her into the bed. His power holding her in place. His touch igniting her.

His mouth was on her neck. Kissing. Biting. Sucking. His tongue soothing his harsher touch. Her hands clutched his hips as she tried to angle his body where she wanted it to be. He was too heavy, too strong to manoeuvre, and for some reason her frustration amped up her desire.

"Flynn?" Her head was back, her neck exposed for his kiss.

"What do you want? Tell me. I'll give it to you, Abby love. Tell me."

Her mind was spinning. Thought was hard. There was only need. Desperate, aching need that clawed at her stomach and propelled her deeper into him.

"You," she gasped. "You. Need you. Now."

His lips were on her breast. He sucked a nipple hard and a moan ripped out of her.

"Now," he agreed.

Her legs parted as his weight settled over her. "So beautiful." His words a whisper of wonder.

Abby's heavy eyelids struggled to open. When they did, it was impossible to breath. He was there. In the moment with her. There was nothing else. Only Flynn. Making her desperate. He pressed into her. Her hands flew to his arms. Her nails dug in. Her back arched.

"Abby," he groaned.

Every inch of her skin was on fire. She couldn't think. All she could do was feel as he filled her. His weight heavy against her. His strength holding her in place. She wanted to taste, to smell, to feel. She wanted to lose herself in Flynn. She wrapped her arms around his shoulders, buried her face in his neck and licked his salty skin.

"Damn it, Abby, I can't hold back when you do that."

"Don't." She nipped his corded neck. So much strength. Just for her. "Don't hold back."

He cursed. His forehead touched hers. A pause. A sigh. His hips began to move. Propelling into her. Each stroke taking her higher, making reality spin. There was nothing to do but hold on to him.

"Yes." She felt it build. A storm inside of her.

"Let go, love. Let me see you."

Suddenly she fell back into the bed, her hands beside her head. No more strength to hold on. All she could do was feel. And she felt every delicious inch of him as he moved inside her. Her body clenched. Her breath stopped. She heard the roaring in her veins. Felt his skin burning hers. Felt herself spiral upwards. Gasping. Moaning. Straining towards him. Claiming him as her own.

Flynn roared. His body clenched tight above her. And as she floated back to earth, his weight fell over her. His arms wrapped her tight and he held her close, still joined with her. She felt muscles pulse and clench. She heard pants and gasps as the world began to materialise again.

A tight fist of reality formed in her chest. A feeling she couldn't quite explain, let alone understand. It was relief at moving on, at feeling alive. At the same time, it was deep grief over letting go. And to her shame, she started to sob. Not gentle tears, but great, rasping sobs.

Flynn rolled them, wrapping her tight at his side, one arm curled around her waist. The other held the back of her head, pressing her into his chest. He nuzzled her hair and kissed her head.

"It's okay, Abby love." His voice was soothing. "It's okay. I understand."

Abby couldn't stop her tears as she inched closer to him. She wanted to curl up inside him. Protected. Hidden.

"It's okay." His hands gently stroked her back.

It wasn't okay. She didn't even understand it herself. "It isn't you. It isn't what we did." She had to force the words past sobs. She had to reassure him.

"I know." He kissed her hair again as he squeezed her tight. "It's just the first time since your husband. It's change. It's loss. It's letting yourself live. I get it. I'm here. Don't worry, Abby, I'm here."

She buried her face in his chest and let the tears flow. Safe in the cocoon of Flynn's warm embrace. Soothed by his musky scent. Listening to his heartbeat under her cheek.

Safe to grieve.

Safe to start again.

Safe with Flynn.

CHAPTER 28

"Okay, so we lost, but good things can come from it—negative and positive." Glenn Hoddle, former England manager

"Muma, Muma, wake up! The circus is here!"

"What the hell?" Flynn mumbled into the pillow.

Abby shot upright in bed, throwing off Flynn's arm, which was wrapped tight around her waist holding her down like an anchor.

"Muma, the door is stuck. Open the door."

There was thumping at the door and the full horror of the situation slammed into Abby. She was in bed. Naked. With Flynn. And Katy was at the door.

"Get up," she snapped at the man who was sprawled on his stomach beside her. He was on the edge, one foot and one arm dangling to the floor.

"Muma! Open the door!" There was more pounding.

"Make it stop," Flynn grumbled.

"Get up, right now." Abby put her hands on Flynn's side

and pushed. Hard. There was a grunt, some cursing and a loud thud as he tumbled and hit the floor.

"What the hell?" Flynn shouted.

"Muma?" Katy shouted. "Are you okay?"

"I'm fine," Abby called. "I'll be out in a minute."

"What's going on, honey?" another voice said in the hallway—Jena.

"Muma's stuck in her bedroom and the circus is here," Katy said.

"I know, I saw it, that's why I came over." Jena made no sense at all.

"Why did you shove me out of bed?" Flynn complained as he stood up.

He stretched his arms above his head, showing off every inch of his lean, muscled frame. Flashes of the night before popped into her mind. Of crying in his arms, of mind-blowing sex, of him waking her later to make love to her slowly. A wave of need swept over her, making her freeze in place.

A gentle knock jarred her back to reality. "Abby, honey, you okay in there?" Jena sounded worried.

"Why is my cousin's wife in your house?" Flynn said.

"Flynn? Are you in there?" Matt boomed from the hallway.

Abby groaned as she stared up at Flynn.

"Why is Matt in your house?" He scratched his stomach.

"Where's Abby?" Victoria's voice snapped through the air. "Has she seen what her neighbour is doing? I knew his behaviour these past few days was an act."

Flynn shook his head in disbelief. "Did you even bother to lock the front door? Is the whole of Invertary in your house?"

"Damn it, Flynn, you are in there. I'm going to rip your head off," Matt said.

"Why's Flynn in Muma's room?" Katy said. "Were they having a sleepover?"

"They better not have been," Matt said.

"The footballer is in there? With Abby?" Victoria almost screeched.

"Calm down," Lawrence said. "I'm sure this all has a reasonable explanation. Why don't we go downstairs and make some tea while Abby gets ready."

Abby jumped up at the sound of yet one more person outside her bedroom door. She grabbed Flynn's jeans from the floor and thrust them at him. "Jump out the window," she said. She should have known better than to think anything she did could remain a secret in this town.

For a second he seemed too distracted by her swaying breasts to register the order. He reached for one and she batted his hand away with a growl. "Out. Out the window now. Jump and run for it. I'll tell them they were hearing things. This will all be okay."

He looked at her like she'd lost her mind. "We're on the second floor. Do you want me to trash what's left of my leg? There would be no running away if I jumped. There would just be writhing in agony."

"Then sit on the ledge until they're all gone. I'll get rid of them. Somehow. Once I do, you can come back in and leave through the front door."

"Sit on the ledge? Have you lost your mind? There isn't enough ledge to sit on. Look." He threw back the curtains to show her what he meant. "What the hell?" he bellowed. "What's with all the people at my place? What are those trucks doing there? Somebody get those morons out of there, they're scaring the donkeys!"

"Shh!" Abby held up her hands. "They'll hear you." She turned to the door. "It's just the TV," she called.

"You don't have a TV in your room," Jena called back.

"Radio?" Abby said.

Flynn pulled on his jeans. "Get dressed. I need to find out why there are trucks and strangers all over my place. That bloody weasel has been up to something. I'm going to wring his neck."

"I knew there was more going on between those two than neighbourly good manners," Victoria said.

"And what if there is?" Lawrence said. "They're adults. It's none of your business."

"This is just what Mother feared. Look at this mess. It's no environment for a child."

Abby wanted to rip her hair out.

"The child is fine," Flynn shouted. "The child is made of bloody Teflon. She wasn't in the room. If you lot hadn't broken into Abby's house, she wouldn't even have known I was here."

"I'm going to kill him," Matt shouted. "Take Katy downstairs, Jena. Lawrence, take Victoria. I'll deal with this. Couldn't keep it in his pants for one bloody week."

"Are they kissing in there?" Katy asked. "Do they have to get married now? I can't get a sister until Muma gets married. I told her it's okay if she marries Flynn. I can't think of anybody else for her to marry anyway."

Flynn stared at the door. "What the hell? I'm a last resort?"

"Come on," Jena said. "Let's go make breakfast. Your aunty Victoria looks like she could use a cup of tea." There was a pause. "Is it too early to add vodka?" There was silence. "Okay, no vodka. Let's go, kid."

There were protests as Jena led Katy downstairs.

"You too," Lawrence said. "You achieve nothing by standing guard outside Abby's bedroom door."

"What am I going to tell Mother?" Victoria sounded genuinely distressed.

"We'll talk about it downstairs," Lawrence said softly.

"Matt," Flynn called. "There's no way I'm coming out if you're waiting there to punch me."

"Damn straight I'm waiting here to hit you. Somebody needs to knock some sense into you. I knew the intervention was a waste of time. I should have just taken you to the gym and pummelled you until you understood things had to change."

"Oh yeah, I really want to come out of the room now." Flynn hunted around for his shirt while Abby pulled on underwear.

"There." She pointed to the shirt poking out from under the bed.

"Thanks, sugar." He shrugged it on.

"What am I going to do? I don't know how to fix this," Abby muttered as she pulled a plain navy dress from her closet.

"Don't worry, it'll be okay," Flynn said gently.

"How?" she screeched.

Flynn scanned the area around her.

"Stop looking for weapons. I'm not going to turn homicidal."

"I believe you." Although his tone made it clear he didn't.

"It's okay, Abby," Matt said. "I'll hit him for you."

"Shouldn't you be outside dealing with the trespassers setting up home on my property?"

There was a snort. "Absolutely, your highness. Watch me run off to do your bidding."

"Poor bloody excuse for a cop. I'm not coming out until you go downstairs." Flynn folded his arms and stared at the door. "Do you think I'm stupid enough to walk into a fist? I stopped falling for that crap when I was twelve. You never did fight fair, you big bastard."

"And you never grew up," Matt shouted. "Get out here."

"Oh, for goodness' sake." Abby pushed her way to the door. "Matt, get downstairs. We need to get out of this room to deal with things."

"Fine." Heavy footsteps faded away.

Abby stared up at Flynn. Her stomach was on spin cycle. He put his hands on her shoulders and pulled her against him. His heat soaked into her and calmed her slightly. He felt familiar now. He felt like he was hers. She blinked the thought away. It was just as insane as the million other thoughts rushing around in her head.

"It's going to be okay." Flynn kissed her hair. He gave her one last squeeze before reaching behind her to open the door. Abby frowned when he moved her out of the way. "In case he faked us out," he said.

"You're both children," Abby snapped.

Flynn turned the lock, opened the door and a fist hit him square on the jaw. Abby screamed.

"Bloody faker," Flynn shouted at his older cousin. Then he launched at him.

"Sissy boy," Matt shouted as he hit back.

Abby watched as the men fell to a tangle on the hall floor. They wrestled and grabbed, trying to get each other into a stranglehold. She blinked several times, unsure whether she was watching reality or a three-dimensional delusion brought on by an overstressed brain. As they tumbled away from her door, Abby stepped around them and headed down the stairs, leaving the idiots to duke it out on her landing.

With as much dignity as she could muster, Abby entered the kitchen. Four sets of eyes shot to her.

"Good morning." She gave them what she hoped was a calm smile.

Before she could say anything else, Jena had her by the arm.

"I'm just gonna take your mom into the living room for a

minute. Why don't you tell your aunt all about the circus?" Jena hauled her out of the room.

As soon as they were in the living room, with the door firmly closed behind them, Jena spun on Abby. "You slept with Flynn?"

"I can't think about that right now." Abby sat on the couch. "I'll schedule it for Tuesday."

As though reminding her there were other more pressing issues, loud music started in the direction of Flynn's place.

"What the hell?" Flynn shouted upstairs, which was followed by a loud thud.

"There are two grown men fighting in my house," Abby said. "My mother wants to take my daughter. A camera crew is hounding me. I'm trying to start a new business. My daughter wants me to marry someone, anyone, so she can have a father. I just had sex for the first time in four and a half years. And instead of it being a private affair, I wake up to half of Invertary outside my bedroom door."

"Yeah, when you put it like that, things don't sound so great." Jena gave her a sympathetic smile. "On the plus side, you had sex for the first time in four and a half years." She grinned. "So you were busted by your family. It's still a win. Go you!" She held up her hand for a high five.

Abby looked at the hand, looked at her friend's smiling face and burst out laughing.

The two women held on to each other as they laughed hard.

As Abby wiped tears from her face, gasping for air, she caught sight of the open doorway. Bruised and bloody, Matt and Flynn stood glaring at the women. The sight of the men set the two of them off again. As the women clung to each other, Katy pushed her way between the men.

"Are they hysterigiggle?" Katy asked Flynn.

"I think your mother may have lost her mind," Flynn said.

Katy shrugged. "That happens all the time. Want some Coco Pops? I need to talk to you about a sister. I've decided you can marry my Muma, but only if I get a sister. You have to promise me or the deal is off."

Katy grabbed Flynn's hand and dragged the scowling man towards the kitchen.

Matt pointed at Jena. "Five minutes to calm down," he ordered before disappearing.

"Does that work for him?" Abby asked through giggles.

"The ordering around thing?"

Abby nodded.

"No."

They both started laughing again.

CHAPTER 29

"He's got his legs back, of course, or his leg; he's always had one but now he's got two." Bobby Robson, former England manager

Flynn let Katy drag him out of the room.

"I can't talk right now, I need to go to my place and find out what's happening."

"Do you promise to talk later?"

"Aye."

She narrowed her eyes. "Say the words."

"I promise to talk to you later."

"You didn't cross your heart."

Flynn glared at her. "Cross my heart and hope to die, I promise I'll talk to you later about whatever crazy topic you're concocting in your tiny, evil mind. Good enough for you?"

"Okay," Katy said. "It isn't a crazy topic. I want to make a deal for a sister. You better talk to me later, Flynn. I won't forget."

"Kid, elephants have a better chance of forgetting than you do." He put up a hand to ward off more questions. "I don't have time. I need to go see what's happening outside."

"As though you don't already know," Victoria snapped from behind him.

"No," Flynn said with all the patience he could muster. It wasn't much. "I don't know what's going on."

"A leopard can't change its spots, Flynn Boyle. I suspect you're playing Abby while you pretend to reform. It would be entirely too easy for you to string her along while you carry on living the debauched life you normally lead."

Flynn counted to ten and told himself the woman was Abby's sister. And you had to make allowances for family. He frowned at Matt, who leaned beside the front door. You had to make allowances for *all* family members. He ran a hand through his hair.

"I don't have time to argue this with you. I've got people setting up equipment on my lawn. I have no idea who they are or what they're doing. There are two camera crews out there and I need to keep them away from Abby. If you want to help, that'd be great. If you don't, then stay out of my way."

Victoria's cheeks flushed red as she started to bluster. Lawrence put a hand on her shoulder.

"He's right," Lawrence said to Victoria before turning back to Flynn. "I can help. I don't work for Abby's mother anymore."

"Great, call Mitch Harris. He's an entertainment lawyer…"

"I know who he is," Lawrence said.

"Good. He's probably staying at the castle with Josh. Or in the hotel rooms above the pub. He's got to be somewhere. I know he's still in town. He dealt with this the last time the camera crew invaded Abby's privacy. If the two of you get together and build a legal wall around Abby and the kid, that would be great. Bill me." He turned to Victoria. "I know she's laughing right now, but it's hysteria. It could turn to tears at the snap of your fingers. This is a lot to cope with. Can you look after Abby while I deal with this? I know you aren't close, but…" He looked around, searching for the words. He felt a tug at his hand as Katy slipped her fingers into his.

"Don't worry, Flynn. I'll look after Muma while you sort out the circus." She gave him a wide-eyed smile meant to reassure him and he felt his chest clench.

He ruffled her hair, making her frown. "Thanks, kid."

"Want me to call Lake?" Matt said. "Get some extra muscle out here in case we need it to clear your place? If we wait for police reinforcement it could be hours. This isn't high priority, and they would have to come from Fort William."

"Lake's guys are great." He felt relief just thinking about backup. "Tell him to bill me. Can you get someone to come here, keep an eye on Abby's house too? I don't know what's happening, but better safe than sorry."

Matt nodded. He already had his phone to his ear. The noise outside grew louder. Cars revved. Music blared. Someone spoke over a sound system, testing it. Flynn clenched his jaw, worried about how terrified his animals would be. He hoped like hell the goat was eating her way right through the crowd—the mob deserved it.

"Let's go." Matt hung up. "Lake and the boys will be here soon."

"Right." Flynn crouched down to face Katy. "Watch your mum. Give her chocolate. Chocolate always helps women when they're upset. And don't let her do anything stupid."

"Okay," Katy said solemnly.

Flynn rolled his eyes. "What am I doing? You wouldn't know stupid if it bit you in the a—"

"Time to go." Matt hauled Flynn back to his feet.

"Wait." Victoria rushed forward. "You really do care about Abby, don't you?"

Flynn felt something shift within him. He looked at Katy, who was staring up at him with unwarranted faith in her eyes. "Aye, I really do."

"And this new leaf of yours, it isn't pretend?"

"No, it isn't a ruse. I'm trying really bloody hard here and it keeps getting screwed up."

Victoria stared at him for a moment before nodding.

"We need to go. More cars have arrived." Matt tugged Flynn away from Victoria and they headed out of the house.

The minute they set foot outside the door, a camera crew rushed forward, followed closely by the woman who accused him of fathering her child. Flynn cast a nervous glance back towards Abby's house, but saw someone had the presence of mind to shut the curtains.

"No comment," he said as a microphone was thrust in his face.

"Back off," Matt growled. As he was dressed in full police uniform, people did as they were told. "Who organised this?"

Flynn cocked an eyebrow at him. "You mean you actually believe it wasn't me?"

"I never said it was."

"You never said anything. You hit first. No questions asked."

"And I'll hit you again, once this is over. It's the least I can do for Abby. You can't screw around with her. She's a mother. She's serious about everything. She doesn't do casual anything. You crossed a line seducing her."

"What makes you think I seduced her?"

Matt shot him an angry glare. "Do you want me to hit you again? We'll deal with the Abby thing again later. Right now, we need to sort this mess."

"We need to find the weasel. He hates me and wants to

make his mark. This has got to be him."

"Got it."

They scanned the crowd. It was barely nine a.m. and already alcohol was flowing. There were cars parked everywhere. Vans near the road were being unloaded by tattooed men. A stage was being set up near the stream. People were tramping over everything. Strangers were coming out of his home. Flynn clenched his jaw at the sight.

"There." He pointed to the woman cowering beside his van. "That's Julia, the production assistant. She'll know what's going on."

They headed straight for her. People shouted out to Flynn, praising him for staging such an "epic party." Yeah, he was being set up, all right. Even though there were attempts to waylay them, they cut a straight line to Julia. Mainly because the crowd parted like the Red Sea for Matt's police uniform.

"What's going on, Julia?" Flynn said as soon as they were in front of her.

"I didn't know." She spoke to her shoes. Her voice so quiet he had to strain to hear it.

"What didn't you know?" He put a finger under her chin and tipped her head up to look at him.

"He called everyone. He told them you wanted to burn the town up. Show them how to live right." She leaned forward. "I think there are people with drugs in your motorhome."

Flynn clenched his jaw as he watched Matt morph into super cop.

"You find out the rest," Matt ordered. "I'll clear the van." He disappeared inside.

Drugs were the last thing Flynn needed to be associated with. He never touched the damn things, and he sure as hell didn't want them in his house.

"What else?" He worked to keep his focus on Julia instead of his rising anger. She was like one of his animals. The slightest scare could spook her into running.

Her eyes welled up. "He booked Royal Flush."

"Royal Flush?" The name rang a bell in the back of his mind, but he couldn't come up with anything solid. "I need more info, honey."

"They're the band that were arrested last year. Really anti-women. Nasty music. Nasty people." She pointed a shaky finger to the vans being unloaded. "He promised them plenty of publicity and said you'd pay double their appearance fee if they played today."

Flynn ground his teeth together so hard he was sure he'd need a dentist as soon as this was cleared up.

"Where's the weasel?" His voice was cold, harsh, angry.

"Weasel? You mean Brian?"

Flynn nodded tersely.

"There." She pointed to the fence beside a swath of parked cars. The man was on the phone and he looked smug. Flynn took a step towards him.

Small fingers curved around his arm. Julia held him tight. Her eyes were wide.

"Remember, everything you do will be filmed. Everything. Think carefully. He wants you to blow. He wants to ruin you on film. Don't play into his hands." She was shaking by the time she stopped talking. Her hand dropped from his arm and she wrapped her arms around herself.

The woman was right. He couldn't give the weasel what he wanted. He needed to think. He needed a plan. And he needed to get Julia out of the line of fire.

"Do me a favour," he said. "Take the donkeys and the goat to Abby's place. Tie them up on the other side of the house. Then I need you to come back with two cardboard boxes. There's a duck in the van. She needs to be moved to Abby's."

He ran a hand through his hair. "And, um, there are three baby hedgehogs in the compartment under the van. I want them safe too."

The woman stared at him for a minute. She was still shaking, but now she looked dumbfounded. "Duck? Hedgehogs?"

"Babies." He smiled at her. "Can you do this for me, honey?"

She cast an anxious glance in the weasel's direction. Flynn pursed his lips.

"I'll deal with him. You don't have to worry. Once the animals are safe away from here, you go into Abby's house and have her make you some tea. Okay?"

She nodded, wary but relieved.

"One more thing," Flynn said. "You'll want to start looking for another job. This one isn't good for you."

"I know." Her shoulders slumped further as she headed for the donkeys. The sight renewed Flynn's need to hit the weasel.

"Hey, hey, Boyle Boy," a voice called out.

Michael was heading towards him. Flynn clasped the man's hand and patted his shoulder.

"What's going on?" Michael's eyes were on the crowd. "I thought you were keeping a low profile. I thought that was why you sent the Ball Babes to me."

"I am. I was. The weasel is playing with me. He wants me to lose the plot on air and make his career for him."

"Hell." Michael toed the grass in front of him. "You didn't arrange this?"

"Nope." Flynn clenched his fists.

Michael went tense. "If I'd known, I wouldn't have come. This situation isn't good. It won't take much to set off the crowd. What can I do to help?"

Flynn patted him on the back. "Hang around. I'll let you

know. In the meantime, you could spread the word to the guys we trust. I don't know half this mob. Talk to the ones we do know. Tell them it's a setup. Matt's in the van. The asshole brought drugs into my house."

Michael shook his head. "I've got your back." He headed off to a cluster of players from his old team.

Flynn watched the crowd. He didn't like the atmosphere. It simmered with violence. Matt came out of the van a minute later.

"I've cuffed them. I had to call for a pickup. The van will take time to get here from Fort William." He let out a growl. "This is why we need another officer here. I keep putting in requests. This town sees too much trouble for one man to deal with. I can't keep pulling in civilians."

"Even if they are ex-special forces?" Like most of Lake Benson's security team.

"Aye." Matt looked out over the crowd. "How many of them do you know?"

"About a quarter."

"Damn."

Flynn folded his arms. He noticed a camera pointed in his direction and angled his body so they couldn't film his conversation with his cousin. "I spoke to Julia. The weasel wants me to blow my top. This event is staged to make me lose it on tape. The band were chosen specially. They've already been arrested this year. I've never heard of them. Apparently their thing is misogyny."

Matt cocked his eyebrow. "With your reputation, no one would believe you'd book that band."

"Aye, I love women. I have the tabloid reports to prove it."

"I don't like the look of the guys setting up the band."

Flynn followed his gaze. Tattoos, leather, patches and skinheads.

"This whole thing is primed to blow."

Julia came up to them. "Can I go into the van?" she asked Matt.

"Why?" He narrowed his eyes.

"Relax," Flynn said. "I want her to get the duck to safety."

Matt stared at him for a minute. "The duck?"

"Hey, don't judge me. You wanted me to be a good guy. Good guys are nice to animals. The duck is nursing a broken wing. She doesn't need the stress of this situation. Julia's going to take her over to Abby's for me."

"Fine." Matt sighed and waved Julia on. "Get the bloody duck."

She scurried away.

"She's in the wrong business," Flynn said.

"No kidding." Matt kept his eyes on the crowd. "Got any ideas?"

"I'm worried if we start to strong-arm people out of here, things will blow. We need to defuse the situation. We need to do something that won't cause violence. I especially don't want to do anything to give the weasel what he wants. We need to turn the crowd around, make them leave on their own."

In the distance, Flynn spotted Lake's car arrive. Whatever they did, they had to do it soon, before Lake and his muscle inadvertently started a riot. What he needed was a miracle.

A miracle?

Flynn grinned slowly. He turned to his cousin, pleased to see the black eye he'd given him was filling out nicely. "I have an idea."

Matt was suspicious. "Is this like the ideas you used to have when we were teenagers?"

"Better. Hold the fort with Lake. I need to make some calls. I know exactly how to defuse this bomb."

CHAPTER 30

"Chile have three options—they could win or they could lose. It's up to them, the tide is in their court now."
Ron Atkinson, former England manager

"You have a decision to make, Vicki," Lawrence said softly as they sat side by side in the window nook in the kitchen. "You need to decide what you're going to tell your mother. Are you going to stand for Abby, or against her? Time is running out."

Katy was playing on the floor in front of them. It was a complicated game involving lots of marbles, each of which she'd named.

"I know," Victoria said.

Lawrence reached out and covered her hand with his. Victoria jerked, looked around to see if anyone was watching and tried to move away from him.

"Nobody's here. You can let me hold your hand."

"What if someone comes in?"

"I doubt anyone would be shocked at this timid display of public affection, but I promise to move away as soon as the door opens."

She relaxed slightly and he almost smiled. His Vicki would never be good at touching in public.

"Mitch is working on the TV angle," he said, getting back to the most pressing issue. "But no matter what we do, some of the footage being shot out there is going to make it onto the internet and possibly the news. Your mother will know about this by the end of the day."

Victoria didn't say anything. She just stared at Katy with sad eyes. His heart broke for her, this woman who kept everything tightly locked behind a polite veneer.

"You know your mother is wrong. She can't take Katy away from Abby. The child is well loved. I suspect even Flynn loves the girl. He certainly made it clear this morning that he would do whatever he could to shield them from harm."

"He brings the harm," Victoria said, but there was no malice in the words.

"He's trying to change. Everyone deserves a second chance, don't they? He made stupid mistakes in the past and now he's trying to make it right."

"What if it isn't possible to make it right? What if the consequences of some decisions can't be rectified?"

He wanted to weep for her. She wasn't talking about Flynn, that much was clear. He squeezed her hand, knowing she wouldn't take kindly to being wrapped in his arms. Not here, where someone could see.

"There's always that risk. Sometimes we can never get past the consequences of our foolish pasts. Sometimes people can't forgive us for the decisions we make."

To his surprise, her grip tightened on his fingers.

"I know you're scared," he said. "All I can tell you is I'm

here for you. You can't let your mother keep pushing you into doing things you know are wrong. You have a way out now. Choose it. Choose me. Choose getting to know your sister and your niece. Choose starting afresh and being the person you were meant to be."

She gave a shallow laugh. "You make it sound so easy."

"I know it isn't. But you have a job with me. You'll have a place to live, with me, if you want it. You just have to reach out and take it."

"What if you hate me too, once you find out my secrets?"

"What if you hate me once you find out mine?"

She jerked back to look him in the eyes. "I don't see how that's possible."

"And there's your answer. It comes down to trust. You have to take a chance on believing the other person will understand. It's up to you whether you have the courage to try." Her eyes welled with tears, but none fell. "You can't compound past mistakes by letting your mother make another one. She's wrong to go after Katy. You know it. And you can't allow it, darling."

"Darling?" She gave him a shy smile.

"Thought I'd try it on, see how it feels."

"What's the conclusion?"

"I like it." He gave in to his need and kissed her softly. "I like you."

They sat quietly holding hands for a long time. The soft chatter from Katy as she played was relaxing. Lawrence smiled down at the child. This was what he'd missed out on. He'd missed out on family. But if he was lucky, maybe this thing he felt with Victoria would turn into something more and he'd be allowed to become a part of her family. And by her family, he didn't mean her mother and brother. He meant what she'd found here. A home for her heart in the Highlands—if she was brave enough to take a chance on it.

"She looks so much like her mother did at the same age." Victoria's eyes were on Katy. "Abby was full of life, always dancing and singing. She was constantly in trouble with Mother for her inappropriate behaviour. She had the courage to be herself. And later she had the courage to break free. Such tremendous spirit. It's irrepressible. Katy has it too, doesn't she?"

"Yes." Lawrence smiled.

"Even now, with everything Abby's been through, everything that's happening, she's standing strong." She looked up at Lawrence. "I admire her so much."

His heart clenched. "Then fight for her, not against her."

"Yes. You're right." Victoria's eyes returned to Katy. "I just need a little bit more time."

"Time's running out. This will hit the news tonight. If you're lucky, your mother won't hear about it until tomorrow."

"Then I'll take the few hours I have until she finds out."

"Vicki…"

"Please, Lawrence." She looked up at him. "I know what I have to do. Just not yet. I'm not ready yet. I need a bit more time to become stronger."

"Okay, but remember this—you aren't facing the future alone. I'll be there."

"You are such a wonderful surprise," Victoria said. "I never thought someone would be with me the way you are. I never thought I'd be given this gift."

"It goes two ways. I see something wonderful in you. Something just for me."

"Foolish man. I'm no prize."

"Oh, sweet Vicki, how delightfully wrong you are."

To his utter shock, she rested her head on his shoulder, a smile curling her lips. And in that moment, Lawrence wondered at the blessing he'd received. A second chance at life, in this woman who had yet to learn how to live.

But she would learn. They'd do it together. They'd help each other.

"IT'S SORTED," Flynn announced as he limped back around the van to where Matt was talking to Lake.

There were several men standing around. All of whom worked for Lake's security firm. He recognised most of them from around town and knew they were all ex-military. Including his cousin Claire's fiancé, Grunt, who was currently frowning his censure at Flynn. It made him want to shout, *It wasn't me!* He ignored the impulse for immaturity and instead joined the huddle with Lake and Matt.

"Police reinforcement is forty minutes away," Matt said.

"People are getting edgy." Lake's eyes were ice, trained on the crowd and missing nothing. The tall Englishman was wearing a black T-shirt over jeans; his arms were folded, muscles bulging. His blonde hair was military short. His blue eyes narrowed.

Flynn knew very little about Lake's background except he was ex-SAS, a security specialist and a scary dude.

The band started a sound check behind them.

"We clearing the place out?" Lake asked.

"We're waiting. Backup is coming in about five minutes."

Matt cocked an eyebrow at him. "What backup? As soon as those guys start playing, they're going to wind up the folk who are already halfway to tanked, and the weasel producer is walking through the crowd stirring things."

Flynn followed Matt's gaze to see the gleeful expression on Brian's face as he "interviewed" some of the guys with scarier tattoos. It was obvious from the angry reactions his questions were designed to antagonise.

"Spill," Lake ordered. "What's the plan?"

Flynn heard a familiar car engine sputtering along and pointed. "That's the plan."

The men turned as one to see a station wagon coming down the drive. It was followed by several sensible cars and two people carriers. The station wagon swerved off the road and squeezed through a gap in the fence someone had taken down earlier to make space for parking. It drove at about two miles per hour straight through the crowd, aiming for the stage and blasting its horn to warn people to move out of the way.

Matt started to laugh. Lake's lip twitched in his version of hysteria.

"You called the vicar?" Matt said. "I take it back. You do have a brain."

"Thanks."

"I'll get the boys to position themselves beside the band and their roadies. From the looks of it, if there's trouble it will start there." Lake waved his hand at his men. They nodded, seeming to know by telepathy exactly what their boss wanted. Flynn was impressed. It was one scary talent.

"Is that the knitting group?" Matt asked with a grin.

"Yep."

Matt patted him on the back. Flynn wasn't ready to celebrate just yet. Things weren't anywhere near under control.

"Excuse me, gentlemen," he told them. "I'm the MC." He headed for the stage, nodding and smiling as he went.

By the time Flynn got there, the local vicar was already standing on the platform, glaring at people. He wasn't angry —that was just his face. Flynn smiled at the lead singer of the band.

"Glad you could make it," he told the guy. "When I heard you lot were turning over a new leaf and looking for some good publicity, I was happy to help out. One reformed bad boy to another."

The tattooed skinhead scowled. "What the fuck are you talking about?"

"Language," snapped the vicar, giving the guy his own scowl.

The look of confusion on the singer's face was priceless.

"My producer, Brian—he's the guy over there." Flynn pointed at the weasel and waved. Brian looked confused. Good. Scared would be better, but hopefully that would come later. "He set this up. He said after last year's arrest you were having trouble. I believe in second chances, so when the vicar here organised this rally, I suggested you guys. I'm grateful you could make it. Did Brian mention you'd need to tone down your lyrics? Wouldn't help the cause if we offended the local women's group." Flynn pointed to the mass of middle-aged women approaching the stage.

The singer's jaw dropped as Flynn's aunty Heather waved at him.

The women of Knit or Die, plus quite a few others from the church who'd been roped in, filed onto the stage. Each of them held a small bucket, and they were wearing matching pink shirts with *Knit or Die* in bold over their chests. They were also giggling like schoolgirls.

"What the fuck?" the singer said again.

The octogenarian vicar reached up and smacked the guy on the back of the head. "God is listening, boy. Have some respect."

The singer actually seemed a little ashamed. Flynn grinned at him before tapping the microphone. He looked out over the crowd, noticing Lake's men and his ex-football team members were dispersed throughout, ready to quell any trouble before it broke out.

"Hello, everybody," Flynn called. "Thanks for coming out

today. This event means a lot to me, and I can't tell you how happy I am to see you here."

The crowd roared. He spotted Matt laughing, and ignored him.

"I think there might have been a bit of a mix-up in the information you got along with your invite," Flynn said. "It looks like some of you are here ready to party hard." Another roar. "And that's great. You can get to it, as soon as you've supported the cause." There were murmurs of confusion. "Before I give the mic over to Reverend Morrison, I want to thank the boys of Royal Flush for coming out at such short notice. The church and I really appreciate the time you're giving up for this worthy cause.

"I realise that, like me, you boys have had some bad press. Maybe made some decisions resulting in fallout you weren't expecting. Well, that's all behind us here. Today we're starting again. We're turning over a new leaf. United in helping the church of Invertary get back on its feet. Reverend Morrison is a great believer in second chances. That's why this cause is a perfect fit. The church building needs a second chance at life too. And with your donations today, they'll be one step closer to achieving that goal. Thank you all for coming. The church ladies will be here later on with cake and tea. In the meantime, let's show this town how fundraising is done! Reverend, the microphone is yours."

Flynn stood beside the lead singer of the band while the vicar grabbed the mic. Shock rippled through the crowd like a Mexican wave at a football match. The sight made Flynn want to grin, but he didn't. He kept a look of serene conviction on his face and reminded himself the old bugger talking had conned him out of a fortune for his appearance at this fundraiser.

"The church needs a new roof," the vicar barked. "And we need new carpet. I'm told the chairs are so old they've retained the bum shapes of some of the parishioners, which makes them uncomfortable when other people use them, so new chairs would be good. Our sound system is rubbish. We need a new one. I put it on the list, but the church committee took it off. Some of them like that they can't hear my sermons. Oh, aye, and we need a new organ." He glared around the crowd. "For you young folk who don't turn up at church, an organ is like a piano—only louder. It isn't a body part."

Some people stared at the minister open-mouthed, while others chatted in confusion. No one quite knew what to do.

"Now, as the ladies move through the crowd with their buckets, make sure you give generously. And smile while you do it. The Lord loves a cheerful giver," the vicar said with a growl and a frown. "I'd like everyone here to know that all donations to the church refurbishment fund come with a ten percent discount on any weddings held in the building." He pointed at a couple who were locked at the lips, the guy with his hand in the back of the girl's shorts. "You two," he shouted. "Save it for your wedding night."

Matt's laughter could be heard in the ensuing stunned silence.

"Now," the vicar continued. "I know you young folk expect more than one act at a gig." He turned to the singer. "That's the right word, son, isn't it?"

The singer just stared at him. The minister rolled his eyes and muttered something about a mind ruined by drugs. He turned back to the microphone.

"We brought along an opening act to warm you up for the main event. I want you all to give a warm welcome to our very own church a cappella group. They're going to sing a medley of popular hymns while the women collect your money. Thanks again for coming out. And thanks to Flynn for letting us use his land."

He pointed at three women who stood behind the Knit or Die group. Flynn almost choked when he spotted one of them was Morag McKay, owner of the town's only bakery and leader of the local morality society—a group made up of Morag and her two best friends picketing anyone they disapproved of. Those friends were on the stage with her now. The women wore matching polyester coats in shades of blue. Their grey heads were permed with tight curls in the fake, no-movement look some old women thought was the height of fashion. They adjusted the microphone as the crowd fell into stunned silence. As one, they started a harmonised rendition of "The Old Rugged Cross."

"Is this a joke?" the singer said to Flynn. "Is there a hidden camera somewhere? Are we being Punk'd?"

"Sorry, mate, this is real. I thought you knew. I thought we were on the same wavelength here."

"No way in hell is this happening." The guy looked like he was about to explode. His neck turned beetroot red.

Flynn faked confusion. "I thought you wanted to change your rep? Brian Flannigan insisted you needed a gig like this. He was the one who called you. There he is, over there." Flynn pointed at the weasel again, before giving him a cheery wave.

The weasel looked ready to spit his dummy out the pram.

The women started singing something about the joy of the Lord—without cracking a smile between them. Meanwhile, the women of Knit or Die were shaking buckets under the noses of the crowd.

"I'm not playing," the singer said.

"But you're the main event. We need you." Flynn hoped he sounded sincere. "You'll be on TV."

"We don't want airtime if we need to share it with them. Our rep will be trashed." He cocked a thumb at Morag and her friends. "We're outta here." He unhooked his guitar strap from his neck and nodded to his band. The looks of disgust were priceless. "We still get paid, right?"

"I'll make sure Brian pays you every penny you're owed. It's the least he can do."

With growls and cursing, the men started packing equipment back into the vans. In the distance, Flynn spotted cars sneaking away as the crowd thinned. By the time Morag had finished her set of classic hymns, the only people in the field were his football mates, the women from Knit or Die and the church, the vicar and Lake's boys.

Flynn sat perched on the edge of the stage.

"I'm impressed," Lake said as he came up to him. "Next time I need a crowd cleared, I'll give you a call."

"Don't call me. Call the vicar."

Lake actually grinned outright. Such a rare occurrence that Flynn checked the sky for an eclipse.

"Did you tell someone to watch Abby's house?"

"Ryan."

Flynn narrowed his eyes. Ryan was as big a player as he was. "You told him he was just watching, right? Not flirting."

Lake shook his head as his lips twitched, his yearly smile obviously over. "You are so going down."

Flynn frowned. "What are you talking about?"

Lake patted him on the back. "Remember my business when you're booking security for the wedding. I'll give you a discount." He wandered off, leaving Flynn to scowl after him.

"We made a fortune for the church." Flynn's aunty Heather bounced over. Her grin was sparkling and it eased something in Flynn's chest to see it. Eight months ago he'd watched her face crumple when she'd buried her husband, and Flynn had wondered if he'd ever see her smile again.

"Don't forget your donation," the vicar ordered Flynn from his chair by the stage. He was eating carrot cake and drinking tea.

"You'll get your money, old man."

"This is the best fundraiser we've had since Josh put on a concert for the town." Heather grinned widely. "You and Josh should get together for the next fundraiser. Imagine the money you'd raise. I'll talk to your mother and we'll set it up. The town needs a new youth centre. I bet we could raise enough for one."

"I had nothing to do with the money pouring in," Flynn said. "People were paying to shut Morag up."

"Forget about a youth centre. We're sorting the church first, woman," the vicar snapped. "I need a new armchair in the vestry. The one I've got has a stray spring that digs into my back. A man can't focus on his prayers when he's in agony."

"You mean you can't nap in the chair, more like," Heather said.

The vicar ignored her while he polished off his cake.

"Thanks for helping out, Aunty Heather," Flynn said.

"That's what family is for." She patted his hand. "If your mum wasn't running errands in Fort William she would have been here too. You did a good thing here. I'm proud of you."

Her words produced warm fuzzies in him he wasn't used to feeling. "It's not enough, though, is it?" He nodded towards the two camera crews and the woman with a baby on her hip. "We're still going to be on TV. Abby will still get hit with the fallout."

"It's not your fault," Heather said.

"Aye," Flynn said. "It is. I get it now."

"You're a good boy, Flynn Boyle. You're trying hard and I'm proud of you. We all are." Heather gave him a quick hug before trotting off to shake her bucket with the other women. The group were toasting their success as extortionists with cake and tea.

"Don't get discouraged," the vicar snapped at Flynn. "Abby needs someone in her corner."

"Maybe I'm not the right guy for the job."

"Ha! Of course you aren't. But you're the one she wants."

"Thanks. Did you learn this encouragement technique in vicar school?"

"Vicar school?" The minister threw back his head and laughed. "Young people know bugger all." He shuffled over to the table with the cakes, lifted a plate with an unsliced chocolate cake and took it to his car.

Flynn smiled at the sight of his friends and family. People who'd come through for him. He should probably hang around and socialise. But he didn't want to. There was only one place he wanted to be.

With a nod at his teammates, he headed towards Abby's house.

CHAPTER 31

"Until we're out of the Champions League, we're still in it." Bobby Robson, former Newcastle manager

Brian wasn't sure how Flynn had pulled it off, but the event he'd staged fizzled out like the Alka-Seltzer he needed for his stomach. Even the band, with its reputation for destruction, left without damaging a thing. There should have been a fight. A drunken showdown or two. At least one shot of Flynn losing his cool. Instead, he had hours filled with women singing dirge after dirge and speeches by a minister who needed a personality transplant.

"You promised me this would be good for my career." Peaches pouted beside him.

The woman was an abomination. She used her kid as an accessory. She freaking matched the boy to her dresses. Right now they were both sporting bling-embellished denim. He vaguely wondered who the father of the baby was. He wondered if she even knew. He expected she didn't care either way. Poor little bastard. If the woman got even a whiff of fame, he'd be left in the dust.

"Brian," she whined. "You promised, and this isn't working out. I can't get any time alone with Flynn. He won't even look at Georgie." She held out her baby in case there was any doubt who Georgie was. "I need to get a DNA test to get a headline. It doesn't matter if it's negative; the test will still make the news." She pushed her collagen-enhanced lips out even further. "You need to give me the money for a test. My production people won't pay for one. They said Flynn flattened the last girl who told him he'd knocked her up. They don't want to risk losing money." She ran a talon down his bicep. Her false lashes batted. "They don't see how important it is, but you do. Don't you, Brian?"

He shook her off. "We don't have the budget for one either. You were supposed to distract him with your charms, make him forget about playing nice."

She looked down at her ample cleavage. "I did use my charms. I think he's gay. Are you sure all these women he boinks aren't a cover?"

"I'm sure." Brian watched as Flynn hobbled back to his girlfriend's house. Fury coursed through him. He would *not* be bested by an idiot like Flynn Boyle. He signalled to his cameraman.

When the man sauntered over, Brian glared at him. "Did we get anything of use at all today?"

"Depends what you were hoping for," the guy said. "We mainly got what you saw. Church fundraiser. Grumpy-arsed band."

Brian clenched his teeth. "What about the other crew. They get anything useful?"

The guy shrugged. "They got Flynn and the chick making out Hallmark style at her house last night. It isn't much."

Brian grinned as his world righted itself. "Get the footage. Cue it. I want to see it all."

"There's nothing in it. They just get all mushy, then she invites him in for coffee, if you get what I mean."

"Go get the footage ready." Brian stared the man down.

With another shrug, the cameraman wandered off.

"Is this good?" Peaches asked. "Will it help get us more airtime? Should I put it on my Instagram account?"

"Yeah." Brian grinned as he dialled a number in London. "Put it wherever you like. Make sure to mention the father of your baby won't deal with you because he's too busy screwing his neighbour."

Her frown was calculating. "I can do that."

Brian turned away from her as the person on the other end of the line answered.

"I'd like to speak with Lord Montgomery-Clark. I have information his mother would very much like to get her hands on. It concerns her daughter Abby and her relationship with Flynn Boyle."

A moment later, the lord himself came on the line.

"I thought you'd like to know," Brian said, "that Victoria is keeping things from you. Things that could bring a lot of bad publicity your way."

The outraged bluster demanding details made Brian's heart sing.

CHAPTER 32

*"If you're in the penalty area and don't know what to do with the
ball, put it in the net and we'll discuss the options later."*
Bob Paisley, former Liverpool manager

It was the calm before the storm.

And the storm was coming. Abby knew it deep in her
bones. Flynn might have headed off trouble at his place, but
the event had still attracted too much attention. It was only a
matter of time before her mother stepped up her attack. And
Abby didn't know how to prepare for it. As she sat on the top
steps at the back of her house looking out into the darkness,
she heard the familiar lopsided tread on the floor behind her.
A throw blanket covered her shoulders and she smiled up at
Flynn.

"Better be careful. You keep doing thoughtful things for
people and you'll blow your reputation as a narcissistic
child."

"Aye, that would be tragic." He lowered himself to sit

behind her. He slid a leg either side of her and wrapped an arm around her shoulders to pull her back against his chest.

Abby was snug in his embrace, warm against the chill night air. It felt like a scarily normal place to be.

Flynn rested his chin on her shoulder. "Everyone's gone home."

She'd noticed the last car leave, followed closely by the police van from Fort William. Jena had told her about the people shooting up in Flynn's home—just one more violation to process.

"What did your sister say? Does she plan to advise your mother to file for custody?"

Abby shrugged. "I don't know. She didn't tell me. She was acting strangely." Abby paused as she thought about earlier when she'd walked Lawrence and Victoria to their car. "She put her fingers to my cheek."

Flynn stiffened. "She hit you?"

"No, I think it was a caress. Her version of a hug. She didn't say anything, though."

Flynn relaxed again. "Maybe it was her way of apologising for throwing you under a bus with your mother."

"I don't know what it was." She stared out into the darkness as Flynn held her close. "I know this sounds weird, but it kind of felt like an apology."

They sat silently, soaking each other in, letting their minds order themselves in the peace of the night.

"Mitch and Lawrence couldn't stop the TV production companies using the footage from today." He sighed heavily. "It's my fault. I signed a stupid contract. I didn't think."

"To be fair, your agent and lawyer railroaded you into a deal that was lucrative for them. You were out of your mind on pain meds when you signed the contract. So it isn't entirely your fault. Not this time, anyway."

Flynn twisted to look down at her. "How do you know about this stuff?"

"Matt and Mitch. They did some digging and were talking about it. I was making tea. People always assume the folk making tea are invisible. Well, except for the Montgomery-Clarks. We were raised to remember servants had ears and weren't to be trusted."

"Servants, huh?"

"It sounds great, but trust me, it isn't. Most people only think about the fact they don't have to cook, or fetch their own dry cleaning, or tidy their bathrooms. They forget there are always people watching, listening, waiting. It's impossible to ever completely relax. You're always on guard."

"I can see the pitfalls. No running around the house naked when the feeling strikes."

She laughed. "Not unless you want to pay the medical bills when the staff have heart attacks."

"We had a servant too," Flynn said, but she could hear the teasing in his voice. "She did all the cooking, cleaning and fetching. Was really efficient until she deemed us old enough to do it ourselves."

"Ah, the joys of motherhood." Abby smiled wryly. "I know them well."

Flynn nuzzled the side of her head, making her snuggle into him. "You know, you're doing good as a mother. With the kid, I mean. She isn't as annoying as she could be."

Abby couldn't stop her laughter. "High praise, thank you."

"Okay," Flynn grumbled. "That came out wrong. She's okay, you know. She's kind of growing on me. She's pretty funny and more than a little evil. We'd get on great if she wasn't so obsessed with painting the Premier League pink."

"You're peas in a pod." Abby shook her head with amusement. "You share the same mental age and know exactly what buttons to push to wind each other up. It's quite entertaining to watch. I'm never quite sure who'll come out on top."

"I will, Abby. You can count on it. There's no way I'm letting a five-year-old get the better of me." Flynn's outrage made Abby chuckle.

"Be sure to tell her when she wakes up."

Flynn ran his fingers along Abby's arms in an absent-minded caress. "Katy asked me if I was staying the night again tonight."

Abby heard the question in his voice. She bit her lip as she thought it over. The cat was already out of the bag where Flynn was concerned. Really, there was nothing else they could do to make matters worse in her mother's eyes. But did she want him to stay? Did she want him in her bed? The answer was a no-brainer. Ill-advised or not, she definitely wanted Flynn in her bed.

"Two nights? Are you sure you can cope with such a commitment? I thought this was a casual fling."

"Do you have any idea how many people have told me you don't do casual? Even if they hadn't, I would have figured it out for myself."

Her heart tried to climb out of her throat. "So, this isn't casual?"

"Abby love, this is something I can't define. It isn't like anything I've experienced. I don't know what's going on here. I don't know where this is heading." He shifted her until she sat sideways in his arms, her legs over his thigh, her back resting on his other thigh. "All I know is I don't want to stop. I don't want to go home alone. I want to spend the night with you in my arms. I want to touch you and taste you and breathe you in. And in the morning, I want to listen to you and the terrorist argue about something stupid over break-fast. I don't know where we'll be tomorrow, or next week or a year from now. I do know I want to be around you all day long, just so I can touch you when I want. And so I can catch those secret smiles you flash at me when you think no one is looking."

With his words, he cracked her chest wide open and made a place for himself right beside her heart.

"So, this definitely isn't casual, then."

"Not for me." He ran a finger lightly across her cheek, over her jaw and down her throat. "Not for you, either. But I can't give you any guarantees on the future. I don't know what it will bring. You might wake up tomorrow and decide I'm not worth the effort." He grinned. "Although I plan to make myself so invaluable in bed you wouldn't dare."

"Invaluable, huh?" Her eyes went to his full lips.

"Totally." He flashed his sexy smile, which undermined her thought process. "I have skills you haven't experienced yet. You've barely touched the tip of this iceberg."

"Mmm." Her eyes were still locked on his mouth.

Flynn's smile remained in place as he trailed his hand slowly across her collarbone and under the blanket to skim her breast. Her breath caught as his hand tested the weight. His thumb stroked the tight peak of her nipple through her dress. Abby felt the world fade away. She nuzzled the crook of his neck, breathing him in. How could he do this to her so easily? Each time he touch her, it made her step through a door to another place. A magical place. Where only Flynn existed.

"Give me your lips, sugar. I need to taste you." His voice was rough and deep. Pure sin to her ears.

She peeked up at him through thick lashes as she angled her face towards him.

"Beautiful." With reverence, his head bent and his lips claimed hers.

. . .

Touching Abby, kissing Abby, made Flynn want to beat his chest and roar. He wanted every touch on her skin to turn into a brand, letting the world know she was his. An overwhelming need to imprint himself on her soul beat at his mind. A relentless drum. Insistent he claim her. Own her. Keep her. Every time she melted into him, he became drunk on the power to make her giddy. It was addictive. She was addictive. As he held her close, felt her respond—he knew he would never get enough of her.

A cool breeze teased hot skin as Flynn deepened the kiss. She tasted like lemonade and warm summer days. She tasted like Abby. He clasped her tight against him, but it wasn't close enough. He felt he'd never get close enough to Abby, but he desperately wanted to spend a lifetime trying.

"Come with me." It was a primitive demand.

She blinked, her movements languid, her gaze hot with need. Flynn nipped her bottom lip then soothed the bite with his tongue. Everything about her was summer for him. The heat of her skin, the heady scent of florals, the taste of relaxing in the sun.

It took great self-control to stop kissing her long enough to help her stand. She grasped his hand tight and headed for the door to the kitchen.

"No," he said. "Over here."

"We're not going to bed?" Her disappointment was sweet.

"Something better." He tugged her towards the old wooden swing seat tucked under the porch eves.

Flynn sat in the middle of the swing, his feet firmly on the deck, keeping the seat steady. Abby moved to sit beside him. His hands grasped her waist to stop her.

"Take your underwear off and straddle me."

She gasped. Her eyes darkened. "Flynn? You can't mean…" She looked around, into the darkness. The sounds of the night made the moment seem even more intimate.

"We're alone. Don't worry. Even if someone was here, they wouldn't see anything." He stared into her wide, expressive eyes. "Trust me."

She blinked several times. He watched as her pulse fluttered at the base of her throat. Slowly, she pulled her hands out of his and reached up under the full skirt of her dress. Flynn stopped breathing. Abby's eyes never left his as she removed her white lace panties. In the muted colours of night, he couldn't see her darkened cheeks, but he knew they were there.

"Come here, Abby love." He reached out for her, and without any hesitation she climbed onto his lap.

Her knees sat snug either side of his hips. Flynn wrapped one arm around her waist, and the other he wove into her hair, clenching it tightly as he angled her mouth towards his. The stiff set of her back melted at once. She wrapped her arms around his shoulders and pressed into him.

Flynn let the swing sway as he trailed his lips over her throat. He felt her fingers dig into his shoulders. His hand cupped her breast through her dress and he kneaded, making her groan.

"Please," she whispered. The word seemed to echo through the night.

His head lowered and he bit her nipple through the material.

"Please, Flynn."

"Kneel up." He held Abby at the waist, guiding her exactly where he wanted her to be.

Flynn held her tight with one hand as he flicked open the button on his jeans with the other. A second later, he lowered Abby onto his length. Her head fell back and Flynn nuzzled the crook of her neck. Heartbeat by agonisingly slow heartbeat, he joined with her. Their bodies pressed flush against each other, their limbs wrapped tight. They were one body. The rightness of which made Flynn groan.

Using his toes, Flynn rocked the swing. Abby's little whines sailed into the darkness as her hips began to move in time to the rocking swing.

"Perfect," he said.

He moved them faster as his lips found hers. He kissed to consume as their bodies swayed together in a rhythm intended to push them higher into the oblivion of ecstasy.

Abby broke from his lips, gasping. "I need, I need…"

Her eyes closed, her mouth open. Her cheeks dark with passion. Her body vibrated with his touch. She moaned and moved erratically against him.

"Shh, I know what you need," he murmured.

His hand slid down between them to caress her secret spot. Her breath stuttered. With one loud moan he felt her explode in his arms. The beauty of it pushed Flynn over the edge after her. His body clenched, his muscles became unbearably taut and he roared his release.

Abby collapsed into his arms. Flynn held her tight against his racing heart. He kissed her hair. His head fell back against the swing. His fingers traced lazy circles on the small of her back.

For a few moments they swayed gently in place, listening to the stream trickle by in the distance, picking out the gentle hoot of an owl, the snuffling of animals in the under-growth. The heady scent of night flowers floated over them on a cool breeze, soothing their heated skin. Abby shivered and he wrapped her tighter. Loath to let her go.

"I really need a shower." Abby paused. "And a snack."

Flynn tried not to laugh out loud, but she must have felt his chest shake under her cheek.

"What's so funny?"

She sat back to look at him. The pout was endearing. He trailed a finger down her cheek.

"You." He grinned. "You've got to stop being so romantic after we make love. I can't cope with it."

She frowned. "I wasn't being romantic."

Flynn laughed. "I know. Last time you offered me tea and cake; this time it's a shower and a snack. My ego can't cope with all the praise you heap on me."

"Idiot." She smacked his chest.

"Your idiot." The words were out of his mouth before his brain had a chance to vet them.

They stilled. The silence loomed around them. Abby's eyes were wide as she stared at him. He couldn't quite read the expression in them. He was too busy coping with the fact his heart was beating like mad and his palms had started to sweat.

"Are you?" she said at last. "Mine?"

Flynn leaned forward to rest his forehead against hers.

"Would it freak you out if I said I was?" Because, even though it scared the life out of him, he couldn't get past the resounding rightness of the words. He was Abby's.

"A little bit," she whispered, but her hold tightened on him.

"Then forget I said it." Flynn smiled at the possessiveness of her hold.

"I might be yours too," Abby whispered.

Flynn froze. "Fuck me," he breathed.

"Yeah," Abby said.

His hands clenched on her hips and he kissed her hard.

CHAPTER 33

"Actually, I never make a mistake, because it takes a huge effort for me to be wrong." Johan Cruyff, Dutch national player

She was a coward. Victoria would have laughed at herself, only she'd forgotten how to laugh a long time ago. Of course she was a coward. She'd always been a coward. This idea was just the latest incarnation of an inborn trait.

She eyed the phone in her hand, then the door in front of her. She resisted the urge to chew her bottom lip. Ladies did not do such things. Instead she placed one perfectly mani-cured hand on her roiling stomach and focused on breathing in and out.

Everything was crumbling. It was all falling down around her. She felt as though she was in an earthquake zone. The ground beneath her feet wasn't stable any longer. The walls she'd built were cracked. Each day brought more aftershocks. Her world was coming down.

And this was the proof—she wanted to lean on someone.

Not someone—Lawrence. Victoria counted her breaths as her blood thundered through her veins. It had been almost thirty years since she'd last let someone close to her. Since she'd last trusted anyone. Thirty long years since she'd had anyone to give her strength. And now there was Lawrence. Offering everything she'd never dared hope to have. Making her dream again.

She let out a long, silent breath. She couldn't do this. She couldn't knock on the door. She couldn't ask him to stand with her while she spoke to her mother. It was cowardly. What kind of woman needed support to talk to her own mother? Coward. She was a coward.

And yet…

Was it so wrong to need someone? So wrong to ask for help? Was it a sign of weakness to need support? Lawrence didn't think so. Abby had no problem asking for help. And they were two of the strongest people she knew.

Before she could stop herself, she reached out and knocked on the door. The urge to run almost won her over. She clenched the phone in her hand as she stared at the door. It felt like an eternity before it opened.

"Vicki." Lawrence's whole face lit up at the sight of her.

His obvious pleasure at her appearance almost eased her fear.

"I…" The words dried up in her mouth. How foolish. She should never have bothered him.

"What is it?" He took a step towards her. The frown lines between his brows deepened.

She loved the lines on his face. The crinkles around his eyes that said he knew how to laugh. The grooves that appeared when he was concentrating. The wrinkles on his brow that spoke of experience. She watched as his eyes took in everything about her. He smiled with realisation when he saw the phone in her hand.

"Have you called yet, or are you about to? Do you want to talk about it, or do you want company to make the call?" There was only genuine affection in his eyes. No censure. No judgment.

She felt her shoulders relax as she swallowed, her throat painfully dry.

"I was hoping for company while I made the call." It was a relief to hear her voice was as solid as usual.

"Come on in." He stepped out of the doorway and motioned her into the room. "How about a drink first? I asked Dougal to send up a bottle of scotch at the start of the week and there's plenty left." His eyes crinkled at her. "The Scots do whisky very well indeed. It's another plus for moving here."

"Thank you." Victoria stood stiff inside the doorway.

"Sit." Lawrence pointed at the chair in front of the desk. His confident stride took him over to the small fridge. He grabbed two glasses from the shelf above it, filled them with ice from the fridge, then topped them up from the bottle of single malt on the counter.

Victoria perched nervously on the edge of the chair as she looked around the room. It was a mirror image of hers, decorated in creams with a touch of red tartan to accent it. A lovely room. Comforting. And neat. For some reason it reassured Victoria to discover Lawrence was neat.

"Here you are." He handed her the glass.

They sipped as they watched each other. Lawrence seemed to be considering something. "Do you want to put the call on speaker, or would you rather I didn't listen to both ends of the conversation?" He pointed at his laptop. "I can busy myself with work, if you'd rather I didn't hear the whole thing. I can even pretend I'm not listening, if you think it will help." His mouth quirked up into a charming smile. The sight of it disarmed her.

"Speakerphone, I think. If you don't mind?"

"Not at all." He pulled the other chair over so he was sitting beside her at the desk.

There were so many things she wanted to say to him, but none of them would come out of her mouth. She looked at him as she sipped her drink and willed him to read her mind. To know without her saying how much she appreciated his being there. She wanted him to somehow translate her confused and chaotic thoughts, so she didn't have to give them voice. How could she talk to him about things she didn't have words for?

With a shaky hand, she placed the glass on the desk, the phone beside it. Lawrence nodded his encouragement as she dialled her mother. Victoria could actually feel the blood drain from her face as she listened to the ringing.

"It's about time you rang." Her mother's voice flooded the room, turning the air to ice.

"Hello, Mother." Victoria's voice was devoid of emotion, as it usually was. It had been such a long time since she'd let any of her feelings surface. She wasn't sure she knew how to let them out anymore. She felt like they were all stuck inside her, in one big ball in her chest. Taking up space and making her ache with each breath.

"Why haven't you returned my calls? I left several messages. Honestly, Victoria, if this simple task is too much for you, I can easily send someone more capable to get the job done."

"I—" Victoria started, but was cut off.

"I received a call today. I'm told Abigail is intimately involved with Mr Boyle. I was also informed that Mr Boyle's last partner had appeared, demanding he claim his child. Why didn't you tell me about any of this?"

"I didn't tell you because those stories aren't true. Who informed you they were?"

"Someone who's obviously much more diligent in their tasks than you are. This is exactly what I thought was happening. The sooner the child is taken into my care, the better. The Montgomery-Clark legacy is at stake here. What must people think, knowing I have a grandchild who's being reared in such a common environment?" Her mother's voice was like an ice pick, chipping at Victoria's soul. "I want you back here immediately. Tell Lawrence we'll start proceedings for custody straight away."

Victoria's whole body was tight with tension, making her certain she'd snap if she moved. She felt the air shift and looked down to see Lawrence's fingers curl around her hand. Her eyes snapped to his as he held her tight in his grip. He smiled his encouragement. Victoria stared at him. It was a gift. He was a gift. Such an unexpected one.

"Victoria." Her mother's voice demanded attention. As usual. "Are you listening to me?"

"Yes, Mother," Victoria said, tangling her fingers with Lawrence's as she stared at the phone. "I won't tell Lawrence to file for custody." Her mouth went dry. She actually felt the room shake and roll as more cracks appeared in her pristine life. "I think you're wrong. I think this course of action is wrong. Katy should stay with her mother. Abigail is doing a fine job. There is no need to interfere with it."

She was shaking by the time she finished talking, but she knew it wasn't evident in her tone. Her voice was its robotic norm. She was vaguely aware of Lawrence shifting his chair; she felt his body heat as his arm went around her shoulders. She stayed stiff, unable to relax her guard.

"Have you lost your mind? Fetch Lawrence at once. I'll tell him myself. You are obviously too weak to get the job done. You've let yourself get led astray by Abigail and the reprobate she's entangled with. I should have known you weren't able to get this done. I shouldn't have trusted you with it. Honestly, Victoria, you are beyond useless."

She felt Lawrence stiffen beside her. Her head snapped to face him when he cleared his throat.

"Mrs Montgomery-Clark, this is Lawrence. I'm sitting beside Victoria and I've heard the whole conversation. I have to say I agree completely with your daughter. You have no case here. No court in the land will take custody away from Abby. I strongly advise you give up on this plan."

"And I strongly advise that you do the job I'm paying you for, sir. File the papers at once. I want my granddaughter in my custody as soon as possible."

"No." Lawrence stared at Victoria as he spoke. His eyes were steel. She shook beneath his touch, shocked at the strength she saw in him. "I've spoken with my partners and we agree your desires are not in the best interest of Maynard-Fraser-Grayson. Formal notice will arrive in the mail, but please be advised we are no longer willing to represent you, nor your family."

There was an outraged gasp. "Do you have any idea who you're dealing with, young man? I will ruin you and your firm. You have no right to withdraw representation. You should feel honoured I allowed you to act on my behalf in the first place. This is outrageous."

"Take it up with your new solicitors," Lawrence said. "If they have any sense at all, they'll tell you the same thing we're telling you. Drop this plan. Leave Abby and her daughter alone."

Before her mother could say anything else, Lawrence let go of Victoria's hand, reached over and broke the connection.

Victoria stared at the phone in shock. "You hung up on Mother."

"Somebody should have hung up on her a long time ago."

Fury emanated from Lawrence, pulsing off him like a beacon to warn the wary away. It had the opposite effect on Victoria. It made her want to curl up against him. Of course she couldn't. She didn't know how.

Lawrence moved away from her, removing his arm from her shoulders to reach for her drink. He placed it in her hand. Victoria felt a little lost now he wasn't touching her. She tried to hide her disappointment.

"What will she do now?" he said.

She stared at her drink. "I don't know. Get another lawyer. Start again." She looked up at him. "She might try suing you as well."

He smiled, his eyes sparkling with the delight of a predator. "Now, that would be fun."

They sat in silence for a few minutes.

"If I go back now, she'll make me pay." Victoria watched the ice melt in her glass.

"Then don't go back."

Her eyes snapped to his. Everything he was shone from him—strength, honour, courage, hope. He was hope.

"Is it really that simple?"

"It is if you want it to be."

"I'm scared," she confessed.

"Want to hear a secret?" He leaned over and took her glass from her, placing it back on the desk. He held both of her hands in his, resting them on her knees. "I'm scared too. Change is a scary thing."

"And you're going to do it anyway?"

He nodded, a knowing smile on his lips. "So are you, sweet Vicki, so are you."

He closed the distance between them and captured her lips with his.

His kiss was a promise.

It tasted like freedom.

. . .

FLYNN AND ABBY heard Katy calling for her mum as they walked up the stairs to Abby's bedroom. There was no hysteria, no urgency present in the cry, so Abby knew she hadn't been awake for long.

"There goes my shower time," she grumbled.

Flynn tugged her close and pressed a kiss to her bruised lips. "Go shower. I'll deal with the terrorist."

"I don't know. She probably got a fright. Or had a bad dream. She'll want her mum."

"Why don't you stand in the door, and if it looks like I've got it under control, you can shower?"

"You're humouring me, aren't you?"

"Aye." He grinned as he turned the handle on Katy's door. "What's up, terrorist? What's with all the shouting?"

"There's something under my bed." There was a tremor in her voice. It took all of Abby's self-control not to push Flynn out of the way and gather Katy to her.

"Do you need your mum?" Flynn asked.

"No. You can look under the bed and scare away anything there. You're bigger than my Muma. You'd probably be more scary to monsters."

Flynn flicked on the light and Abby peeked inside as he knelt beside Katy's bed. "I'd have nightmares too if I had to sleep in a room painted Pepto-Bismol pink." He flicked the covers up and peeked under your bed.

"Is there a monster?" Katy clutched her favourite toy, her eyes wide.

"Aye, there's a monster, all right. It's Eric Cantona." He sat up and cocked an eyebrow at Katy.

"Eric Cantona is not under my bed. You told me he spends all his time on trains, reading poetry. Plus he's not a proper monster. He only kicked one man. Jonathan used to kick people all the time until he got in big trouble, and he isn't a monster either."

"I can't believe you're defending Cantona. Sure, he was a great forward, but he was also more than a little nuts. It's a damn shame what happened to him."

"Is he dead?"

"No, he's an actor. But he might as well be dead. How can a man go from playing for the French team and leading Man U to victory, to prancing around in a bunch of arthouse movies? That's no way to end a soccer career."

Abby covered her mouth with a hand to stop from laughing. Katy just glared at Flynn, her arms folded over her princess pyjamas.

"There's nothing wrong with acting. Jonathan's mum said you could act in films. She said you're pretty enough and you're going to have to do something with your life now you can't play football. She says you can't sit around all day tanning your belly."

"I really need to have a long talk with Jonathan and his mum." Flynn tucked Katy in. "Everybody is an expert. Everybody thinks they know what I should do with my life. I'm supposed to have a plan, but what people don't get is that I was going to plan in a few years' time. This whole injury thing happened before I had time to get to it."

"Don't worry, Flynn. Jonathan's mum said you can always get work being a giggler."

"Giggler?"

"Yes." Katy nodded solemnly. "We weren't supposed to be listening, but we were. We heard her tell her friend a giggler makes ladies happy. Jonathan said you must know a lot of jokes."

Abby snorted and Flynn's eyes shot to hers. She made a point to Google gigolo options for him later. Flynn frowned at her in warning, but Abby just smothered a laugh. Gigolo. It was the perfect fit. He narrowed his eyes at her before turning back to Katy.

"How about we read a bit more, then you can go back to sleep?"

"Okay. Are you having a sleepover with Muma again?"

"Aye. Don't go banging on the door in the morning. I thought the house was coming down around my ears this morning. I'm surprised there weren't any dents in the door."

"I'm strong. I have muscles. See?" She flexed her biceps.

"Impressive." Flynn opened a book. "Right. Where were we? David Beckham." He let out a long sigh. "Now before we go any further, I want to point out we're talking about Beckham's football career. I don't want to hear any of Jonathan's mum's opinions on his modelling career, or how hunky she thinks he is, or anything else. This is a serious topic. We're talking about one of the best midfielders England has ever produced. It isn't about how he looks in his underwear."

"Okay, Flynn." Katy snuggled down under her duvet. "I'm listening."

"Good." Flynn cleared his throat and started to read. And Abby tiptoed to the shower with a silly smile on her face and a heart ready to burst.

CHAPTER 34

"Football is a simple game made complicated by people who should know better." Bill Shankly, former Liverpool manager and Scottish national player

A storm broke over Abby's house at eight thirty the following morning. It seemed fitting that the day brought thunder and rain. The heavy clouds over the hills were just one more ominous sign things were going to get bad. The rain fell heavily all morning, weighing her down with each drop.

At lunchtime, Victoria and Lawrence arrived and Abby was prepared to hear the worst.

"I won't make you wait," Victoria said as soon as she entered the house. "I spoke with Mother and told her not to file for custody."

The air went out of Abby in one great whoosh. She had to place her hand on the wall beside her to stay upright. Lawrence smiled at her and squeezed her shoulder as he passed on his way to the kitchen, leaving the sisters alone in the hall.

"Thank you." Abby felt tears prick at her eyes.

Victoria's lips pinched, but her cheeks were flushed and her eyes seemed glassy with emotion.

"I won't lie," Victoria said. "Mother is beyond furious. She won't let this matter drop. Lawrence and his firm have cut ties with her, but I expect she will hire another solicitor and carry on with her plans."

Abby's stomach lurched. "So, it isn't over."

"No." Victoria hesitated. Her hand twitched towards Abby, as though she wanted to touch her, but didn't quite know how. She cleared her throat and stood straighter. "Lawrence and I have agreed to support you. We will stand in your corner on this issue."

She couldn't stop it. A tear escaped and slid down Abby's cheek.

"You won't be able to go back if you do." Abby, more than anyone, knew disobeying Mother meant cutting all ties with her.

"I know." There was no emotion in Victoria's answer, but Abby spotted the small tremor in her hands. Victoria's eyes flicked back up to Abby's, and she swallowed hard, as though steeling herself for something. "I have to speak with you about another matter."

"Okay." Abby drew out the word. From the look on her sister's face, the other matter wouldn't be good.

"After lunch, perhaps?" Victoria said. "We could take a moment in private to talk."

"We can talk now."

Her sister couldn't meet her eyes. "No, later is fine."

Abby desperately wanted to demand to know now. If the blade was going to fall on her neck, she didn't want to wait to find out how. But the anxiety radiating from Victoria made her hesitate. What difference would another few minutes make? It was the least she could do, considering everything Victoria had sacrificed to help her.

"Okay," Abby said. "Let's go get some tea."

Her sister was visibly relieved by the reprieve. "Tea would be lovely."

They walked side by side into the kitchen only to find Lawrence, Flynn and Katy discussing football around the dining table.

"Everything okay?" Flynn said when he saw her.

"Yes. It's all good."

He gave her the sort of private smile that made her heart clench hard. Victoria sat at Lawrence's side. Lawrence shocked Abby further by taking her sister's hand. The way he smiled at Victoria made Abby ache with hope. He was a good man. And after a life living for their mother, Victoria deserved a good man to help her heal.

Abby served tomato soup with crusty bread, and the conversation flowed easily while they ate. As Abby cleared the table, the doorbell rang. As though he lived there, Flynn went to answer it, and Abby didn't think twice about it. It felt like he belonged there.

Katy gestured widely while explaining why David Beckham was a great footballer to Lawrence, and her drink went flying. As Abby mopped up the mess with a cloth, Flynn came into the room. She stilled at the look on his face. It was a combination of anger, resolve and trepidation.

"Abby," he said. "Your mother and brother are in the living room."

It was Victoria's turn to spill her drink.

"Calm down, Vicki." Lawrence placed his hand on her shoulder. "It's going to be okay."

Abby didn't move. "Mother?" It'd been eight years since she'd seen her last. "Charles?"

She couldn't quite get her head around them actually being there.

"They have a new lawyer with them." Flynn looked at Lawrence. "Merser and Bannister?"

Lawrence nodded sombrely. "They're a good firm."

"Mother is here?" Abby said.

She looked over to Victoria, whose face had drained of all colour. Their eyes met in a moment of brutal understanding.

"I thought she'd just call," Victoria whispered.

"Yes," Abby whispered back.

"She wants to talk to both of you." Flynn's lips thinned as though he were readying for an argument. "There's no way you're going in there without me."

"Nor me." Lawrence looked equally determined.

Abby's eyes hit her daughter, who was sitting wide-eyed, soaking in every word. What about Katy? She couldn't be anywhere near the toxic air her mother generated. Before she could formulate a plan, Flynn was talking into his phone. The call ended quickly.

"Matt and Jena will be here in a couple of minutes," he said. "They're going to take Katy to their house to play."

"Can Jonathan come too?" Katy's enthusiasm was at odds with the strain in the air.

"I'll tell Matt to make sure he picks up Jonathan." Flynn's face softened as he spoke to Katy.

"Can I show him my new football book?"

"Course you can, monster. He might learn something. Go get it and I'll keep an eye out for Jena. Hurry up; they'll be here soon."

Abby was happy to let Flynn talk. All of her words seemed to have dried up.

Katy whooped and ran at Flynn, her arms up wide. Without pausing, he lifted her to his chest. Katy put her arms around his neck and hugged him tight.

"You're the best, Flynn," she said.

"I know. Now don't forget to tell everybody." And to Abby's shock, he kissed Katy on the cheek before putting her on the floor. "Get moving. Time's running out if you want to take the book with you."

"And the DVD too," Katy shouted as she ran full speed from the room.

Without a word, Abby walked to him and wrapped her arms around his waist. She pressed her cheek to his chest and counted his heartbeats as she waited for her mind to restart. Flynn held her without comment, gently stroking his hand down her back. There was no censure. He didn't try to take over. He was just offering his strength. And she was eager to take it.

"I'm here." Flynn pressed a kiss to her head.

Abby was pretty sure those words wouldn't be reassuring to most people. For most people, Flynn's presence was the harbinger of disaster. For her, he embodied security.

The back door opened and Jena walked into the kitchen, followed closely by Matt. The cousins shared a grim look.

"Take as long as you need." Jena pulled Abby from Flynn to give her friend a hug. "Katy can always have a sleepover at our place if she needs to. Don't worry about her. We'll be fine. Just concentrate on sorting this out."

"Thanks." Abby squeezed her tight as Katy came running back into the room.

"Can we watch this?" She held out a DVD to Matt.

Matt grinned at her. "Highlights from the last World Cup? Sure you wouldn't rather watch Winnie the Pooh?"

"No." Katy shook her head. "I need to study up so I won't embarrass Flynn when we watch the next World Cup."

"Flynn told you you'd embarrass him?" Matt glared at Flynn.

Katy nodded. "He said I don't know anything about football and he doesn't want me making a fool of myself when we talk about the World Cup."

"You're five." Matt glared at Flynn. "She's five."

"Age is no excuse for ignorance," Flynn said, but his eyes sparkled with mischief while he did it.

"Don't worry, Uncle Mattie," Katy said. "Flynn doesn't know anything about Barbies. So we're going to watch all the Barbie movies together so he won't embarrass me with my friends."

"Hey, I didn't agree to that." Flynn glared at her.

"Suck it up," Katy said.

"Katy!" Abby snapped. "Where did you hear that?"

Katy pointed at Flynn with an angelic smile on her face.

"Tattletale," Flynn grumbled at her.

With a giggle, Katy took Jena's hand and pulled her from the house, babbling on about how they needed to pick up Jonathan. Jena gave Abby a reassuring smile.

"It'll be okay," Matt said. "Just be yourself." He pulled Abby into a hug, which Flynn broke with a growl.

"Mine," he told his cousin.

"Yours?" Matt cocked an eyebrow at him.

Flynn pointed in the direction of the back door. "Don't you have more important things to deal with?"

With a laugh, Matt headed after his wife.

Abby looked at Victoria. "This is it," she said.

"This is it." Victoria seemed to steel herself.

"Let's do this." Flynn took Abby's hand in his.

Holding him tight, she went to have a reunion with her mother.

CHAPTER 35

"I can see the reports weren't exaggerated," her mother said as soon as she spotted Abby holding hands with Flynn.

The woman was perched on the edge of one of the armchairs, her back perfectly straight, her ankles crossed with her legs tucked under her. Her hands were clasped on her lap. Her makeup was perfect and understated. Her jewellery far from gauche. Her silver hair was styled into an expensively cut bob. Her dress was a grey shift, the subtle detail in the stitching giving it away as designer. Everything about the woman was elegant sophistication. Everything except the nasty look of disapproval on her face.

"Hello, Mother." Abby was pleased her voice didn't shake.

"Abigail, I am sorely disappointed in you." Her mother frowned at Flynn. "I thought you'd fallen far enough with your last romantic entanglement. It seems I was wrong. You've managed to fall even further this time."

"My last romantic entanglement, as you so rudely call it, involved the man I married. The same man I buried. A man I loved dearly. A good man."

Her mother sneered before dismissing Abby entirely and turning to Victoria. "I should never have sent you to do this task. I should have known it was far too difficult for you."

Abby watched as Victoria seemed to fold in on herself, her pale skin appearing paper-thin.

"And you?" She eyed Lawrence. "If you hadn't resigned, you would have been fired." Abby's mother motioned to the stranger standing behind her chair. "My new lawyer is looking into whether or not we have cause to sue you and your firm."

"Good luck," Lawrence told the new guy before staring at the older woman. "You don't scare me, Millicent. You don't intimidate me, either."

"We'll see about that." Abby's mother waved a hand dismissively.

She turned her cold glare back on her daughters. Through all of this, Charles, the brother Abby hadn't seen in years, sat silently staring at his shoes. Probably waiting for mother to pull his strings and make him dance. Abby's memory of Charles were generous—she'd actually thought her brother had a backbone. She'd been wrong.

"Why are you here?" Abby said to her mother.

"I'm here to see the mess you've made of your life. I'm here to see the damage you've done to my granddaughter. And I'm here to serve notice. I intend to fight for custody of the child. You've made it clear through your decisions and behaviour that you are a bad influence on her. She needs to be removed from your...friends." She scoffed at Flynn. "A Montgomery-Clark does not associate with people like this."

"Katy isn't a Montgomery-Clark." Abby felt her cheeks flush with fury. "She's a McKenzie."

"Her blood is Montgomery-Clark." The words froze the air. "You never did understand the importance of heritage. Blood means everything. That child is the embodiment of the Montgomery-Clark legacy. Charles is biologically impaired and unable to father a child." Charles' neck turned red, but he didn't object to his private life being made public. In fact, he didn't say anything at all. He didn't even look up from his shoes.

"Victoria," her mother continued, uncaring at the impact her words were having on her son. "Victoria, as this task has proven, is completely useless. She's well past her best child-bearing years, in any case. Which means I am forced to turn to you for the continuation of the Montgomery-Clark legacy. If your child is to carry on the family name, she needs to be raised properly. By people who know how to provide an appropriate environment for a child of her standing."

There was a moment of what Abby could only assume was stunned silence. The horror on the faces around the room was a comfort to Abby. It meant she wasn't the only one repulsed by her mother. In fact, the only two faces not showing disgust belonged to Charles and Victoria. Abby was angry to see they were both staring downwards, taking the verbal abuse as though it was normal. Which, Abby knew, it most likely was.

"You look exactly like Helen Mirren." Flynn broke the silence. "Doesn't she look exactly like the actress? They could be dead ringers. Except for the personality. I've met Helen. She's a great laugh. Funny, smart. While your mother is pretty much Cruella de Vil."

Shocked at Flynn's levity, Abby turned to find him smiling at her, but there was a hard, violent look in his eye. He knew exactly what he was doing and she loved him for it. Something clicked into place within her at the thought. She loved Flynn. Unfortunately, it wasn't the time to wonder at the revelation. Instead, Abby focused on his wicked smile and felt an answering grin break free. The mood in the room shattered under the weight of Flynn's words. She heard Lawrence chuckle behind her. And she could have sworn she heard Victoria breathe again.

"I know she makes a *wonderful* case for looking after Katy." Flynn's sarcasm made Abby's grin widen. "But I don't think you should give her the kid. She'll probably skin her and turn her into a coat."

"You are a poor excuse for a man, Mr Boyle," her mother snapped.

"Aye, I get that a lot." Flynn grinned widely. But his eyes were dark, flaring with barely contained rage. He tugged on Abby's hand. "You got something to say to your mother, sugar, because I'd like this over so I can go watch football with the kid."

Abby squeezed his hand. "Don't worry, baby, this will be over soon."

His eyes flashed at the endearment. Abby turned back to her mother.

"If you've said everything you came here to say, you can leave."

"Not without seeing the child."

"Not going to happen." Abby shook her head. "You're poison. I won't let my daughter anywhere near you."

"How dare you?" Her mother stood. "I will ruin you. I will tie you up in court for years. I will have child psychologists testify you're ruining the child. I'll have investigators dig up every tiny detail of your past, and Mr Boyle's past. By the time I'm finished with you, you won't have a penny to your name." She waved an elegant hand. "You won't have a house. You won't have a business. You will have nothing. You will be nothing. Are you entirely certain you want to challenge me, Abigail?"

"Yes. I'm certain," Abby said calmly. "If you take this further, I will fight. I'll start by demanding you testify in open court. Five minutes listening to the poison spewing from your mouth and no judge would hand any child over to you."

"You have no idea who you are dealing with, child." Her mother's face spoke of pure cruelty. "You think I unleashed hell on you before now, it will be nothing compared to what I will do to ensure this matter ends the way it should."

"You mean the way you want it to end?" Abby shook her head.

"That's what you've never understood, Abigail. In this family, the only way that matters is my way. Do you really think any of you *children* have the backbone or intelligence to deal efficiently with family matters? You'd best learn now that I will get what I want here, and I want the child."

Abby took a step backwards at the ferocity of the venom in her mother's voice. She felt Flynn tense beside her and knew he was about to jump to her defence. Before he could get there, Victoria spoke.

"No, Mother, you won't get her." Victoria's voice was small, the words trembling.

Her mother sneered. "Stay out of this, Victoria. You've proven your lack of usefulness in this situation. It is time for you to be quiet. I'll deal with you when we get home."

"I'm not coming back." Victoria didn't sound so sure, but Abby willed her to stay strong.

Lawrence took a step towards her sister and placed a hand on her lower back. A subtle mark of support.

"Of course you are. Don't be ridiculous," her mother snapped.

"No. I'm staying here. I plan to work for Lawrence and get to know Abby and Katy."

Her mother's eyes went hard. "You do and you cut all ties with me. No money. No home. Nothing. I own everything you hold dear and I will take it all away, Victoria. You won't have any security at all. And don't think you can come crawling back to me. I won't change my mind and take you in. Your name will be wiped from the family and you won't be welcome in polite society. How do you think you will cope, exactly, without your shopping trips to Harrods and your afternoon teas at the Savoy? Work for Lawrence? Doing what? You have no skills. You are barely of any use to me."

Victoria faltered. The shock on her pale face was horrifying to watch. Abby reacted to her pain without thinking, and reached out, wrapping her fingers with her sister's. Giving her strength. Victoria's eyes snapped to hers and the agony in them was unbearable. Victoria squeezed Abby's hand with trembling fingers as she faced their mother.

"No, you won't, because if you do, I will go public. A Montgomery-Clark shouldn't be in the newspapers. Isn't that what you taught us? Not unless it's the business section, a story on philanthropy or an obituary. You've drummed that into me my whole life. If you do this, if you fight for Katy, if you try to take her away from Abby, I will speak to any newspaper I can get to listen to me. I will tell my story."

"You will not stand between me and my granddaughter." Anger flashed in her mother's eyes.

"Katy isn't your granddaughter," Victoria said, her voice devoid of emotion. "She's mine."

Abby dropped her hold on her sister. She staggered back, hitting Flynn's wide chest. She stared at Victoria. Saw the look of shock on Lawrence's face. Felt Flynn tense behind her.

"Your granddaughter?" Abby whispered. It didn't make sense. None of it did.

Victoria had tears in her eyes, but she held her chin high. She stood as though expecting a blow. But she didn't look away from Abby. Abby's eyes stuck on Victoria as her world crumbled and everything she knew to be true fell away.

"I'm not your sister," Victoria said. "I'm your mother."

CHAPTER 36

"They say Rome wasn't built in a day, but I wasn't on that particular job." Brian Clough, former England player

"You're my mother?" Abby's shocked question cut through the stunned silence like a sharpened blade.

Everyone spoke at once as Abby stared at Victoria.

"Victoria, how dare you?" her mother shouted. No. Not her mother. Abby's head began to spin.

"Deep breaths, sugar," Flynn mumbled behind her. His hand was firm against the small of her back.

"How dare I?" Victoria's agony-filled eyes were wrenched from Abby. "How dare I? How dare you? You took her from me when I was barely more than a child myself."

"Took her," Millicent scoffed. "You hardly put up a fight to keep the girl, now did you?"

"What choice did I have, Mother?" Victoria's eyes blazed. "I was fifteen. You whisked me away to Switzerland for the duration of the pregnancy. I was cut off from my friends.

From Robert. You signed papers on my behalf. By the time I knew what was happening, it was too late. You told the world Abby was yours, and I was told to behave myself or I would be shipped away for good."

"Poor you," Millicent sneered. "I saved you from the shame of an illegitimate child. I raised your daughter as my own and gave her the Montgomery-Clark name—not that it had any impact on the child." She shook her head at Abby. "She never did live up to the name. Hardly unexpected, considering your father was the son of the gardener."

Abby's head reeled. Her father? Robert? Not George Montgomery-Clark. Not the man who was always so distant, so critical, so cruel. She watched Millicent's face as the pieces fell into place. No wonder they resented her. No wonder she'd always felt like they didn't want her, like she didn't belong.

They *hadn't* wanted her.

She stared into the eyes of the woman she knew resented everything about her. The eyes of the woman who no longer deserved to be called Mother. "You only took me on to save face. To protect the family name."

"Of course, why else?" Millicent said.

"You never wanted me," Abby whispered.

"I did," Victoria answered before Millicent could say anything. "I wanted you. I never stopped wanting you."

Abby spun to Victoria. "You gave me to them?" She couldn't keep the pain out of her question. Victoria alone knew what that meant. She knew the cold, unfeeling family life Abby had endured. She heard the disapproval in every word spoken to Abby. Victoria knew.

"I didn't have a choice." Victoria's face was blank, her voice even, but her eyes were full of emotion. "I was fifteen. I tried to be in your life. I spent as much time as I could steal with you."

"The playing, the dancing." Abby felt her eyes well with tears over what might have been. "We used to laugh."

"You were my heart." Victoria's voice was a whisper. "You still are the one good thing I have managed to do."

"But you went away. I remember, the playing and laughing suddenly stopped. Where did you go?"

"Mother and Father shipped me off to stay with cousins in South Africa. They said I was a bad influence on you. By the time I was allowed to return, you were in boarding school."

"You rarely visited when I was in school."

"It was made clear to me I would be cast out with nothing —no resources, nowhere to go and no skills—if I interfered in your upbringing." Victoria took a step towards Abby, but stopped dead, as though afraid to come any further. "This is what I planned to explain to you today. There's no excuse for how I behaved, for what I did. I should never have given in to blackmail. I should never have given you up in the first place. It's unforgivable."

"How very touching," Millicent said. "You may as well tell her all of it, now you've started. Tell her how your young beau wanted nothing to do with you once he found out about the child. Tell her how you were too stupid for further education and unable to amass any sort of skill. Tell her how easily you gave in to our requests. It wasn't like you fought to spend time with her, was it, Victoria? No, you kept your head down and carried on with your life. Content to allow your daughter into our care."

"There was no care," Victoria snapped. "There was provision, which is nowhere near care. You never showed any of us any affection or compassion. I don't understand why you even had children."

"It was expected," Millicent said. "We had to carry on the

family name. If I'd known you would turn out to be such disappointments, we may have thought otherwise."

"Enough," Abby said.

Everyone quietened, their attention on her. She took a deep breath, aware Flynn stood silently behind her, offering his strength.

"Enough," she said to Millicent. "This is my home and it's past time you left."

"I will not be moved until this matter is settled," Millicent said. "I will not leave until you understand the child belongs to the Montgomery-Clarks."

"If you don't leave, I'll call the police and have you removed. Better yet, I'll have Flynn pick you up and toss you out like rubbish for the camera crews to film."

"You wouldn't—"

Abby cut her mother's bluster off. "I have had enough of you. I have had enough of your vile and nasty manipulations. Of your threats and selfishness. Of your cruel behaviour. If you want to take me to court, take me. I will turn it into the biggest media circus you have ever seen. Flynn here will help me to set up interviews with everyone he knows. In fact, I expect he wouldn't mind lending his notoriety to a campaign to drag your good name through every muddy field in England."

"I'd enjoy every minute," Flynn said.

Millicent's face paled but her shark-like eyes were still determined. "You will bankrupt yourself paying for legal counsel. Is that what you want? For you and the child?"

"She won't bankrupt herself," Lawrence said. "I'll take the case and run with it for free."

"And how will you live while you're fighting me? There won't be any time to work. You'll be out of house and home within months."

"No she won't. She can have my money," Flynn said. "I'm not doing anything with it anyway."

"Flynn, you can't…" Abby whispered.

He shrugged. "I'm behind you, sugar. Whatever it takes to make this go away. It's only money." He smiled at her, a soft, intimate caress of a smile. "Don't stop now. You're kicking ass."

Abby smiled back at him before turning to her unwanted guests. "I don't need to explain anything to you. All you need to know is this—if you start a war, we will wage a war. I will fight you until my last breath. I will do everything within my power to ruin your name." She scoffed. "Now isn't that interesting? Turns out I am a Montgomery-Clark after all, because when it comes to getting what I want, I will not lie down until you are ruined and bloody. Doesn't that sound familiar, *Mother?*"

Abby didn't wait for an answer—she looked at Millicent's new lawyer. "Leave. Now."

The man bustled and flushed, but he headed for the door. Abby looked at Charles, who was still staring at his feet.

"Charles, take your mother and get out."

His head came up slowly. There was nothing but blank acceptance in his eyes.

"Let's go, Mother," Charles said, his first words since entering the house.

Millicent stood, her back straight, her air regal. "You'll regret this, Abigail." With one last glare, she swept out of the door.

The air in the room eased as Flynn pulled Abby into his arms.

"You were amazing." He held her tight.

"She'll still fight," Abby said into his chest.

"Probably. She's a vindictive old witch. But we'll fight back."

Abby let her head fall back to look at him. "It isn't your fight. You don't have to do this. I can't take your money, Flynn."

Flynn rolled his eyes. "Daft girl. If it's your fight, it's my fight. I can't let them take the terrorist from us. Not when I'm on a roll with her education. Anyway, I invested in Harry's company when he first started out. He made a mint. He can always make more if we need it."

Abby felt her bottom lip tremble as she looked at all the things left unsaid in his eyes.

"You love me," she said with absolute conviction.

And Flynn Boyle, bad boy of soccer, actually blushed. "Aye, but don't rub it in."

"You love me." Abby grinned. "Your head must be spinning. Bet you never thought it was possible to love someone other than yourself."

"Funny, oh so funny." Flynn tugged her back into his chest.

"Are you feeling okay? Do you need to lie down?" Abby's voice was muffled against him. She was grateful for the teasing, as it cut through the horrors Millicent left behind.

"I am seriously regretting falling for you now," he grumbled.

And against all odds, Abby started to laugh. She felt Flynn lean down and whisper in her ear.

"I do love you, Abby."

She held him tight and felt his muscles tense beneath her hold.

"Aren't you going to say it to me?" He sounded so affronted at the thought she wouldn't that it made Abby laugh harder.

She looked up from him to find the room empty. "Where's Victoria?"

As she spoke, they heard a second car's engine start. Lawrence walked into the room, grim and worried.

"She's made a run for it," he said.

"Lawrence?" Abby said.

"Don't worry, I'll go after her." Lawrence patted Abby's hand.

"Tell her…" Abby bit her lip, her mind a jumble of emotions and thoughts that might never be properly processed. "Tell her we need to talk."

Lawrence nodded firmly, then headed out of the house.

As Abby watched him go, she felt pain overtake her.

"You do love me, right? I mean what's not to love?" Flynn's voice jarred her back to the present.

"I think you love yourself enough for both of us, Flynn," Abby teased.

He narrowed his eyes at her. "Evil woman. I will make you say the words. You can count on it. I haven't lost a challenge yet."

"Shut up and kiss me." She needed him to whisk her away from everything—if only for a moment.

And thankfully, he complied.

CHAPTER 37

"Football is simple, but the hardest thing to do is play simple football." Johan Cruyff, former Dutch national player

"I saw her heading to the loch," Dougal said to Lawrence as soon as he entered the pub.

"Thanks," he told the man behind the bar, as his shoulders sagged with relief. He'd feared she'd run further. Somewhere he'd never catch her.

"She was crying." Dougal's usual boom was toned down to almost normal levels. His face, which was a carbon copy of Santa Claus, held worry. "She seemed lost, as though she didn't know what to do with herself or where to go. I don't like seeing anyone in that state." He eyed Lawrence speculatively. "Are you taking care of this?"

"Yes." He headed for the door, before turning back to the pub owner. "Don't give away our rooms. We're moving to town and it will take a while to find a place to live."

Dougal's face broke out in a wide grin. "Will you be opening an office here?"

"When I can. There are a lot of loose ends to tie up in London."

"We need a good lawyer in town. Anything you need. Let me know. Welcome to the family, son."

Lawrence couldn't help grinning at the man who wore a yellow shirt with a red tartan bow tie. Without another word, he jogged off in search of Victoria.

She wasn't hard to find. She wasn't hiding at all. She was sitting stiffly on the wall beside the loch, just out of sight of passersby. Her arms were around her waist and she was curled in on herself, as though she hoped to become as small as possible until she disappeared entirely. Lawrence hated the sight.

He felt her stiffen as he sat down beside her. He didn't touch her, unsure what the reception would be. She didn't look at him, but he noticed she tried to sniff discreetly to hide her tears. For a long time, they sat side by side, looking out over the water. The grey of the vista was soothing. The air still heavy after the storm. The sounds of gently lapping waves and ever-present gulls were a balm to open wounds. Lawrence fought the urge to pull the woman who had become important to him into his embrace. He wanted to fix things for her. At the very least, carry her pain. But all he could do, he knew, was be there for her.

"You were terribly young." Too young to stand up against her parents.

She jerked at his words, and for a moment he thought she might ignore him. Her eyes stayed firmly on the water as she spoke. "I'd just turned fifteen." She gave a very unladylike snort. "I thought myself in love. We had one night together before he disappeared. Father paid the family off. He told me it was an awful cliché to get knocked up by the help."

He knew from the look on her face she wasn't seeing the loch anymore. She was watching her past.

"You must have been afraid."

Victoria stared at him for a long time, her eyes welling with fresh tears. But they didn't fall. She cleared her throat. "I didn't have anyone to lean on. I was sent to finishing school in Switzerland, or at least that's what everyone was told. It was a clinic. Private. Very exclusive. I stayed there for the whole pregnancy."

"Alone?" Lawrence wanted to hurt Victoria's mother so badly it ate at him.

"Of course." Victoria looked back out over the water. "My parents turned up a month before the baby was due. They had a team of lawyers in their wake. The papers were already drawn up. They were going to take my baby, raise her as their own. I would be allowed to spend time with her, under the proviso I never revealed our true relationship. If I didn't agree, the baby and I would be cut off without a penny. All family connection would be withdrawn. I would have been asked to leave the clinic and have the baby elsewhere. They did say they'd take me back to London. It was their only concession. Although they made it very clear that once in the city, I would be on my own."

Lawrence couldn't take it anymore. He wrapped an arm around her waist and pulled her into him. His anger towards her parents was a visceral thing. He wished he could rip them apart with his bare hands.

"I signed away my baby." Her whispered words were warm against his chest.

"Of course you did." He squeezed her hard. "They didn't give you a choice. You were a child. How would you survive alone with a baby?"

She pushed back and looked up at him. "You don't hate me for making the decision to give her to them?"

Tears bit at his eyes as expletives fell from his lips. "Of course I don't hate you. Why would you think that?"

Silent tears fell down her cheeks, cracking his heart with each one. "I did a terrible thing. I gave my baby away. I let her believe that people who didn't love her were her parents. I let her suffer. They were so cold to her. So horrible, and I stood back allowing it. I hurt her. I should never have given her away." Her voice broke as she buried her face in his shirt and sobbed.

Lawrence soothed her with meaningless words mumbled as he stroked her. Rage at the people who damaged those they should have loved and protected the most was a fire inside him. He buried it deep. Promised he'd ruin them at a later date. Right now, Victoria needed him.

A noise behind them drew his attention, and he stilled, ready to protect Victoria from gawkers. It was Dougal. He held a tray. It had takeaway cups with warm drinks, bottles of water and a plastic-covered plate of cookies. Without a word, the man placed the tray beside them, smiled softly at Victoria and left. In that moment, Lawrence knew they'd found a real home. Him and Victoria both. They belonged in Invertary.

"Here, darling, have a drink." He reached for one of the warm cups and held it out to her. "You'll feel better." He noticed Dougal had left a pack of tissues on the tray, and silently blessed the man.

As Victoria held the drink, he used a tissue to wipe her tear-stained face.

"Sip," he ordered.

She did as she was told, and for some reason he hated to see her obey. *His* woman had spent her life obeying orders. Terrified of being cast out and rejected if she didn't. It would take time, but he'd teach her there was nothing wrong with standing up for herself. She wouldn't lose him if she did.

"You did a good thing today, darling," he told her as he held her close. "You stood up to your mother. You gave her a reason to stop her pursuit of Abby. You made sure Abby didn't lose her daughter the way you lost yours. You were very brave. I'm proud of you."

She leaned into him. So small and fragile in his arms. How she'd managed to live under the evil will of a tyrant and still manage to keep a semblance of herself, he had no idea.

"She must hate me."

He knew she didn't mean Millicent. "I don't think Abby has it in her heart to hate anyone."

"I wouldn't blame her." She held the warm cup tight to her chest. "I tried in the beginning. To love her. To spend time with her. I would read to her. Cuddle her. Play with her. She was amazing. Beautiful, warm, loving. She was perfect, Lawrence, utterly perfect." She wiped at her eyes. "I remember how it felt to wrap her tight in my arms. I never wanted to let her go. I hated being apart from her. I'd cry for hours when we were separated. I loved her so much," she whispered. "She was my baby." She looked up at Lawrence. "I still love her so much my heart aches with it, but over the years it became easier to be distant. It hurt too much trying to be close when I knew I could never be what she needed."

"I know, my darling, I know."

Victoria turned back to look at the loch. "I visited with David, Abby's husband, once when she wasn't there. I think he suspected something, but he never said. I wanted to make sure he would be good to her. I had to see for myself that he was a good man. He was, Lawrence, he was a very good man. And he loved my Abby. I never went back. Mother would have had a fit if she'd found out there was contact. She..."

Her words faded. Lawrence didn't need them. He'd had enough experience with Victoria's parents to know they must have made her suffer daily for her childhood indiscretion. He could only imagine the mental abuse she'd endured over the years.

"Charles?" He wondered if the brother had known. If he'd ever done anything to help.

"Charles only cares about Charles. He does whatever he must to keep Mother out of his business." She shook her head. "Charles has some interests Mother would disapprove of."

Lawrence nodded. He'd heard rumours. The man's tastes ran to the twisted. He definitely wouldn't want a spotlight on them. Neither would he want the funds available to pursue his interests cut off when his mother found out.

"You've been alone such a long time."

"It's no more than I deserve."

"No." He shifted to look her in the eyes. "You're wrong. You didn't deserve any of this. It was done to you. Your choices weren't choices at all. You were a child, and then you were an abused adult dealing with the only world you knew. You don't deserve this. You don't deserve any of it."

"Abby?" Victoria's voice cracked as the tears started again.

"We'll deal with it together. You're not alone anymore." He kissed her hair and wrapped her in his arms.

Where she belonged.

CHAPTER 38

"A penalty is a cowardly way to score." Pelé, greatest footballer ever

Flynn made a call to his cousin and told him what happened. Matt offered to keep Katy overnight, but Flynn knew Abby would want her baby. After everything he'd heard, Flynn couldn't bear the thought of the terrorist being out of his sight. They should be together. Where they belonged. Matt promised to bring the kid home as soon as her play date with the famous Jonathan was over, which gave Flynn some time to care for Abby.

Adrenalin-fuelled emotions had worn her out. When she crashed, numb and bruised, he'd put her to bed and told her to sleep for a while. The whole situation was a mess. A nasty, ugly, screwed-up mess that left a foul taste in his mouth. One he just couldn't get rid of.

Flynn was sitting on Abby's front step, nursing a beer and wondering who to kill first—the list of prospects was pretty damn long—when Mitch drove up. The American was wearing one of his usual power suits, although he looked more rumpled than pristine.

"It's Sunday—what the hell kind of meetings do you have on a Sunday? Give your backside a day off and wear a pair of jeans." Flynn grinned at the man. They'd become friends over the past few years, catching up when Flynn was in Invertary or Mitch was in London. He liked Mitch. For a lawyer—especially one in the entertainment business—he wasn't half bad.

"I had a meeting with your agent, asshole." Mitch threw a folder at Flynn as he came up the steps. "Where's the beer?"

"Kitchen fridge." Flynn opened the folder and sucked in a breath. It was the contract he'd signed for the TV show. He looked up to ask Mitch what this meant, but the man was already inside the house.

Flynn read, hope bubbling up inside him. When Mitch came back out, his jacket and tie were gone, his white shirt sleeves were rolled up and he was holding an ice-cold beer. He sat on the step beside Flynn.

"You broke the contract?" Flynn said.

"You are now agent-less, lawyer-less and you no longer have a camera crew up your ass." Mitch clinked their beer bottles together. "You're welcome."

"How the hell did you manage this?" Flynn was in awe. Seriously. The guy deserved his complete adoration.

"I am just that good." Mitch stretched his legs out in front of him. "I also put Lake on the case. He's going to do some digging. You were being fleeced by your agent. I'm pretty sure the lawyer was in on it, but I don't have any proof—yet."

"I figured as much when they stopped answering my calls." Flynn's jaw clenched. "Guess I need a new lawyer."

"Don't look at me." Mitch held up his hands. "I'm up to

my ears dealing with Josh. Without me he would be broke and singing for food."

Flynn laughed, because it was most likely true.

"Thanks," he said.

Mitch shrugged. "No biggie. We're friends."

"Aye." And it felt damn good to have people around him, watching his back. He'd spent most of his life in the cutthroat world of professional soccer, where each man looked out for himself. He hadn't realised until recently just how much of an impact his upbringing and professional life had on his character, or the people around him. As much as he complained about coming home, Invertary had given him back his life.

And it'd given him Abby.

They sat quietly for a while, staring at Flynn's state-of-the-art motorhome. The land looked bare without the donkeys, who were currently eating their way through the field between Abby's and Matt's houses.

"You ever going to build the house you're supposed to be building?" Mitch asked.

"Don't think so." Flynn grinned at him. "I like this house. Think I might just move in here. Will save a load of effort."

"And another one bites the dust." Mitch shook his head. "I stopped drinking the water in this town years ago. There's something in it that makes the men sign away their freedom and shackle themselves to the first woman who falls at their feet."

"One." Flynn held up a finger. "Abby didn't fall at my feet. If she heard you say that, she'd sock you. Or set the terrorist on you. So I'd keep the thought to myself if I were you. Two." He held up another finger. "I'm not shackled. I'm still a free man. I just choose to spend my freedom enjoying one woman instead of millions."

"Millions?" Mitch scoffed. "Your ego knows no bounds."

"It's my superpower," Flynn said solemnly. "And three"—he held up another finger—"I intend to be the first one laughing when you get shackled."

"Don't hold your breath. Many women have tried to pin me down. I'm unpinnable."

"What if it happens the other way round? What if you meet a woman *you* want to pin down?"

"Never. Going. To. Happen. There isn't a woman alive I'd chase hard enough to catch."

"Famous last words. I might get them printed on a T-shirt for you."

Whatever Mitch was going to say was lost in the sound of an engine revving. The two men watched as a car sped up the road. It cut across his field and headed straight for his RV.

"I think your producer just found out his show's been cancelled."

"Pity I'm not home to take his call." Flynn sipped his beer.

"I don't think talking is what he has in mind." The car's speed increased. The engine roared.

A few seconds later there was an almighty bang as the car rammed the side of the van. It reversed out, tyres squealed and it hit the van again.

"I'm really glad the animals are out of there," Flynn said.

Mitch cocked an eyebrow at him. "You got insurance?"

Flynn nodded. "Good job, too." A thought hit him. "There's no way Abby can send me home after this."

"Dumb ass." Mitch shook his head.

"Got to look out for those silver linings."

They drank their beers as they watched the car hit the van again. Metal ripped. Tyres burned. It was nasty.

"What the heck is going on?" Abby came running out onto the porch.

"Hey, sugar, you feeling better?" Flynn moved over to make space for her, on the side of him away from Mitch, who laughed when he saw the move. Flynn ignored him as he tugged Abby down to sit beside him. She looked delightfully sleep-rumpled.

"Aren't you going to stop him?" She pointed at the car, which was ramming the van again.

His poor van wasn't designed to take that sort of abuse. It was crumpling before his eyes. The car didn't fare much better, but it was still in one piece. Pretty much.

"Nope," Flynn said. "Better he gets it out of his system on an object rather than a person."

"He's damaging your home?" Her incredulous look made it clear she thought he was insane.

"Guess I need to find somewhere else to live." He gave her a hot look, heavy with meaning. "Got any ideas?"

She flushed pink, making him smile wickedly. There was another crash.

"I can't believe you're sitting here doing nothing when a madman is trashing your RV. Do you have so much money you don't care when it's wasted?"

"It isn't wasted." He pointed across the field. "Look."

Abby looked where he pointed and spotted a camera trained on the producer. She stilled in confusion. "Is this part of your documentary?"

"Nope—the show's been cancelled, sugar. The producer isn't happy about it." He turned to Mitch. "How much do you reckon it will cost me to make the footage as public as possible?"

"Want me to go find out?"

"If you don't mind. Add this service to my bill."

"Smart ass," Mitch grumbled, but he pushed to his feet and sauntered over in the direction of the cameraman.

"This will ruin his career." Abby watched the motorhome crumple under the assault.

"We can only hope," Flynn said as he finished off his beer.

. . .

Abby leaned into Flynn. "You know there's a duck in my downstairs bath."

"Aye, but she's on the mend. She won't be there long."

"You're just a big softie, Flynn." Abby nuzzled the point where his neck met his shoulder, breathing the musky scent of him in deeply.

"Don't tell anyone," Flynn whispered.

"Flynn Boyle," a voice shouted. "I'm going to ruin you. You'll wish you were dead. I'm going drag your name through the mud. I'm going to sue you for every penny you have. I'm going to..."

Flynn looked completely unconcerned as he turned his back on the weaselly producer who was jumping up and down in the middle of the field. Everything out of the odious little man's mouth was being taped for the viewing pleasure of the British public. Good. It was the least he deserved. Once the thought was in her mind, she wondered exactly when she'd become so bloodthirsty.

Mitch sauntered back, handed his empty beer bottle to Flynn and winked at Abby.

"The footage will be on the web within the hour. Should be on the news tonight. You'd better call Matt about the damage. Without a police report you can't claim insurance."

Flynn sighed, like it was too much effort, but pulled his phone out of his pocket. A minute later he was talking to Matt.

"You need to come arrest someone," he said. "The producer just trashed my van."

There was silence. Then outrage. "What do you mean you thought the noise was me? When are you going to get it through your thick head I've turned over a new leaf?"

Mitch and Abby started to laugh.

"No," Flynn said in answer to whatever Matt said. "We'll come get her in a wee while. I don't want her staying at Jonathan's overnight. His mother will just feed her impressionable mind with more crap about Beckham."

He turned to Abby. "You don't want Katy having a sleepover at Jonathan's house, do you?"

"No. And thanks for asking after you'd already made the decision."

He ignored her and wound up his conversation with his cousin. Abby grinned at Mitch, who was shaking his head at Flynn.

"You sure you know what you're doing?" Mitch asked her.

"Does anyone?" Abby said.

"Fair point." Mitch waved at them both before he climbed into his car.

On the way down the drive, he passed another car coming up. It was Lawrence. And he wasn't alone. Every muscle in Abby's body instantly vibrated with tension. Her eyes stayed fixed on the car as she held her breath. Lawrence got out first. He flashed a reassuring smile at Abby. Her heart stuttered at the sight. Flynn came up beside her and squeezed her hand tight.

"We all make mistakes, sugar," he whispered to her.

As Abby stared, Victoria climbed out of the car. She looked smaller. She looked beaten, drawn and depleted. Her every move was hesitant. Fear and defeat radiated from her. Even from a distance Abby could see her red, swollen eyes. When those eyes looked up at Abby, her whole body shuddered. The pain was like a beacon, there for everyone to see.

I'm sorry, Victoria mouthed.

And Abby was running, down the steps, over the grass and into the arms of her mother. The two women stood clinging to one another, sobbing loudly.

"I'm so sorry, I'm so sorry," Victoria whispered over and over.

"Don't leave me again," Abby said. "I want to know you."

Victoria stroked a hand down her hair, and Abby remembered all the times she'd been in the woman's arms when she'd been a child. When Victoria had barely been more than a child herself. She'd been so happy then. She'd felt so loved. Wanted.

"I need to explain things." Victoria's voice cracked. "I know you will never be able to forgive me, but I need to explain."

"Then stay. Stay here in Invertary. Take your time. Explain it all."

"I never stopped loving you, my baby," Victoria whispered. "I'm so sorry I wasn't strong enough to hold on to you." Victoria's tears fell.

"You were strong today. Strong enough to stand against Millicent. Strong enough to give me the ammunition I need to fight her. That counts for something."

There was too much to say. She remembered a time, long ago, when David had told her Victoria had come to visit him.

"She loves you deeply," he'd said. "I don't think she knows how to show you, but that sister of yours loves you a lot. I got the impression she'd have me dealt with if I wasn't good for you."

"She was always there for me when I was tiny," Abby had said. "She was more of a mother to me than my own mother. I miss the closeness."

"Maybe it will come back." He'd kissed her then. "Don't give up hope. It took guts for her to come to me. Maybe one day she'll have the guts to come to you too."

Abby leaned back and looked in Victoria's eyes. "We'll take our time," she promised. "We'll get to know each other again. I want you here. Stay in Invertary."

"It's more than I can ask." Victoria's lips trembled.

"Then don't ask. Just stay."

"Okay."

As they stood there hugging, Abby's eyes met Flynn's over Victoria's shoulder and she realised she had something she'd always longed for.

She had family who loved her.

CHAPTER 39

"We're taking twenty-two players to Italy, sorry, to Spain...Where are we, Jim?" Bobby Robson, former English manager talking about the 1998 World Cup in France

Flynn moved into Abby's house. She didn't invite him. He didn't ask. He kind of hoped she just wouldn't notice. He'd been there six weeks and she hadn't mentioned it so far. He figured if he was lucky, he'd be there another fifty years without her bringing it up.

"Are you going to marry my Muma?" Katy asked him over their usual bedtime story.

This one was about Brazil's spectacular record in world football, followed by their equally spectacular screw-up when they hosted the World Cup. Flynn had moved on from players to teams, in the hope Jonathan's mother would stop comparing him to every player Katy mentioned to her son.

"Do you want me to marry your mum?" He was surprised to find he was actually quite anxious about the answer.

"It's okay with me if you want to. I know you like kissing her."

The relief Flynn felt was a solid lump in his throat. "I think you're a little obsessed with kissing. Are you and Jonathan kissing at school and not telling me?"

She scrunched up her nose. "Ew, no. I still haven't decided if I want to marry him or not. He says I have to, but I want to wait and see. I'll kiss him if I marry him, but I'm not doing it before then."

"Good plan. Let's keep it that way with all future boys too." Flynn thought he heard laughter coming from downstairs. Sometimes Abby still listened in to story time because she thought they were funny. Katy and Flynn kept explaining to the woman that there was nothing funny about football.

"If you get married, can I have a little sister?"

"That's up to your mum, but there would be no guarantee you'd get a sister. These things are a crapshoot. It could be a boy."

"Don't bother, then," Katy said in disgust. "Just get me a puppy."

Flynn rolled his eyes and carried on reading about the Brazilian national team.

"Flynn?" Katy said when he was mid-sentence, making him wonder if she was even listening.

"What now?" he whined.

"I think you make a good daddy."

His heart stopped dead. He swallowed hard.

"I love you, Flynn." Her eyes were wide and sincere. And damn if she didn't look exactly like the evil, conniving cat in *Shrek*.

"I love you too, kid."

Her whole face lit up and he felt like he'd been handed the world. "If you *really* love me, you'll make sure I get a baby sister. Or a puppy." She batted those eyelashes at him. "You can get me a sister, Flynn. I know you can."

Flynn found himself wondering if a fertility clinic could get Abby pregnant with the kid of his choice. A girl. For her sister. His eyes narrowed. The evil genius was messing with him.

"Time to go to sleep, monster." He put the book on the shelf and she did what she did every night. Sat up, opened her arms and waited for her hug. He held her tight to him, this precious little bundle, and hoped Abby would be open to adding to the family. He'd love another ten just like the terrorist—enough for his very own football team.

"Sleep well," he ordered as he kissed her cheek.

He tucked her into her bubblegum-pink bed in her Pepto-Bismol room and went to find her mother.

She was standing in her office, a look of shock on her face and the phone in her hand.

"What is it?" He rushed to her side.

Her wide eyes blinked at him, filled with disbelief. "That was Millicent's lawyer. She's giving up on taking Katy from me. He requested neither Victoria nor I ever contact her again."

"That is fantastic news." Flynn swept her up into his arms and spun her around.

"It's over," she breathed against his neck.

"About bloody time."

He kissed her gently, then put her back down at her desk where she'd been working on her designs.

"We should celebrate," he said.

"What do you suggest?"

"Well, we could celebrate horizontally. Katy wants a sister." He grinned at her. "I'm worried if we don't give in to her demands she'll take the animals hostage until we do."

Abby pushed away from her desk and smiled up at him.

Her business would start trading online in a couple of weeks, and already she was planning her next season line of products.

"Tell her to save up and buy a baby at the supermarket." Her eyes sparkled.

"That's exactly the kind of thing I'd say to her."

"I know. You're corrupting me. I used to be good and now I'm borderline bad."

He perched on the edge of her desk, tugging her hand to make her stand between his thighs. She wrapped her arms around his neck without hesitation. His woman.

"Only borderline? I'll have to work harder."

She faked a sigh. "I just don't think you're up to putting in the effort."

"You're right." He nuzzled the spot behind her ear that made her weak, and was pleased when he felt her weight press into him. His Abby was easy, although he'd never tell her. It was his secret to delight in. "It would take a serious time commitment to corrupt you fully."

"Twenty-four hours a day," she mumbled.

Her head fell to the side to give him greater access to her throat. He sucked the spot that made her tremble.

"Aye, it would take years of round-the-clock effort to corrupt you properly."

"And how do you suggest you start this intensive corruption?" She popped the top button on his favourite blue tartan shirt as she peeked up at him from under those thick lashes of hers.

"I think the only way to do it is to sign on for the long haul." His heart raced as she froze in his arms. Flynn was done playing. "Marry me, Abby love," he whispered.

She leaned over, kissed his throat and inhaled him deeply. "Name the time and place. I'll be there."

He couldn't stop a grin. "Is that a yes?"

"Always." She kissed his lips softly. "It's always a yes for you, Flynn Boyle, because I love you."

"I knew it!" He pounded the air. Challenge won. Again. He was a freaking legend.

With a growl of victory, Flynn slanted his mouth over hers and took control of their kiss. And, as always, Abby melted to a puddle of desire in his arms. Just the way he liked her.

EPILOGUE

FOUR YEARS LATER

"Flynn?" Abby's voice had a hint of hysteria in it.

Flynn looked over at his eldest daughter and winced. "Think she saw them?"

"Kind of hard to miss three alpacas, dad," Katy said with a laugh.

"I really hope she doesn't look out the windows on the other side of the house. I was hoping to get her in a good mood before I mentioned the other stuff."

"What you got?" Little Vicky looked up at him with exactly the same shade of chocolate eyes as her mother. "Muma said no more puppies. You got a kitten, Daddy?"

Flynn ruffled his daughter's hair, only to have her twin

climb up onto his knee and demand her own cuddle. "Is it a pony?" Josie said.

"No ponies, puppies or kittens this time."

The three-year-olds bounced on top of him, demanding he tell them what he was hiding on the other side of the house. He wasn't about to give in. Neither one of them could keep a secret worth a damn. Katy laughed, and he narrowed his eyes at her.

"This is your fault," he told her. "You wanted a sister."

"One," his nine-year-old reminded him. "I only asked for one. The other one is your problem."

"Damn terrorist," he mumbled.

"Goal!" Katy shouted at the screen, bringing Flynn's attention back to the replay of the Arsenal game they were watching.

"I like the look of the new midfielder," Katy said.

"He's got potential." Flynn wouldn't let anyone convince him the team wouldn't have been better off with him in it. Although they were doing well this season.

Katy grinned at him, probably knowing exactly what he was thinking. She insisted on dressing in head-to-toe pink for every Arsenal game they watched—just to cheese him off.

"Jonathan wants to play midfield this season," she told him, mentioning the little league team he managed.

"Not happening. You're the strongest player we have. If he wants another position, he'll have to work for it."

Katy nodded. She took the game very seriously. As she should.

"Daddy?" Josie put one of her tiny palms on each of his cheeks. "What do you got in the garden?"

He couldn't help beaming at her. His girls were perfect, and he'd hit anyone who told him otherwise. But perfect or not, they still couldn't keep a secret. "I'm not telling you."

She pouted, followed closely by her twin. They reminded him of his younger twin cousins, a very scary comparison.

"Have Aunty Claire and Aunty Megan been giving you two tips again?" He made a mental note to talk to his cousins. Again.

Identical twin heads shook in unison. Katy had styled their hair with pink glitter and bows for the game. They were innocence personified, but he had years of experience with his eldest daughter. He knew they could be just as much of a terrorist as Katy had been.

"Flynn," Abby called. "Get in here."

"Oh, you in trouble," Vicky said.

"You gonna have to sit on the naughty step," Josie added.

"Not again." Flynn moaned. He looked at his eldest. "You told them to say that, didn't you?"

She nodded with a bright grin. "You never sat on it for me. They might have better luck."

"Flynn. Don't make me come get you." Okay. Abby had reached her limit.

"I need to go deal with your mother." He lifted Josie off his knee and placed her on the couch. "Be good and shout loudly if Arsenal scores again."

He found his very pregnant wife staring out of the living room window. Her mother, Victoria, sat on the sofa with her husband Lawrence at her side. She looked amused, which wasn't a good sign for Flynn.

"What is it, Abby love?" Flynn wrapped his arms around her, rubbing her belly while he did it.

They'd had three scans this time. It was definitely a boy and definitely wasn't twins. One shock like that in a lifetime was enough for both of them.

"Don't you 'Abby love' me." She frowned. It was cute. "Why are there alpacas in our garden?"

"Because I couldn't get a hold of an elephant?"

Lawrence barked a laugh, only to cut it short at Abby and her mum's looks of censure. Flynn gave the man a sympathetic smile. When mother and daughter teamed up, they were a force to be reckoned with.

"I thought we agreed you wouldn't bring home any more animals?" Abby said.

"Technically, I didn't bring them home. They were delivered."

"You can't keep taking in people's strays. We're getting overrun here."

He nuzzled behind her ear, delighted when she gasped. "I promise no more animals after today." It wasn't a lie. The animals on the other side of the house had been delivered already.

She narrowed her eyes. "What have you done?"

"I don't know what you mean." He tried to pull off an innocent look. The one the girls got away with all the time but never seemed to work for him.

"Flynn Boyle, what else did you bring home from the surgery? I know that look. Where did you hide it?" She turned in his arms, her full belly pressing into him and making him feel the same surge of protectiveness he usually felt when she was near.

"Have I told you how beautiful you look today?" He kissed her delicious lips.

She smacked him on the chest. "Stop dodging the question. Everyone in the Highlands knows you're a soft touch for abandoned and injured animals. It's only gotten worse since you started training to become a vet. We're running out of space to put all the rejects you keep bringing home."

"It was your idea to study veterinary medicine, Abby. If you hadn't pushed me, I wouldn't have done it."

"Is it also my fault our house is being overrun by everyone else's unwanted animals?"

"I didn't say that." Flynn looked at Lawrence for help. The man held up his hands to tell Flynn he was on his own. Flynn gave him a look he hoped conveyed he was going to find himself a new lawyer. Lawrence just laughed.

"I'll stop, I promise." He'd try hard, anyway. She was right. He was a soft touch.

"Muma." Josie ran into the room, followed closely by a grinning Katy. "There's big birds in the garden. Can I ride them, can I?"

Josie wrapped her arms around Abby's legs and begged with her eyes, while Vicky climbed up onto her namesake's lap and snuggled in. Vicky and her grandmother were pretty much inseparable.

"Big birds?" Abby snapped at him.

"Tattletale," he told Josie, making Katy laugh.

Abby shrugged out of his arms and stomped to the back of the house, closely followed by the whole family.

"Ostriches?" It was a screech. "There are ostriches in the garden." She spun on Flynn. "Why are there ostriches in my garden? Why are there ostriches in Scotland?"

"Calm down, Abby love. Think of the baby."

"Idiot," Katy said. "Dumb thing to say."

Abby kicked him hard on the shin, making sure to aim for his undamaged leg. Although he could walk and run fine now, it still ached now and then. Hence Abby's consideration.

"It's like this," Flynn said. "Ostrich farms were fashionable a few years ago. Same with owning alpaca—having exotic animals was trendy. But there isn't any market for them now, and people don't want them anymore."

"And you thought our house was the best place for these animals to retire?"

Flynn tried his charming smile, hoping it swayed her. "I

can't take them back now. I promise to try to find another home for them. This is only temporary."

"You've been saying that since the goat." She pointed to the animal who was currently eating the washing from the line.

"Aye." Flynn pulled her into his arms. "I'll admit the goat might have been a mistake."

"What am I going to do with you?" Abby said.

"Love me forever?" Flynn said hopefully.

Abby smiled up at him, her anger gone.

"I think I'm going to puke," Katy said.

Flynn ignored the terrorist and kissed his very pregnant wife.

"When I grow up, I'm going to rule the world."
Abby and Flynn's daughter, Katy, aged five

HERE COMES THE RAINNE AGAIN

"Why did you pick Betty for your best man?" Matt Donaldson grumbled over his beer.

The stag party had taken over the only pub in Invertary and the entertainment had fallen to the best man—eighty-nine-year-old Betty. Or as the locals called her—Satan.

"He picked me because I have bigger balls than the lot of you," Satan said, followed by her trademark cackle. "Look at you. Bunch of wee boys whining and complaining. There isn't a proper man amongst you."

There was a grunt. Betty's head spun towards the behemoth known as Grunt. "Okay," she conceded. "Maybe you can pass for a man. Or a mountain. Whatever."

The huge, taciturn American grinned at Betty.

"Seriously." Matt leaned across the table towards Lake. "Why?"

The town's only cop had known Betty his whole life. He spent most of his time trying to avoid the woman, or jail her, whichever was easiest.

Lake snorted. "Like I had a choice. It was this or she wanted to be father of the bride. Seeing as I actually want to marry Kirsty and she would kill me if I suggested Betty step in for her dead father, that narrowed the choice down."

"You made the right decision, son." Betty patted him on the head, like he was her dog, and then she waddled off towards the buffet table the pub's owner Dougal had laid out.

Lake grinned after her. It'd been three years since he'd inherited her along with the shop he'd bought, and he still got a kick out her. It was like having his own gremlin. Entertaining but kind of scary.

"Your relationship with that woman is sick and twisted," Josh McInnes said from the other side of the booth.

Lake couldn't argue with the American singer, so he said nothing. He was well aware that he was possibly the only person on the planet who appreciated Betty. He'd long thought her talents were wasted in the Scottish Highlands. If she'd been born elsewhere, or in a different era, she'd have been ruler of her own regime—or have given Mata Hari a run for her money. Under her tartan tent and hairnet was the mind of a criminal genius.

"Are we just going to sit around here and eat all night?" Mitch asked.

Josh's manager and best friend was one of the few unattached men in attendance. His idea of a party was living it up in Las Vegas, not eating chips at the Scottie Dog.

"Betty has entertainment planned," Lake said.

There was a unanimous groan.

"No," Harry, the resident boy genius, protested. "It will be fun. You'll enjoy it."

"What did you do?" Harry's brother, Flynn, said with a sigh. "What did Betty con you into this time?"

"Hey, I resent that." Harry glared at his brother. "I didn't do anything, and Betty isn't capable of conning me."

They all stared at him.

"Fine." Harry's shoulders slumped. "But I'm older and

wiser now. I know to be suspicious of everything she says." His eyes went wide with sudden panic and the men groaned. He had totally fallen for another con. "No," Harry said. "I checked out everything she said this time."

"And?" Flynn prompted. Like the rest of the men, no one was appeased by Harry's conviction.

"All she wanted was to use my credit card to book strippers. See, now the surprise is ruined." He threw up his hands in disgust. "They're coming up from Glasgow." He checked his watch. "Should be here any minute. They're probably delayed because of the weather."

Everyone looked out of the window at the snow. It was coming down thick and fast, almost obliterating the view of the streetlights glinting off the black loch.

"Wind's picked up," Matt said.

"Blizzard," Flynn said. "Weather forecast said it was coming. Said it was the worst to hit Scotland in decades. They advised we all stay indoors."

Mitch's head hit the table in front of him. "Just when I think this can't get any more lame, we start talking about the weather."

Lake's lip twitched at Mitch's pain. The guy was right. This was the worst bachelor party Lake had ever attended. The fact it was his own was kind of amusing. Apart from his friends, the pub was empty, as people had stayed home because of the snow. In all honesty, Lake would be home too, wrapped up with Kirsty, if he could. He'd been hassled into having a stag party, and only the fact Kirsty was holed up at the castle with the women kept him from staying home.

"Caroline will kill me if I watch strippers," Josh said.

"If Jena was here, she'd join in. She'd get up on one of the tables and dance for us." Matt obviously missed his wife as much as Lake missed Kirsty. "She's a great dancer."

"Yeah," Harry said. "But maybe not on the tables. Dougal's still upset about the last time."

"It wasn't her fault she fell off and people got injured. She can't help that she's accident prone."

"Maybe if she stopped wearing stilts for shoes, she wouldn't fall over so much," Harry said.

Mitch hit his head on the table again. "Now we're talking about shoes. Why don't we braid each other's hair and get this over with? Betty is right. She has more testosterone than the lot of us."

"Interesting group of friends you've got here," Callum McKay, Lake's buddy from when he was in the SAS, commented drolly.

"He collects us," Josh said. "We're his hobby. Lake would be lost without us."

Lake's lip twitched at Josh. Mitch sat back up and rolled his eyes at his best friend.

"He doesn't collect us. He makes no effort to be friendly. It's as though his lack of response acts like Velcro to all the needy people around him. *We* attach ourselves to Lake."

"Who you calling needy?" Flynn said.

"I don't need anyone," Matt said. "Well, maybe Jena." He leered. "But that's a good kind of need."

"I need people." Harry's fingers tapped on the table as though they couldn't function without a keyboard under them. "No man is an island."

Flynn grinned. "I'm an island. I'm bloody Ibiza!"

"*About a Boy.*" His brother high-fived him. "Classic movie. Even with Hugh Grant."

Lake shook his head at the brothers as Callum watched in bewilderment. "Are you sure this guy is cut out for business?" He nodded at Harry.

Lake had spent the afternoon in a meeting with Callum and Harry, hammering out a business proposal that would make the three men partners. He knew Callum was still undecided, and part of that was due to working with Harry. At twenty-six, Harry had nowhere near the life experience of Lake and Callum. But they had nowhere near his genius. No one wrote security code like Harry. The guy was a programming genius and an asset they couldn't afford to exclude.

"This guy," Harry said without taking offence, "hacked into the Ministry of Defence when he was eleven and they never caught him. I confessed after I rewrote their security program for them. This guy heads a billion-dollar company. And this guy"—he pointed at himself with pride—"knows how to keep a secret. Anyone want to know who really killed Diana? Well, tough. These lips are sealed." He folded his arms and grinned at the men.

Flynn groaned. "Way to prove you're mature, bro."

"Was that what I was supposed to do? I thought I was proving I was skilled." Harry turned to Callum. "If you're looking for serious and mature, you're better off with Grunt."

Grunt grunted helpfully to prove Harry's point.

Callum shook his head. "What the hell am I doing here?"

"Having fun?" Mitch said. "No. Me neither."

Callum stared at Mitch, but Lake knew he was amused—his way of showing it was to frown less. Lake watched as Callum's hand twitched on his thigh and his jaw tightened slightly. Lake knew his friend was fighting the urge to rub his leg. He'd recently been fitted with two new prosthetics and they were giving him some trouble. Not that Callum would admit it.

"This is mind-numbing," Josh complained. "I would have arranged a much better party. Bet the women are having more fun at the castle. Who did you leave to guard them?"

"Ryan and Joe." Lake sipped his beer.

Josh shot up out of his chair. "No! You left two womanisers with the women. What the hell were you thinking? If those guys seduce my Caroline, I'm going to have a hit put out on you." He pointed at Lake.

There was a moment of silence before everyone burst out laughing.

"What the hell?" Josh demanded. "What's so funny?"

"Caroline," Mitch sputtered.

Josh looked ready to thump his best friend. "You think Caroline isn't attractive enough to seduce?"

"Get a grip." Flynn wiped his eyes. "What he's saying. What we're all thinking. Is that Caroline is unseducable. She would never cheat on you. Her head would explode even thinking about it. Not only that, she'd lecture the ears off any man who tried to seduce her."

"Damn straight." Josh slumped back, mollified.

"That's if she even noticed she was being hit on," Matt said.

Josh grinned. "There is that."

"You're not wrong about the party, though," Flynn said. "This is mind-numbing."

"Don't worry," Harry said with a grin. "It'll pick up soon. Strippers. Remember?"

"Let's get this party started," Betty shouted. "The entertainment is here."

"See?" Harry said.

They all turned towards the door and collectively groaned.

"She booked *male* strippers?" Harry wailed.

Four buff guys, dressed in fake fatigues with Velcro seams, swaggered into the middle of the room.

"She ordered soldiers?" Grunt spoke for the first time that evening.

"Lake's ex-forces. What else was I supposed to order?" Betty demanded.

"Well, duh, women," Flynn pointed out.

Betty cackled as she dragged a wooden chair into the middle of the room and positioned herself between the strippers. "Ready when you are, boys."

"I'm going to vomit," Matt said.

The music kicked in and the men started gyrating. Their packages inches from Betty's grinning face.

"Make it stop," Josh wailed.

"I need to call a therapist." Mitch turned his back in disgust. "I can never unsee this."

"I can't believe she conned me into paying for male strippers," Harry said.

Callum looked from the strippers to Harry's stunned expression, then to Lake. "Are you *sure* he'd make a good business partner?"

Lake tipped back his head and laughed loud and long.

Get Here Comes The Rainne Again now and keep on reading!

ABOUT THE AUTHOR

I'm a Scot, living in New Zealand and married to a Dutch man. I write contemporary romance with a humorous bent – this is mainly due to the fact I have an odd sense of humour and can't keep it out of anything I do! If I wasn't a writer, I'd like to be Buffy the Vampire Slayer, or Indiana Jones. Unfortunately, both these roles have already been filled. Which may be a good thing as I have no fighting skills, wouldn't know a precious relic if it hit me in the face and have an aversion to blood. When I'm not living in my head, I'm a mother to two kids, several pet sheep, one dog, four cats, three alpacas, two miniature horses, eight guinea pigs and an escape artist chicken.